De

MW00452411

This tale is dedicated to my brother Walks in Dreams and all those nameless boys who carried their drums fearlessly into the face of certain death and never turned aside from their duty. A mention should also be made to those special friends that set aside their time and talent to aid in the publication of this trilogy; you know who you are.

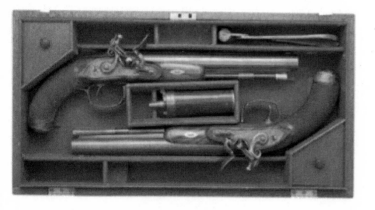

CHAPTER 1

Lieutenant Oliver Perrin led his men at a fast pace away from the growing battle behind him. Deep inside he felt as though he was betraying the young men left behind but Captain Marking's orders had been succinct and to the point. Lieutenant Perrin was to be responsible for getting his men and the Engineers back to the Marshal's lines and warning him of the approaching French; he was not to turn back to help with the fighting under any circumstances.

The guilt Oliver felt as he heard the loud crashing of the many guns and the volleys of musket fire behind him only went to spur him onward. Oliver not only had his own men to get back to the lines but the Engineers also. It was to be more than two hours later when they stopped for rest that he discovered that young Lieutenant Carterton was not with them but it was far too late to return to look for him.

The distant sounds of battle receded the further they moved towards where Marshal Beresford had hopefully set his lines. Lieutenant Perrin knew that at best they would only have little more than a day to ready for the oncoming French army; that the French numbered well over the estimated sixteen thousand that the Marshal was expecting could set back the Marshal's plans.

Oliver Perrin pushed his men forward and well into the night as he tried to save as much time as he could. With only a few hours sleep Oliver Perrin got his men up and pushed on into the dawning light, the sight of picket fires in the distance led him to push harder.

The breakfast fires were sending smoke into the air as he brought his tired men to the edge of the picket line; once the challenge had been met and they were allowed through, Lieutenant Perrin went in search of the Marshal to report while his men were sent to find a place to rest. Oliver Perrin noticed a number of strange looks as he and his men entered the camp; it took him a moment to realise they were still wearing the odd assortment of jackets and not the bright red ones of the army. It was one more thing he would have to correct later in the day after he had reported.

Lieutenant Perrin finally found himself outside the Marshal's tent. He felt tired and dirty as the dust that had accumulated during the fast run was now making him look like a ghost. Oliver Perrin was met by the Marshal's second in command; the Major took one look at the young Lieutenant and frowned.

"Yes! Who are you?"

"Lieutenant Perrin reporting as ordered Sir."

2

"Ordered? Ordered by whom Lieutenant and you are out of uniform Mister Perrin."

"Ordered by Captain Marking Sir and I apologise for the lack of uniform, it was necessary for our journey back to the lines."

"Since when did Captain Marking have the right to give orders Mister Perrin? Your orders were directly from the Marshal and his were to be obeyed above and beyond any others."

"Sir Captain Marking sent me back to report the enemy's movements to the Marshal so he would have his lines set in time for their arrival."

"Well then you better come in and make your report but this will not go unnoticed nor will it be forgotten Mister Perrin."

It was only a few seconds before Oliver found himself standing at attention before Marshal Beresford; the Marshal did not seem amused at Oliver's presence.

"You are?"

"1st Lieutenant Perrin of the 29th Regiment of Foot Sir. I have been sent back to make report of the French advance Sir."

"Ah yes, Perrin. Were my orders not clear enough Lieutenant?"

"Yes Sir they were but Captain Marking changed them in the interest of advising you of the situation to your front Sir."

"Well Lieutenant, apart from you being out of uniform of which we have taken notice; Captain Marking does not have the authority to change my orders regardless of the situation. This, Lieutenant could mean a Courts Martial for all of you once I have taken care of the French and that should be in short order Lieutenant. Now then have you anything else to report?"

"Yes Sir. The French number somewhat more than the estimate given to you and they shall be here as early as the morrow. We have estimated their number to be over 24,000 plus their baggage and supply train. They also have some 48 heavy guns at their disposal as well as some 19,000 Infantry and approximately 4,000 Cavalry. Captain Marking thought you should be made aware of the increase in numbers so you can reset your lines."

"And just where did the Captain get these numbers Lieutenant?"

"Captain Marking sent out mounted scouts and had been shadowing the French column for some days before he made his stand on the plains at Olivenca."

"So the Captain did stand and fight then?"

"Yes Sir. When I led the Engineers and escort from the field, Captain Marking had started his attack on the French lines of advance Sir."

"Attack! What do you mean the Captain attacked? His orders were to hold and defend the redoubt and nothing more. You will please give me a full account of the Captain's actions so I may set up an inquiry when he returns; if he returns. Proceed Lieutenant and do not forget your reputation as well as your future depends on your words so think carefully Lieutenant."

"Yes Sir. Well Sir, Captain Marking looked at the plans for the redoubt and considered them to be insufficient to hold the French back for more than a few minutes at best. After talking it over with the Engineers he changed the plans so that the line of advance was better covered."

"He changed the plans of the redoubt? Please explain his actions Lieutenant?"

"Sir the original plans would have put the redoubt well to one side of the roadway. Captain Marking supposed the French could very easily bypass his redoubt without slowing their advance. If this had occurred Sir the French would already be at your lines. To this end he revised the plans for the redoubt so they encompassed a width of one hundred yards either side of the roadway. The French would have no option but to spend the time to attack and clear the redoubt before they could advance further."

"I see, and did this work Lieutenant? And I still do not see where the Captain would have forced an attack?"

"Yes Sir the new design worked a treat. Captain Marking had every uniform stand at the redoubt until every musket had fired its last ball in the defence of the redoubt; it was not until the French Cavalry had made a large charge that the redoubt fell Sir. Not a single uniform survived the charge Sir."

"I see, well at least they all fell with some little honour. So Lieutenant, if the redoubt was overrun, how then did the Captain mount his own attack?"

"The Captain's attack was separate from the defence of the redoubt Sir."

"Separate! How so Lieutenant? Also, if the redoubt had fallen, how did you manage to escape Mister Perrin?"

"It was all in the Captain's planning Sir. Captain Marking had set his guns above the valley leading to the redoubt; he also had his men behind stone walls that they constructed on both sides of the same valley. When the French began to set their guns to fire upon the redoubt, the Captain's gunners fired down upon them and the French pulled them back so they could be saved for their attack upon your lines. With the lack of guns the French had no option but to charge the redoubt with Infantry and Cavalry. As the Cavalry rode down on the redoubt I had been ordered to withdraw and escort the Engineers back to your lines; our withdrawal was covered by the Captains own Cavalry while he and his men held the heights on both sides of the valley behind the French."

"Wait, wait. The Captain had Cavalry and guns? I was informed that he had no heavy guns, in fact Lieutenant he stood on that very spot and told me he did not have any heavies at all. Cavalry, where in the blue blazes did he get Cavalry? I distinctly remember him saying he had only a few men; can you explain this anomaly for me Lieutenant?"

"Yes Sir. Captain Marking did indeed only have a few men when he arrived here at your camp but his main force was at Elvas. The Captain's forces are made up of Drummers,

English and Spanish Axillaries and Spanish and Portuguese Irregulars. His guns are; I am assured by his Artillery Officer, only light French guns he took during other campaigns. The Captains Cavalry is made up of a mixture of his forces and are used as mounted musketry. They are commanded by a young Spanish Colonel and I must say Sir, they are very effective and wreck havoc among the French forces."

"Mounted musketry! That's preposterous Lieutenant, muskets cannot be fired from horse back; are you trying to fudge the disastrous attempt of the Captain to avoid a fight with the French with untruths Sir?"

"No Sir, you asked for the truth Sir and I can only relate what I saw with my own eyes."

"Well Lieutenant I am having my own doubts as to your veracity but continue, although I must warn you to keep to the truth Lieutenant and no more speculation about the impossible."

"Sir every word I have spoken is the truth and the rest of my report is incomplete as we were ordered from the battle by the Captain once the redoubt had fallen. Captain Marking took position on the upper slopes of the valley and attacked from there. To the best of my knowledge he was holding out against at least one third of the French Cavalry when I lost sight although we could still hear the guns in the distance some two hours later. My estimation Sir is that the Captain managed to hold the French for at least four hours which means they will be at your lines on the morrow. What happened to the Captain and his men is not known by me Sir."

"What their fate is, is neither here nor there Lieutenant; we can only hope they held their lines to the last man and delayed the French long enough for my purposes. I never really thought they could do much anyways Lieutenant. Why the Viscount sent me damn Drummers and misfits is really beyond my understanding. Very well Lieutenant, you have made your report, you may leave and see to your uniform and those men who retreated with you. I hope for your sake Lieutenant that you and your men do not have ideas of running away again when the French arrive on the morrow; I expect to see you and your men on the front line at best Lieutenant. You are dismissed."

Oliver could feel the heat of anger rising in his belly as he saluted the Marshal and smartly turned about and left the tent with his rage building by the second; the Marshal had blatantly accused he and his men of cowardness in the face of the enemy; it did not sit well with Oliver and a new plan began to develop in his mind as he went in search of his men. If any of them survived the upcoming battle then he would put his developing plan into action and the devil can have his day with the Marshal.

Oliver first went in search of his friend Conrad Wainright. The two young Officers had shared Conrad's tent ever since they had landed on the Peninsular even though they were both in different Brigades. Each had become familiar and good friends and saw no reason to change old habits just because of a change in units.

Once he had found Conrad's tent he entered and talked with his young friend; it was Conrad who supplied Oliver with one of his spare uniform jackets to wear the next day. Neither of them were really looking forward to the battle now that they had been noted by those who ranked above them; there was an uneasy feeling between the two as the time of fighting drew closer.

5

Once in his borrowed jacket Oliver went in search of his men whom he found among the lines of the 29th Foot. Oliver noted that all his men were now wearing new red jackets which they had been issued from the Quartermasters; Oliver knew that the cost of the new jackets would be deducted from the men's pay each month until paid for. The army did not appreciate the loss of a soldier's equipment for any reason.

Oliver walked into the large group that made up his B Company area and what he saw made him look around for his Sergeant Major. The men were all huddled over upturned crates in groups of five. On the crates they had what appeared to be waxed paper sheets as well as powder horns and wooden dishes full of musket balls

When the Sergeant Major joined him, Oliver asked what the men were doing.

"Well Sir, it's like this. Them boys we was with had some right good ideas. The men noticed what they was up to and for the time we was with them they joined in the training the boys was doing. It was them boys what showed the men how they could load their muskets faster and send out a better rate of fire Sir; right smart them drummer boys was Sir."

"I see Sergeant Major, and how does it improve your rate of fire?"

"Well Sir, I was talking to some of them youngsters at night time and they was right forthcoming. If I may suggest Sir, if we was to form three ranks instead of the usual two, then the men would be able to keep up a steady rate by firing volleys in rank. Those youngsters told me they could keep up a continual fire rate with three ranks that they could not do with just two."

"So what is it the men are doing then?"

"Making cartridges from paper Sir. They put the ball in one end and twist it closed, next they put in a measure of powder and twist close the other end. When it comes to firing, they just bight off the top and hold the ball in their mouths; pour in the powder and spit the ball in then hit the butt of their musket hard on the ground to settle the load. It remains only for them to charge their frisson and they are ready to fire in less time. We watched the youngun's doing it; they was so fast it was like eight rounds a minute Sir."

"That sounds like what we may need on the morrow Sergeant Major, tell the men I approve and we will form three ranks when we see the French."

"Well Sir, it may cause trouble with other Officers Sir."

"Don't worry Sergeant Major I'm sure that what tomorrow brings will give us more cause than to worry about others. Tell the men to carry on as they are and be ready to set ranks of three when we go to lines."

"Yes Sir, thank you Sir; we will do our best."

"Thank you Sergeant Major, I'm sure the men will more than do their duty."

Oliver returned the Sergeant Major's salute and returned back to Conrad's tent for the rest of the evening; he did not even feel like going to the mess for dinner, he would have Conrad's batman find him something to eat later.

The morning of the 16th of May dawned clear and dry; the rising heat of the new summer sun was already making the men's uniforms uncomfortable as they began to form the lines in readiness for their French enemy whom they could see on the distant side of the plain. Oliver went in search of his Commanding Officer to find out where he and his men would stand in the line.

Oliver found Lieutenant General Houghton standing among the other Senior Officers of the Second Division; after snapping to attention and saluting the Senior Officers Oliver asked.

"Sir, 1st Lieutenant Perrin reporting for line assignment. Where do you wish my men to stand Sir?"

Lieutenant General Houghton looked Oliver up and down with a frown on his face before answering.

"Perrin, yes I have word of you Lieutenant, the Marshal has ordered that you will stand at the centre of the line with the men of the Second Brigade. The Marshal's orders are that you and your men will stand to the last and, if in the unlikely case of a retreat you and your men will hold the line until all others are safe. Is that clearly understood Lieutenant?"

"Yes Sir, my men and I will do our duty as ordered Sir."

"I should damn well think so Mister Perrin and I hope your efforts are better than those you showed at Olivenca. You are dismissed Lieutenant, go and see to your men."

Oliver was not happy at all but there was little he could do at this stage; he and his men were being put in a position of sacrifice so that those senior to him can sleep better at night. Oliver returned to his men and led them towards the lines waiting for the French. He had now settled in his mind that, should he survive the day his plan would be put into action on the completion of the battle.

Oliver set his ranks in three as he had said he would, he was not surprised at the looks of the other Junior Officers further along the lines when they saw the unusual formation but before a word could be said against him, the distant sound of cannon were heard from the French lines. The battle had begun.

There was little that could be done by the Infantry as the cannons of both sides sent their barrages of shot into the large formations. To the left flank of the three main brigades the French could be seen wheeling around until they eventually faced the red coats waiting for them.

Lieutenant General Houghton's Brigade was at the centre of the three that lined up along the slight rise; it was the position that was to be hit the hardest by the advancing French. After the battle it was discovered that the French had mounted the largest ever Infantry attack of the war on the hapless English. Lieutenant General Houghton, due to an errant cannon ball, was not to live to see the end of the battle but many thought it was perhaps better that he did not when the dead were counted.

Oliver's Company was positioned at the centre of the Brigade which always was the hardest hit on any attack; as he stood waiting for the inevitable, his Sergeant Major came up beside him with a small implement in his hand.

"Sir, I thought you may like to keep this close; there is blood to be lost today and this may give you a fighting chance once the French are amongst us."

Oliver looked at the thing in the Sergeant Major's hand; it was a peculiar type of mace. The handle was of wood with a leather thong through the top of the handle. The iron head was something that could do real damage if used correctly. On one side it was shaped much like a hammer but a little larger; the other side was a deadly looking spike and the whole weighed about three pounds. Oliver hefted it in his hands before giving the Sergeant Major a thin smile and tucked the strange weapon in his waist sash.

As the French drew closer to the main lines; Oliver gulped and tried to moisten his dry throat; he had only seconds before he began to give fire orders to his triple ranks. It did not take long before the noise and smell of battle filled the air around him and his men; for the long hours that the battle ensued it was a simple case of kill or be killed.

For Oliver it seemed that the battle raged around him for days and finally, when the French began to retreat under the ever stiffening defence of the red coats; Oliver had time to look around him. Oliver could not believe he had survived when all around him were the broken and bloodied bodies of men he had known.

As the din of the battle receded and the full impact of the slaughter began to take its effect, Oliver could only marvel that he was still standing albeit in a bloody and dishevelled state. Oliver gave thanks for the thoughtfulness of his Sergeant Major and would have to look for the man to thank him. The mace had saved his life many times as he used it with deadly effect at close range; especially when the enemy was too close for his sword.

Oliver Perrin could only gasp for breath as he saw the ranks of blue coated French retreat from the field. All around him were the men he had marched and trained with; most were now lying still amongst the blood and dirt of the place they had held so valiantly. Oliver was to find that his Company of one hundred and thirty five men now numbered only twenty seven and four of those were seriously wounded and may not live through the rest of the day.

Oliver's Company was now no more; how he had survived through it all was to be a mystery to him for the rest of his life. Oliver's only regret was that he was never able to thank the Sergeant Major for the gift of the strange weapon that had been the saviour of his life more times than he could count.

With the devastation of his Company and the few friends he had made in it; Oliver finally made his decision on the plan that had been forming before the battle. There was now only one thing left to do when the remnants of the army went into bivouac for the night. On finding that his friend Conrad had also fallen only went to cement his decision.

Oliver knew he would not be given another Company while he was under the orders of Marshal Beresford and yet he did not want to leave the peninsular while the French were still there. There was only one thing he could think to do; he would resign his commission and go looking for his brother's army. With luck he would never again have to see the waste of human life as had been done this day.

CHAPTER 2

16th May 1811: Somewhere in Seville.

'Pain...grey mist...pain...floating...pain...blackness.'

'Can't breathe...pain...floating...ghostly voices...pain...blackness.'

'Can't move...young boy screaming far away...pain...blackness.'

'Foggy light...pain...faceless heads...bloody fingers...pain...blackness.'

22nd May 1811: Near Cordova.

'Can't see...numbness...floating...too hot...hands holding tight...hot, too hot...blackness.'

'Far away voices...cold...oh so cold...murmuring voices...blackness.'

'Smell...bad smell...pain...hurts...red fingers...pain...blackness.'

25th May 1811: Hacienda Juan Rodrigo Hermosa, Andalucia.

'Light; I can see the light...dimming, the light is dimming...no, no wait for me...must get up...yelling voices...blackness.'

'Hot...so hot...water...thirsty...must get up; French attack...blackness.'

2nd July 1811; Hacienda Juan Rodrigo Hermosa, Andalucia.

'Voices, whispering voices. I think I know those voices...who are they...must wake up the French are coming...too many...too many must run...get up...get up must run...blackness.'

'Voice, young voice...I know that voice but!'

"Go and call Mister Grey I think the worst is over and he's coming around."

"Yes Sir."

"Thomas...Thomas...can you hear me; come on old man time to wake up, you've been resting long enough. Open your eyes Thomas; time to stop playing dead."

Thomas's eyes fluttered as he tried to open them; it seemed like such an effort. The voice! He knew that voice it was...it was...Jervis, yes Jervis; he was still alive and Jervis had fixed him but why could he not move?

Thomas groaned as his eyes opened to slits; his right leg was stiff and he felt as though he was tied down. The bright light that shone into his eyes made him squint as it reflected off what appeared to be very white walls. He had no idea how he got to be in a place with white walls; the last time he saw anything it was the dirt and stones of the battle field.

Thomas let another groan come from his dry lips as he tried to turn his head for a better look; the mistiness that had distorted Mister Jervis's face was clearing and he could see the worry lines on the young Surgeons face.

Thomas opened his dry mouth and could not believe the croaking voice that came out.

"Where am I? What happened?"

"Well it's nice to see you're not playing dead anymore; you caused us quite a stir. Are you ready to rejoin the world now?" The acerbic sound of Jervis's voice was almost comforting to Thomas's ears.

"Water, thirsty."

"I suppose you would be; wait a minute and I'll get some brought to you; we weren't expecting you to be awakening just yet."

Thomas sighed as he settled back on the clean white pillow under his head; in his mind he was almost smiling. The bloody French had not got him yet but he could not understand why he was so tired and felt so weak; it was something he would have to wait to find out when he had had a good long drink; his throat felt not only dry but also raw.

Thomas tried to lift himself up from the pillow but could only hold his head up for a brief moment before collapsing once again and breathing heavily; he could not understand how much effort that simple action had taken.

"What's wrong with me; why can't I sit up?"

"Well Thomas, that's a result of many things; if you can wait until you have had a little water then I will go through it all for you."

Thomas watched as Jervis turned his head as Fairley entered with a large glass of water; at last he could drink. Fairley was very careful as he held Thomas's head up for him to take a small sip of the cool fresh water. Thomas was not allowed to gulp but only take a few small sips at a time and Fairley was careful to keep watch as Thomas cooled his parched throat.

When he felt he had had enough, Thomas slumped back onto the pillow in exhaustion; he could not believe it had taken so much effort to sip a glass of water. Once he was lying back and feeling better, Thomas looked up at Jervis with a questioning look in his eyes.

Thomas's voice was still a little croaky as he asked the most pressing questions.

"How is the battle going? Are the men safe? Where are the French? Can we escape now? Where the hell am I?"

"Well Mister Marking, I see it didn't take you long to get feisty; perhaps it was a mistake to stop your Laudanum. So many questions and you haven't even eaten yet. Private Fairley will you go to the kitchen and tell them the Captain is awake and hungry; if they would make a bowl of soup for him I would be grateful."

Fairley left hurriedly as Jervis turned back to Thomas; he wondered if the Captain would ever know how close he came to death but this was not the time to bring it up.

"Well first off Captain, you are now at the Hacienda Juan Rodrigo Hermosa, or as it is known in these parts; The Hacienda Don Thomasino de Toro. This is the land that the Cortes awarded you and is now your home in Spain. It is in the south of Andalucia and you have the lands of Don Estaban Colosio five miles to the east and the lands of The Prince of Anglona to the south and west and some two days march away. Here you are safe from even the most adventurous Frenchman. Next, you have been in a state of delirium for nearly six weeks and your weight has suffered hence your weakness. The battle is well and truly done and most of the men escaped but we did have bad losses and many wounded as well as losing all your guns. You will be confined to this bed for the next week at least before I will let you up for a short time each day until you regain your strength. Ah here comes young Fairley with your soup; I'll tell you more after you have eaten."

Fairley arrived with a steaming bowl that smelt like heaven to Thomas's hungry belly. Fairley rearranged his pillows and added an extra one so he could be propped up for him to eat. Next Fairley placed the tray carefully on Thomas's knees and gave him a spoon with a warning to sip slowly as it was not only hot but his stomach was not used to food and he would get sick if he ate to fast.

"Right Private Fairley, when Mister Marking has finished you can inform his Officers that they can see him but only for a brief minute; I will attend to the rest of what we have spoken of before." Jervis then left the room after issuing his orders as Fairley sat and watched over Thomas with a sharp eye and one of Thomas's Manton's in each hand.

After the first two or three spoons of soup which he took slowly and carefully; Thomas was feeling a little better. As he sipped another spoon of soup, Thomas tried to look around the large room the big bed was in. Along one wall there were huge tall glass doors that led to the outside and let in the bright light of the midday sun. Fairley sat in a straight backed chair close to his bed, the pistols seemingly at the ready as the young man's eyes kept their vigil of the outside.

Thomas looked down to see why his left arm was not working and saw that a white bandage not only encircled his chest but also tied his upper left arm to his side and a loose sling kept his wrist in place across his bare stomach. Below the white sheet his right leg throbbed and felt stiff as he tried to wriggle his toes; the fact he had been freshly bathed completely missed him.

Thomas had only taken about ten spoons of the thick vegetable soup before he felt bloated; it was a disconcerting feeling to know he could not eat like before, after such a long time without food he should have been able to eat a horse. It was just another mystery he would have to get answers to.

Thomas dropped the spoon into the half empty dish and settled back against the pillows as Fairley laid his two pistols on a side table and took the tray away. When Fairley had disappeared through the large Oak doors, Thomas tried to look around the room for more details. It was a short time before he saw the strange long wall painting at the end of his large bed and on the opposite wall. At first he thought it was some type of painting but the subject was like no other painting he had ever seen before.

At the centre of the painting there was a large ornate bed which had small bedside tables on each side. There was a single wooden chair on the left of the bed and a pair of long benches off to one side. In the bed was what appeared to be a gaunt figure that was all bones and seemingly made a very small impression to the white bed cloths covering it.

The figure was of a young teen although he looked as though he was right at deaths door. His hair was cropped short; the face was nothing more than sallow skin spread over the bones of the skull. The dark eyes were sunken deeply into the sockets and had thick black rings around them. Across the bony bare chest was a thick white bandage and the figures ribs stuck out as though the figure had been staved almost to death.

Thomas gazed in awe at the details of the fine painting; his next actions though would bring a cry of alarm. As Thomas looked at the fine painting, he lifted his good right arm up to scratch an itch on his nose; that was when he gave a shout of alarm. The figure in the painting moved in just the same fashion. It took a few seconds before Thomas could reconcile that the deathly figure was in fact himself being shown in a tall wall mirror.

At the strangled sound of Thomas's yell, Fairley came running into the room and went straight for the pistols at the bedside just as the glass doors were thrown open and six heavily armed men rushed in with pistols and cutlasses drawn. Jervis was just rushing in the door when he saw the armed men in the room and instantly began to look for the threat as he made his way to Thomas's bedside.

After a quick check to see that Thomas was alright and had just been shocked by his image in the mirror; Jervis turned to the six armed men.

"It's alright Perkins, Mister Marking just got a shock when he saw himself in the mirror. If you would take the men back outside I can explain it to the Captain."

The man Perkins, gave one more look around the room to make sure all was well before nodding and ordering his men back outside. Jervis sighed as he turned back to the still staring Thomas as Fairley sat back on his wooden chair with the brace of pistols again at the ready.

"I'm sorry Thomas, it's all my fault. I was going to have that mirror covered before you woke but forgot in the excitement of having you back with us. Come on old man, lay back you need the rest."

Jervis lifted Thomas's head and removed one of the pillows so his Captain could lay back down and rest; the look of horror was still on Thomas's face and Jervis knew the time had come for explanations; it was sooner than he wanted but now it would not wait. With Thomas settled back and looking a little better, Jervis sighed as he began to tell Thomas why he looked so bad and how he had got to the Hacienda.

"Well Thomas, I wanted to put this off until you were stronger but now that you have seen yourself I think you need to know." Jervis paused as he tried to gather his thoughts; there was so much to tell and he was not really sure that Thomas was ready for the news, both good and bad. With another deep breath he began his explanation.

"Maketja was blowing the French withdrawal on his bugle when one of the Cavalry fired his pistol at you, when you went down the ten men who were your guard surrounded you. While one of them lifted you the others formed a circle around you to protect you both. Four of them lost their lives protecting you but the others got you out of the line. Carmelo took over command as the French withdrew while you were carried back to me; we really thought we would lose you. The sword cut was deep but had not hit anything vital but that's only half of the story. The ball in your chest was in itself a miracle. The Cavalry rider must have either short charged his pistol or he was at maximum range. The ball entered your chest right where your heart is but was deflected by one of your ribs and ended up higher in your shoulder. Had the shot been closer or of full power it would have struck your heart."

Jervis paused once again as he watched Thomas's reaction closely before continuing.

"We got you back to my wagon where I started work on you. The leg wound did not look too bad so I sewed it up smartly and then started on the wound in your chest. The ball had cracked the rib but I had the devil of a time trying to get it out without doing anymore damage. After taking out the ball and unfortunately adding to your scar by having to cut deeper than I wanted to; I made sure it was clean of any cloth pushed in by the force of the ball and then sewed you up and got you ready to take to safety. I used the laudanum to keep you unconscious as I didn't want you to move around and tear open the work I had done. On the way to safety, Carmelo suggested we come into Andalucia instead of trying to go through the French lines to Vimeiro."

Jervis paused again and took a sip of water as he thought out what he would say next.

"On the way here you went into a delirium and we had to stop until it was over; the fever was bad and the only way we could keep you in good health was to feed and water you through a tube; that's why your throat is a little hoarse but it will get better as you heal. We made it back here to the Hacienda and His Highness the Prince met us here and organised with the Cortes for it to become your home in Spain. Not long after we got you settled in bed another fever hit you and it was then I saw that the wound in your leg had become infected and I had to operate again. The infection was really bad and I had to use a large number of maggots to clean out the dead flesh. Once clean I used the last of my sulphurous powder and sewed it up again, since then I have kept you under the influence of the laudanum. Fairley has been taking care of you for everything and would not leave your bedside for a moment. You can thank him for keeping you clean and fed."

Thomas listened to his trials and tribulations while under the influence of the laudanum but his eyes could not leave the ghost like figure in the mirror; he instinctively knew he would never be the same again. Jervis continued with his recitation.

"I had to tie your left arm down so you would not open the chest wound when you were thrashing around in the fever but if you promise not to jump around I can cut the bandage and let you use your left arm. The wound is mostly healed but you may find your left arm is a little stiff from now on and any cold weather and you are going to feel it a little. Your leg wound is better now and I have taken out the stitches but you have to take it easy until you have rebuilt your strength. Any questions?"

"What of the men? Did we lose many?"

"Yes we lost seventy six and another one hundred and thirty five wounded; five of them seriously and I have had to do amputations on them, they will live but not be able to fight anymore. Estaban has taken all the wounded and a large number of others back to Vimeiro, they will wait for you there. Estaban lost his right hand and young Maketja lost two fingers when a Frenchman shot his bugle out of his hand and his other arm was hit but it has only made him madder, if that's possible."

"Who did we lose?"

"Of your Officers there was Lieutenant Croxley but Lieutenant Morgan has taken over the gunners but he has no guns anymore, Mister Croxley had to spike them when the French got too close. Lieutenant Allen fell defending your Colours but somehow the young Lieutenant from the Engineers showed up and took command of the Colour Guard just in time to hold back the French."

"Where are the others?"

"Jones, Lorenco and Carmelo have stayed here to watch over you as have the six remaining guards, the others are back at Vimeiro, most should be well healed by now, I sent all three of my assistant with them. I'm just about out of the medicines we had so we will have to do something to get more in time. Now I think that's enough for one day; let me take that bandage off but no getting out of the bed. Carmelo and the others can come in for a brief minute to see you but then I want you to rest."

Thomas could only nod his head as even now he was feeling tired and it was an effort to keep his head up; the ghostly figure in the mirror had him worried and he lowered his head so he would not see it until he slept.

Jervis saw the direction of Thomas's eyes and, once his captain was asleep they would cover up the damned mirror before it scared his patient into a state where he would not heal.

As promised, Jervis let his young Officers in for a quick greeting and not much more before he chased them out to let Thomas sleep; it was going to be a long slow time for him to heal and the less worries he had to contend with the better he would get.

CHAPTER 3

As Thomas lay back on the plump pillows he could hear a number of voices outside his room; it was not long before the first of his friends walked in to greet him. Carmelo looked a little tired but his smile was wide and welcoming as he carefully grasped Thomas's right hand.

"Patron, both the Devil and God are on your side; it would seem neither want you in their realms and have left you here to make the French Puta pay their dues. We are all glad you are back with us and soon; when the time is right, we will make them pay a hefty price for what they tried to do. This I swear on my honour."

Thomas tried to smile at Carmelo's words; it was so typical of his friend to want instant revenge on the French. With his voice still being a little hoarse he thanked Carmelo as he saw Fairley reach for the glass he had replenished so that Thomas could have another small sip of the cooling water.

"I must go now Patron, the surgeon has given us only a minute with you for now; he says you must rest to get strong again. There is much news to tell when you are stronger but for now know that we are all at your command and that your Hacienda is safe from any who would do you harm."

Thomas thanked Carmelo again and his friend left so others could come to visit. One after the other, those Officers still here with him came and went after making sure their Patron was going to get better. It was not long before Thomas was again alone except for the ever vigilant Fairley. The boy flatly refused to leave and sat by his bed with the brace of Manton's in his hands.

When next he awoke it was to see darkness had arrived and the young figure of Fairley was dozing in the hard wooden chair; the two pistols were still firmly in his hands. Thomas gave a small groan as he tried to ease the stiffness in his limbs; all he wanted now was some solid food and more water. The groan, as light as it had been; was enough to waken Fairley and the boy instantly looked at Thomas in askance.

"Hungry and thirsty and I need to pee."

Thomas was surprised that young Fairley did not even blush at his request; had he known the youngster had been the one looking to all his needs during his recovery, he may have understood better. Fairley smiled as he lay the two pistols aside and took a strange ceramic bottle from under the bed. It was Thomas that suddenly blushed as Fairley lifted the blanket and began to take care of business. It took Thomas a little time before he could release his flow but the relief he felt soon made up for the embarrassment.

Once Finished, Fairley left the room to empty the bottle and find Thomas some food; from the darkness outside his room that was now lit with many candles; Thomas could hear men walking back and forth. He still had his guards to protect him.

For Thomas that first day was to continue in the same manner for another four days. Jervis's instructions were followed to the letter by all in the Hacienda. When Thomas had asked to be let up from the bed, the answer he got from Jervis was succinct and brooked no argument.

"Captain, you will stay in bed until I decide when you can get up and not before. It is my duty both as a friend and your surgeon to make sure you are fit enough to be able to move around on your own; and frankly Captain, that will not be for some time to come. Is that quite clear Captain?"

"Damn it Jervis, there are things I need to see to and I outrank you and will get out of bed when I am damn well good and ready."

"I would not push your luck if I were you Captain; I am the surgeon and in the case of sickness or injury I have final say. Now keep your skinny arse in that bed until I say different or I will have you tied down. Is that clear enough for you Captain?"

"You're a bloody bully Mister Jervis, you just wait until I can get up and around and then we will see who has seniority."

"Don't you try and scare me Captain, it won't work. Now lay back and do as you're damn well told."

"Bully."

"And you are a pain in the arse Captain now do as you're told."

It was to be another three days before Jervis would relent and let Thomas be taken outside to sit in the shade of the wide and expansive veranda that ran right around the large Hacienda; Fairley was always within call or reach.

Thomas had not even been allowed to get out of bed on his own; instead Jervis had called for Perkins and had Thomas lifted from the bed and placed carefully into a strange wicker chair with small wheels under it. Thomas was not a happy chappy at being wheeled around wherever he wanted to go but Jervis had said it was either that or stay in bed; Thomas accepted the strange chair.

Each day he was visited by a number of his men but they were never allowed to stay more than a few minutes before Jervis pushed them from the room. If Thomas had any intentions of asking about the Battalion he was sorely disappointed. Jervis told the visitors that under no circumstances could they discuss anything to do with the Battalion until Thomas was a lot better; no one wanted to go against Jervis while their Patron was under his care.

It was almost a week later and Thomas was now allowed to go for very short walks as long as he had two grown men with him at all times; not for security but in case he felt weak and could not make it back to the safety of the wicker chair. On the fourteenth day after awakening in the bed, Thomas was informed he had a special visitor on his way.

Jervis warned him not to get over excited and was to stay seated at all times or it would be back to the bedroom for another week.

While Thomas was finding Jervis's mothering a little too much to take, he also knew that the young surgeon would make good on his threats. Thomas was again settled under the shade of the veranda when he saw the black coach drawn by six black horses turn into the gateway of the Hacienda; the coat of arms on the door told him all he needed to know about his visitor.

Thomas watched as the Prince of Anglona stepped from the coach accompanied by four of his Generals; the young Prince had a wide smile on his face as he looked up to where Thomas was seated in the shade. Moments later and the Prince was standing above Thomas with his slender hand held out as he said.

"Well Don Thomasino, for a dead man you look remarkably well even if you could do with some fattening and sun. You had us all at the Cortes very worried when we heard the reports. It was only the quick thinking of Don Estaban who told us all what had happened and that you would need time to rest and that it would be better if no one knew of your miraculous escape."

Thomas shook the offered hand and smiled as Fairley appeared with a chair for the Prince to sit on, the Generals all stood a little distance off to let the two speak with a little privacy.

"Thank you Your Highness, I think it's as much a surprise for me as anyone else. I thought the French had done for me when I saw the Dragoon shoot and the ground rush up at me."

"Ah Don Thomasino, only the good die young and as far as the French are concerned, you Don Thomasino are a very bad young man so you should live to a ripe old age."

Thomas had to smile at the Princes jest; he was grateful that no one around made too much of how serious his injuries had been, he did not want to feel like an invalid even though he truly was one.

"Now Don Thomasino, I have been told by your surgeon not to speak of war or anything that may tax you but, as a Prince of Spain I am allowed to break the rules. There has been much speculation over your demise. It would seem the French thought you had been killed during the battle and sent reports to Napoleon saying as much. From what I have discerned, your English Command saw a copy and also had it posted in that newspaper they love so much. Now this may be good or bad but it must be said. The English, believing you killed in action have held a large memorial for you and their orders have gone out to the effect that your Battalion of drummers has been disbanded. It would appear Don Thomasino that you are now dead and unwanted by them."

Thomas could not believe his Battalion was no more as he looked up into the Princes face and saw concern and worry written all over it.

"I know this comes at a bad time for you Don Thomasino but there is also a silver lining should you wish to make use of it?"

"What would that be Your Highness?"

The Prince of Anglona saw how the news had affected Thomas even though the young man did his best not to show it.

"It means that you are now free to join our forces if you wish to still go after the French."

"But what of my men, I can't just leave them to the mercy of those Generals?"

"What men would they be Don Thomasino?"

"All the men of my Battalion of course."

"But I just told you Don Thomasino, there is no more Battalion and there are no more men although I do know of a force of rebels living near Vimeiro that would welcome a General of the Spanish army if he were to join them against the French."

"But how?"

"Well Don Thomasino, as I heard it; when the Battalion was disbanded all of the young Officers tended their resignations immediately and, as for the rank and file; well they seem to have just disappeared into the hills somewhere behind Vimeiro and no one can find them. An interesting situation don't you think?"

"If I am considered dead to the English then what do I have to do for Spain to get my men back?"

"Why Don Thomasino it has already been done. Are you not truly a General in the Spanish army; if this is so then you have the right to at least a Regiment if that is what you wish, it is entirely up to you how you would continue to harass the French. That Don Thomasino is the advantage of being a General; if it so happens that you have a friend in the Cortes, well then anything is possible. Do you have such a friend Don Thomasino?"

"I would sincerely hope so Your Highness."

"Good then it is settled and I can report back to the Cortes that the report of your demise was at best faulty. Now then we have things to do. Firstly, next week when you have gained a little more weight I will send my tailor to have your uniforms measured and made. I will also send my coach maker, a General of such importance must have a coach, don't you agree General Don Thomasino de Toro?"

"A coach Your Highness? What would I do with a coach; I march with my men Your Highness as you well know and as for a uniform; the one we all wear has been fine for nearly three years now; what use would I have for any more?"

"Aha I can see you are not up with the times Don Thomasino. Your need for a full uniform is to impress the English, flashy but important when needed. As for your daily needs, then I will leave it up to you but it must be something that makes you stand out a little more; tiresome I know but needed when in the field. Now as to the coach, it is expected by those of rank to have one, of course if you were to leave it at your

Hacienda when you went into the field then there is little others could say. That is a matter for your own conscience or needs."

"What of the need to arm and provision my men; the English will not help in that regard and I know that the Spanish do not always have the monies needed for such things?"

"I have been told Don Thomasino, that you have friends in some very strange places; perhaps you should contact them and see what they can accommodate you with. I believe you know a certain Colonel Cruickshank; perhaps he may have a few ideas but I would keep it very quiet if you know what I mean. There will come a time when you must face the English Officers once again; in a time of war it is impossible not to so you must be prepared for when that happens. Perhaps should we say at the end of January? I am told you will be fifteen then; it is a good age to be a General in Spain while still young and feisty as you have a reputation for."

"I have to go back to the English in January? Why?"

"Because it is the beginning of the spring and soon after the fighting begins once again. It is necessary for all of us to show our colours at that time and begin to make plans for the season ahead. Do not worry Don Thomasino, you will be among friends and; as the English have declared you fallen in battle you are now free to do as you please. I am looking forward to seeing their faces when a dead man walks amongst them."

Thomas could only look at the Prince with his mouth open as he heard the man saying things that he had never thought about. As he watched the Prince, the other man reached into his jacket and took out what looked much like a newspaper. Unfolding the paper the Prince gave it across to Thomas as he stood up and looked down at the young seated figure.

"I saw this and thought you may like to have the copy; it is an interesting read and it raises some doubts as to the veracity of some English Officers. You may find it interesting to know about before we must meet them in January. Well my dear friend Don Thomasino, use your time well and rest as much as you can. The winter is not far away and it will give you time to organise for your new command. One more thing Don Thomasino!"

"Yes Your Highness?"

"Please, for the sake of the Spanish people and your many friends who have supported you; learn to duck when attacked by a Dragoon with a large pistol; you have given us quite a scare General and we do need your peculiar type of warfare if we are to rid ourselves of the French locusts."

Thomas could not hold back the smile as he looked up at the Prince of Anglona.

"I shall try my best to learn Your Highness."

"Good then I will not have to come all this way to see a ghost again. I will probably not be able to see you much before mid January when we shall prepare to speak with the English, until then Don Thomasino de Toro I hope you will keep your head down; the surprise for some should make it an interesting meeting when they see you."

"Thank you for your visit Your Highness, I shall do as you ask. I may have to move back to Vimeiro around October or November but I will keep myself hidden until I see you again."

"Good that is all I ask. The Cortes sends you their best wishes for a speedy recovery and they all look forward to you taking over our need for your special type of warfare. Their orders are that all Spanish forces are to provide anything and anyone you want. There will be a written order to that effect sent to you in a few days. Don Thomasino, the Cortes is giving you full Carte-Blanc to command your unit anyway you see fit. Now then I must get back to the politics of war, stay well Don Thomasino; until we meet again."

Thomas waved as the Prince left the veranda followed closely by his four Generals. Somehow Thomas felt a new lease on life even though it appeared the English had written him off; it was a heady thought that he could now do as he pleased. Perhaps there was now a way to make his men even safer and they would no longer be at the beck and call of Officers who had ulterior motives for the use of his small army.

As Thomas watched the Princes coach disappear, he opened the newspaper; as expected it was an older copy of the Times. The headline was boldly printed across the front page.

"GREAT VICTORIES CLAIMED BY VISCOUNT WELLINGTON AND MARSHAL BERESFORD IN SPAIN"

Thomas read through the front page article as it described in detail how the two great men had beaten the French in what they claimed to be decisive victories but, it was not that that really interested him; it was a small footnote at the end of the article that drew his eye.

"FALLEN HERO"

Thomas read through the short piece and found he did not know whether to laugh or cry but one thing was for certain; someone had stretched the truth a little too far. Thomas began to reread the article so it was clear in his mind.

"This correspondent has also learned of the demise of the young Captain often called the Hero of Rolica. A report from Marshal Beresford has told of the tragic death of Captain Thomas Marking in a small battle at Olivenca before the plains of Albuera. From Marshal Beresford's report it would seem that our very valiant young Captain volunteered for an impossible mission to delay the advancing army of some 25,000 French troops so that the Marshal had time to form his defences. There have been no reports on any survivors of the small battle at Olivenca and so most if not all have been presumed dead. The Captain's once renowned Battalion has since been disband. We are all sure that the valiant young Captain will be missed by many. A sad ending for an honourable young man."

Thomas could not believe what he was reading. Deep in the pit of his stomach a small fire was lit; the blatant lie by a Senior Officer was plain to see, his respect for the English armies Senior Officers took a sudden and different turn. If they wanted to play it like he was of little importance then there was only one thing for him to do. The return of fire in his belly only made Thomas more determined to get well and reclaim his name and, if that meant he would fight for Spain, then so be it.

Thomas was about to screw the paper up but then changed his mind. He would keep it as a reminder that there were those who held little honour in the search for their own glory; he was not going to let that get in his way anymore. From this day forward Thomas was going to play the part of Don Thomasino de Toro and, if it meant he had to go over and above what was expected then so be it.

The following week, just as promised; the Princes tailor arrived in a small coach. It took only minutes before Thomas was standing and being measured from head to foot. The tailor had tried to insist that Thomas would need at least ten uniforms and it took Thomas a little time to convince the man he did not. Finally a compromise was met and Thomas would accept two dress uniforms and two day wear uniforms, once the decision had been made it then took another hour before Thomas got his way on the design and appearance of his day uniforms; on his dress uniforms he got little if no say; the tailor was adamant that he knew best about what would be required for a General of Spain.

With the tailor gone Thomas could settle back to getting well. Each day that passed he got stronger and he was sure it was the renewed fire in his belly that was responsible for his fast recovery; that and the insistence of Fairley that he eat four times a day and rest for no less than two hours in the afternoon.

It was nearing the end of September and Thomas was now fit and well although he walked with a small limp; the added surgery on his infected leg had shortened his muscles a little and the limp would stay with him for life as would the slight stiffness in his left shoulder. Thomas was now able to walk or march longer distances and he would often be seen watching the tenant farmers at work in the fields. The peacefulness of the scenes gave him a pleasure he did not know existed and he would watch the hard working men and women for hours at a time.

He had found that if he went too close to them they would all stop working, turn towards him and bow to their Patron, Thomas often felt embarrassed and so now kept his distance as he watched.

Thomas was sitting under the shade of the veranda when he saw a stranger approaching; the man looked to be dressed in simple clothes although they were of a better cut than those worn by the farmers he still looked to be of the land, it was to be the first time he was to meet his overseer.

Carmelo appeared and stopped the stranger in the centre of the courtyard. Thomas saw from the corner of his eye the ever present Fairley straighten up and take the musket off his shoulder. Thomas had reclaimed his pistols and had now got back into the habit of wearing them when outside; it had not stopped the young Fairley from feeling he still needed to protect his Captain.

Thomas watched as the two men in the courtyard talked for a few minutes and then saw Carmelo signal the man to follow him up to where Thomas sat sipping his morning cafe. When the two men were standing in front of him he saw the sparkle in Carmelo's eyes as he bowed to Thomas and then said.

"Patron, this is your overseer Senor Delgado; he is enquiring if you would like to join him tomorrow morning for the tax collection?"

"What tax collection Carmelo?"

"The taxing of your tenant farmers Patron. It is done each three month and tomorrow is the time for the next collection."

Thomas sat and looked at the man Delgado; there was something about the man that raised the hackles on the back of his neck.

"Yes Carmelo, I think I would like to see that. Senor Delgado I will meet you at the gate at 10 of the clock, we will take the collection there. Carmelo can you show Senor Delgado to the gate and then come back, I have a few questions to ask."

"Yes Patron."

Carmelo gave Thomas a faint raising of his eyebrows as he turned and led the new man away to the gate; he was back in a minute or so.

"So my brother; what has caught your eye?"

"I don't like him Carmelo; there's something just not right about him."

"Ah my Patron, so you saw it to. He is one not to be trusted Thomas, he was the overseer of the previous landholder and I am sure he had something to do with the French being able to take the Hacienda from Don Juan Rodrigo Hermosa. What do you wish to do about him?"

"Tomorrow have Mister Jones come and take charge of all the man's ledgers and look them over. I want at least four of the guard there as well. One thing more."

"Yes Patron?"

"I have seen the farmers gathering in the feed for the winter but we have no stock to feed, why would they do that?"

"Ah...yes I have forgotten to tell you so much because we were all worried about your health; perhaps now is a good time to tell you things."

"What things?"

"The stock for your Hacienda is hiding in the mountains. You see my Brother, when the French came to take the land, there were those among the farmers who did not want it to happen so they rounded up as much of the stock as they could handle and took it all up into the mountains and hid them in a canyon. They have been watching over them ever since. I will send word out today that they can come home and that you will keep them all safe."

"Yes do that. Now what if my suspicions about Delgado are correct, what am I to do about it?"

"If they are correct Patron then you will do what must be done or; if it is your wish I am sure there are those around that can take care of the problem for you. It would not be wise to have him roaming around the country and informing the French about your survival."

"Yes perhaps you are right Carmelo. Tomorrow we will see. Where does he live on the estate?"

"Not more than five minutes walk from here, he has a small home and keeps to himself most times. It is said he has a very young wife but few see or have ever talked to her. That is perhaps why you have not seen much of him. It appears most only see him at the time of taxing."

"Thank you Carmelo, tomorrow we will know for sure and then make our decisions about his future."

Carmelo smiled as he turned and left Thomas to finish his morning cafe in peace; that his Brother in arms was now almost fully recovered and feeling the need to be busy pleased Carmelo no end. If they were lucky they may be able to leave the Hacienda and make for Vimeiro and the rest of their friends before too much longer; it would be a welcome change.

The next morning just before 10 of the clock saw Thomas and Jones sitting at a small table that had been brought from the kitchen for the collection of taxes. Behind Thomas stood four of his older guards and Fairley was standing close by his side as they watched the tenant farmers begin to congregate for the tri-monthly taxing. Thomas noted that Senor Delgado had not yet put in an appearance and it was not until nearly all of the sixty or so farmers were gathered that the man was seen striding towards the table at the gate.

Thomas was still feeling a distinct dislike for the man as he watched him stride towards him; that the farmers must have also felt the same dislike was not hidden from Thomas. It was plain to see the difference between the clothing of Senor Delgado and the common farmers. Delgado's clothes were of a better cut and cloth whereas the farmers were dressed in not much more than old and worn clothes which could be remarked as being close to tattered rags. Thomas was not impressed and, with a very casual flick of his fingers called Perkins to his side.

Thomas also noted that Delgado's well fed stature was in sharp contrast to the weather and work worn gauntness of the farmers; he almost felt like growling with anger at the difference.

After a short whispered conversation with Perkins, Thomas turned back as Delgado gave a perfunctory bow and took a seat in the third chair; no one noticed two of Perkin's men disappear down the road.

Delgado placed two large thick ledgers on the table and opened one of them at a new page; there was a long list of names and numbers filling the page. Thomas kept his face blank as he watched Delgado get ready to call the names of the tenants and to tell them what their tax was for the period.

Before Delgado could call the first name, Thomas stopped him with a gesture before speaking.

"Senor Delgado, before you begin perhaps you can explain how the taxation works and what you use to rate the taxes?"

"Yes patron. Well Patron it is worked out on the basis of the farmers land holding, his cottage rental and the number of children in the home. If the farmer is unable to pay his full dues he then has to give free labour on your lands until the difference is paid in full. It is a simple and productive way for your lands to be tended and saves you from having to pay for labour; it is an accepted practise Patron."

"Thank you Senor Delgado, please continue with the collection but I would like you to tell them all not to leave after the collection; I wish to have a few words before they go back to their homes."

Delgado nodded and then turned to the waiting farmers and their families to relay the message, most just nodded; there was little they could do if their new Patron wanted it so.

When Delgado called the first farmer to the table he kept one eye on Jones as the young man ran through the pages of the older ledger, he noticed a number of very small crosses being marked along the edge of each page. Delgado seemed oblivious to Jones tinkering with the ledger.

"Farmer Paulo?"

Thomas watched as a man who must have been in his sixties slowly walked to the front of the table and stood with his old worn hat in his hands as Delgado told him what his tax was.

"Paulo, I see you have had your daughter and her husband join you in cottage number ten as well as their two children. I also note you have now got seven goats and two sheep. Your tax has been raised to seven silver, can you make payment?"

Thomas looked at the work-worn face of the old farmer and saw that under the subservient facade was a strong proud man; he watched and listened as the man told his story.

"No Senor Delgado, I have only four silver as it was necessary to use a little to settle my daughter and family."

"Paulo, you well knew that the tax would be more if you had new people staying in the Patron's cottage, why were you not prepared?"

"It is what it is Senor Delgado; I cannot produce silver coins at will and feed my family at the same time."

"Then you will have to give your labour free to the Patron for two months if you can only pay four silver."

Thomas watched as the old farmer stayed silent, it was as though the reply was what the old man was expecting. Thomas watched and listened as each farmer was taxed, he noted that very few had the means to fully pay the tax demanded and all of them would now have to give free labour so they could keep a roof over their heads and the heads of their families. Thomas was not impressed but stayed silent as the last of the tenants paid their dues.

Delgado placed the last entry into his ledger and added the few silver coins to the leather bag he had carried. Before the man could stand to leave and thinking his business of the day was over, Thomas placed a hand on his arm to indicate he should stay seated before he stood to address the tenant farmers.

"Thank you all for your hard work, I know I am new here and do not expect you to want to welcome me on this land that I am sure you have all worked for many years. It has come to my attention that all is not right and I want to make some changes. Before I say more I would ask you to show patience as my man finishes his work on the ledgers. Senor Delgado you will stay until the end just in case I have a question or two. If you all wish to take time to eat while we wait then I have no objections, thank you."

Thomas at back down and watched as Jones ran through the second ledger; Thomas did not miss the faint sheen of nervous sweat on Delgado's brow as Jones turned page after page and added his little crosses.

Ten minutes passed before Jones closed the second ledger and signalled to Thomas that he wanted to talk in private; it was easier than most might have thought as they just changed to their normal language of English leaving those around them in ignorance.

"Well Jones what have you got for me?"

"The bastard has been stealing the Hacienda blind Thomas. These farmers have been working for not much less than nothing for at least the last four years and the amount he has taken from them would have fed their families in style. I hate people like him; I thought it was only at home that there were such greedy people."

"Thanks Jones, oh and by the way; if you were to also resign your commission in the English army I have a position for a good Captain to take charge of the new forces administration."

"Accepted Thomas, or should I say General. I resigned along with all the rest some months ago as did everyone else."

Thomas smiled as he changed back to Spanish.

"Senor Delgado we have certain inquiries to make of your actions. You are hereby placed under arrest until we can investigate further."

Before Thomas could say much more, Delgado jumped to his feet with anger showing on his heavy features. It did not last for long as he felt something cold and hard press against the back of his head, the distinctive sound of two hammers being draw back also caught his attention. When Delgado took the chance to glance behind himself he could only see the hard pale blue eyes of the young boy who had been standing to the left of the Patron; that the boy would pull the triggers on his unusual musket there was little doubt. Delgado sat back down while his face grew red with pent up anger.

As if on cue there came a loud screech of a woman's voice from further down the road leading to the Hacienda. When Thomas saw how young the girl was he could only gasp but it was not just her age that had caught him by surprise; it was her words.

The young girl was struggling in the grasp of Perkin's two men as she screamed and kicked while she tried to free herself from the tight grasp of the two guards. Finally the girl was standing in front of the table; Thomas could feel the rage coming from the silent Delgado beside him.

"Who is this Delgado?"

"It is my wife and you can let her go immediately, I will not allow nor want your barbarians laying hands on her."

"So she is your wife! How long have you been married Senor Delgado?"

"Five years if it's any of your business."

"Everything on this Hacienda is my business Senor Delgado or have you forgotten who is the Patron here?"

Delgado stayed silent but his wife was still spouting curses and screaming at the top of her voice; even the farmers looked at her with distain.

"Perkins can you shut the damn woman up for a minute; we have all we need to know."

Perkins nodded at one of the two guards and he quickly placed his hand over the mouth of the girl and silenced her immediately. Thomas turned back to Delgado.

"Tell me Senor Delgado, how long have you been an agent of the French and yes, if you are wondering how I know then you should know that I speak French and recognised her language immediately. It is also easy to guess why you are both here."

There was silence in the crowd of farmers as they heard Thomas's accusations; had they really had a French spy in their midst for the last four years, what was more surprising was the fact their new young Patron had so easily caught them out, there was a sudden whispering in the small crowd of farmers as Thomas gave Perkins a small signal.

It took less than a minute to have both spies tied tightly; the girl had to be gagged to stop her screaming. Thomas turned to Perkins once again.

"Perkins, I was told you were once a Bosun's Mate on the HMS Carlisle; is that true?"

"Aye Cap'n, true it was."

"Well Mister Mate, what would the men do with a thief amongst the crew?"

"Well Cap'n, there is two ways we would look to him. One is that we report him to Officers and then keelhaul him and make no mistake on the end result."

"And the other?"

"A sharp knife in the middle of the night Cap'n."

"Very good Mister Mate, I will leave Senor Delgado in your tender care."

"And his missus Cap'n?"

"I think it only fitting she be handed to the women of this Hacienda and for them to decide her fate."

"Aye Cap'n, done it is."

It took only seconds for Perkins and his three man guard to lead the prisoner away; it was the last he was ever seen. Thomas turned to the waiting crowd as their eyes followed the disappearing Delgado; as the conversation was held in Spanish, they all knew what was happening.

Thomas looked at all the women that had been silently waiting at the rear of the farmers.

"Ladies I will give you the responsibility of taking care of this French spy; after all it was you who have suffered under the hands of the pair."

Thomas stood silently as all the women of the farmers slowly began to encircle the struggling French woman. Thomas tried not to be too concerned as the farmer's women pulled and tugged at the spy as they led her away and out of the sight of the men; she also was never seen again. Thomas turned back to the waiting farmers but before he could say a word they all heard the sound of a large number of horses trotting towards the gates of the hacienda.

When the horses appeared there was almost a sigh of relief from the farmers. Thomas looked at the riders, each of which rode as though they had been born in the saddle; which was quite possibly true. The sameness of their features, whether old or young told of their relationship with each other. The oldest was an upright older man who seemed to be in his sixties and those following ranged in age from forty something to as young as mid teens.

Each rider was mounted on a jet black horse which had the same lines as those of Estaban's white horses. The riders all carried the long lance like pole and were dressed almost identically in a brown homespun jacket and trousers with worn black calf length boots. It was only the older man that wore the typical flat crowned black hat while the others all wore floppy woollen caps with a small ball at the end.

The riders pulled to a halt just short of the table and the older man looked down at the men gathered there. With little preamble, the older man looked at Thomas and spoke with a strong steady voice.

"You are the Patron El Toro, called Don Thomasino de Toro?"

"Yes Senor, whom do I have the pleasure of addressing?"

"We are the men of the family of Ortega. We are responsible for the livestock of the Hacienda Hermosa. We have returned to bring back your livestock and take up our previous position as protectors of the horses and bulls of Hacienda Hermosa."

"Then I would ask you to join me to tell me more about why you found it necessary to take the stock away and hide them?"

The older man looked down at Thomas with the eyes of a hawk; it was as though he was reading Thomas's most inner thoughts as he looked the young man over. With a slight nod of his head and a small grunt, the older man stepped from the horses and walked to the table in front of Thomas.

"How do I call you Senor?"

"I am Rafael Ortega and these are my sons and grandsons; if you are truly the Patron then we are at your service, Senor."

"I am Thomas Making and the Cortes has given me the title of Don Thomasino de Toro and I have been offered this Hacienda for my lands. These other men are with me but will soon be departing to fight the French once again."

"Thank you Patron, it is what I have heard. My sons and I are at your disposal, you have only the need to ask and it will be done."

"Thank you Rafael Ortega, if you would kindly join us along with Farmer Paulo, there are things I would like to discuss with you both."

Thomas called for the old farmer Paulo to join them and once the two older men were seated, Thomas began to tell them his ideas.

"Senor Paulo, how long have you been on these lands?"

"Patron, we have worked and farmed here for four generations; it is all we know."

"And you Senor Ortega?"

"We have also been here for the same time Patron. I am the Master of the Bulls and my eldest is the Horse Master."

"Thank you Senor's. From the day after tomorrow Senor Paulo, you will take the position of overseer of the farms and, when we have completed the search of Delgado's cottage you will move your family there. Senor Ortega, I would ask you to once again take your rightful place as Master of the Bulls and that your eldest retain his position as well."

Both men gave their thanks to the new Patron and waited for him to continue.

"Senor Paulo I would ask you to inform the tenants that as long as the French have one foot in Spain they will not have to pay taxes again; when the war is done then we can discuss this further. Are you both in agreement?"

Both men looked at the strange young man that was now their Patron; it was something that had never been done before, most Patrons depended on the taxes to improve their own lives but they were not about to reject his expansive and generous offer, they both agreed with a will.

"Senor Paulo I will let you go and tell the other tenants about the new arrangements while I talk further with Senor Ortega."

Old man Paulo rose and then bowed to Thomas before leaving to spread the good news. Thomas turned again to the older man Ortega.

"Senor Ortega, what stock did you manage to save from the French?"

"Patron we were unable to escape with all of it but we did manage to save seven bulls and fifteen cows as well as twenty of your horses, those we left behind were not of the same quality and, while their numbers were a great loss to you the ones we saved are of the finest lines. I personally selected those we would take and made sure they were your finest."

"Thank you Senor Ortega, from this moment on they are your only responsibility. As I have already stated, I will soon be returning to the war with the French and I will need men of the quality and honesty of you and Senor Paulo to watch over these lands while I am away. Now Senor Ortega, there is something you may be able to help me with. His Highness has ordered a carriage for me and I am not certain I know much about them, can you make a suggestion of what horses I should have to pull the coach?"

"Patron I will inform my eldest and he will see to the horses and make sure they are trained for your use. Is there anything else you may need of us?"

"Thank you Senor Ortega, now all I have to do is find a driver as I have no idea at all about driving a carriage."

"Patron, if you will leave this small thing in my hands I will see that you have the best driver I can find; on this you have my word."

"Thank you once again Senor Ortega."

"Is there anything else you may need Patron?"

"Yes Senor Ortega, there is one more thing. For some time I have been in thought about my return to the battle field and I have a small plan that may make the difference."

"May I ask what the Patron has in mind and how I may help?"

"Yes, I am thinking of turning most of my force into a mounted one, it would give us more mobility and hopefully less losses but I will need a lot of horse to do that. Would you know how I would go about getting the many mounts I will need?"

"If the Patron will give me a little time I will ask questions of all those I know; if it can be done then I will do it, this I promise. The people of Spain know of your reputation and I am sure they will help where they can to rid themselves of the French."

"Thank you Senor Ortega, I will let you look to your duties and thank you again for your honesty in saving what you could in the face of the French."

Rafael Ortega stood up and bowed before rejoining his family on their horses. With another small bow from the saddle, Senor Ortega turned his horse and went back the way he had come. The first part of Thomas's new plan had been put into effect, all that remained now was to get completely fit and healthy and return to Vimeiro to be with the men that waited there for him.

The following week his new uniforms arrived and a few days later his new coach also rolled into the yard of the Hacienda. The sight of his dress uniform gave Thomas a sense of dread, there was so much gold braid on it that he thought it may be too heavy for him to wear. Fortunately the tailor had obeyed Thomas's orders for his day wear and he felt much better with the little braid that had to be on it.

The dress uniform was a black tailed jacket with the waist cut short so his sash could be seen around his waist, the front panels of the jacket were heavily braided with gold braid which covered it from top to bottom and, when the jacket was fastened it made the braid look as though it was a continuous line right across the front. The sleeves were also covered in gold braid around the lower cuffs and had patterned swirls that went almost to the top of the sleeves. The collar was high and stiff and again had far too much gold braid for Thomas's liking.

The trousers were also black and on the thighs was more swirling gold braid and his new boots were almost knee high and had an added piece that covered his knees at the front. Thomas could not see where he would be able to put his boot knives and the toes and heels had no steel in them. The hat was another bone of contention. It was in the shape of a sliced fruit and had the cockade of red and gold on the right side and a long white feather set in the brim; for Thomas it was just too much to take in and he hoped he did not have to wear the strange looking uniform more than needed.

The coach was smaller than the one he had ridden in with Mister Percy but could still carry four grown men with space at the rear for two guards to stand. On the door was a crest that Thomas almost found silly at best. The crest was in red and gold paint, at the top was the same symbol that was part of his medallion as a Cavalier de Espana, below that was the head of a bull painted in full detail and it was all surrounded by gold laurels. Below the crest were the words *"Honor a la Valentia y Verdad"* Now that Thomas was so fluent with Spanish it was second nature to translate it. "Honour, Bravery and Truth" Thomas wondered who had thought up that one for him.

Winter was making itself felt in the latter weeks of October when Thomas felt he was ready to make the long trip back to Vimeiro but he would first have to satisfy Mister Jervis; that alone could be a problem if he did not handle it properly.

Jervis finally agreed that it was time Thomas returned to his waiting men at Vimeiro but he made one stipulation that Thomas was entirely not happy with. Thomas could only leave for Vimeiro if he rode in the coach and did not try to march or ride with the others. It took some time arguing but as usual Thomas lost to the more aggressive Jervis. The thought of having to ride in the new coach made Thomas's mood a little darker and; while others around the Hacienda went around with smiles, Thomas more often than not wore a frown.

It was almost the last day of October when they were ready to leave. The coach was pulled by a very dark brown, matched pair of horses. Philippe was the young drivers name and he was about twenty years old and showed the hard calloused hands of a farm worker; he was also one of Senor Ortega's nephews. Before they could leave, Senor Ortega arrived with a large jet black stallion on a lead; with a small bow to Thomas, he said.

"Patron, this is Santana, he is to be your war horse. He is courageous and full of fire just like the Patron. When you go into battle against the French he will keep you safe. Don Hermosa had him trained for one of his sons but now neither of them are with us anymore; it is only fitting that he should carry you against the French pigs."

Thomas looked up at the huge horse; it looked to be at least sixteen hands and its wide chest was very muscular along with the solid looking hindquarters. The horse's neck was a thick curving band of solid muscle and the slightly smaller head was almost strange looking on such a heavily built horse. The jet black mane was long as was the flowing tail and it made the horse look a little wild and yet it stood steadily amongst the many men.

Senor Ortega handed Thomas a few apples which would have been the last of the season and said.

"Patron, if I may suggest that you feed these to him as you travel, by the time you are back in your home at Vimeiro he will know you well. There is no need for steel in his mouth; he is trained to obey your commands by foot and knee. I have been told that Don Estaban Colosio is with you; ask him and he will know what to do to help you learn Santana's ways."

"Thank you Senor Ortega, I will follow your suggestions. Have you had much luck in the search for extra horses?"

"I have put the word out with all the families who are faithful to Spain; when I have an answer I will send a rider to you. How many horses do you think you may need Patron?"

"I am thinking that it will be at least a hundred Senor Ortega, if that is possible?"

"It shall be as you ask Patron."

Thomas thanked the man once again and then looked around as the rest of his men began to form up for the long trip to Vimeiro. There was need for an extra wagon to carry all their needs; four of the large travelling trunks and a number of strange hat boxes belonged to Thomas and he was not even sure what was in them as Fairley had taken charge of all of it for him.

Thomas's new coach sat waiting as the others formed up around it. Lorenco had taken his men out ahead almost an hour before; again they would play vanguard for the column. On the coach sat Philippe along with young Fairley beside him. At the rear on a narrow bench seat were two more of the guards and one more waited to be seated inside the coach so he was close enough to protect Thomas.

Carmelo had his men lined up along both sides of the coach and about ten paces out to the side. Lieutenant Jones was to ride with Thomas in the coach as would Jervis. With a resigned sigh as he looked up at Jervis sitting with his back to the horses, he stepped up into the coach and took his seat. Thomas would sit beside Jervis so that the guard could see any possible threats ahead from his place facing forward just the same as the two seated at the rear on the narrow jump seat.

As the coach finally pulled out of the Hacienda, Thomas saw what must have been every man, woman and child at the Hacienda was lined up along the road to wish him luck. As the coach passed the people would all bow and then call out words of good luck for their new Patron; Thomas almost felt guilty leaving in the way he was. After his latest near death experience he only hoped he would live to be able to return to this new home he had been given.

It was mid-morning on the fourth day when they finally came in sight of the town of Vimeiro. Thomas called a halt and stepped down from the coach as the escort surrounded him in a protective screen. During their travel they had tried as best they could to avoid any large towns or encampments stopping only in smaller villages or on open ground when the need arose.

Night camp was always made somewhere where there were no prying eyes and usually in some small canyon or gully for protection. With Vimeiro finally in sight, Thomas wanted to march in like they had always done and Jervis was not going to get any say in the matter. The wagon and coach were situated to the rear of the column and Carmelo took his place at Thomas's side as the others all formed up into ranks behind them. Thomas's one regret was he had no drummers with him but he still wanted to enter the village in a manner to show respect for the people that had made a home away from home for him.

Lorenco pulled his sharpshooters back so they were only yards ahead of the column and waited for Thomas to give the order to march. It was only moments before Thomas was to give the order that his eye caught movement up by the village; when he saw what was happening his jaw dropped open and tears filled his eyes.

The road leading into the village was being quickly filled with what must have been every person in the village; what happened next just caused more tears to fall as Estaban led his mounted muskets out to either side of the road and formed up in ranks. Next came the masses of infantry and gunners that quickly formed in front of the riders and the final place of honour at the front was given over to Thomas's original drummers.

The drummers lined up in two ranks about five paces ahead of everyone else. When Thomas heard the long drum roll that was the prelude to the Della Guerra he had to gulp and call the order to march. Thomas and his small column began to advance to Vimeiro just as the full force of the Della Guerra filled the valley with its sound. As they marched forward, Thomas saw that the Colour Guard had formed up in the middle of the road with the three flags fluttering lightly in the soft breeze; it did not go unnoticed that the English Union Jack was missing.

As they marched towards the village that they called home and the many friends they had missed for so long, Thomas could not stop the tears that fell on his cheeks. He would never have thought he was such a person as to shed tears just for a home coming or that he had missed all his friends so much.

It was a good ten minutes before they came close to the massed ranks and Thomas was sure his tears could be seen by everyone there. When the small column was only twenty yards away, Thomas heard the voice of Estaban call out above the sound of the drums.

"The army will salute."

Thomas watched as every man except the drummers, aimed their muskets into the air and; at the command from Estaban fired a massed volley that resounded all through the valley. From the villagers there were great cheers and calls of praise for the return of their Patron; that he had survived death at the hands of the hated French was for them the only proof they needed that the Patron El Toro was under the protection of the hand of God.

Arriving before the Colour Guard, Thomas halted and looked at the new commander Lieutenant Carterton as he stood at attention and gave the salute. Thomas still could not stop the trickle of tears both at the return to his many friends as well as finally arriving at his second home.

"Sir, do you wish to lead the Colours into Vimeiro?" Lieutenant Carterton asked Thomas.

"Thank you Lieutenant but I wish for you and the Colours to lead the way. The guard will take station at the fountain and render the salute to the people of Vimeiro."

"Yes Sir. The Colour Guard will advance; about turn, quick march."

Thomas and his friends took a place behind the Colours as they were lead into the small town of Vimeiro. The drums and the applause never stopped for a second as their returning Commander marched with a small limp to the centre of the town with the rest of the army following shortly afterwards.

CHAPTER 4

With the final act of the salute to the people of Vimeiro it was quickly decided that the rest of the day should be a fiesta to celebrate the return of their protector. Within an hour the town was filled with laughing and happy people. The women and mothers of Vimeiro were soon at work preparing food for the hundreds of their young soldiers while the men saw to the slaughter of enough sheep and cattle to feed the masses.

Thomas was quickly led to a place of honour under the shade of a wide veranda that stood out from the front of the only tavern. For the next hour Thomas was beset by friends and villagers as they passed on their congratulations on his return to health and the safety of his adoptive home. Thomas noticed that even here in the safest place he could be in Portugal, his guards were still only steps away and Fairley was once again hovering nearby with his musket on his shoulder.

As Thomas sat in the shade and with the last well wisher gone, it was finally time for him to start working on what he was now going to do. Thomas had some ideas now that he no longer had to report to the Viscount or any other English Officer but it would still take more thought to finalise what he wanted to accomplish.

As he sat with a cool drink in his hand he began to watch the others as they laughed and joked all over the square of the town. As he watched, Thomas started to put things in order; his first duty would be to promote new Officers and set out how he wanted to reform his small army. Now that he was back on his feet and had sole command, he wanted to have more mobile forces so they could hit the French over a wider area. There was also the need for some new guns if he wanted to hit any of the more stationary targets the French had built in Spain over the years.

As Thomas looked around he saw that there was something markedly different about the town. It took him a few minutes before he saw what it was. The town of Vimeiro looked as though every house or shop was newly built. Every surface he saw was freshly white washed and the doors and window trims had been freshly painted. Above every door that he could see was the caricature of the bulls head and a copy of their battle flag flew high on the spire of the small church that serviced the people.

Outside the town were new stone fences holding large gardens and there seemed to be more animals in the open fields; there had been many changes since the last time he had been able to come home. Thomas would find out more the next day when he returned to their valley.

There was just enough of a view from where he sat that Thomas could see the far off rise where his many friends were now buried; he would go the very next day to visit each and every one of those lost; it was the very least he could do for those who had stood by him even at the worst of times.

The fiesta went long into the night although Thomas was ordered to rest by Jervis well before the others called it a night. The next morning Thomas called for his new horse Santana to be brought for him; it was time to visit the fallen and remember who they were and why they had fallen. The losses at Olivenca stilled played on Thomas's mind and he was determined to never let it happen again on such a scale.

With his duty done to the fallen, Thomas returned to the town just as the others were starting to form up for their march to the valley. There were some very sick looking men and boys amongst them but not one of them complained; their El Toro had returned and it was now time to turn their thoughts to defeating the hated French and seek some revenge for those lost at Olivenca.

As the long column entered the valley that was their home Thomas once again saw more changes. The number of small houses had been increased and the older ones now had well built tile roofs or had been freshly thatched. At the far end of the valley was a strange new construction, it had been suggested, designed and finally constructed under the expert eyes of Lieutenant Carterton.

It was an area that had a flat space at the base of the rise of the nearest wall. At the centre was what appeared to be a table made from three large pieces of stone; two upright in the ground with the third lying on top. Around the curve of the wall were set a large number of rough but flat stones in four tiers that faced the stone table. Thomas pointed to the new addition and lifted an eyebrow at Estaban.

"It is now for all meetings Patron. While you were healing we decided it would help to include all of the men when making plans. The Lieutenant has a name for it but I cannot say it; it is a foreign language."

Thomas nodded, he would have to ask Mister Carterton what it was called at some later date but he did like the idea of everyone being able to speak their piece and be heard by all. Finally Thomas arrived at his cabin but now it was nothing like the one he had left all those months ago. The once small cabin had been increased in size and freshly white washed. He was to find that the inside had all his furniture and two extra rooms had been added, one obviously for his war room as there were two large trestle tables covered in newly made maps. Mister Smithson had been a very busy young man in the time Thomas had been away.

Thomas was surprised that he felt so tired as he dismounted from Santana in front of his rebuilt house; it made him think that perhaps he was not as fit for duty as he first thought but there was still much to do although his closest friends flatly told him to rest for the remainder of the day and start fresh on the morrow. Thomas sat on the large chair that was always set aside for his use; it was only moments later when one of the wagons pulled up to his door and Fairley jumped down and began to give orders to three other men.

Thomas watched as the men began to unload several large chests and place them near the open door. Looking at Fairley, Thomas asked him.

"What the devil are all those Fairley?"

"Your travelling trunks Mister Marking."

"What travelling trunks Fairley?"

"The ones His Highness had made for you Mister Marking."

"What the hell do I need travelling trunks for, everything I need can fit into my panniers."

"Not all of it Mister Marking."

Thomas watched as Fairley stepped over to the growing pile of expensive looking trunks and began to explain them.

"This tall one is for your Generals uniforms and boots along with your under cloths; there is also new hose just for your uniform. Now this one Mister Marking is for your everyday uniforms and other things you need on a daily basis. These Mister Marking, are your hat boxes; the Prince wanted to make sure you had all of your hats even from when you were just starting as a drummer Sir. This last one is your arms locker Mister Marking."

Thomas looked at the oblong chest with wonder. It was well made and looked to be very solid. The timber was well finished and the whole was about four feet long, two feet deep and another foot and a half wide. Thomas looked at Fairley and could only shake his head.

"I don't really see the need for all this Fairley. What happens when I have to go into the field, do I have to carry all this with me?"

"No Sir, most of it will stay here in safety; you will only need to take what you need but the Prince insisted that you have everything you may ever need."

"I can see I will have to have words with the Prince before much longer. Show me the Arms locker if you please Fairley."

Fairley called two of the men to carry the large crate inside, once it was on the floor in front of Thomas; Fairley knelt down and opened the padlock before handing the large metal key to Thomas. Thomas watched as Fairley opened the locker, the lid was a few inches deep and lined with fine green baize. Fixed to the lid were Thomas's pair of pocket pistols that were held in place by a metal clasp. Next to the pocket pistols were Thomas's spare knives.

The first shelf in the locker had two wooden pistol cases; one belonged to his Manton's and the other to his double barrelled Purdy's; the rest of the top shelf was filled with all the cleaning and loading kit for his weapons. Fairley pulled out the top shelf and revealed the second one. This shelf had his two spare swords; The Toledo which had been a gift to him as well as a new one that he had not seen before but it was so fancy he surmised it was to wear when he had his formal uniform on. Skully's sword was still worn by Thomas but there was a space set aside on the shelf for it as well.

Fairley removed the second shelf and revealed the bottom of the locker. Sitting in a set of wooden slots was his Livorno musket and beside that an empty place for his double barrelled Purdy musket, Thomas saw that there were still two spaces empty for any new muskets he may acquire over time.

Thomas looked at Fairley and said.

"And just how am I meant to move that bloody thing?"

"It stays here Mister Marking, but if you need to take it then just call for some of the men, they will take care of it for you."

"Well thank you Fairley but I still don't see why I need all this stuff; we came here to fight the French not look like peacocks."

"Yes Mister Marking, what do you want done with it all Sir?"

"Put the damn things in the back somewhere out of sight. Is that all there is Fairley?"

"Yes Sir, these are the last of your trunks. Will you want anything else Sir?"

"Yes Fairley, a bloody large brandy and ask the kitchen if they have a snack I can have before dinner. The ride has taken a bit more out of me than I thought it would."

Fairley smiled as he gave his boss a wave and went looking for some food for him; at least it almost sounded as though the old Captain Marking was back again

Dinner that night was a small affair and only Carmelo and Estaban joined him although Fairley was once again hovering in the background; he seemed to just not trust that his boss was safe unless he was around to watch over him. During the dinner Thomas told his two closest friends what he had been thinking about and asked them for suggestions. For the two hours that dinner went on, the three friends talked about what they would have to do to get their small army ready.

Thomas had shown them both the written orders from the Cortes and they now had to decide what, when and how they were going to make use of all the talents they now had at their disposal. First on the list was a need to appoint new Officers and reform their army into a different type of force; he wanted them to be more mobile and be able to strike at far off targets that the French would never suspect to be under threat. Unknown to Thomas he was about to have a meeting the next day that would answer one of his most pressing needs and would change the game even further in his favour.

The three old friends had only just started eating when they were interrupted by one of the guards from the entrance. When the young guard was beside the table he looked at Thomas for permission to speak; it was given immediately.

"Patron, there is the youngest son of the cobbler wishing to speak with you."

"Bring him here quickly." When the young guard had left Thomas called out for Fairley.

"Can you set another place for our young visitor?"

"Yes Sir."

Fairley quickly set about making an extra place at the large table and had just finished when the young ten year old was led to where the three old friends sat waiting.

The boy smiled as he saw the great El Toro, Patron of Vimeiro. With a small bow of his head he said.

"Patron, I am Emanuel, son of the cobbler and I carry a message from my Papa."

"Come and sit with us Emanuel so you can eat while you tell us your important message." Thomas said.

Emanuel looked please to be invited to sit with the Patron; he would have a great story to tell his friends when he returned to his home that he had sat with the Great Patron and supped at his table. After taking the empty seat and filling his plate, Emanuel looked over at his hero.

"Patron, my father has sent me to tell you that there are three strangers in the town asking for you. They are not of Spain or Portugal and we think they are English but they have no language that we can understand. My father heard them asking for El Toro but that is not the name they used and he only heard the word Toro and so thought of you."

"Can you tell me what they looked like Emanuel?"

"Yes Patron. They are very rough looking men and walk strangely, not like real men but as though they were rolling from side to side. My father thought it very strange Patron and so sent me to tell you."

"Thank your father for his very important message Emanuel and you can tell your Papa that I will send the cart for the men tomorrow. Now then eat with us and Don Estaban will find one of his men to take you home on one of his fine horses."

"Thank you Patron, when I am older I will come and fight the French by your side; this I have already told my Papa."

"Thank you Emanuel but I can only hope we have sent them back to France before you have to do that."

Thomas saw a small frown cross the boys face at this news but Emanuel turned to his plate and said nothing. If the Patron hoped to have all the French sent from their lands before Emanuel could fight by his side then perhaps it was a good thing although he felt a little disappointed that he would not be there to help his Patron.

When dinner was over Estaban called for one of his cousins to take the young boy back to his home, it would be far safer and faster than letting the boy walk alone at night. When Emanuel had disappeared, Thomas told the others what he had been planning and how they would do it all. Thomas got the full co-operation of his two old friends and they set about planning how and what to do the following day.

The small donkey cart left before the sun rose to go to Vimeiro and collect the strangers; Thomas had little doubt they were sailors and probably sent by Mister Percy for some reason. He would have to await their arrival and see why they were looking for him.

Thomas was also up early and was seated under the small veranda when he sent word for Jones to join him for cafe.

Jones arrived quickly although only partly dressed and carried with him a pile of papers with his ever present quill and ink. As the two sat and drank their cafe, Thomas went over what he wanted to do and how he wanted it done. Jones carefully kept detailed notes of everything his boss wanted; there was a lot of work for him to do before late afternoon which is when Thomas was going to inform all the others at a general meeting.

It was mid morning when he saw the small cart arrive back from the town; sitting in the back were three older and rough looking men, that they were sailors was easy to see even without them walking around with their strange rolling gait. It was their mode of dress that gave Thomas all the answers he needed. Thomas was still sitting at the table when the three men were driven close to his house; he had asked for Carmelo and Estaban to be present.

Carmelo and Estaban were sitting at the table with a second cafe and had their jackets open and their legs spread out in front of them as though relaxing and well at ease. Thomas was only in his white shirt and his black jacket was resting on the back of his chair, he also had a fresh cafe at his hand. The three friends watched the strangers dismount from the cart rather stiffly; the long drive had left them stiff and sore.

Thomas and his friends watched as the three obvious sailors made their way to stand in front of the table and look at the three young foreigners; which was the one they had been told to come and see was anyone's guess. The sailor in the lead looked at the three young men. Two of them wore black jackets with a thin curl of gold braid on their shoulder tabs; the other was a little younger and wore only a white shirt. The leader of the sailors turned to look at the oldest of the three; he had to be the one that was in charge. The sailor turned his eyes to Estaban and, along with the other two; bowed their heads slightly and touched their foreheads as though saluting in the manner of a sailor.

"Cap'n Toro, I be Second Mate Bowden of the ship Mary Rae. I be under orders of Cap'n Rat to carry a message for ye."

The three friends looked at one another and each saw the glint in the other's eyes; it was time for a little fun. Estaban's English had improved greatly over time even though his accent was heavy and he still mispronounced some words. As though he was in charge, Estaban turned to Carmelo and gave out a long spiel in Spanish. When Estaban had finished, Carmelo turned to Thomas and told him about a joke he had heard but said it all in Portuguese. Thomas could not help the rather childish giggle that came from his throat and turned to Carmelo and made another bad joke in French which caused the other two to also break into a boyish giggle.

The eyes of all three friends never left the faces of the three sailors as they joked around in languages they knew the newcomers would not understand. After a few more choice words between them, Thomas nodded to Estaban to ask the question he had posed for Second Mate Bowden.

"What is report?"

At hearing the heavy accent of the young man, Bowden was not sure he had the right person; he was sure that Captain Rat had said the person he was looking for would be easily recognisable; this young Spanish lad did not seem the right sort but he still had his orders and the Spaniard had not said he was not Captain Toro.

"Cap'n Toro, Cap'n Rat said to report to you that the Mary Rae has been lost with all hands and all cargo, Sir"

A frown came over Thomas's face as he heard the news; why they were being told he could not for the life of himself understand; it was time to own up to the confused older sailor. Thomas reached down to his left boot and took hold of his black baton; as he straightened up he saw the look on the face of the Second Mate.

Second Mate Bowden looked at the youngest of the three as he bent down for something under the table. The younger man looked to be of lesser years than his two companions but there was a hardness to the young features; it was the look of someone that had seen far too much death for his tender years. The lad could be anywhere between fifteen and eighteen; with the hard bitten look the lad could really be of any age.

Bowden watched as the youngster straightened up; it looked as though the lad was favouring his left arm as he placed a familiar black baton with a silver slave head on top of the table; the lad's voice soon confirmed the lad's heritage as the familiar English accent was plainly heard.

"I'm Captain Toro Mister Mate; sorry for the deception but we have learnt to play it safe with strangers. Now then what's all this about. You say a ship has been lost but it has little to do with us, shouldn't you be reporting it to the Admiralty?"

The shocked look on the Mates face only brought another smile to the three friend's faces as they watched the man try to recover his wits.

"Sorry Cap'n didn't really know who we was speaking to. Cap'n there be a problem with reporting to the Admiralty and Cap'n Rat said we was only to talk to you."

"Then why can't you report to the Admiralty Mister Mate?" Thomas watched as the three men shifted uneasily; he also saw them glance at the half finished mugs of cafe sitting before the three young men. Taking a more relaxed attitude, Thomas called for Fairley who he knew would be well within ear shot as was his habit.

"Fairley could you go and ask Corporal Morgan to make three fresh cafe for our visitors; make sure he adds Colonel Grey's tot as well." There was no reply but Thomas heard Fairley's steps going back into the house; he turned back to the three sailors.

"Mister Mate, perhaps you and your two friends would like to join us for cafe while you tell us why you cannot tell the Admiralty?"

"Thankee Cap'n."

Thomas waited for the three men to sit at the table and it was only moments before Fairley arrived with three fresh mugs of cafe; once the mugs had been tasted by the three sailors, much to their delight by the look on their faces; Bowden looked at Thomas and began.

"Well Cap'n, ye see we can't report to Admiralty as we is all dead. Drowned we was when ship went down and carried us all to Davey Jones locker it did Cap'n"

Thomas watched as the Second Mate took another large sip of the hot cafe; it was obvious the three men had not tasted it before and the addition of the rum only went to make it more tasty for them.

"Well then Mister Mate, if you are all in Davey Jones locker then how is it you sit before us. You don't strike me as one of those ghosts?"

"Well Cap'n if I may have a little of your time, perhaps I can explain it all; of course if your man was to get another mug of this here drink then me throat may be able to spill a little more of the tale Cap'n?"

Thomas smiled as he saw the Second Mate lift his now empty mug; Thomas was sure it was the rum the Mate wanted more of and not the cafe. Thomas nodded to the ever waiting Fairley and then sat back to wait for the Man to continue.

"Well Cap'n, it's like this you see. We was all aboard the Mary Rae when we left Portsmouth to carry supplies for the war. Now we was carrying a full hold of dangerous stuff so was put at back of convoy like. Well Cap'n, as we was getting close to this here Portugal the old girl started to take on water. Well Cap'n, as you may know, we was carrying far too much in holds and the water was rising right fast. Now our Master was an old sea dog and could see there was no way O' saving ship and crew. Well Cap'n, the Master sent up rocket to warn convoy of trouble and; as it was approaching night he called for all to take to the boats."

The Second Mate paused to take a deep drink of the cooling cafe before continuing.

"Now then Cap'n, the Master took his boy what was working his way as cabin boy to his Da and also had two men to man the oars. As they pulled away into the dark the rest of us prepared the ship and watched as the skiff was swallowed up in the dark. Now once the skiff was not to be seen no more we went back below and closed all the cocks and began to pump out the bilges. The escort had come in close just before dark and saw we was low in the water and then left to protect the rest of the convoy as they had been ordered. Well Cap'n, here we was all alone in the dark and the last of the convoy had disappeared so it was time to save the ship and make for a safe harbour."

"I don't see how you could have sunk and all died then Mister Mate?"

"Ah now Cap'n, I be coming to that right soon. Well Cap'n here we was all lost in the dark of night and we hear this loud rushing of water, now we all knows what that was; rough water ahead it was Cap'n. Now the old girl was labouring hard to hold tack when we see's this here wild water ahead. Well Cap'n caught us fair and square it did and so down the old girl went with all hands and cargo. Right nasty time it was Cap'n. We be thinking that the army was going to be right put out by the loss of the old girl being as we was carrying such valuable cargo."

"So I assume you must all have swum ashore and been saved as you are here right now?"

"Not atall Cap'n, drowned we all was, the old girl hit bottom as we was shaking hands with Davey Jones himself."

"Uhm Mister Mate it still does not tell me how you got here?"

"I is coming to that part Cap'n. Well you see Cap'n, here we was waiting for old girl to sink right under us all when she hit bottom; seems we accidentally got into this here small bay and the ship was sitting on bottom with her bow on the shore. Right strange how she got there Cap'n but ours is not to reason the way of Davey Jones. Well Cap'n we waited for the light of day and then seen we was in this little bay and all hidden away from the open sea so I got out small letter written by Cap'n Rat and did as it said. Took us five days to find yon village and then get brought right to you Cap'n."

"You have still not told me why Captain Rat asked you to find us Mister Mate?"

"Oh aye, right you are Cap'n. You see Cap'n as I said before, we was carrying right important supplies for army but as how we was now sunk and all on board is dead, Cap'n Rat told us to find a place to unload said supplies where they would do most good."

"And what are these supplies Mister Mate?"

"Did I not tell you Cap'n?"

Thomas did not miss the twinkle in the mate's eye.

"No Mister Mate you overlooked that part."

"Well bless me Cap'n, must be old age catching up to old bones. Well Cap'n we was carrying twenty of them twelve pounder gun's aboard deck with four caissons, the rest being aboard another ship; and our hold was filled with powder and shot. I was told there is enough there for two or three big battles were it to be saved from a watery grave Cap'n."

Thomas's jaw dropped at the news, it seemed Mister Percy had his own way of helping Thomas and the Council of the Black Hand had done the rest. Thomas smiled at the Second Mate and then asked.

"That's indeed fortunate that your ship sank right on the shore of a hidden bay Mister Mate. How long do you think it would take for someone to help you unload your cargo so you can take to the sea once again?"

"Well Cap'n, if my timing is right I would hazard a guess that the men have mostly unloaded the cargo or a fair amount at least. If you were to have enough men and horses to make the bay I would say about four to five days to get there and then perhaps another day to refloat the old girl. Once that is done we may be able to spend a little time to change her look so the crew can find other employment with a new ship under them. If my memory serves me right I seem to recollect that the old Master did sell off all his rights to old ship before he went to look for safety with the convoy in the skiff."

"I see Mister Mate; so If I knew where to get about seven hundred young men to help refloat the ship we could have all the cargo for payment?"

"That's the thinking I was having Cap'n."

"Well you may be in luck Mister Mate; I just happen to have a few men free in a day or so. This afternoon we have an important meeting with all the men and then we should be free to assist any sailors that may have been accidently put ashore with their ship."

"Thankee Cap'n, right happy we would be to get back asea; this here land walking is not good for old sea legs."

"Then I will ask you and your friends to stay here for the night and we can make our way to your bay tomorrow with men to spare."

"Thankee Cap'n; if you will tell us old sea dogs where to sling hammocks we will let you get back to your business of making the French run for their lives."

Thomas gave a snort of laughter as he asked Fairley to take the three sailors to one of the barracks where they could spend the night; for himself there was still the need to finalise the meeting for this afternoon.

As lunch was served to the three friends, Jones arrived with a stack of papers and three new ledgers which he placed on an empty section of the large table; his blush also told the three that he had also had a small surprise from the new orders.

"So everything is finished Mister Jones?"

"Yes Sir, all is ready as you wanted. Uhm...Sir?"

"Yes Jones?"

"Is it real you want me to have that rank and position?"

"Was it written in those notes I gave you Mister Jones?"

"Well yes Sir."

"Then it must be true, I need you to fulfil that position for us Mister Jones; if you need help then find some of the others to help you; perhaps one or two of the wounded that can no longer fight. I feel bad that there is little for them now they are unable to march or help and I want to keep us all together like always."

"Thank you Sir, I will do as you ask. Sir there is one thing that I think you should be made aware of."

"What's that Mister Jones?"

"The young lad that lost his leg Sir. Seems it has hit him pretty hard and I have fears for him Sir."

"Thank you Mister Jones, perhaps you can find him for me and bring him to lunch with us; there has been enough losses for us without losing one more for no reason. I'll look over these papers while you go and find him; if everything is right then we can tell everyone that the meeting is for 4 of the clock."

Jones nodded and turned away to go and find the young teen he had seen looking very morose and lost as the lad sat all alone and well away from all the other troops. Jones found the teen still sitting alone, the look on the teen's face was one of hopelessness and Jones was sure his fears were well founded. Jones asked the teen what was wrong but all he got was a forlorn look and more tears to join those already on the teen's cheeks.

Jones sat beside the teen and then said.

"The Patron asks if you will join him for lunch."

The teen looked over at Jones and, through the light sobs asked.

"Me, the Patron asks for me? Why would he be concerned for a cripple?"

"Because he cares for all his men even if they can no longer fight they are still his friends and he feels it is his duty to watch over every one of them."

The teen nodded slowly and then struggled to rise as he hooked his crutches under his thin arms; he had lost so much weight after his injuries that he was no longer as strong and fit as before the battle and the loss of his left leg. Jones slowly kept pace with the teen as they moved towards the home of the Patron.

Thomas watched the two men approach where he and the others were sitting at table for lunch. Thomas almost let a tear slip as he saw the young Spaniard hobble on his crutches towards them; his left leg had been amputated above the knee and the teen looked underweight and weakened by the surgery. Thomas waited until the two were standing beside the table before asking the wounded teen about himself.

"What is your name? I have seen you many times in the front rank and you were always a brave and hard fighting member of my army."

"I am Flores De Silva Patron."

"Come and eat with us Flores De Silva, you are welcome at our table."

Flores blushed at being singled out by his Patron; he could not understand why such a great commander would be bothered with him, he could no longer fight and seemed to have little use for any future battles. Flores sat a few places away from his Patron so as not to seem to familiar; he was in a position that he was not used to.

"So Flores, I have heard you are troubled because you were injured in the battle at Olivenca; why would you feel like that, are the other men giving you trouble?"

"No Patron, the others have tried to help me many times, it is only me. I feel I have no use anymore. With no leg I cannot fight for the Patron so there is no use for me here and there is nowhere else for me to go. The Patron's army was my only home."

"Nonsense Flores, for my men there is always a place for them in our army. What did you do before fighting for us?"

"I found work on the farms when I could Patron. The pay was small but enough to put food on my plate and clothes on my back."

"So you know about farming Flores?"

"A little Patron, mostly I watched over the sheep and goats and took them to market for the farmer; he would sometimes let me do the selling for him but under his eye; I found it exciting to bargain with the others."

"Were you good at the bargaining Flores?"

"The farmer said I was very good Patron. I would often get him the top price for his sheep."

Thomas sat back as he watched the underfed teen fill his plate while Fairley poured a glass of wine for the injured teen. Thomas went through his mind and the list he had made for the promotions; in all honesty he could not ignore one of his men just because he had been wounded. Thomas looked at Jones and then pushed the paper of Promotions towards him.

"Mister Jones please add the name of Flores De Silva to the list of promotions. He is to be given the office of Procurement Officer and the rank of Lieutenant. Flores De Silva, from this day you are responsible for obtaining all the livestock for the armies needs. Mister Jones will give you the purse each month and it will be your duty to make sure there is always enough meat on the table for the men. You will deal honestly with the people who sell to you and will make a report of your spending to Mister Jones each month. Do you accept this post Flores De Silva?"

"But Patron, how will I move around, with my legs missing it would take months to walk to the farms that are selling stock?"

"The small cart will be yours to use from this day on; Don Estaban will find a good mule for your use and it will be stocked with what you need to set camp each night. I will also find you a boy to help with the camp if you like or perhaps you have someone in mind to help you?"

"There is one of the younger boys who helps in the kitchen that is from the same place where I was born Patron, I am sure he would help me."

"Then it is settled Lieutenant De Silva; you are now in charge of all live stock procurement. Your duties will begin tomorrow so that Don Estaban has time to get your cart ready. Now then eat up and tell us more about your life."

Thomas tried to ignore the free flowing tears on the cheeks of Flores as the teen gulped before trying to swallow his food. Thomas suddenly felt a great deal better now that he could finally see the results of doing something good for one of his injured; he promised himself he would spend more time looking at ways to help those who could no longer fight due to wounds.

After the slowly eaten lunch, Thomas and his friends went to find somewhere to spend the next two hours of siesta as the torrid heat of the middle of the day shone down on them. This year it was unseasonally hot and should have already gotten colder this close to winter even though the days were shorter and in the far distance was the ever present threat of rain or snow.

Once he had awoken from his afternoon nap, Thomas began to dress in his work day uniform; once finished he went to read through the papers that Jones had prepared for the meeting. Thomas hoped he was doing the right thing by re-organising the army along new lines but he also wanted a more mobile force for what he planned in the not too distant future. There would have to be minor changes as he now would have the use of twenty guns; they also would need a new organisation for what he wanted to achieve.

As the time for the general meeting approached, Thomas saw all of his army making their way to the newly built construction at the end of the valley. There was a lot of light laughter and speculation as to what the Patron was going to do now that he had returned to them. The last few months had been hard on all of the men even though they had much to do under the ever watchful eye of Don Estaban.

Many days had been spent building the new additions to the camp as well as others going out to help the people of Vimeiro. They all felt like the people were now part of their own family and they also felt it was a small way to repay the village for the aide they had freely given when the small army had first stood to the guns on that far off day.

Now that their Patron had returned to them in good health, they all wanted to get back to their main job of harassing the French in their own unique way. There was also the factor that they could once again seek their revenge on the French for past grievances done to their families or to their country as a whole.

Thomas took one last look in the small mirror on the wall of the front room. While he did not like the idea of being stood out by the attachment of the gold braid; he at least had kept it to the minimum for his day uniform.

His overall uniform was still the same cut and in the same black cloth. His sash was the same one he had now had for three years and was showing its age as some of the edges were a little frayed and; even though there had been many attempts to clean it, it still showed faint smudges where dried blood had been cleaned off. His hat was once again the same flat crowned black one that had been worn since the first time and his boots were also the same. There was no way Thomas would part with them if for no other reason than they held his hidden knives and were comfortable.

Thomas's new jacket was the same style of Bolero but now it had three thin rings of gold braid around the edge of his right hand cuff and his thin shoulder tabs also had finely worked gold braid on them. Even this part had been remade for Thomas, there was no longer the usual pins, medallions or heavy braid covering any of their uniforms; Thomas had been happy to pare it all down to what was now seen.

For the Colonels there were two rings of gold braid on the sleeve and the new Majors would have one. The new Captains would have three silver braid rings; the 1st Lieutenants would have two and the 2nd Lieutenants would have a single ring.

For the soon to be new Sergeants there would be three white cloth rings and the Corporals would have two or one depending on their seniority. Thomas had determined that his Originals would still wear their special badge but now placed on their chest as a mark of their service to the little army of guerrillas as they were still highly respected by all those who came along later. All the men would have to re-sign articles for their inclusion in a Spanish force but their pay would not be altered although Jones would now keep a new set of ledgers for the new force but carry over all that was owed to the men from when they were under English orders.

Thomas heard a soft cough at the front door and turned to see Carmelo and Estaban waiting for them in their new uniforms; it was time to tell all the men what was going to happen from this day forward.

As Thomas and the other two approached the new meeting place; he saw that all of the flat stone seats were filled and there was a hub-bub of talk going on as the mass of his army tried to work out what it was all going to be about. Thomas walked to the flat stone table set up below the new seating; he found he could easily see everyone from that central point; it was a well planned addition to the valley.

It took only seconds for silence to descend as Thomas, who was flanked by Carmelo and Estaban, laid the papers on the stone table top; with a last glance at all the men gathered he gave a soft cough to clear his throat before beginning.

Much to Thomas's surprise and before he could say a word, all the men jumped up and stood at attention; after giving a smart salute they all called out as loud as their voices would allow.

"Viva Patron, Viva Patron, Viva Patron."

The loud sound reverberated around the valley as Thomas felt a tear dribble down his cheek; the outgoing of welcome and friendship was not lost as the men finally sat back on their seats to wait for his words.

Thomas unconsciously wiped the tear from his cheek with the sleeve of his jacket before getting down to business; with a final glance at all the expectant faces before him he began.

"Thank you all for the welcome home, I'm really glad to be back with you all. Over the last few months I have been giving a lot of thought about how we should continue and in what form we will fight the French. His Highness the Prince of Anglona and the Cortes of Spain have given us a new name and new direction. As most of you may already know, the English have forgotten about us and declared that we no longer exist in their army. The Cortes has seen fit to give us new hope and for that we have to reorganise and fight in a new way. The Cortes has said we have free reign to fight the French in any manner we wish as long as it rids Spain and Portugal of their presence. Now then, towards this end I have new promotions and new formations for us to use."

Thomas paused to take a breath and wait for everything to sink in before continuing.

"Before we go further I would like to tell our gunners of some news we have just received. It appears that a ship has gone aground in a bay only a few days from here, on board the ship are twenty new guns that we can use and all we have to do is go and get them. Mister Morgan I would like you to arrange for your gunners and the horses for twenty guns; Colonel Colosio will see to the wagons needed to bring back the powder and shot."

Thomas paused again as the talk went around the men at the news they would once again have guns to help them. When there was silence once more, Thomas continued.

"I have here a list of the new Officers and the new arrangement of the army, as I read out the new Officers names I would like you to come up here so the men can see who is who."

Thomas stopped once again as he sorted through the papers on the table until he had the one with the promotions written on it along with the new formations before beginning again.

"Firstly we will now be known as the 1st Regiment of Spanish Guerrillas, we will keep our colours as they are except for the English flag which will no longer be flown alongside our own. If, when you have all heard what I have to say, you no longer wish to fight with us then Mister Jones will see to your payment of all money owed to you; if you wish to stay and fight them we will need for all of you to re-sign articles as members of the Spanish forces. The final decision is yours alone and we will not interfere with any man or boy who wants to leave."

Thomas paused again before taking up the two pages he wanted.

"I am staying to fight and will accept the rank given to me by the Cortes as will Colonel Colosio and Colonel Grey. The following promotions will be effective from today if they are accepted by the men concerned and they wish to stay and fight. The following are the new formations and the new Officers who will take charge of them."

Thomas looked at the expectant faces of the men on the stone seats around the meeting place; it was time to tell them what was ahead.

"Colonel Colosio is now overall Commander of the Cavalry. Colonel Grey is overall Commander of Infantry and Colonel Lorenco will be overall Commander of Scouts. Lieutenant Morgan will be promoted to Major and will Command the guns and the following men are promoted also to Major and take charge of their respective forces and positions."

Thomas then read out the rest of the new promotions and their place in the new forces. When he had finally finished this first part of the meeting he stopped and waited while the mass of his army talked over the new promotions and renewed types of forces and what it would mean for them all. When the men seemed as though they had accepted and were also mostly in favour of the new forces and Officers, Thomas began again after raising his hands for silence.

"I see that most of you think the new ideas are better than being under the orders of the English. Before I continue I would like to ask all those who no longer wish to fight to come and tell Mister Jones so he can see to your due payments of wages so you may leave when you feel ready."

Thomas stopped and waited but was not really surprised that not a single man wanted to leave; some had nowhere else to go and felt that this strange little army was their family; others wanted another chance at revenge on their French invaders but whatever the reason no one wanted to leave, they had all thrown their lot in with the young Patron and where not about to change anything just because they now had a new name.

"There is one important promotion that needs to be mentioned and is under the direct orders of the Cortes. Private Maketja! Please come to the front."

Thomas and the others waited until the young figure of the gypsy boy stood before them; he had a rather nervous look on his young face as he watched his friends standing before him. Thomas raised his voice as he looked around the tiered seating at the expectant men.

"Maketja, you came to us as a prisoner and with little hope for a future. Over time we have all come to accept you and many of us owe you our lives more than once. At Olivenca you stood alone and exposed to the French Cavalry so you could help to save all of us from a sure defeat and death; for these acts of bravery, the Cortes of Spain has given a special decree that you be promoted to Captain and awarded the medallion of a Hero of Spain. Captain Maketja your duties will now be as the Scout Commander of the Cartographers. Your duty will be to see to the safety of the new formation to be known as the Cartographers under the command of Major Smithson. All of your duty will probably be behind the French lines so that Major Smithson can make detailed maps of all the possible sites where we may face the French. The lives of Major Smithson's men will be entirely in your hands and in those who you wish to select for your force. Captain Maketja: Every man here thanks you for what you did to save us all at Olivenca; we will never be able to repay you for saving so many."

Thomas watched as Maketja blushed for the first time that Thomas could remember. For Maketja it was a new feeling that he had never felt before. The Romani were usually the object of jibes and curses so it was completely new for him to be the centre of attention and pointed out as someone special; it got even more pointed when Thomas called out loudly so everyone could hear.

"Men of the 1st Regiment of Spanish Guerrillas: Attention. Three cheers for Captain Maketja: hero of Olivenca and saviour of the Corps. HIP, HIP?"

All around the valley the echo of every voice in the camp was heard as they answered. "HUZZAH" Thomas called the cheer three times with the same result and all Maketja could do was blush as he felt a tear run down his face; nowhere had he ever felt so welcome as he did at that moment. Gone was any suspicion that usually hung around the Romani gypsies when they made contact with outsiders, here he was truly one of them. At last Maketja had found his home and now he had even more reason to rid the land of the French.

Once everyone had settled down Thomas went back to reading out the new promotions and how they would now form up the army. There was to be an increase in the number of mounted musket riders and the Infantry was reduced to two smaller Corps but would now follow a new and tougher training regime. The soon to be new guns would now be changed into four batteries of five guns even though a battery was normally only two guns but there was also now a special battery made up of the newly used rockets but it would have sixteen frame launchers so that they could fire thirty two rockets in a barrage.

Estaban as Commander of Cavalry was now tasked with finding enough mounts for the extras he would have to train as; even with all the French horses they had captured there would still not be enough for the planned three full troops that they hoped would be of one hundred men each. Thomas soon passed on to Estaban about the collection he had started back at the Hacienda; it would only need for Estaban to take enough men back there to bring the horses through to Vimeiro.

Finally as the afternoon grew towards dusk Thomas closed the large meeting; he now needed to organise for the march tomorrow to get their guns and supplies from the waiting ship in the bay north of Peniche where it was hidden from prying eyes by the men with Second Mate Bowden. It turned out that when they left the following morning with the many empty wagons and unencumbered artillery horses, they were to make the bay in only two and a half days.

The speed at which this young army of men, many of whom were not much older than boys totally surprised the Second Mate and his friends; they had had to ride on one of the wagons as they would have had little hope of staying the pace with the others. For Second Mate Bowden it had been a real eye opener; he could now understand the awe in which this young army of misfits had been held by the powers that be and now he could see why they were able to harry the French for more than three years and not be caught.

As they came in full sight of the small bay Thomas was able to see the full vista before him. For some little time they had been able to make out the two tall masts of a ship in the distance but now he could really see what was lying in wait for he and his men. The ship was, just as he had been told; slipped with its stubby bow on the beach but there were two thick rope cables laying out to sea from the stern which was still in the water.

At the bow ran two more cables which ended in two large and heavy anchors set into the deep sand of the beach. Above the beach were huge stacks of what appeared to be many kegs and boxes under the canvas of what must have been spare sails. It was easy to pick out the covers of the guns by their shape and the way they were neatly lined up in two ranks on the more solid ground above the sand.

Thomas was awed at the amount of cargo he saw and it was still being brought ashore by means of the main masts being used as cranes and then the crew would either carry the boxes or; if they were too large or heavy; roll them on smaller spars across the sand. Thomas knew that the ship's crew must have been working like slaves to get so much ashore with so few men. It was time to meet the crew and see to their windfall. Craven Morgan looked as though he was chomping at the bit when his eyes settled on the two lines of covered guns; Thomas was not going to keep him waiting any longer.

CHAPTER 5

NEW PROMOTIONS OF THE 1r REGIMIENTO ESPANOL GUERILLAS.

GENERAL

THOMAS MARKING: DON THOMASINO de TORO.

CAVALIER de ESPANA (ORDER OF SPANISH KNIGHTS).

COMMANDER: 1r REGIMIENTO ESPANOL GUERILLAS

COLONEL'S

DON CARMELO GREY: COMMANDER OF INFANTRY

DON ESTABAN COLOSIO: COMMANDER OF CAVALRY

LORENCO SOUZA: COMMANDER OF SCOUTS

MAJOR'S

OWEN JONES: ADJUTANT AND QUARTERMASTER

CARTRIGHT JERVIS: SURGEON GENERAL OF INFIRMARY

CRAVEN MORGAN: COMMADER OF ARTILLERY

OLIVER PERRIN: COMMANDER 1ST CORPS OF INFANTRY

BENTLY TRENT: COMMANDER 2ND CORPS OF INFANTRY

THIMOTHY CARTERTON: COMMANDER OF THE COLOUR GUARD AND REGIMENTAL ENGINEER

JEREMY SMITHSON: COMMANDER OF CARTOGRAPHY

CAPTAIN'S

SERGIO MARKING (ADOPTIVE): ASSITANT CARTOGRAPHER

CARLITO MARKING (ADOPTIVE): GUARD COMMANDER OF CARTOGRAPHERS

MAKETJA (UNKNOWN ROMANI): SCOUT COMMANDER OF CARTOGRAPHERS

TOMMY PERRIN: COMMANDER 1ST PLATOON 2ND CORPS OF INFANTRY

PABLO CAVALINO; COMMANDER 1ST TROOP OF CAVALRY

THOMASINO CAVALINO: COMMANDER 2ND TROOP OF CAVALRY

DIEGO CAVALINO: COMMANDER 3RD TROOP OF CAVALRY

LIEUTENTANT'S

"SNOT" MORGAN: VICTUALLING OFFICER

SIMON CROXLEY: GUN COMMANDER 1ST BATTERY

BEN CROW: GUN COMMANDER 2ND BATTERY

STANNARD SMITH: GUN COMMANDER 3RD BATTERY

SIMON KENT: GUN COMMANDER 4TH BATTERY

PETER WRIGHT: GUN COMMANDER 5TH BATTERY (MOBILE SWIVEL GUNS AND ROCKETRY)

FLORES DE SILVA: PROCURMENT OFFICER FOR VIMEIRO

SERGEANT'S

TOM FAIRLEY: BATMAN (COMMANDING OFFICER)

Thomas and his Senior Officers had gone ahead of the long convoy of wagons and men to see the beach landing and to find the First Mate Mister O'Grady. Thomas had been told the man's name by Bowden and it was O'Grady that had taken over the ownership of the Mary Rae from its former Master.

The first of the gun train horses were just coming into view when Thomas asked one of the sweating men on the beach for First Mate O'Grady. After he had been told he would find the man up on the beached ship's deck, Thomas went looking for him as Craven Morgan made a direct line for the two rows of guns; they were all that interested him at that moment.

Thomas found that walking through the sand made his limp more noticeable but he tried to ignore it while Estaban kept a close eye on him. Finding a rope ladder leading up to the ship's deck, Thomas began to climb it as a large net filled with casks of powder was swung out above his head. For some reason Thomas tried to duck as it flew above him and then began to descend towards the waiting men on the beach.

As he climbed the last few swaying rungs, Thomas thought how hard the sailors must have worked to get the cargo out of the ship and onto the beach with such a tough way to unload. Once on deck Thomas did not take long to see the man he was looking for.

O'Grady stood on the aft deck and watched every part of the ship as the men below decks waited to refill the thick and heavy cargo net.

At the appearance of the two newcomers, First Mate O'Grady took only a glance which was enough to see the small silver head sticking up from the boot top of the younger of the two men; this was the man he had been told to wait for.

Thomas made his way through the men on the deck until he was at the foot of the steps leading up to where the First Mate stood. When Thomas and Estaban had made it onto the aft deck Thomas looked at the heavy set Mate. The Mate's face was scarred and his hands looked as though they had done a lifetime of hard work; the shoulders were thick and strong and he stood alone with an air of authority that was backed by a hardness rarely seen.

First Mate O'Grady watched the two young men step onto his deck; without thought he drew himself up to his full height and gave a small bow of his head as he touched his non-existent forelock.

"Be you Cap'n Toro, Sir?"

"Yes Mister Mate and I want to thank you and your crew for what you have done for us."

"Aint never no mind Cap'n; just following orders of the council we is."

"Never the less Mister Mate, you have our thanks. Now what can we do to help get you back to sea Mister Mate?"

"Well Cap'n if you can spare a few men we can have the hold empty in a few days or so; it will only be then we can get her off the beach and back into deep water. Once that's done Cap'n we can work on making her look like something else. I have the ships carpenter working on some of it now but with only one apprentice to help him its slow going Sir."

"The rest of my men should be here soon Mister Mate, once here I can let you have as many as you need."

"Can I ask how many that will be Cap'n?"

"I have brought about five hundred with me Mister Mate, some will go back with the guns straight away while others work on loading the wagons, the rest will help you where they can."

"That's a fare number of men Cap'n; where did they all come from?"

"Let's just say they had nothing else to do at this time and the extra effort is good for their training. Now then Mister Mate, what are you going to do once you leave here?"

"That depends on the owners Cap'n."

"And who are they Mister Mate?"

"Well Cap'n, if you can wait a little I will get the orders from Cap'n Rat, I got them down below so if you can excuse me Cap'n I'll go get them for you to read?"

When the First Mate had disappeared down the steps and below deck Thomas stood with Estaban and watched the men working on the deck. There was a continuous sound of creaking ropes and the occasional squeal of a wooden running block as the heavy cargo net was swung out of the hold with its full cargo. On the foredeck the men who worked the large capstan were cursing and sweating as they grunted to turn the capstan under the heavy load. It was a scene of orderly chaos until there was a sudden pall of silence that seemed to swiftly take hold of the entire ship. Even those on the beach had stopped their cursing as they tried to move the heavy cargo through the softer sand and above the high water mark.

Thomas was taken aback at first until he also heard the reason for the sudden stop in the working routine. From below deck there came the urgently running footsteps of the First Mate at the sudden silence. When First Mate O'Grady suddenly appeared holding a rolled parchment in his hand, Thomas now saw and heard the reason for the silence.

Just coming into sight were the first of the horses for the guns and just heard in the distance was the creaking and rumble of the twenty wagons. First Mate O'Grady was the first to understand and started yelling orders to his men as the long column of newcomers came further into sight. With a voice that to Thomas's ear sounded much like his old Sergeant Major in the 33rd, O'Grady began to shout orders.

"WHAT'S THE STOPPING YE BLOODY LUBBERS; GET YOUR BACKS INTO IT OR BY GOD I'LL HAVE THE SKIN OFF YE AFORE THE SUN SETS."

The sudden loud orders soon had the seamen back at work as the column drew closer; Thomas thought it must have been quite a surprise for the few sailors who had laboured so hard to see so many arriving to help.

First Mate O'Grady stepped up to Thomas and handed him the rolled up orders from Mister Percy.

"This be the Cap'ns orders Sir."

Thomas took the scroll and unrolled it. There was no address or heading on the top of the scroll only a single round black spot which explained everything to those who knew what it meant.

Thomas began to read it slowly; his ability at reading was little better than his ability at writing when it came to fancy orders although these were put in plain terms so the Mate could also understand them.

First Mate O'Grady, under the orders of the Council you will take command of the ship once known as the Mary Rae. When the unloading of cargo is complete you will rename said ship the "Avante" and take command. The Avante will now come under the ownership of Marking Shipping Company and you will proceed to employ the ship in the manner of a merchantman. If there were occasion that you came across any French shipping that you surmised could be of benefit, you are hereby given permission to take her and add her to the fleet. After disembarking from your present location you will make your way to Oporto where a refit of sixteen guns will take place. As of the receipt of these orders you are promoted to Captain and will take full charge of the Avante and her crew. Upon meeting with Captain Toro you will ask him for advice on your first cargo and any requirements he may have for you. Should you take a foreign ship once your guns have been set aboard, the prize money will be divided equally among the crew. Any trade done by the Avante will be divided as follows. From the total will be deducted the cost of cargo, from the remains of all monies, half will go to the company of Marking Shipping Company with the other half being equally divided by the officers and crew of the Avante.

So Ordered by the Council.

Thomas saw that the scroll was signed with a simple drawing of a rat sitting in the centre of a black hand. After reading the scroll, Thomas looked at O'Grady with a smile before saying.

"Captain, thank you, it would seem that the Council has taken care of everything; my congratulations. Now then Captain, what do you need from us?"

For a few seconds the new Captain seemed a little flustered as he heard a Council member defer to his needs.

"Well Cap'n we could do with extra hands to unload the rest of the cargo, once that's done we will need strong backs to help get her off the beach and back into deep water. The high tide will help as we have her anchored by the stern and will only need block and tackle to help her back until we can use the windlass on the stern anchors. With that done then it will only be a matter of a few weeks with the few hands I have to make her ready for sea once again."

"What if I was able to give you as many men as you need, when can you be at sea again?"

"Well Cap'n that would depend on how hard and fast they can work, but with extra hands for the carpenter and others on the blocks we could cut that time by a fair amount. Now then Cap'n, the Council says to ask you for advice on cargo once we gets to Oporto. What do you suggest Cap'n?"

"I will have to give it some thought Captain but I am starting to get some ideas. There is however one thing that we desperately need. Our surgeon is very low on medicines for the wounded; I would like to ask him for a list so you can procure it in England. The cost can come from any cargo we ship over there and I will send a message to a friend on the London docks to meet you there, he will organise everything we need. I would suggest Captain O'Grady that we make this bay our own base for unloading anything we need. Do you have any suggestions on how we could make it more accommodating for the ship to unload here?"

O'Grady at first seemed a little taken aback at being asked what he wanted but he soon recovered and began to look around at the small hidden bay; it took only a few minutes before he decided what could be done and turned back to the young Councillor.

While O'Grady had been thinking, Thomas had watched the arrival of the rest of his small army of men. There had been little preamble when they arrived and their officers immediately got them to stack arms, although they still wore their pistols, and then they were sent to help the sailors on the beach with the older and stronger men going to start loading the arriving wagons. Major Craven Morgan was already at the guns and setting the men to arranging them for the journey back to the valley.

Major Morgan had set only four horses to each gun as they did not have to pull any caissons with them; the extra horses he sent over to the wagons as the loads were going to be heavy and would need the extra power as the wagons only had four horses to pull them. Lorenco had sent his scouts out into the countryside to watch for any attempts against them. It was not long before the once quiet bay was again a hive of activity as the five hundred extra men and boys added to the noise of unloading the ship and making the wagons ready for departure to the valley.

Thomas took his eyes away from the orderly chaos below and waited for O'Grady to tell him what he was thinking.

"Well Cap'n, if it was possible there is one way to help with any unloading but it would take time, hard work and an Engineer to do it so mayhap it's too much to ask."

"Tell me what you're thinking Captain?"

"Well Sir, if you look down yonder near the far end of the bay."

Thomas followed O'Grady's finger and saw where he was pointing. At the far end of the bay it cut back into the towering cliff and formed a smaller bay that would be hidden from any searching eyes from almost any direction. Thomas nodded that he saw where the Captain was pointing.

"Well Sir, if we was to get a dock built down there we could unload much more quickly. The water there is very deep, even at low tide so we could make it in and out with little trouble but the making of a dock there would take men and a good plan to complete. I don't see much in the way of timber around this part to make the piles so it may not be much we can do. We can just unload by long boat; it will take longer but better than beaching the old girl each time."

"Leave it with me Captain; I think I may have someone that will fit the bill and more than enough men to build something for you. Do you know how long you will be in dock at Oporto?"

"I don't know Sir but my guess would be that the Council will have something to say about the refit so it could be less time than most would have to spend."

"Well when you leave ask someone to send a message to me; the Council know how to find me. Once you have had your refit I would suggest that you ask around for a full cargo of the Oporto wine; it should fetch a good penny or two in England and give you coin to buy cargo for your return."

"I will look to that Sir; now then as it is getting on to dark perhaps you would like to join me for dinner?"

"I have a better idea Captain. My own men will have a good hot meal ready by now so I will ask you and all your crew to join my men. After seeing what they have done this last two weeks I think they all deserve something special and that's what my boys are good at."

"Thank you Sir, I must admit that pickled pork and hard tack becomes a little hard to take after such hard work and nothing else to relieve it."

"Good then call your men to the beach and we'll go see what the boys have got for us."

O'Grady called to all his crew to stop work and gather on the beach, it was not difficult to get the crew to agree to eating with the newcomers; the heavy smell of fresh cooking food had been in the breeze of the offshore wind for some time.

The well cooked dinner was enjoyed by the crew and it also turned out that, as many of Major Morgan's gunners were all ex seamen that some of the crew had old friends to explain the strange army to them and who the young leader really was. There were more than a few awed looks among the rough crew when they found out who Thomas really was.

The next day was to see the last of the cargo unloaded now they had so many extra helpers. All the guns had left but there was still a large pile of cargo under the heavy canvas that would take far longer to transport by wagon back to Vimeiro; it was to be a long journey to get the last of it back to safety as Thomas only had the twenty wagons to use.

With the cargo now unloaded and the ship much lighter it took only half a day to ease her back into deeper water off the beach where the carpenter and a new horde of youngsters helped him to make the necessary changes before she could once again take to the sea and start her new life as the first ship of the Marking Shipping Company and registered under the flag of Portugal.

With the ship almost ready to leave and the second arrival of the wagons, there was little left for Thomas to do. After calling Estaban, Thomas mounted his horse Santana and began to take a leisurely ride at walking pace as he let his thoughts turn to the new problems that had now arisen due to his name being used for the new company. It seemed to Thomas that the Council had once again taken things into their own hands.

As he rode Thomas began to form some ideas as to what he should do with the new situation, that he now had his own means to replenish any of his needs via the ship was one of the good points; all he needed now was a way to purchase what he may need from England and still keep his secret from others that he was still alive and ready to fight.

As Thomas rode back into the temporary camp above the beach, he saw what could be the simple answer to his plans. Riding towards the tent kitchen he called for Snot to come and see him. When the ever smiling boy arrived beside his horse; Thomas looked at him with a smile of his own.

"Lieutenant Morgan I have a special job for you."

Thomas saw the smile widen as Snot was told he was now needed for something special; Thomas thought the boys face would split in half as he waited for Thomas to tell him what was needed.

"Lieutenant do you have another boy who can take over the kitchen duties for a while?"

"Yes Sir, all of them can work without me around; they might even like it for a change Sir."

"Good then I have something for you to do and it will mean you will be away for some time. Can you come over to my tent and we will discuss it further."

Snot Morgan jumped to attention and saluted while Thomas chuckled and turned the horse for his tent where Estaban was just sitting down at the small field table. Thomas soon had one of Estaban's boys arrive to take the horse back to be rubbed down while Thomas sat with Estaban to wait for Snot to arrive.

The young teen arrived moments later and Thomas told him to sit while he explained what he wanted him to do.

"How is your riding ability Snot?"

"Quite good now Mister Marking; Colonel Colosio's men have been good at teaching me."

"That's good; now what I want you to do is ride back to Vimeiro and get a change of clothes, pack them in a pannier and then ride for Lisbon. I'll give you a message for Major Jones and he will give you some coin. When you get to Lisbon use what coin you need to find passage on a ship that's going back to England. I'll give you a paper that may help you to find a place on a ship. When you get to England I want you to go to your father and give him a message from me then wait for his answer and return here. I want you in uniform at all times and take your firearms with you. I want you to try to be back here within three or four weeks if you can."

"Yes Sir, when should I leave for Vimeiro Sir?"

"Go and collect anything that belongs to you and come back here, I'll have the papers ready for you then and Colonel Colosio will find a good horse for you."

Snot saluted again and ran off; it was not often someone trusted him to do something so important all on his own. Snot determined he would not let his General down.

Thomas was just finishing the letter to help Snot find a ship passage. He had written it just as Percy had shown him all those long months ago and was signed with a black outline of a hand with the number 13 at the centre.

When Snot entered his tent, Thomas gave him the three messages. The first was for Jones and would get Snot the coin needed for his journey; there was also a foot note for Jervis to make a list of his medical needs. The second was for Peter Morgan with a message about the soon to arrive new ship and what Thomas hoped Peter could find for him as a cargo. Thomas was going to have the Avante loaded with Oporto wines and anything else the new Captain could find to fill his holds.

On the return journey the ship would hopefully carry the needed medicines that Jervis had asked for and the rest of the back loading was left to the wits of the new Captain. The last note was for Snot to use at the docks in Lisbon which Thomas hoped would help to get him on a ship quickly.

Thomas explained it all to a very alert Snot. The young teen saluted and before he ran for his waiting horse that Estaban had allocated for his use, Thomas told him to ask Mister Carterton to come to the bay for a special meeting. Snot's horse was to be stabled in Lisbon to wait for Snots return from England.

Thomas could finally sit back and take a breath as he saw the first of the wagons returning from Vimeiro. Thomas saw that there were now extra horses attached to the wagon and as soon as it stopped near the huge pile of cargo it was swarmed by his men and reloaded in very quick time. Thomas saw that the driver changed places with another man so the wagon could move off as soon as it was fully loaded.

It was only an hour before dark when the second empty wagon arrived to get its second load. The same procedure was followed and the wagon was moving out towards Vimeiro just as darkness fell an hour later.

A number of wagons continued to arrive one at a time through the night, they were also reloaded quickly and the driver changed before starting their return to Vimeiro. Thomas's men at the bay would keep up this system until the full cargo had been taken back to their home valley. Thomas had not intended to stay for such a long time at the bay but once he had asked Mister Carterton to look at some type of dock for the ships return it was decided to stay so all the men he had there could help to build Carterton's design.

The weather had also turned for the worse and, although the bay was protected from the sea by the unusual shape of the headland, the camp was still battered when the wind rose and came off the landward side. There were days when the heavy rains made working on the emerging dock almost impossible yet the men struggled on with Mister Carterton's design as well as reloading any wagons that made the trip back from Vimeiro.

Craven Morgan had stayed back at Vimeiro to retrain his men on the new guns but had sent all of the horses to work on the wagons as the loads were far too heavy for the normal four horses.

It was the last days of December when the final wagon left for home and Thomas decided it was time for the men to get back for some well earned rest; the only ones to stay were those asked for by Mister Carterton to finish off the last of the work on the dock. When the last fifty men finished the topping of the dock with cut stone, they would come back to Vimeiro and have extra time off to rest.

With everything in order and those staying behind had been given enough supplies to keep them going for the estimated extra week, Thomas led the rest for home. Although most of the returning men were tired they were also now very fit and had worked hard both during the day and many times late into the night when wagons had arrived.

It did not take much urging to get the men to increase their pace so that in only two and a half days they were marching through the pass and into their home valley for some well earned rest; for Thomas it was just the start of more long hours of planning. It would soon be time for El Toro to reappear and harass the French like never before; there were debts of blood to be paid and they were to be paid in full.

It was at the end of the first week of January 1812 and Thomas was now almost fifteen although many said he looked older than his years; Thomas put it all down to his injuries and the cost it had taken to heal and get back to his normal self.

The previous night there had been another large party set out for him to celebrate his birthday a little early and the arrival of Mister Carterton and the fifty men left behind to finish the dock earlier on the same day made Thomas twice as happy. The next morning he was alerted by the guard that a rider was approaching at speed and he asked for him to be sent right to him.

The rider was one of Prince Pedro Pimentel's messengers. The message was both welcome and yet unwelcome as Thomas read the parchment. The Prince was asking for his appearance at an estate just outside Lisbon in two weeks time along with all of his officers. Thomas was informed that it was to be a Ball in celebration for the start of the campaign season and would be attended by all of the English, Spanish and Portuguese Officers and their ladies; Thomas was asked to be there at least a day early for meetings with the Prince before the Ball.

Thomas had Jones write a reply to say he would be there on time and sent the tired rider off on his return. It was two days later that he saw the returning men of the map making troop come through the gate at the head of the valley.

Jeremy Smithson looked worn as did all the others, Thomas was to learn they had been moving at their best speed to make it back with all the new maps so Thomas could see what had so far been accomplished. Maketja was in the lead with his twenty men of the scout squad while Carlito, Smithson and Sergio led the three pack mules and urged them to hurry as they finally closed on their home valley and some well needed rest.

Thomas saw how tired they all were and told them to go and rest, they could tender their report the next day when they had time to think and get their thoughts in proper order. The large barn at the end of the valley was now almost bulging with the tightly packed supplies from the ship; they had even had to use two of the smaller houses as powder stores to get it all under cover.

Craven Morgan was working his gun crews mercilessly and in all conditions while the rest of the small army went through their own training in readiness for the upcoming attacks behind the French lines. Thomas had been surprised when Mister Oliver Perrin asked for permission to train his men to a new way of climbing. Oliver went into an explanation of how he had seen the men of Austria climbing tall mountains with the use of ropes and strange thick leather belts.

Olive told Thomas that his old Patron had taken him a number of times to Europe during the summer months where he had seen many things not known in England; the climbing was one of them. Thomas agreed that Oliver could train his full corps in the hope that one day it could be used to their own advantage. Thomas was not really enthused when he found out that the men would be swinging down high cliffs at the end of ropes but Oliver told him it would be perfectly safe as long as the men followed Oliver's rules.

Winter was almost over and it was only days before the Celebration Ball; Snot had not yet returned but Thomas could not wait any longer if he wanted to be on time for the meeting with the Prince. Thomas assembled all his Officers and told them to pack their best dress uniforms; those who had not had one had asked the Mothers of Vimeiro to make them one. Using the patterns from Carmelo, Estaban and Thomas, the Mothers were soon hard at work and had the uniforms ready well before they were needed.

The need to inform the men of what was to happen caused Thomas to call for a general meeting where he informed the rest of the men that they would be under the orders of their Sergeants until the Officers returned in a few days. Thomas also told them that, if Snot returned before he was back then the young Lieutenant was to stay and wait for Thomas's return and then give his report.

The next morning and in the very early light of dawn Thomas led all his officers out of the valley and onto the road for Lisbon. They would ride hard and hoped to make the Capital before dark which would mean they would not be stopping for lunch but eat in the saddle as they went. All of the officers wore their normal arms as they travelled and would only change into their dress uniforms once it was time to go to the Ball.

They all arrived in Lisbon just after dark which for Thomas just suited him fine, the less number of people that saw them at this stage could only be better for them all. There had been no arrangements made for their stay in Lisbon and so it took another hour for them to find an Inn that could accommodate them and their horses; it also suited Thomas that the Inn was more towards the outer edges of the main city.

The next morning Thomas told the officers to take the day off; only Carmelo, Estaban, Lorenco and Thomas had to go to the meeting and he would tell the others all about it when they returned. The other officers were to use the time off to go about the city and have fun, there were many places they could spend some of their coins that they had amassed over time and not spent. Thomas gave strict orders that the older officers were to watch over the younger ones as they may have ideas of using some of their youthful exuberance to cause trouble in the city while Thomas and the Senior Officers were away.

Thomas and the other three rode off towards the Estate where the Prince waited for them. The message Thomas had received gave instruction on how to find the Estate which proved to be on the other side of Lisbon, which did not make Thomas exactly happy as he did not want to be recognised by any of the thousands of English soldiers now in the city.

It would have set Thomas's mind to rest had he known that no one would have recognised him nor that as everyone thought he was now dead, there was no one looking for a young Spanish Officer; even so Thomas kept his black hat pulled low over his face and his head down a little as they rode at a quick trot through the city until they could see the large Estate in the distance.

Thomas and his three friends were ushered through the large gates without pause and directed towards the rear of the huge Hacienda where their horses would be taken care of while they were in their meeting. The estate was well guarded by a huge number of soldiers which were on constant patrol around the large high walls of the hacienda as Thomas and his friends found their way to the rear.

Once the horses had been handed to a number of hostlers, the young Officers made their way to a side door that had the Prince standing outside and waiting for them. The four young Officers stopped and saluted the partially dressed Prince as he stood with a mug of cafe in his hands; had anyone been watching they would never have thought the half dressed young man was a Prince by his casual demeanour.

"Welcome Don Thomasino, you and your friends are just in time for Cafe. Will you join me?"

"Thank you Your Highness; we didn't stop to have ours this morning." Replied Thomas.

"Good, then it is just the right time for us to relax before we have to talk about more serious things. How is your little army coming along? Do you have everything you need?"

"The men are training well Your Highness and want nothing more than to repay the French. As to supplies we have been fortunate enough to have an English ship come into our hands, it had much of what we needed."

"Ah yes, I did hear of a ship hiding in a bay on the coast, my informants thought it may have been smugglers trying to bring in supplies for the rebels that fight with the French but once I had a description of the men unloading her I had an idea it may well be you and your men. Did they have everything you needed?"

"Just about Your Highness, we were in need of medical supplies but that is now being taken care of as we speak."

"Good, now then here is your cafes, let's sit and talk of other things while we drink."

The conversation now turned to more mundane things, the weather, the influx of troops into the city and anything else that was not directly about the upcoming campaign season. The Prince was relaxed and seemed to have an air about him of a normal trader talking about business rather than one of the most important men in the Spanish forces.

It was fully an hour later and after a light breakfast had been served and eaten before the Prince asked them to follow him into his temporary war room off to the side of the main house. The room had been set up with huge maps of Spain which marked where they thought the French had bivouacked over winter and where they were thought to try to attack in the spring.

Thomas looked at the many maps and realised how much better and more detailed Mister Smithson's were. Thomas and his friends were pointed to chairs around a large table and the Prince took the one in front of the largest map; it was time to get down to business. Thomas and the others had just taken their seats when a side door was opened and a number of Spain's Senior Officers walked into the war room.

Thomas and his friends rose from their chairs and waited for the men to enter as the Prince smiled at the newcomers before saying.

"Don Thomasino, I presume you know some of these men? General Cuesta, General Martino and of course our most valued ally General Livorno so let me introduce you to the others." Thomas smiled at the three Generals as they also returned a nod and smile before the Prince continued.

"Don Thomasino this is General Braun and General Arriaga of the Portuguese Artillery and finally General Joaquin Blake y Joyes, Commander in Chief of all Spanish forces. As you may know Don Thomasino, the English have insisted we use their Senior Officers to command most of our troops but I can assure you we also have our own small cabal of selected Officers that report directly to the Cortes. Gentlemen; General Don Thomasino de Toro Commander of the 1r Regimiento Espanol Guerrillas, better known as the Patron El Toro."

Thomas was surprised when all of these high ranking Generals snapped to attention and saluted him before they broke into smiles and went about shaking his hand. General Blake y Joyes spoke for the others.

"Don Thomasino we are glad that the report of your early demise was it seems, a little premature. I personally would like to extend my thanks for all you have done to save our homeland and hope that you can now once again become the terror of the French. Your reputation and that of your unusual army has put back bone into our own men and they now meet the French with far less hesitation."

Thomas blushed at the fine words and then replied.

"Thank you Sir, I also hope we can once again take revenge on the French invaders for the people of Spain and Portugal."

"I'm sure you will Don Thomasino and if there is ever anything I can help you with then please send word and it shall be done."

The Prince now interrupted as he indicated the open chairs for the new Generals to sit at.

"Gentlemen we have business at hand if you would take your seats and we can bring our esteemed friend up to date with the current situation."

There was a shuffling of chairs as everyone found a place at the table to sit in comfort before the Prince continued.

"Don Thomasino, I am not sure how much you know about the current situation as I know you have been well out of sight and sound for most of your time spent recovering so I shall tell you what has happened so far before we get into what is to come. Ten days ago Viscount Wellington defeated the French at Ciudad Rodrigo and has pushed them back towards Salamanca where they are resetting their lines. At the moment he is moving his forces south towards Badajoz; I am told he hopes to also defeat them there to protect his rear before turning back north and taking Salamanca around the middle of the year."

The Prince paused as he watched Thomas take in all the new information before continuing.

"Now the main reason I have asked you here is that once again we are in need of your special talents. As I have already said, our Generals are somewhat hampered by the English Officers need to command most of our forces so it leaves us little lee way to do things for ourselves. Now then Don Thomasino, as you are; to the best of the English Army's knowledge now dead, we have a chance for you to be totally free to do what you and your men do best. The French forces far outnumber ours and the English so we are in bad need for you to hunt them behind their lines as you have before. As you also achieved the objective of pulling large numbers of troops back to guard their lines of supply, we are hoping you can do it once again."

Thomas watched and nodded as he listened to the plans of the Prince.

"We have heard vague rumours of Napoleon wanting to attack Russia; if he does this then he will not have reinforcements for Spain so the more disruptions you can cause for them the less men we will have to face on the battle field. Do you think you can achieve this for us Don Thomasino?"

"We will give it our utmost best Your Highness."

"I'm sure you will Don Thomasino. Now then let me show you what we have so far."

The Prince followed by all of the others, stood up and went to the largest map hanging on the wall. Prince Pedro began to point out the area he wanted Thomas and his men to disrupt.

"The area here behind Salamanca is where we would like you to strike, there are many other places but your small force would be stretched too far for safety so we thought you would be better used just behind Salamanca until it is taken then you could move on to other areas to do the same once again."

"What are the other places you had in mind Your Highness?"

"Well it is a large part of Spain and the distances may even end up being your defeat if you tried to spread your men too thin."

"Perhaps you could just show me Your Highness and then we will see what we can do about them?"

"Well if you think so Don Thomasino?"

Thomas smiled as he nodded; it almost seemed that the Prince did not really grasp what he and his small army could really do if they had free rein. The Prince looked deeply at Thomas as though trying to gauge his sincerity but he then sighed and turned back to the large map.

"The easiest way would be for me to tell you that the Viscount has ideas of entering Madrid before the campaign season is over, possibly around August or September depending on the French resistance. It leaves the question that any area that could be a supply line or line used to bring in reinforcements would be a possible place to attack."

The Prince showed Thomas the placing on the map of Madrid and the outlying areas that could possibly be resupply lines. Thomas stood silently and looked over the map as his brain went into planning mode. After a few minutes of inspecting the map and letting his imagination run wild he turned back to the Prince and began to ask questions.

"Your Highness, do you know what roads they are using for supply lines to the north and east of Madrid?"

"Well yes Don Thomasino, we have quite detailed reports on their movements of supplies. It would seem Don Thomasino that you have inspired many of the ordinary people to rise up against the French now that they are being pushed back by the English forces. There were tales of some fifty thousand peasants around the country making raids on small patrols of French troops all over the country. It seems their favourite thing is to leave behind a certain small red and gold flag with a bulls head on it. From some of the reports I have seen the French are not happy to have El Toro still in the field and spread all over the countryside; especially as they reported that you were killed at Olivenca."

"The people are raiding them on their own? What about reprisals, the French are known for taking revenge on any rebellion by the people."

"There have been some reprisals but it seems the French are not as avid about going into small towns as they once were so many of the people have gone unpunished by them, something that could work in your favour. So Don Thomasino, what do you think?"

"Our plan since we first started is to disrupt the French over as wide an area as we can at the same time; it has worked for us in the past and keeps the French on their toes as they never know when or where we are going to strike. I think Your Highness we have to continue as we always have."

"So you plan to divide your forces and attempt to make the French run all over Spain hunting for you?"

"Yes Your Highness but we also plan to do far more damage than they can sustain. If I may Your Highness, I will show you what I have thought out so far."

The Prince stepped back from the map and let Thomas move in close. After a few more minutes of thought, Thomas began to give a rough outline of his plan.

"I think we should start here at Medina del Campo, it is close to Salamanca and must be on their main supply route. As this must be a very important place for them we will hit it hard and very fast then disappear before they can bring troops up from Salamanca. Next we will hit Tudela, Aranda, Somosiera and Toro all at the same time. As you can see on the map Your Highness it is in the form of a circle that covers a wide area behind their lines; it may hopefully give them the idea they are now surrounded to the north and east. Even though we don't have the numbers it should play on their minds that it would appear they now have no line of retreat."

The Prince and other Senior Officers looked at the map and Thomas saw them all nodding their heads at the audacious plan, it was once again the Prince that brought up what he perceived as a problem for Thomas.

"Don Thomasino, what you plan will take thousands of troops and you have only a few hundred, how can you hope to carry it out without being annihilated. At the first sound of a shot they will have troops all over you. Medina del Campo must be one of their staging areas as close to Salamanca as it is?"

"Surprise Your Highness, I am hoping it would be the last thing they would think we would do so close to their main lines, that and the fact we will be long gone before they can send reinforcements."

"A bold plan Don Thomasino, we can only hope you know what you are doing, on the other hand; if you were to get away with it then it would put the fear of God into the French when they realise they are not safe anywhere in Spain. How will you be able to attack all of the other places with so few men?"

"Our mobility Your Highness. Each place will be attacked by some of our best men who can move with surprising speed when the need arises. Our way of fighting Your Highness is to never stop and fight a battle; you know the outcome of that type of fighting for us after Olivenca. We move in fast, do as much damage as we can then disappear before they can organise their defences or come after us."

"I see, well Don Thomasino what do you have planned once the French are running around the north looking for you?"

"We will then attack both Molina and Villaviciosa, again at the same time and draw more of them to the east, hopefully from around the Madrid defences and, as a last needle for them, when we have a date for the attack on Salamanca we will then attack in the Guadarrama Pass near Escorial, it should make them feel that the pass to Madrid is closed off and they will feel more isolated."

"You have described a large area of Spain Don Thomasino, if you succeed then the French will certainly be on the back foot as it were; I hope you can make it work, the more of them running around the country chasing you then the better we will all be when it comes time for battle. Now Don Thomasino, there is only one thing more to discuss."

"And what is that Your Highness?"

"The celebrations for tomorrow. We are planning a long day of entertainment for our English friends. I know they traditionally have a ball in the evening but this year I have prevailed upon the Viscount to let me host the festivities. It will start in the afternoon once the heat of the day is past and then continue on into the evening with the main Ball. Here is what I would like from you Don Thomasino, it should make the day even more enjoyable and I cannot wait to see the looks on certain people's faces."

For the next hour, Thomas and his friends listened and planned with the Prince for the next day. While the Ball was the last thing Thomas wanted to look forward to, the plan set up by the Prince had a certain amount of fun in it and that Thomas could not ignore or even want to avoid.

When the planning for the celebrations was finally done, the Prince called a halt to the rest of the day and then led Thomas and his friends outside to see where the beginning of the celebrations would be held and the large garden area that the guests would be making use of until the evening Ball.

Once outside of the main Hacienda, Thomas saw that they were standing on a huge patio paved with granite and at the centre was a wide set of stone steps which led down to a wide expanse of green lawn. There was space enough for hundreds of people on both the patio and the immaculate gardens. Prince Pedro spread his arms and smiled at Thomas as he explained what he had in mind for the next day.

"I will have my men appear from over there at the far corner of the Hacienda, they will form ranks at that end of the gardens. If you are in place inside I will have one of my servants bring me the message and when my men begin I would like you to lead your officers through the main entrance and out here onto the top of the patio close by those steps. I will be standing at the top with some of the most Senior Officers and it will be from there I will start the introductions; if there is some way for you to hide your features until the last moment it would add to the fun."

Thomas had a broad smile on his face as he caught onto what the Prince was trying to do, the idea of causing a little discomfort to any English Officers that may be within sight was just another added benefit for Thomas.

"I will do my best Your Highness. This may be the first time I am looking forward to an official function."

The Prince clapped his hands and smiled widely as he then clapped Thomas on the back with a glint of humour in his eyes.

"Good then we will see you and your Officers at about 4 of the clock. I have asked the guests to arrive for the festivities at 3 of the clock so with luck most will be here before you put in your appearance. Well my young friend, it is time for rest. Until tomorrow and we shall see what we see. I must confess I am looking forward to this with great anticipation."

"As am I Your Highness. Until tomorrow and thank you for all you have done for myself and my men."

The two shook hands and then Thomas did the same with the rest of the Senior Officers before he turned and left the open patio with his friends as he heard the Prince and the Officers chuckling about the plans for the festivities.

CHAPTER 6

The next morning dawned overcast but by midday the sky had cleared and the prospect for the rest of the day was good. The first of the Princes guests started to arrive a little before 3 of the clock and continued over the next hour. Most of the married Officers had brought their wives with them on this, one of the most important days of the year. The beginning of the new campaign season was always a great time for the military men and was seen as a chance to make a good impression on those who held their futures in their hands.

On the garden lawn below the wide patio the women had been ensconced in a large marquee where they would be protected from the glare and heat of the bright Spanish sun. The ladies were attended mostly by their husbands but the younger unmarried Officers had made a home for themselves in the second marquee that was set aside as the main bar area.

A large number of the Princes servants were circulating with large silver trays of small finger food for those who felt a little hungry. To the far left on the patio a small quintet played the popular music of the time while the most Senior Officers stood in a group at the top of the wide stone steps that led into the garden below. Prince Pedro Alfonso Pimentel stood with his own Senior Officers and was chatting amiably with those of Viscount Wellington.

The Prince was the epitome of politeness and cordiality as he made sure all his guests were fully enjoying themselves as he talked to the specially selected and invited guests.

"My Lord Viscount, firstly I must apologise that not all of my guests are here on time; especially one of my own Generals who, unfortunately has quite a distance to travel and has been away for some months. I am hoping he will show shortly as I wanted you to especially meet him, you may find you have a little in common with him as far as your unorthodox manner of fighting the scourge we have been invaded with."

"And how would that be Your Highness?"

"Why my Lord Viscount, was it not yourself that noticed the young drummer boy in the first place and then saw the possibilities of how he could be used to better your campaign?"

"Ah yes I see; well Your highness he did show some little promise and was even able to carry out some small attacks to disrupt the French. A pity really Your Highness that he volunteered to confront the full force of the French in the manner he did; he could have made something of himself eventually had he not been so rash." The Viscount turned to the General beside him.

"What do you say Beresford? That young drummer had some little potential don't you think?"

"Well My Lord he was rather brash but then he was only a ranker and we all know they cannot perform the real duties of a true Officer. Personally My Lord I think he overstepped the mark and got his just deserts."

"Quite true Beresford, quite true. Well Your Highness you can see that we tried to improve his lot in the world, however some people of low birth just do not have what it takes when the fighting starts. Did you know Your Highness that his father also served under me out in India; much like his son he was also one of those brash sorts; cost him his leg in the end. Blood will out Your Highness."

"Yes my Lord Viscount I tend to agree with you, blood will out in the end." The Prince turned slightly to his right and spoke to the portly man standing beside another younger Colonel. "Ah I see that you were able to attend Colonel Cruikshank; it has been some time since we last had time together. What are your opinions on the young man we were just discussing?"

Percy Cruikshank smiled at the Prince and then looked at the English Officers all standing around waiting for his opinion, most knew of his friendship with the deceased young man and wondered what he would say in front of so many Senior Officers.

"Well Your Highness, as you know I was quite taken with the young man and I could never really say he was the type to be brash, especially when it came to the lives of his fellow troops. But as we have seen; sometimes things just do not work out as we plan them. I do agree that for him to volunteer to meet the full force of the French head on doesn't really sound like the sort of thing he would do, but then I was not there so perhaps he overestimated his abilities and perhaps not. I suppose we will never know unless he returns from the grave to tell us."

"Well put Colonel, I must also admit I was quite taken with him and his new but strange ideas on how to conduct a battle but there was something rather novel about his approach to all things military."

"Tell me Your Highness." The Viscount asked. "What made you think this General of yours was similar to the drummer boy?"

"Oh he uses much the same type of offensive against the French. He has few numbers but his results are quite remarkable for what he has to work with; he is also quite an ingenious young man and that is why he rose in our ranks so quickly. Amongst the general population he is quite revered; his name is often spoken by the ordinary man and it is only because of his feats behind the French lines that the people avidly follow him. I am sure you will find him entertaining. Perhaps my Lord Viscount you would even impart some helpful advice to him when he gets here; I'm sure he will appreciate your help and knowledge"

"Well I shall surely try Your Highness. Does he speak English Your Highness? Sometimes things can be lost in the translation if he does not?"

"Oh yes my Lord Viscount, in fact he is also quite the scholar for one so young. If I am correct I believe he can speak some four languages almost fluently although I must admit his English is perhaps not of the highest calibre but he does try his best."

"Thank you Your Highness, I am sure I can cope if it comes to that. Tell me Your Highness, is he high born, we have found that the best officers have to be high born so they can command the respect of the lower ranks. I really don't know what the army would come to if just anyone was promoted above their station."

"Just like that young drummer boy do you mean my Lord Viscount?"

"Exactly Your highness, we all saw how badly that ended."

"Well you need have no fear on that count My Lord Viscount. He is not only a Knight of Spain but he also has his own Hacienda and more than five thousand acres of land, I'm sure you will find he is quite well adjusted in matters pertaining to correctness."

Percy shuffled his feet before speaking.

"Excuse me Your Highness, but it would appear one of your servants is trying to attract your attention."

"Thank you Colonel Cruikshank, I will have to see what he wants; the cook has probably burnt the bread once again. Will you gentlemen please excuse me for a moment; I shall try not to be too long."

The Prince gave a small bow and smile as he turned towards the open doorway of the Hacienda and went to speak with the waiting servant. The conversation took only a few seconds before the Prince nodded his head and the servant returned inside to the shadows of the great hall that ran the length of the main building. Prince Pedro turned back to his important guests and smiled as he walked towards them; no one saw the small nod he gave to a young Lieutenant that was standing at the far end of the Hacienda as though on guard.

At the Princes nod the Lieutenant suddenly came upright and disappeared around the far corner as the Prince waved a hand at the small quintet at the other end of the patio; the silence was immediate and the large crowd below suddenly also grew quiet as the music stopped. The Prince took his place at the top of the steps and looked down on the assembled crowd; he was just beside the Viscount as he began to speak louder so that everyone could hear him.

"My Lords, Ladies and Gentlemen Officers, my apologies for disturbing your enjoyment but it has just come to my notice that my special guest has finally arrived and I am sure he would like to be introduced to you all. Before he appears I have a little entertainment for you in the form of my own drum troop who wish to mark this special occasion with their rendition of our most famous martial music; the De La Guerra. I am sure some of you have heard it before although I believe it is sometimes called the Della Guerra by some English folk. My Lords, Ladies and Gentlemen, the De La Guerra."

At the far end of the large Hacienda came the sound of a single drum marking the time to set the pace for marching. From behind the Hacienda came a troop of thirty drummers accompanied by a single young Officer who was carrying a long silver staff.

The drummers marched with perfection as they finally formed up in three ranks at the far end of the large garden.

When the troop was in ranks, the young Lieutenant stepped to the front, placed the butt of the long silver staff on the ground with his left hand and snapped a very smart salute to the Prince. With a return of the salute and a small nod of his head, the Prince stepped back a little so he was standing almost beside Mister Percy.

As the first drummer began the long drum roll, one at a time the others began to join in. While the drum roll was being played, the Prince saw Mister Percy pull a handkerchief from his pocket and cover his lower face as he pretended to cough.

"Is there something disturbing you Colonel?" The Prince asked with a smile on his face. Percy looked at the Prince and even the crinkles at the corner of his eyes told he was trying not to laugh out loud in front of all the Officers.

"Not at all Your Highness, I just had a sudden thought of what we are about to see and the reactions it may cause."

The Prince smiled as he turned back to watch the drummers and his guests. Percy felt a slight nudge on his elbow and looked up at the Colonel standing close beside him.

"What's going on Colonel Cruikshank?"

"What makes you think there is anything going on Colonel Lewis?"

"Something is going on Colonel Cruikshank and it has the smell of something a certain young drummer boy would dream up if he were still alive."

"I really don't know what you mean Colonel Lewis, but if it were true a wise man would have his handkerchief ready in case he had to cover his smile in a hurry."

Colonel Lewis nodded and stayed silent but Percy noticed the younger man reach into his pocket for his handkerchief as the voice of Marshal Beresford was heard at the front of the watching Officers as the drums drew closer to the full rendition of the De La Guerra.

"Your Highness, does this piece of music have a story about it like most martial music?"

"It certainly does Marshal Beresford. When our troops hear this they know the order has been passed that there will be no quarter given, no retreat and no prisoners taken. We use it to instil fear into our enemies by making it known that when they hear our drums they will only be carried off the field in a dead man's cart."

"Ah I see Your Highness and tell me, does it work?"

"Undoubtedly Marshal, did not your own young drummer use it to great effect at times?"

"Yes Your Highness but it did him little good in the end. Playing a drum is far different than meeting the enemy eye to eye and bayonet to bayonet Your Highness."

"So I have heard Marshal Beresford, I am led to believe that Albuera was such a battle, you must have been very lucky to take the day Marshal if all I have heard is true."

Before Beresford could reply the drums started fully into the De La Guerra and their thunder filled the gardens and echoed out into the open countryside surrounding the large Hacienda. At the end of the De La Guerra there was only a single drum marking the time while the rest stayed at attention; it was then that those standing on the patio heard the unmistakeable sound of booted feet on stone flooring; it was coming from behind them.

As though they were all tied with the same piece of rope, the Officers turned towards the sound of marching feet as they moved closer in time with the single drum beat. From the shadows of the great hall came a sight that almost overawed the watching Officers.

The Officers approaching the waiting men were in a phalanx and three abreast, at their head was a youngish man of medium height and his fancy uniform looked just a little too large for his slender frame. Neither Percy nor the Prince missed the sarcastic comment from behind them; the voice betrayed the person as Marshal Beresford.

"If they are going to wear such outlandish uniforms they should get a man that can wear it to effect. The General looks as though he could do with a damn good meal."

A whispered reply was heard by those closest.

"It would appear that these foreigners think looking like a popinjay will be enough to win their battles for them, too flashy for my taste if you ask me."

Some of the other Officers nodded in agreement as they watched the youngish General march towards them. He was dressed in the usual over fancy uniform that the foreigners seemed to prefer. It was all black and his knee length boots were much like those worn by the cavalry. On the thighs was a very intricate pattern of gold thread and around his waist was a sash of red and gold; it looked to be a little the worse for wear and detracted a little from the overall effect.

The jacket was a masterpiece of heavy gold braid and finely worked gold threads on the two front panels. The sleeves were also covered in the gold braid and there was a strange red patch on his left shoulder which none of the watching Officers could quite make out. On his shoulders were a pair of very heavily braided epaulets which almost looked too heavy for the slender figure to carry.

The Generals hat was a Bicorn and was worn fore and aft and pulled down a little low so it covered most of the Generals upper features. Around the curved brim of the hat was heavy gold braid and a white feather was nestled along the upper part of the upturned brim. On the right hand side was a red and gold cockade but at the very top was a circle of black. The high collar of the jacket kept the General's head up but the hat still hid most of his upper features.

For those watching it appeared the slender General was carrying far more braid than he could handle but the lower part of his face was firm and the lips pressed together in a straight line. It was noticed by those watching that the General walked with a limp to his right leg and his left hand appeared to be also suffering as his hand rested on the hilt of a very fancy and expensive looking sword.

Behind the General were three Colonels and the only difference was a little less braid and they wore their Bicorn's sideways. From the ranks of watching Officers there came a few soft whispers as some of the older Officers recognised the three Colonels but mostly it was missed by many.

Behind those four in front were the rest of the Officers of the strange group and they appeared to number about twenty four in all. Behind the Colonels were seven Majors, following them were seven Captains and bringing up the rear were seven Lieutenants that appeared to be mostly very young. The Majors and Captains wore black Shako's with the red and gold cockade tipped with black and the young Lieutenants wore a familiar flat crowned black hat with a red and gold band.

When the group was only a few steps from the large group of Senior Officers they all came to a halt just as the single drum finished its rata-tat-tat. With the precision of well trained troops, the new arrivals came to attention and saluted in unison and waited for the Prince to return the salute before dropping their arms. The Prince turned back to the waiting English Officers just as Mister Percy heard a sharp intake of breath from Colonel Lewis and saw the younger man lift his handkerchief up to cover his lower face.

Colonel Lewis at first did not recognise the young General but he did recognise some of the Officers with him; for Colonel Lewis it could mean only one thing so he quickly covered his growing smile so as not to spoil the surprise that was coming for the other Officers. Colonel Lewis kept his head down to hide the ever growing smile as the Prince began the introductions.

"My Lord Viscount and Officers of His Majesty King George of England, I would like to introduce General Don Thomasino de Toro; Knight of Spain and commanding Officer of the 1r Regimiento Espanol Guerrillas. Don Thomasino these fine English Officers are sent to help us rid our lands of the accursed French."

As the Prince finished his introduction the General reached up with his right hand and removed his Bicorn to reveal his face. As he tucked the hat under his left arm the look on his face was cold and his eyes were like sharp pin points as he looked over the stunned English Officers.

"Thank you Your Highness but I have made the acquaintance of most of these...er...Gentlemen previously, I am sure they are well known to me."

Thomas found it very difficult to keep a straight face as he heard the splutters of surprise and disbelief coming from most of the Officers as they took in the young General before them; if he had truly been a ghost it would not have caused as much surprise; or in the case of Marshal Beresford, concern.

Viscount Wellington was the first to recover from the shock of seeing a ghost from the past.

"Captain Marking!"

"No Sir, I am now known as Don Thomasino de Toro, a Knight of Spain and a Landholder."

"Ahh...well...err yes, well Don Ahm Thomasino, I'm sorry young man but you are still an Officer of England as you have never rescinded your rank in any formal manner so I must insist on calling you Captain Marking."

"Sir you may insist all you like but it will not make it true. You yourself declared me dead at Olivenca and that means I no longer have a duty to England. Sir a corpse cannot be an Officer; unless I am mistaken and the English army has taken to enlisting the dead."

"Young man you are being impertinent and I must ask you to retract that statement or face courts martial for your unseemly actions."

"Sir you seem to not understand, I am no longer duty bound to your laws. I'm a Knight of Spain and answer only to my adopted country and the Cortes. If you wish to lay a complaint I suggest you make contact with my superiors. There is also the matter of the misreporting of the situation that took place at Olivenca as I am sure Marshal Beresford knows."

"What's this? Are you accusing one of my most senior and trusted Officers Sir?"

"Yes Sir I am. Marshal Beresford has reported that I and my men volunteered to face the French army in an attempt to slow their advance. These facts are not only incorrect but tantamount to a downright lie Sir. The Marshal was the one to give explicit orders for my corps to stand against the French in a temporary redoubt which would have been nothing less than a death trap. I had tried to dissuade the Marshal from insisting on this action but was completely ignored and threatened with courts martial and cowardness if I refused to obey his demands."

"I have heard nothing of this and I trust my Officers to know what is right and most beneficial for the army. Do you have any proof of what you accuse the Marshal of or even a copy of the supposed orders?"

"Yes Sir I have a witness to the orders even though the Marshal refused to present me with written orders and I was dismissed before I could insist on receiving any. If I may call Major Perrin of the 1st corps of infantry he will verify the verbal orders given to me and could also state what he saw at Olivenca prior to the French attack. If you desired further proof I also have available Major Carterton who also stood with me at Olivenca."

The sudden loud voice of Marshal Beresford was heard before the Viscount could reply to Thomas.

"My Lord I must protest, Carterton is nothing more than a cowardly deserter and, as for Perrin the man ran from Olivenca when he had been ordered to stand and fight by me personally. His cowardliness was continued when he resigned his commission the moment the battle was over at Albuera. Neither of these men have any veracity what so ever My Lord."

The distasteful discussion had caused voices to be raised and there was a total silence in every part of the large gardens as everyone tried to hear without missing anything. The accusations being raised caused some concern in certain areas, the least of which was the ever silent and watchful Colonel Percy Cruikshank. Viscount Wellington was known for his hard stand on cowards but he was also well known for his sense of justice where any accusations were made whether it was against an ordinary soldier or one of his Officers.

Viscount Wellington looked at the two main protagonists, of them both he was for some reason more inclined to believe the young man who had saved his bacon more than once; it was time to make a decision.

"Gentlemen it appears we have something of a situation here that needs further investigation. As I was not personally privy to what went on or the orders given I will need some time to find out what exactly went on. General Marking, at this stage I have to accept that your reported demise at the hands of the French does allow you to accept the position you have now found yourself in and we must all accept that you are now the responsibility of the Cortes of Spain. The two Officers you mentioned may have to be called for their report should it come to a courts martial but I also have to accept that they were free of re-enlist with the Spanish forces. Marshal Beresford we will have to discuss your report further but I would suggest you withdraw your accusations of cowardness on the two young men mentioned previously unless you have definite proof of their cowardness."

"My Lord I must protest, those two young men failed to carry out my orders which I personally expressed to them, in doing so they showed cowardliness in the face of the enemy."

"What is your proof Marshal Beresford?"

"Sir if I may interrupt?" Thomas said before Beresford could continue with his accusations.

"General Marking?"

Thomas took note that the Viscount was now using his new rank in front of all the other Officers.

"Sir There was no cowardness on the part of either of my Officers. Major Carterton carried out the orders of Marshal Beresford to the letter, in fact Sir had not Major Carterton stayed behind to guard and protect the colours we may all have been lost. Major Perrin was under my express orders to escort the engineers back to Marshal Beresford's line as well as inform the Marshal of the French numbers and route of advance so he could prepare his lines accordingly. Major Perrin did not leave the field of his own accord and twice refused to leave as he felt he and his men would be needed by us against such a large force. It was only due to my insistence that he finally gave in and carried out the duties I had assigned for him."

"Is this true Marshal Beresford?"

"I don't really know My Lord but as far as I am concerned young Perrin turned his back on the redoubt after I had directly ordered him to stay and fight. That the commander of the redoubt ordered him to leave is against my personal orders to both parties; that My Lord smacks of cowardliness in the face of the enemy."

Viscount Wellington looked at Thomas for a reply.

"Sir I have been informed that on his return to the Marshal's lines, Major Perrin was ordered into the front line at the centre of the Marshal's army, it was a blatant attempt to put him in a place of extreme danger in the hope he would not survive the contact with the French; as you can see Sir, it did not work and the Major then resigned his commission and came to join with us so he could continue to fight the French; that is not the actions of a coward Sir."

"Well gentlemen it would seem we have something of an impasse. Your Highness, it would appear I have need of an urgent meeting with my Senior Staff. I would ask you to excuse my Officers and I so that we can get to the bottom of this affair with some urgency."

"Of course my Lord Viscount, I only hope it has not spoiled your day and that you can find a solution quickly and justly. I hope your other men will be allowed to stay and enjoy the rest of the celebrations while you continue with your meeting."

"Yes Your Highness I am sure they would much prefer to stay and enjoy your hospitality. Now Your Highness if you will excuse us so we can work on getting to the bottom of this unfortunate affair."

As the English Officers strode purposefully past the other young Officers of the Spanish corps, one of the young Captains smiled widely at Marshal Beresford. As the Marshal scowled at the youngster he saw the Captain raise his right hand with the forefinger extended and draw it across his throat in a well known gesture, the Marshal noticed the very young Captain had the last two fingers of that hand missing. Marshal Beresford scowled again and grunted as he stomped away to follow the other English Officers from the patio and out of sight.

Thomas watched the men leave and then was surprised when a voice close to his ear spoke quietly.

"I'm damn glad you made it back to us Thomas, if there is anything I can ever do; as little as it may be, then send one of your youngsters to see me. It perhaps would not be a good idea for you to show yourself to often at the Viscounts tent."

"Thank you Colonel Lewis and I shall keep it in mind."

"Good, now I better catch up to the others before the Viscount see's I am missing. Good luck General de Toro, I hope you will keep me informed of your whereabouts when convenient."

"I shall try Colonel and keep yourself safe as well."

Thomas gave the friendly Colonel a wave and then turned to the widely smiling Prince.

"Well Don Thomasino that went better than we expected; I always knew you were made of sterner stuff than the English gave you credit for. Ah Colonel Cruikshank, I see you have decided to stay with us, perhaps you would care to join us for the rest of the day? I am sure Don Thomasino would like the chance to enjoy your company."

"Thank you Your Highness, I think it would be far safer here than anywhere close to the Viscount at this time. So Thomas, at last we meet again. I'm sorry I could not get to see you sooner but certain things kept me out of the country for some time. You know you gave some of us quite a scare, we actually thought we had lost you there for a few months."

"Thank you Mister Percy, it's good to see you once again and, yes there are a few things I would like to get cleared up before the day is out."

"Good then let's enjoy His Highnesses hospitality while we discuss what you have been up to and what your plans are for the future."

The rest of the day and evening went well even though the absence of the Senior Staff Officers was taken note of by those attending the celebrations and it was late in the night before the Ball finally drew to a close and the guests began to make their way back to their homes and accommodations. Thomas and his men soon joined the Prince and Colonel Cruikshank for a late night toddy while they finally relaxed in good company, there were still many things Thomas needed clearing from Mister Percy and so it turned into a very late night indeed.

Thomas, Carmelo, Estaban and Lorenco joined Percy and the Prince in one of the very well appointed studies for their late night toddy's. Before he sat down in the thickly stuffed chair, Thomas ran his forefinger around the tight collar of his jacket, the constriction reminded him too much of the thick hard choker he had to wear as a drummer boy; it was not a pleasant thought or feeling.

Seeing Thomas trying to loosen his tight collar, the Prince looked at the others and said.

"Gentlemen, let's free ourselves of these coats and relax; it is not the time for formality, there has been enough of that for one day."

The Prince smiled as he saw Thomas smile and sigh with relief as he began to quickly unbutton his heavy jacket and free himself of both the weight and the uncomfortable tightness. With his jacket off and his cravat loosened, Thomas took a sip from the fine Oporto wine and settled back into the padded chair with relief. It had been a long and stressful day but the end result pleased him no end.

With all of them now partially disrobed and settled back in comfort, Thomas turned to Percy and asked.

"Mister Percy, why did the Council name the shipping company as they did?"

"Aha straight to the point as usual young Thomas. Well it had many reasons but the main one was that no one in the shipping business really knows who you are so it was safer for all concerned to use your name. I sincerely hope you don't mind. Any ships that join your company will undergo refits under the eyes of the Council whether in England or here in Portugal. There is one thing though and I am sure you can work out the reason for it when I tell you. The Council do ask that you offer them a tithe of 10% of the profits which they will use in various forms to aid those in need. Do you agree?"

"Certainly Mister Percy, it is the least I can do after what they have done for me."

"Good then it is settled, I'm sure you will see the benefit in the long run, especially when this damn war is over and the French have run for home. Now then I want to know where you plan to go from here."

"Our plans so far are to attack the French behind their lines once again. We are going to start to the north of Salamanca and try to infer that we are surrounding them in the rear and cutting off their escape north. If this succeeds then they will have to pull a great number of troops away from the front to protect their rear, we will then move on to other parts and do the same once again."

"That sounds exactly what we need and I also appreciate it is far more your style of fighting so you should have great success. Is there anything you need from me?"

"Not at this time Mister Percy but I may have to call upon you at a later time. The landing of those guns has filled the one weakness we had and the men thank you kindly for what you did."

"Think nothing of it Thomas, I'm sure some damn young artillery Officer would have just wasted them or even worse lost them to the French, better you make good use of them where they will do most good."

"We will certainly make good use of them Mister Percy, of that you can be assured."

"I know you will Thomas, if anyone can do it I know you will. Now then let's see how long this fine bottle of Oporto lasts before we have to go to our beds."

For the next hour the talk was mostly on incidental subjects and any talk of the war was ignored in the welcome companionship of good friends and allies. The Princes celebration and Ball was the talk of the town the next day as Thomas led his men out of Lisbon and turned towards Vimeiro, it was time to get back to the business of war.

Thomas and his men had been back in Vimeiro for five days when he decided it was time to make his move north and once again take on the French. Major Smithson's maps now came into their own and the fine details went a long way to making the planning so much easier.

As on previous occasions, Thomas had his small army split up for the move north. They would leave at different times and advance mainly at night and using the daylight hours to hide and prepare for the next day. With the accuracy of the maps and the distances shown, it was easier for Thomas to set the distance of march each day and pin point their final destination for their temporary camp once inside French territory.

While the final plan had not been set in stone, there was still a general feeling in the little army that they were going to give the French a bloody nose. The final plan would come once they saw the layout of the French camps around Medina del Campo. The retreat from the battle front of Medina del Campo had also been set out so that each force could make its own way if they were cut off or separated during the fighting to the next attack point and camp site.

The movement of the army in its small units would take an estimated five days at their normal fast pace and the need for the new guns to make their way as one unit meant they could only move at night and would have to be off the road before daylight if they were to be of any use to them.

On the 6th of February, Thomas found himself and his army looking down from the high ridges into the large town of Medina del Campo. Far below them on the open plains outside the town, Thomas and his men could see a wide spread French camp. It appeared to be well settled and had obviously been in place for some time. On the eastern edge was a large supply camp but the sheer number of troops made it a bad bargain to just go on the attack with any intent at gaining entrance into the depot to destroy it; it was time for his new guns to find their range.

The plan was for Estaban to send his three troops of 100 cavalry to each of the three smaller towns; Tudela, Aranda and Toro and for them to carry out attacks on any French patrols or smaller guard stations. If they also came across any supply trains that they thought they could attack with relative safety then they would also attempt to destroy or interrupt their travel.

Thomas kept the two corps of Infantry with him to protect the guns which gave him 300 men and Officers along with the 120 gunners if they came under attack. The five gun batteries which also included the single rocket battery would be the main thrust of the attack on the well guarded camp below them on the wide open plains. The ridge they were on was the only high ground for some great distance and Thomas knew he would have to pull his guns out well before they could come under attack by the French.

Major Craven Morgan had assured Thomas they would get the best part of seven or eight shots each before the French would be able to mount a counter attack; it would then be up to Thomas and his Infantry to protect them until they had hooked up their guns for the retreat to the new proposed camp near Somosiera. The run for Somosiera would be hazardous at best but they hoped the confusion they wanted to create below them would give them the extra time needed to make their escape without hindrance.

To add as much confusion as he could, Thomas sent the 5th Battery under Lieutenant Peter Wright to the east of Medina del Campo which had a thick grove of trees on a low rise some 900 yards from the edge of the supply depot; he would be the first one to fire which would then be the signal for the heavy guns to open up from the ridge to the west at a range of 1100yards. It was almost at the upper end of the range for the guns but with four Batteries that were spread out over the full length of the ridge top but they would be well sighted personally by Craven Morgan.

Craven had spent a long time lying beside Thomas on the top of the ridge and taking range sightings during the late afternoon, the plan of attack was for the guns to open up at around midnight when the troops below would be at their most tired. There was also the fact that there had never been an attack on Medina del Campo and it was almost common knowledge that the English army was trekking south and well away from the security of the north.

For the whole of the afternoon, Thomas and his Officers lay watching the camp far below on the plains through a new spy glass that Thomas had been given by Mister Percy as a parting gift. It was a far larger one than his small pocket glass and was often used by sea Captains, the increase in power and definition made for easier watching and pin pointed many things they would not have otherwise seen.

Even at the far range they were watching from, it was obvious that the many guards in and around the camp and supply depot did not think there was much to worry about this far away from the battles of the west and south. There was a distinctive feeling below of boredom and safety, any rebel action had been well away from such a large concentration of French troops and it was felt that only fools would even attempt to make war on such a heavily held camp.

What surprised Thomas the most was the lack of roaming French patrols; it appeared they had not found the need to patrol outside the immediate camp area and so Thomas and his gunners were left undetected as they watched from above.

The 5th Battery had been given extra men so they could carry far more extra rockets; the hope was for them to fill the night sky with as many rockets as they could before having to pull back and make their late night run for Somosiera. Thomas and his friends hoped that the fact of being attacked from two sides in the middle of the night would cause confusion and disruption in any French plans to counter attack in any one direction and would give them the time needed to also make their escape.

The plan to retreat for the gunners was far more dangerous than the 5th Battery as they would have further to go and would have to take a long run around Medina del Campo to the south and try to split the area between the town and far off Salamanca, they would have to be across the River Carrion well before the French could have time to trap them with their backs to the same river.

To make for a faster escape, Thomas asked Craven to keep his horses hooked up to the caissons and close enough for the guns to be hooked up quickly so they could make it out of there well before coming under fire from below. It would be down to fine timing as during the day they had been able to count more than forty guns lined up in the camp below although there did not seem to be much interest shown by the French troops to set them out in Batteries for the defence of the camp.

Lorenco positioned his platoon of sharpshooters about fifty yards below the ridge top so they could act as the first line of defence if the French tried to counterattack during the hours of darkness or once the guns started firing. It was not normal for the French to try to attack at night so it was all to Thomas's advantage to make use of the dark.

Normal army protocol insisted that most fighting was carried out in orderly ranks and depended greatly on fixed manoeuvres set out by well laid plans; in a situation that Thomas was setting up, the French would be at a distinct disadvantage and the lateness of the hour would only add to that confusion.

When the sun finally sank in the west Thomas led his men to the back of the ridge for the first hot meal of the day. When the meal was finished the gunners began to push their heavy guns into place on top of the ridge, once ready to leave they would manhandle them back to where the horses and caissons waited and run for safety during the night.

As the time for the assault drew closer Craven went from Battery to Battery to make the final range checks, all of the guns would be firing solid shot and they had been stacked neatly behind the guns ready for use while the powder monkeys waited to run the powder sacks forward; it did not pay to have the powder sacks too close when the guns were firing.

Thomas peered into the dark to make sure everything was ready. The four Batteries had been spread along the top of the ridge with about fifty yards between each five gun Battery, in the darkness it would give the appearance of a far larger force as the French would only see the flashes of light as the guns fired and the darkness would cover just exactly how many enemy were truly involved.

Thomas stood to the side of the 1st Battery and looked down on the dim outline of the camp below. Most of the cooking fires were now faint glowing embers and only the still burning fires of the picket lines could now be seen in the darkness although there were far more of them than Thomas would have liked.

It was close to the midnight hour when they all saw the first sixteen rockets shoot high into the dark night sky; while the first ones were still in flight they saw the second set fired off, it was time for the guns to add to the coming confusion of a night attack.

Thomas and his friends watched as the first rockets began to drop from the night sky and finally explode only ten to twenty feet above the unsuspecting camp. The shower of small sparks and flaming balls descended on the dry canvas tents in an array of pyrotechnic brilliance. The first sound of the explosions soon filled the still night air and it was only seconds before the shouting started as the French realised they were under attack from the darkness.

Before the second set of Rockets began to land or explode, the third and then fourth were also in the air but they were almost ignored by the panicking French troops as the heavy guns opened up from far away; it was not long before the fires started by the rockets were joined by the sounds of solid shot landing with great gouts of dirt and smoke in the middle of the camp.

Thomas was relying on the wide spread of his five gun Batteries to cause more confusion. The Batteries fired one after another with the first shots starting at the left flank and then moving down the line. With the 4th battery firing their five guns it made time enough for Battery one to have reloaded and take over the next salvo.

In the darkness and confusion Thomas hoped it would look as though there were more guns on the heights than there actually were; with luck the French would think they were under attack from a major force.

The rocket Battery had been instructed to fire into the centre of the camp where most of the ordinary soldiers were in bivouac. The 1st Battery had been aimed at the main supply depot. The 2nd battery had been aimed at where they thought the main headquarters were positioned and the last two Batteries were directed towards the large cavalry lines on the outer edge of the main camp.

Thomas was well aware of the damage the Cavalry could cause them should they be allowed to get mounted and form a counter attack; it was imperative to keep the cavalry units dismounted.

Lorenco had moved his sharpshooters closer to the camp as soon as it was dark enough to cover his movements and he was now positioned within shooting distance of the outer pickets. The number one Battery had just fired its fifth gun when those on the ridge began to hear the smaller sounds of musket shots further to their front; Lorenco had joined the night battle and was hopefully taking care of the wide spread picket lines.

The 5th Battery was still firing rockets into the main area of the camp and the many fires were taking hold on the dry canvas of the massed tents; with all the fires, noise and confusion, the French had yet to try to form any kind of defence or even attempt to form any sort of attacking force to take care of the far off guns.

The 5th Battery had the use of extra bodies to carry spare rockets, they were now firing their third salvo into the dark night sky and with the many fires started they were finding it easier to mark their targets. The panic in the large camp was now almost total as the earth shuddered under the continuous bombardment of the twenty guns on the heights.

The ground inside the camp was becoming more like well tilled fields as the heavy shot ploughed deep gouges and holes into the land while it also tossed bodies around like confetti and the screams of the dying and wounded filled the once quiet night air. Through his new spy glass Thomas could see some of the Officers trying to restore order and form some sort of resistance.

Thomas watched as what he thought were the last of the rockets they had been able to carry take flight towards the now devastated camp. The 5th Battery should now be breaking down their rocket ramps and making the break through the trees towards Somosiera where Thomas and the gunners hoped to once again meet up with them for their next attack.

Thomas and his gunners were still hidden in the darkness and all that could be seen by the French below them was the almost continuous flashes of massed guns; with the distance the French could not work out how many there were nor the exact distance. Thomas kept close watch on the camp by swinging his spy glass from one place to the other. It was fortunate that he did as he saw the French guns finally being arranged to return fire at the far off heights; it was time to make their move to Somosiera and quickly.

Thomas called out for Craven Morgan to retire the guns after their last salvo, ten minutes later and the ridge above Medina del Campo was bare of any guns and in the darkness it would seem there had never been any there at all. When the French guns finally got into position to return fire their first shots hit only empty spaces; their attackers had already disappeared into the vastness of the plains behind the ridge as they made their escape.

Even against the rumble of the fast moving guns Thomas could hear the return fire of the French guns as they sent shot onto the heights where Thomas and his gunners had been only minutes before. As they rode into the darkness the bombardment of the French guns continued to rumble in the night. At the pace Thomas and his gunners were moving it was not long before the French guns faded into the night and only the creaking of the wheels on the Caissons and guns could be heard above the fast trotting hooves of the many horses.

As he rode at the head of the column of fast moving guns, Thomas hoped that Lorenco had pulled out in time and was even now making his way towards Somosiera in a more direct line; he hoped to meet up with him near where they had planned to cross the River Carrion.

As far as Thomas could guess they had made a very good amount of damage to the Medina del Campo supply depot and troop bivouac; he could only hope the other units had also been as successful with their smaller attacks on the other towns and would be able to break away in safety and meet him at Somosiera for the next part of their plan.

While Thomas had insisted that they make as much speed as they could in the darkness, he also thought the French would find it difficult to form any sort of chase, especially if the amount of destruction had been as wide as he had seen through his spy glass. It was a comforting thought that they should be well out of range before the enemy was able to respond and try to follow them.

One and a half hours after leaving the heights above Medina del Campo the guns made it to the west bank of the River Carrion; it did not take long before a large number of dark shapes appeared from their hiding places along the river bank and greeted Thomas and the gunners. Lorenco had been able to make a clean break from so close to the camp and had brought all of his men to the meeting place in good order.

The river crossing took the best part of half an hour but, once on the other side no time was wasted before they settled down to a steady pace towards the east. They would have to find a good place to hide away once the sun rose as it would be too dangerous for them to move towards Somosiera until the following night where they would then have the safety of the mountains to hide in until all the other units had found them and rejoined for the next part of the plan.

Having to turn north once they were over the river to avoid any contact near Segovia only added more time to their long trek. As the first glimmer of dawn broke in the east, Thomas sent some of Lorenco's men out to find a hiding place for the day; it would not be easy to do in the wide open plains but he had little option if he wanted to avoid a head on fight with French troops or patrols.

The final resting place for the day turned out to be a narrow gully that ran from north to south and was barely wide enough for the Caissons and guns to run into in single file but it did offer a very good means of defence with its narrowness. Thomas looked over the excellent map that Smithson had made of the area and saw that they would only be a half a day away from Somosiera when they restarted their march that night; they should be at the base of the mountains some time before midnight.

Thomas talked with Lorenco and asked him and his men to move out two hours before the rest and try to locate a place for them all to camp once in the mountains; but not too close to Somosiera as they did not want to warn any French troops too early of their whereabouts.

Had Thomas known the results of the other attacks he may have been able to relax just a little more as the massed gunners began to settle down for the day and rest until they had to make the final push to their new hiding place.

So far Thomas and his men had avoided any deaths or injuries; he could only hope the others had been also as lucky. The other units had the hardest part as they were smaller units and would have to rely on their mobility to avoid danger or disaster. The mouth of the narrow gully was now well protected by the two Corps of Infantry so the gunners could get as much rest as they were able to. There was still a long way to go for safety so every man on guard was as alert as the long day and night would allow them to be.

Lorenco sent out his scouts to watch their back trail and, if possible, try to gather some information on the results of the attack. Lorenco's men had had a long night but they had been able to get a little more rest than the gunners and Infantry and were able to find the strength to do their duty once again.

It was late in the day and Thomas's men were preparing to continue their trek towards their next destination when Lorenco and his men returned. They all looked tired but the smiles on their faces told Thomas they had some good news and so it turned out to be.

As they all sat around to eat the first hot meal in two days, Lorenco made his report to the other Officers.

"Patron we went as far as the Carrion and the countryside was in an uproar. Everywhere we went there were French Cavalry patrols and they seemed to be in some haste. The ones we watched looked to be very nervous as though they were expecting to come under attack from larger forces at any moment. We kept ourselves hidden and just watched but the number of roving patrols was far more than would be normal so it would seem our attack has very much upset the French who must have thought themselves safe so far behind the lines. From what we saw I don't think they have worked out that we came this way as most of their movements seemed to be working towards the south. It was a good idea to come east and further into their lands, it is the last thing they would think we would do. Two of my men crossed the river and were able to lay out a number of our smaller flags, when they are finally found it should put the French at even further unrest."

"Thank you Lorenco, that was a good idea I hadn't thought of doing it last night but if they think we are once again in the field it should make them draw even more troops away from the English front. All we have to do now is to hear from Colonel Colosio and his men; hopefully they were as successful and can escape without losses then the French should really be at a quandary."

An hour after dark and the main part of El Toro's new army was on the march again but this time not as urgently as before. The news that the French were concentrating their searches further to the south gave Thomas a lift and he hoped it would stay that way until the next time for an attack.

CHAPTER 7

Snot settled into the saddle of the large horse selected for him by Colonel Colosio. He had been instructed to keep the horse at a gentle canter as it would not only cover the ground more efficiently but would not tire the horse as quickly as a gallop would have.

As he rode Snot thought back to all he had learned since joining the army of Mister Marking; the young man was his idol and he would have done anything for him and now, he was given an important job to do all on his own. Snot was determined that nothing would stop him from carrying out his orders.

Snot stopped only for a few hours during the night; it would give the horse time to rest for what Snot hoped would be a last push for Lisbon. So far Snot had not had any trouble and he wanted to keep it that way. For the third time that night Snot checked his weapons as he ate the small meal he had set aside before leaving the valley; it would be the last he got until arriving at Lisbon.

Snot thought back to what he had learned so far with this strange army; there were so many things he had not known until joining up with Mister Marking and now he was able to ride horses, shoot like any good soldier and was also trying to learn something about helping the wounded from Mister Jervis. All in all he felt good about himself and even his older brother Craven often said good things to him.

Snot's duty in the kitchens was not as onerous as some would have found it; with his duties for his father at the tavern, the organising of the camp kitchen had almost been second nature and he liked the idea of making others work to a set time and standard.

It was not long after midnight when Snot remounted for the last run to Lisbon; the valuable papers from Mister Marking were tucked away safely in a leather pouch that was tucked firmly under his shirt and jacket where they would be safe and out of sight.

Snot finally stopped at a small tavern just a few miles from Lisbon as the first rays of the sun showed over the eastern hills; he had decided to get a solid breakfast before making his way to the docks to find a ship; he did not want to waste time in the city and his tired body could rest once he was at sea and on the way to England.

Snot rode through the large city in search of the docks; all it took was for him to keep the smell of the salt air in his nostrils and then follow his nose. As he rode through the city streets he looked neither right nor left; what was going on in the early morning streets meant little to him as he had much more important things to think on.

Snot rode through a wide cobblestone avenue and saw for the first time the high masts of ship above the roof tops ahead of him; he had found the direction of the docks and now only had to work his way there through the building mass of people that were coming from their homes to work another day.

Ten minutes later and Snot had worked his way through the remaining streets and narrow lanes to the edge of the docklands. Ahead of him he saw the massed masts of many ships both at the wharf and anchored out in the stream. Snot yawned widely as he saw what could be the end of this part of his journey; his body was tired but he was not ready to rest yet.

Snot had no intentions at this stage to have the horse billeted until he had found a ship for his purpose, to this end he rode right onto the busy wharf to look for a ship. Snot did notice that as he had always thought, the dock workers were mostly Portuguese although they were working under the ever watchful eyes of English soldiers.

The soldiers were mostly standing at the bottom of the gangplanks as though to guard the ships but they also never missed an opportunity to offer some snide remarks about the workers. Tied at the wharf were four English war ships; three looked to be frigates and the one further along the wharf was a three decked Man-O-War and its decks and the docks were swarming with men loading supplies.

Snot did notice that; as he rode past the Portuguese dockworkers most stopped working and looked at him before bowing as though they knew him. It took a few minutes before Snot realised what the men were doing. The workers did not know Snot but they did recognise his black uniform and the red and gold sash. To the dockworkers the youngster riding along the wharf on such a magnificent horse could only be one of the Patron El Toro's young men and so they showed the proper respect for one of the men that had helped to save their country from the French.

As Snot rode past the last of the four ships and towards a smaller merchantman that was tied up at the very end of the wharf space as though he did not have a care in the world; his peace was broken by a rough sounding voice from behind him.

The Marine standing guard on the gangplank of the Man-O-War watched the young foreign boy riding along the dock as though he owned the place; it did not make him happy even though he had to admit to himself that the horse the youngster was riding was a fine piece of horse flesh but it was the apparent arrogance of the rider that got him all upset and he was not going to allow a bloody foreigner to show up the Royal Navy.

Snot had just passed the gangplank of the Man-O-War so he presumed it was one of the guards but he did not like the tone of the soldier's voice.

"Oi you; foreign boy; what you doing here on yer horse. This here is Admiralty docks so get off afore I come teach you some bloody manners."

Snot signalled the horse to stop by the use of his boot toes; he had been well taught about not having to use the leather reins when giving his mount instructions. Snot was about to turn around and give the man a few choice curse words when a faint smile drifted across his face. Snot was young and not above having a little fun if he could get away with it and, as far as he could tell a good laugh might ease his tiredness.

Snot nudged the horse with his right boot toe and waited as it bent its front leg so that Snot could easily step out of the saddle and onto the cobblestones of the dock; the horse then stood again which made it look as though it towered over the smaller figure.

Snot turned back to the horse and gently rubbed its nose as he pretended to ignore the now approaching Marine. The sound of the heavy boots stopped just behind Snot and a rough finger jabbed him in the shoulder from behind; Snot pretended to be hurt as he spun around and eyed up the larger Marine who was now holding his long musket at the ready.

"You hear me boy? I said you're not allowed on the docks. You understand me boy?" Hey you speak English boy?"

Snot looked the Marine up and down; he noticed the man was wearing Corporal bars. As he looked up at the man he decided the chance was too good to pass; with a faint light in his eye he answered the Marine in Spanish which included more curse words than his father would ever have allowed him to speak. When Snot had finished his discourse on the Marine's heritage and lack of a human mother; Snot stopped and smiled at the Marine as he saw the look of incomprehension on the man's face.

Snot waited patiently as though he was talking to a young child; he did not have long to wait before the Marine started speaking, but not in a friendly way.

"May God bloody save me from foreigners; what's with this damn country. Don't none of your lot speak the King's English?"

From off to one side, one of the dockworkers stepped forward and smiled at the Marine; he had heard the young rider speak and decided to help the Marine although he quite easily picked up on the strange accent the youngster had; he also picked up on the glint in the boy's eye. Stepping forward he asked the Marine Corporal.

"Excuse me Senor Corporal but I think the boy does not speak English; perhaps I can help you with his language?"

"Well as long as you tell the little scouse he can't ride that bloody horse around here." The Marine stayed close by as the dockworker turned to Snot and began to speak to him in Spanish.

"Are you one of the Patron's men?"

"Yes Senor, I am Second Lieutenant Morgan and am on a special mission for the Patron. I have to find a ship going back to England very quickly."

"Ah then my young friend you have just found the right man. Tell me, why are you not using your own language with this oaf of a soldier?"

"I thought it would be great fun to play a game with him."

"Ah yes my new friend, it is a good idea. Now then what should I tell him so we can make his day worse for him?"

"Tell him that I am an Officer and I know he is just a low Corporal so he had better show me some respect and that he is now on our land and does not tell us where we can ride our horses. That should upset him a little."

"Yes my young friend, you are certainly one of the Patron's men. I shall pass on your words and we shall see what he does."

While the dockworker turned back to speak with the Marine, Snot turned back to the horse and once again began to rub its nose gently with his left hand; his right hand was busy undoing the buttons of his jacket. Snot had a funny feeling things were going to turn for the worse once the Marine had been told Snot was actually an Officer; he was not surprised when a heavy hand caught him by the shoulder and tried to spin him around.

"You tell this here boy that I don't give a tinkers damn who he thinks he is; around here he aint nothing but a bloody foreigner and he can take that bloody horse off the Admiralty's docks."

It was time for Snot to do his own talking. As the heavy hand spun him around, Snot reached into his jacket. The Marine soon had a look of utter shock on his face as he looked down into a pair of pistol barrels and the sound of one of them being cocked was enough to make the Marine pull his hand back very quickly. It was time for Snot to end the long exchange; he had other things of more importance to do.

"Corporal I am Second Lieutenant Morgan of the 1st Regiment of Spanish Guerrillas and you have just laid hands on me which by all the rules of any military means I could have you hung or I could pull the trigger on my pistol and put a damn hole in you. Now where is your Officer?"

For the Marine Corporal it was bad enough that he had two barrels aimed right at his head but the sound of the young boy's voice speaking English was even more surprising. The Marine gulped as he realised the boy was more than he at first thought and now he was being reminded that he had laid hands on an Officer. To a Courts Martial it would make no difference if the Officer was foreign or not.

"Sir, my Officer is on board ship Sir."

"Well Corporal then I think that this time your luck is in. If I hear of you abusing others as you have toady I can assure you that next time I will pull the bloody trigger. Now Corporal it would be better for you to return to your duties before I change my mind."

The Marine snapped to attention and lifted his musket to the salute before turning about and marching smartly back to his place at the bottom of the gangway. Snot smiled widely as he looked at the dockworker while replacing his pistol under his jacket. Reverting to Spanish, Snot said.

"Thank you Senor for your help; it will not be forgotten. Perhaps you can help me one more time?"

"Just ask Lieutenant and it shall be done. There is much owed to the Patron El Toro and we are all at his service should we be needed."

"Thank you again Senor. Firstly who am I speaking to?"

"I am Hernandez Diaz of Madrid Senor Lieutenant. I came to Lisbon to work when the French took my city. I could not stay under their yolk and so came here until they are sent back to France."

"Very well Senor Diaz, thank you once again, I will let the Patron know of your help to me. Now then I am in need of a ship that is going to England and in a hurry. My mission for the Patron is urgent. Do you know of one that can take me so I don't have to wait for weeks?"

"Indeed Lieutenant that Merchantman at the far end of the docks is waiting for the tide. I believe the captain is in a tavern around the corner and is not a happy man, I am sure he would find a place for you."

"Why would he not be happy Senor Diaz?"

"It would seem the English Navy does not allow him to find a cargo while at their dock although these docks do not belong to them; he is most angry because he will have to sail his ship back to England without a cargo to help pay for the travel."

"Thank you Senor Diaz, I will go and look for him. The tavern just around the corner at the end of the docks you said?"

"Yes Senor Lieutenant, he has spent many days there so he should not be hard to find."

"Thank you once again Senor Diaz, I hope we will meet again one day so I can repay your kindness."

"It is nothing Senor Lieutenant; we all do it for the Patron."

Snot nodded as he turned back to his horse, a light tug on the reins and the horse knelt down for Snot to climb into the saddle and then quickly stood back up as Snot lightly shook the reins for it to move at walking pace to the far end of the docks. Snot was now feeling the need for some sleep but his determination would not allow him to stop. If he found passage on a ship then he could rest while they sailed for England but not before.

As he rode past the Merchantman he looked it over. The general hull seemed sound although the rigging and some of the woodwork looked a little worn as though it had been some time since coin had been spent on its repairs. Snot rode past and looked for the corner at the end of the dock so he could find the tavern he wanted.

The ship was not fancy but he was sure it would be seaworthy enough for him to make it to England if he could convince the Captain to take him. Snot had also decided he would take his horse with him rather than leave it here in Lisbon in the hands of strangers. The ship's Captain would just have to find enough feed for the horse as part of the deal.

Snot turned the corner and saw the tavern he was looking for only a few more steps along the lane; drawing the horse to a stop, he dismounted and tied the reins to a ring post and prepared to enter. By the raucous noise coming from inside the tavern it was almost as though he was coming home to the Kings Gate. Snot straightened his jacket; made sure his pistol was free in its place under his left arm and opened the door.

It was as though a gun had been fired as he stepped through the tavern door; there was an immediate silence in the barroom as he walked in and looked around the dim room for the man who looked like a Captain; he was not hard to find.

As Snot began to make his way to the back of the barroom the half drunk sailors looked him up and down like savage animals watching their next meal but they all stayed seated as he walked past without showing any fear; the fact he was wearing some sort of uniform also helped to keep the sailors in their seats.

When he got to the table at the back of the barroom, Snot looked to the burly man he guessed was the Captain of the Merchantman. With little preamble Snot looked directly at the man and said.

"Captain, I am Second Lieutenant Morgan and I am looking for a fast passage to England. I have been told that you and your ship are waiting for the tide tonight so I would like to take passage with you."

The burly man looked Snot up and down; it was obvious he had his doubts about such a young man having the needed coin to pay for a passage all the way back to England. As the Captain had not been able to find a cargo to pay the ships way he would have to charge a hefty sum just for one passenger. The Captain took a deep breath which puffed his huge chest out to its limits, took a large sip from the tankard on the table and then spoke to Snot in a very rough voice; one that had seen many storms and had yelled orders into the roaring winds and rough seas.

"Well would you now me lad, and what makes you think you have coin enough for such a passage?"

"I have orders to make for England at all haste and enough coin for that purpose; there is also the need for you to transport my horse as well."

"Is that so Lad, well I can tell you that I am the only one that gives orders as to where and when my ship will go; what makes you think I will do as you ask and not just take you asea and drop your body over the side for Davey Jones?"

Snot realised the whole bar in the tavern had fallen silent as the two exchanged words; carefully he reached under his shirt and brought out the large leather wallet that contained the papers, selecting the one he wanted he laid in on the table so the Captain could plainly see it for himself. One glance by the Captain and his whole attitude altered to one of friendliness.

The paper lying on the table was simple and plain for all those in the know. The paper was a plain white page with the black outline of the hand and at its centre was the simple number 13. No more words needed to be said as the Captain called loudly for the tavern owner to bring food and drink for the young lad standing before him.

"Come and sit with us Lad and tell me what you need; if the Council is behind your needs then there is a place for you on my ship. I have no cargo so we will be travelling light and it would appear there is little profit in this trip but then we have our duties."

"Thank you Captain I do need a rest and the food will be welcome. All I need is to get to England as soon as possible along with my horse. I have some coin with me but if it is not enough then I can come by more once there."

"I see lad, well if it were not for the Council I would have to charge you a King's ransom as I have no cargo but then the Council would probably make things difficult for me in the long run. The ship is in need of work but she is sound although a little slow due to not being careened in some time. It mayhap take us six or seven days to make London Town if that be fast enough for you?"

"What if I could find a cargo for you Captain; would that be of help?"

"You lad? You have knowledge of a cargo?"

"If you were to sail via Oporto I am sure I could find you a cargo of good value even though it may take an extra day or two. I am sure the Council would not want any man to be short changed for his work."

"Well lad if you can do that then I see no reason for us to sit around here all night; you sit and sup your drink and finish your food, I'll send the Mate to ready the ship for sea. The tide is in two hours and we can be away from those blasted Admiralty docks in no time."

"I'll need a bag of oats for my horse if you can manage that Captain?"

"Don't you worry none lad, the Mate will see to it afore we sail, now then what are we to do when in London; it's not been a good place for me to find cargo what with all the big companies holding credit with the War Office to supply the army here."

"If you can trust me Captain I will do what I can once in London, I happen to know a man who may be able to help you with cargo."

"Then you have my thanks Lieutenant, being as I work my ship without contract it is difficult in these times to find a cargo so the men can be paid so any assistance you can offer will be greatly received."

"I will do my best Captain."

"Larkin Lieutenant, Captain Larkin; owner and Captain of the Beatrice Graves."

"Thank you Captain Larkin, I'll just finish up here and we can get my horse aboard and set sail for Oporto."

"You take your time Lieutenant, the tide is not for another two hours and we have time for you to rest a little afore we set sail.'

Snot nodded as he turned back to finishing the meal. It was only a half hour later and he was watching as the men carefully walked the horse up the gangplank and onto the deck where they had hastily built a small section for the horse to be settled in. Snot was surprised the horse did not make a fuss just as long as Snot was close by; it turned out to be fortunate that the whole trip was in fair weather and the stop in Oporto was just long enough for Snot to take the horse for a ride before going back aboard for the final leg to England.

In Oporto Snot used his limited knowledge of his Generals reputation to secure a good cargo for England; dropping the General's name among the dock workers proved to be advantageous when he went in search of the cargo for Captain Larkin. The cargo did not completely fill the large hold but the Captain would certainly make a profit from the trip; with luck Snot hoped his Father would be able to assist the helpful Captain once they arrived in London.

The trip took almost two weeks as a full eight days was spent in Oporto loading the cargo but Snot was not put out about it, the need for the Captain to pay his men had to have consideration if Snot was to need the man again in the future. He had learnt his lessons well from his Father and Grandfather about treating the men of the sea with respect; one never knew when they would be in urgent need of a good ship and crew.

On arrival off the coast of England and with the mouth of the Thames in sight, Snot gave directions to the Captain for his Fathers dock; they would tie up there and unload their cargo while Snot went about his own business.

As the ship came abreast of his Fathers dock, Snot saw a large three masted schooner tied up and loading cargo; he asked the captain to drop anchor abreast of the dock and hoist the pennant to ask for a docking pilot. It was just at the top of the tide and so was easy to drop anchor in exactly the right place before the tide began to ebb which would have made it more difficult.

Snot watched as a few minutes later a small dory with two men at the oars and one sitting in the stern began to make its way towards them; Snot smiled as he recognised one of the Smithy's at the stern and he chuckled to himself as he thought of the man's face when he saw Snot all grown up and dressed in the black uniform; he was not the same small boy that had left so long ago.

The dory tied up alongside the ship and Smithy began the climb up the rope ladder and onto the deck where the Captain and Snot were waiting for him. At first Smithy did not recognise the young man in the black uniform but, once he did his face split with a wide smile as he first nodded to the Captain and then turned on Snot.

"Well bless me soul if it aint young Snot; what you doing all dressed fancy like a little ponce in that there uniform? My your Da is going to be right surprised when you walks ashore all grown up. Now what you be doing here then lad?"

"Hello Smithy, I got some business with me Da and this here Captain Larkin was right kind to bring me all the way from Portugal. He needs docking and unloading then I'm hoping me Da can find him a good cargo. Captain Larkin did not charge me a fare to bring me so we owe him something in return."

"Not to worry lad we will do what's right, you knows your Da. Now then do you want to come ashore in the dory with me; I knows your Da will be right proud to see you?"

"I have my horse on board, when can Captain Larkin dock to unload?"

"See yonder ship, well she will be out on the morning's tide; if the good Captain can wait until then he can have first place right after; the tide be about seven of the clock in the morning, will your horse be alright until then?"

"Yes Smithy, he's done well on the trip and will not mind the wait but I will come ashore with you now, I have urgent business with me Da."

"Right then lad, Captain Larkin I will be back aboard in time to dock you in the morning if it's your pleasure?"

"Thank you Pilot, the morning tide will do us just fine; I have other duties for the crew until then."

"Then thank you captain and I will have the dory alongside before seven of the clock and take you in. Come along young Snot, time for you to see your Da after such a long time; I bet you have stories aplenty to tell and your Granddad will want you to have time for him as well; you know you is his favourite."

Snot smiled as he then followed Smithy to the ladder and clambered down into the waiting dory for the short pull back to the dock, even with the ebbing tide running they still made good time and Snot soon had his feet back on English soil and was walking towards the not too distant Kings Gate Tavern.

As Snot walked towards the familiar door of the tavern he did notice that he was getting some strange looks from the many men and boys that hung around the area. Snot smiled to himself and no longer felt any threat as he once had when confronted by the rough looking people that lived and worked on the docks. Snot's sense of self worth had grown immensely since his time at war; he felt that if he could face French muskets then he could face anything.

Snot ignored the looks and opened the door into the Kings Gate tavern, the familiar smells and noises of the building almost brought a tear to his eyes as he once again took in the long bar and the few customers now sitting for dinner at the small tables; the rest of the barroom was full of drinkers as the dockworkers changed their shifts and looked to a few mugs of ale before heading back to their homes.

There were a few tables of sailors but none of them took notice of the well dressed young man in black; all that is except for one old man partially hidden at the back of the room. Snot was not surprised when a voice called him above the noise of the drinkers.

"Come here boy and let me old eyes get a fill of ye afore you go looking for your Da."

Snot smiled widely as he turned to his Grandfather seated at his special table; with a homecoming tear he almost ran to the older Morgan and sat beside him in the small alcove; with a small sniffle he grasped the old Captain around the shoulders and felt the hard hands of the older man pat him on the back.

"Well now boy you do look all grown up. How is your war going, is it what you thought it would be?"

"Much worse Gramps, much worse but now I know I am doing the right thing. Mister Thomas has been good to me and all the others; it's easy to see why they want to follow him."

"Aye lad, the boy has a way with him. Now tell me why you just popped up like this?"

"Mister Marking gave me an important task to bring a message to me Da."

"Is ye all alone then?"

"Yes Gramps, Mister Marking was getting ready to attack the French once again but wanted me Da to know things so here I am."

"Well you keep doing it honest like youngun and you will do well. What's this here uniform you is wearing?"

"It's our uniform for the Regiment; Mister Marking has made me a Second Lieutenant so I got duties to perform now."

"It's certainly a strange uniform but I suppose if it works for you then it's all good even though it's a bit funny looking when you see our redcoats all lined up and marching. Do you have to march a lot over there?"

"Aye Gramps but we march all different to the soldiers. Mister Marking has his own way and we can march more than twice the distance in half the time of others and we got lots of horses to. Mister Marking even gave me one to ride all the way here, I'll have him off the ship tomorrow so you can look at him. Right nice Horse he is and real smart; better than the old nags we got around London Town."

"Is that so youngun, well I got to see this here horse if he's so special, now I think it's time you went to see your Da; I can almost hear his feet a tapping on the floor above."

"Ok Gramps, I'll come back later and see you to tell you more."

"You do that Snot, you know you be a right good boy so we is all expecting good things from you in time. Have you seen much of your brother; I hear tell he was a big Officer now?"

"Yes Gramps, he is in charge of all of Mister Marking's guns and is now a Major and I look after all the kitchens and supplies for the men but we still have to train like the others and be ready to fight when we have to. It's sort of exciting and frightening at the same time but Mister Marking watches over all of us all the time."

"That's good lad, now off you go and see your Da, I'll be here as you know so there's no hurry to get back. You do your duty first then we can talk more later."

Snot stood up from the table after giving his Grandfather one more hug and then wove his way through the bar to the stairs leading up to his Fathers rooms. As Snot was about to place his foot on the first step a large hand grasped him by the shoulder and began to spin him around. Snot reacted far faster than he ever thought he could as his right hand delved into his jacket and grasped the pistol with the intent on drawing it for defence.

As he spun around to face the man who had accosted him, Snot saw the large barrel chest, the tattooed face and twinkling dark eyes of George. Snot relaxed immediately and then threw his arms around the waist of the large tavern owner as he mumbled into the big man's chest.

"Jesus George you half scared the devil out of me."

Snot took a step back and watched as George used his hand language to speak to Snot.

"Where you been little brother, you did not come to see me first."

"Sorry George I didn't see you when I came in and then I was with gramps for a while. I need to see my Da kind of urgent like but I will come back and we can talk like other times. Have you been well?'

"I am always well little brother, you go see your Da then come back here for your dinner and we can talk more about your great adventure to those foreign parts."

"Thank you George, I'll be back just as soon as business is done."

George smiled and gave Snot a hefty pat on the shoulder as he turned back to watch over his bar; Snot began the climb up the stairs to finish his business. As he walked into the very familiar room that was his Fathers office and living space, Snot saw the other Smithy sitting on the old leather couch, his Father was at his desk with a number of candles burning as the night darkened.

Snot saw his father watching him every step of the way as he crossed the wooden floor and then stopped in front of the desk with a large smile on his face; it was so good to be back in a familiar place with friendly faces.

"So young man to what do to owe the pleasure of your company."

"Hello Da, I'm here on Mister Marking's orders to ask you for help."

"Is that so young man? And why would such a man as Mister Marking be giving you such an important duty? Why I remember that not so long ago you were just a shrimp of a boy who spent all his time making trouble for grown men."

Snot decided to play his Father's game and so straightened up to attention as he had learnt to do and in a strong and steady voice replied to his Father's enquiry.

"Captain Morgan, I am Second Lieutenant Morgan of the 1st Regiment of Spanish Guerrillas and am here at the request of my superior officer to carry an important message asking for your valued assistance."

Peter Morgan put a surprised look on his face as he tried to hold back the laughter; his youngest son had certainly grown up and even at a time like this looked very serious and duty bound.

"Well Lieutenant Morgan, I am pleased to make your acquaintance. Perhaps you can give me the message from your superior and we can discuss this further."

"Yes Sir." Snot was finding it harder and harder to keep a straight look on his face, especially when he heard the chuckling from behind him as Smithy watched the little tableau between the two men.

Snot took out the leather wallet and removed the sheet of paper; making a play of great ceremony, he carefully placed the paper on his Father's desk for the older Morgan to open and read. Peter Morgan looked down at the sealed paper and then back at his youngest son.

"Do you have anything else Lieutenant?"

"Yes Captain, there is a matter of the ship that brought me here. The Captain, one Captain Larkin, was kind enough to run with a part empty ship to make sure I arrived quickly. I would like to ask for some assistance for him and his ship as he did not need to make the trip at a loss just for me. The ship is also in need of some maintenance and I hoped you could help the man."

"I see, and where is this Captain Larkin?"

"He is still aboard ship Sir but will be ashore with the tide tomorrow."

"Very good Lieutenant, I will have one of the men go and meet him for talks. Smithy that's your job first thing in morning."

Snot heard a grunt from behind him as he waited for his Father to continue. It seemed that his Father had decided it was time to have his youngest son back as a wide face splitting smile spread across the older Morgan's features.

"You look good Snot, have you had your dinner yet?"

Snot immediately relaxed and smiled widely back at his Father.

"No Da, not yet; George said to come down when we was all done here."

"Good, then go down and eat and all of us will get together with your granddad and you can tell us all about your travels. I'm real proud of you Snot; you're growing into a good man. Now get out of here so I can read this message then I will come down and join you."

Snot smiled as he turned and ran for the stairs; his narrow belly was starting to rumble with hunger as it would for all growing boys; it was only minutes later and he was sitting at his Grandfathers table and starting on a huge meal that George had placed before him, it was accompanied by a warm mug of old fashioned mead; something not often seen in the tavern unless it was for a special occasion.

Snot sat and ate in silence while his Grandfather watched silently as he also ate a little and sipped on his tankard of ale; it was almost a picture of family peace and contentment.

Peter Morgan opened the message from Thomas and read it silently; he then took the other paper that had come with it and looked over the list of needs written on it. With a sigh Peter looked up at his friend Smithy and said.

"I've got a job for you Smithy. Take this list and see what you can do about it; any costs can be charged to Marking Shipping Company. Let's double the amounts he has written here just to be sure. Next I want you to go down to Harry's and ask him to clear his dry dock just in case it's needed for this Captain Larkin's ship. I'm going to join young Snot for the rest of the evening so you can have the night off but I want you on these things first thing in the morning so don't get too drunk or I will know the reason why."

Smithy stood up and reached for the list before touching his nonexistent forelock and leaving the room; Peter rose and made for the stairs as he wanted to spend as much time with his youngest as he could before the boy returned to the war.

The next morning found Captain Larkin standing at the gangplank as the pilot left the ship to carry out other duties. Captain Larkin watched as the pilot stopped to talk to another man waiting on the dock. After a few words the two men parted and the newcomer looked up the gangplank at the waiting Captain.

"Captain Larkin, permission to come aboard Sir?"

"Come ahead Sir."

Larkin watched the man climb the gangplank, it was immediately obvious the man was familiar with the sea and its ships as he stepped onto the deck and quickly looked around before giving a small bow and touching his forehead.

"Captain Larkin, I am Jonas Smith and am here on behalf of Captain Peter Morgan and have been instructed to offer you all assistance. What is your cargo Sir?"

"A mixture Mister Smith; some wine of Portugal and bolts of cloth. Only a half hold but that was all I could get before making for London Town as young Mister Morgan needed to make all haste."

"Very good Sir. If you could have your men remove the hatches I will call the men to have you unloaded. I have also been told that you may be in need of maintenance on your vessel?"

"Yes she could do with some work but alas I don't have coin enough for such work and be able to pay the crew as well. Times are hard Mister Smith and needs of the crew must come first if I want to keep her sails aloft."

"Captain Morgan has given instructions that your ship is to be taken to dry dock for all work needed to her. It's his way to thank you for watching over his youngest son and delivering him safely. There will be no charge for the work and the Captain would like to make your acquaintance at your earliest convenience; he may have some work for you and your ship if you should so desire Sir."

"Thank you Mister Smith and where would I find Captain Morgan?"

"Just go to the end of number three warehouse and you will see the sign of the Kings Gate tavern, you will find him there Sir."

"Thank you Mister Smith, I will make my way there just as soon as I have the men release the hatches. I must ask Mister Smith; what of my men while the ship is laid up?"

"I don't know of that Captain but I am sure Captain Morgan will be able to answer that for you."

"Thank you Mister Smith, I will do that. I need to get the men working now so if there is nothing more then I will say good day and hope that we can meet again."

"Aye Sir, I will go and get the dockers to start unloading. Captain Morgan will offer you a price for your cargo so you can pay the crew just as soon as it has been valued."

Captain Larkin nodded his head and then turned to call for the crew to remove hatches; it seemed the young Lieutenant was as good as his word and that pleased the Captain; it was difficult in these times to find any honour while the war was on.

Captain Larkin made his way to the door of the Kings Gate tavern. From inside he could hear the sounds of early drinkers settling in for the day. Stepping inside he saw the most unusual sight he had ever seen. Behind the bar was a man who looked to be no more than a savage dressed up as an Englishman; it made Captain Larkin pause in his step and wonder if he was really in the right place.

A young voice caught his attention and it took little time for Captain Larkin to spy the young Lieutenant sitting in a rear alcove with a very old man who was partially hidden in the deep shadow. Captain Larkin made his way towards the young Officer in the hope of finding his Captain Morgan. Snot had watched Captain Larkin enter and; after a short pause, make his way towards him. When the Captain was standing in front of the table, Snot said.

"Good Morning Captain Larkin, are you here to see my Da?"

"Yes Lieutenant that is my instructions from Mister Smith."

"Good then just go up the stairs he will be waiting for you, that is unless you would like to stay for breakfast before you meet him?"

"No thank you Lieutenant, business must come first but I may join you later if it is still your pleasure."

"It certainly will be Captain."

"Then I thank you for your offer Lieutenant and look forward to joining you after business is done."

Captain Larkin turned to the narrow wooden stairs and made his way up; he wasn't quite sure what he was expecting but the wide and well appointed room above was not it. The man he thought could only be Captain Morgan was sitting behind an old wide desk and shuffling through some papers when Captain Larkin stepped through the open door. Peter Morgan was the first to speak when he saw who his visitor was.

"Captain Larkin I presume, come Sir take a seat and let's get acquainted. I must thank you for helping and watching over my youngest; not many would take the chance with one so young and unknown and for that you will have my eternal thanks."

"Think nothing of it Captain Morgan, my ship was lying empty and with little hope of cargo at the time; there was also something about the young Lieutenant that I could not refuse."

Peter chuckled a little before he said.

"Aye Captain the boy does have a way about him when he wants something. Now then Captain, I have the first provisional costing of your cargo; it will probably increase once we are fully unloaded but at this time I have a first accounting for you to consider."

Peter slid a piece of paper across the desk for the Captain to look over before he continued with the discussion. Captain Larkin took one glance at the figure written on the paper and lifted his head to stare at the man behind the desk.

"Is this a true value of the cargo Captain Morgan?"

"At this stage, yes but I am sure as we finalise the unloading there will be some small additions."

"But Captain Morgan this is almost thrice the price I paid for it in Portugal and nearly twice what I expected on the final sale."

"I can assure you Captain Larkin that it is a fare price on today's market place. Your casks of wine alone are in high demand among the gentry and will more than fetch a reasonable price and the added lace and cloth are in very high demand as well by the ladies. You made a good choice in cargo's Captain."

"I must admit Captain Morgan that it was the young Lieutenant that organised the cargo for me, I had little knowledge of where to find one that would pay for the travel to England and thought that as I have less than a hold full I would be hard pressed to make wages for the men."

"So you are satisfied with the arrangements for your cargo Captain?"

"Fully Sir, more than I could have expected."

"Good then I have one more thing to offer you. Should you wish time to consider it then I can wait until your ship is refloated after repairs and you can give me your final decision. Is that fair Captain Larkin?"

"More than fair Captain but what is your offer, if I may be so bold?"

Just as Peter was about to explain what he had in mind, he heard footsteps on the stairs and a moment later he saw the face of Shipwright Harris with a concerned look on his face.

"Excuse me a moment Captain Larkin, Mister Harris has the report on your ship so you may be interested as to what he has to say. Harry! What have you got for us?"

"Well it's not all good Cap'n; that old Barque needs some work and right quick."

"Well don't blather on Harry, tell us what you've got so we can get onto it."

"Well Cap'n we will need to step a new Jib Boom so I can add an extra sail, her foot is rotten and can't be saved. Next she has two planks at the waterline that have sprung; I don't have a clue how she's held together so long. Now then there is the careening and that's long overdue; must have most of the ocean litter hung on her hull. I can see she will be able to carry eight guns and I can add top Royals to the Main and Fore to add a little more speed, the rest is just dressing her up and a good clean inside and out."

"How long Harry?"

"With the men I have now, I would say about ten weeks, perhaps eight unless I can hire extra men."

"Eight to ten weeks, damn it Harry I know you can do better than that."

"Well Cap'n, ifin I was to hire extra men it would add about one hundred guineas to the cost but I could perhaps have her all done in six weeks."

"You have the extra hundred Harry and not a day over six weeks; agreed?"

"Aye Cap'n, six weeks and she'll be afloat, pon my word."

"Good enough, the men should have her free and clear by late afternoon; can you get her in the dock by nightfall?"

"I'll have every man standing by, don't worry none Cap'n, she'll be tied down by dark."

"Good enough, what do you think Captain Larkin?"

"I...I...I don't know quite what to say Captain Morgan. I agree of course, she's been a good ship and I would like to have her at sea for a few more years."

"Thank you Harry, it's all in your hands now and you know what I expect."

"Aye Cap'n, we'll get it done on time and done right."

Harry bowed his head and touched his forehead then turned and left the room to the two Captains; he had his orders and he well knew that no one broke a contract with the Morgan's; not if they wanted to stay in business on the docks.

"Now Captain Larkin, back to our own business. As you can see we look after our friends, is there anything else we can do to make your ship safe and sea worthy?"

"No Sir, in fact it is far more than I would have expected from any man; I'm just not sure how I am going to repay you. My cargo will not cover the costs involved and I still have my men to pay. I fear that if the ship is docked for six weeks I will lose my crew before she can sail again and you must well know how hard it is to get a new crew in these times of war."

"There is no charge for your repairs Captain Larkin, the life of my youngest son is worth far more that the cost of a few repairs so you can put it to rest. Now then as too your crew. If you were to agree to what I am about to offer then your crew would be taken care of with wages until you are once again afloat."

"Well I am prepared to listen to your offer Captain Morgan, it is the least I can do."

"Good then here is what I propose. I am the agent for a new but small shipping company and they are on the lookout to add ships to their fleet. Now before you worry about having to sell your ship let me fully explain. The company would like to offer you a two year contract to sail for them; you would remain in full command and retain ownership of your vessel. The terms they are offering are that from your cargo we will deduct the cost of cargo and then the rest will be halved with you. All your revictualling will be done at the cost to the company so your profits should more than make up for paying half to the company. If you agree to these conditions then we can guarantee that you will have full cargoes for the next two years. There is one more thing that they will require and that is that you sail your ship under their colours when at sea or in foreign ports but here in England you may fly your normal ensign."

"A most generous offer Captain Morgan, one I find very difficult to refuse especially as my crew who have been with me for a number of years are also being looked after. May I ask how many ships the company has and where I may be taking my ship most times?"

"The company has only one other ship at this time, she is a Brig and mounts sixteen guns, the company likes to have all their vessels armed in these times of war. The Brig is being stepped with a third mast along with other alterations to make her faster and most of her work will be across the Atlantic to the Bermuda Islands. If you take on the contract your ship will mostly be running supplies and cargo to Portugal and Spain and that is why we want to arm you. There are still those French around that think they are still winning and an unarmed ship is easy prey for them."

"I can well see the need for the guns Captain Morgan but my men are not trained for warfare, they are just sailors. The rest I can fully agree with and would find it difficult to refuse your offer except for the situation with the guns."

"Have no fear Captain Larkin, you will have the best gunners I can find to fill that part of your ship. So what do you think; is it worth it to you to take the contract and have a guaranteed income for your ship and crew or would you prefer to take to the sea on your own once the repairs are done?"

"If I wished to move on alone, what is the cost to me for the repairs?"

"As I told you Captain Larkin, the repairs are paid for by the Company as a thank you for watching over my son, there is no debt incurred whether you accept or refuse we just will not mount the guns but that is all."

"Then Captain Morgan I offer my sincerest thanks and I will sign articles with you company for the expected two years. The security it offers the crew and myself is undeniable and only a fool would refuse."

"Good then Captain Larkin, welcome to the Marking Shipping Company. Would you like to join me down below for a tot to seal the deal?"

"That I would Captain, that I would"

The two men left the room and made their way down into the bar where the crowd had increased; Captain Larkin saw that most of the men in the bar were from his own ship and were already drinking. He followed Peter Morgan to the rear alcove where Snot still sat with his Grandfather. When the two men arrived, Peter said.

"Captain Larkin you know my son of course and the other old fellow is my Grandfather Captain Henry Morgan. Pop this is our newest Captain and he will be joining Marking Shipping once his ship is repaired."

Captain Larkin could not believe his ears, sitting before him was the convener of the Council himself. It had just not clicked in his head that the name Morgan was the one known for more than a hundred years and that Peter was the same family. Suddenly Captain Larkin understood why it was so easy for Peter to get everything done in such haste.

"Welcome Captain Larkin, I'm sure you will have many questions which I will try to answer for you in full, but for now sit and drink to your success."

"Thank you Captain Morgan, I can now see how your young Lieutenant was able to accomplish all he did in such a short space of time."

"Well captain you will also be a part of it from now on so I hope you will toast to your coming success."

"Thank you Sir. There is one thing I would like to ask."

"Certainly."

"Who is this Marking Shipping Company; it's not a name I have ever heard of before."

"Ah yes, well Captain you may have seen certain newspaper articles on a certain young drummer that did well in the war?"

"Yes I think I remember seeing some writings on his exploits but if my memory serves me right he was killed by the French at a place called Olivenca."

"Well they were a little hasty in reporting that, as it turns out Captain Marking is fit and well; it is his company that you now sail for. He has now joined the Portuguese Spanish alliance as a General and that is why you have been asked to fly the Portuguese colours when at sea. The young man has had a falling out with the English high command and now fights under the Spanish flag and therefore has the need for his own ships to supply him; that is where you come in."

"I see, well if there were a more worthy cause to sail for then I can't for the life of me think of it at this stage. Gentlemen! To our long and successful contract with the young General."

The three men and Snot lifted their glasses and drank the large tot of rum then, as the sounds of loose tongues and happy voices began to fill the bar the four of them settled down to get to know each other better. It was only a half hour later when Snot had to leave to reclaim his horse from the dock as it had been unloaded and was waiting for him nearby.

Peter Morgan had one last offer to make to Captain Larkin and he wished to get it all over and done with before the drinking and celebrations fully got underway.

"There is one more thing I can offer you and your crew if they wish to accept it Captain Larkin. The new Company has available a boarding house for its crews when they are in London. It is just around the corner so is close to the docks. There is no charge for Company crews and as you and your men will be here for at least six weeks I would like to make the offer for you and your men to make use of it until the ship is re-launched. It is called the Copper Key and is easy to find unless you and the men have other plans it is there for your use."

"Thank you Captain Morgan, there are those who will like to visit loved ones but I am sure there are others who would like to make use of it. I will inform the men when I pay them off tomorrow morning."

"It may be better if you do it today and before they are too far in their cups as they won't have a ship to go back to as soon as it's unloaded; it may also pay to have them gather their hammocks now before the ship is dry docked. I will soon have the full total of the value of your cargo so you can pay them today if that will suit your needs."

"Even better Captain Morgan. It will allow them to make plans immediately. I thank you once again; I can see joining the new Company was indeed the right thing to do."

The three men settled back and it was only a half hour later when Peter's cargo manager brought the final costing of the cargo to him. An hour later and the crew had been paid and told about the accommodations available to them if they wanted to make use of it. A number of the crew had nowhere else to go and took up the offer but others had homes and families to visit and were soon on their way to see them. Of those left it was to turn into a very late and drunken night as most sailors were want to do.

The next day Snot soon had his horse under him and was taking a long ride through the packed streets of London. For many that saw the youngster mounted on such a well bred horse and appeared to also be armed to the teeth brought much speculation but no one tried to stop or delay his ride.

It was just after midday when Snot found himself outside the London boundaries; it was then he got an idea of his own. If he was too hurry he could make the small stone cottage before dark and he was sure the occupants would be glad of any news he could carry to them; it was the least he could do for his special hero Thomas Marking.

Even though the roads were still carrying the mud of spring, Snot made good time to the small cottage and arrived an hour before dark; he was just in time to see Thomas's father limping towards the cottage from the closest field. Snot also spied the small brother of Thomas tottering around close the door of the cottage. The waddling walk of the little boy brought a smile to Snot's face as he slowed the horse and then stepped down to lead it into the front yard.

Cromwell Marking saw the rider and had stopped just outside the doorway and turned to watch as the young man in the distinctive black uniform approached on foot with the beautiful horse following on the rein.

"Good evening Mister Marking, I don't know if you remember me but I'm one of your General Marking's Officers. I thought I should come and let you know that he is well and fighting fit. I don't know if anyone has told you yet but thought you should know he survived his wounds."

"Thank you young man, please come in; it's time for supper and you're most welcome. We were told that Thomas recovered but it's good to see one of his friends here. I'm sure his mother will welcome any news you have."

"Thank you Sir, is there somewhere I can stable my horse?"

"Yes just around back there is the barn, put him in there for the night. I assume you would like to stay with us if you have little else to do?"

"Thank you again Mister Marking, I would like that."

"Good then put the horse away and come back and join us, I'll go and tell Thomas's mother we have an extra for supper."

Snot did as he was told and was soon back and being introduced to Thomas's mother. For Snot it was the first time he had really spent time with an ordinary family and they both made him feel like one of the family; it was a new and welcome experience for the boy that had been raised in a tavern in the middle of London Town and one he enjoyed to its fullest.

CHAPTER 8

5<u>th</u> February 1812

Percy pulled his cloak a little tighter as he made his way through the cold and damp streets of London. He was now close to his final destination and was thankful he would soon be out of the miserable weather that was the norm for this time of year in England.

It may have been early spring in Portugal and Spain but here at home it was still like the middle of winter and his bones were feeling it. Only the memory of the warmth of the Peninsular and knowing he would soon be returning gave him hope that he would not have to spend too much time on his business.

Percy made it to the Oak doors of the Carrington Gentlemen's Club and walked into the warm foyer; waiting behind the long wooden desk of the reception was the familiar face of Sterling, it was almost like coming home.

"Good evening Colonel, it's good to see you back once again."

"Thank you Sterling. Did you get my message about the room?"

"Yes Colonel, everything has been made ready for your stay. Would you like a small drink before dining, there is no one in the salon and you will have some peace and quiet before any of the other members arrive."

"Yes thank you Sterling, have my bags arrived?"

"Yes Colonel, they are in your rooms and the valet is unpacking for you as we speak."

"Fine then if you would be so kind as to take my cloak for me I will go and find that Brandy you spoke of."

"Yes Sir. I shall inform the steward that you are here if you would like to make your way to the salon."

"Thank you again Sterling, it's good to be home again and to let the world go by outside."

"That it is Colonel, now if you will excuse me I will go and find that steward."

Percy nodded and, after removing his damp cloak made for the salon where one could smoke a cigar and have a small drink or two in peace. Percy had been sitting alone and sipping his second Brandy when he heard a number of members enter the club. Percy took little notice of the chatter and laughter as the members in the foyer divested themselves of their cloaks in readiness for an evening at the club.

Percy sat in the deep leather chair gazing at the fire as his thoughts turned to the business he needed to take care of. He ignored the voices in the foyer as his mind rushed from one point to another. Percy was suddenly woken from his thinking by the sound of a strong voice speaking his name.

"Percy, Percy Cruikshank; well I never. How long has it been?"

Percy turned to the vaguely familiar voice and then stood up as he recognised the man standing in the doorway.

"Lord Belmont! Well My Lord it must be all of twenty years at least. May I offer you a Brandy that is unless you are already committed to your friends?"

"Nonsense Percy old man, they will go ahead and I can join them later; they will only be talking politics and you know how I feel about that subject."

Lord Belmont joined Percy in the salon and waited for the smaller man to pour him a good sized Brandy before loosening his cravat and settling into a chair facing Percy.

"So old man what have you been up to?"

"Oh you know me My Lord, a little of this and a little of that."

"Well the first thing you can do old man is to drop the title. We didn't share rooms at Cambridge for three years that we now have to get all carried away with titles."

"Thanks Sebastian, it's been a while and I did hear you had taken over the title. Now then what have you been up to?"

"Not a lot Percy, you know how it is in the House. Damn it all if the Pater had not fallen from his horse on that damn hunt I could be out in the Peninsular earning my way."

"I'm sure you more than earn your way in the House Sebastian."

"That's tommy rot and you know it Percy. Damn it man I wanted to make my own way just as you did but no, the old goat had to chase just one more bloody fox. I don't know how many times we told him to stop hunting."

"Your Father was a stubborn man Sebastian but it was his pleasure so you can't really blame him. When a man gets to his age there is little left to bring a smile to your face."

"HA, and how would you know that my old friend. There is barely two months between us so you surely are not that old."

"There are times I feel fifty years older than I am Sebastian."

"Is that the sound of defeat I hear in your voice? Perhaps I have been mistaken and you are only pretending to be Percy Cruikshank. The Percy I knew was full of spit and vinegar. Think back old son to that day you stood up to Winthrop and his little gang of wastrels; by the Gods old son I have never seen the likes of that day, especially after all you went through in the first two years at school."

"That's true Sebastian but I was younger and not at all wise then."

"Well you certainly upset a few of the boys when you turned up. What happened to that savage that looked after you? George, wasn't it?"

"Oh George is still around, I do admit he made for good company and the looks he garnered from some of the toffs was rather amusing."

"That I would have to agree with, he certainly scared the hell out of me the first time you brought him into the room. I couldn't sleep for three nights worrying if he was going to serve me up for supper while I slept."

"Ha and now you know he was just a softy as long as you didn't get on his wrong side."

"Yes I do have to admit he handled those two ruffians to save my bacon in the street that night. If you see him again tell him I was asking after him; I still owe him for saving me."

"I'll do that. So Sebastian, what are you up to in the halls of power now that you carry the title and have your duty to perform for the Government?"

"Oh just the same old thing Percy. Half the time I think it's a damn waste of time and the other half I really think we are accomplishing something. You know old man there has always been one question I wanted to ask you but never got the courage or the chance."

"Well now is your chance Sebastian, I have all night and seeing you after all this time and having the chance to renew an old friendship is more important than dinner."

"Well Percy, I have always wanted to know how you managed to get into Cambridge. When you look at those times it was almost impossible for a young man of seventeen who had no title and no money to join the school. I remember the day you arrived; not only did you look as though you had just stepped off some old ship but your clothes were not exactly fashionable for the times. I can still remember the smell of the sea on you."

Percy couldn't restrain the laughter as he looked at the only person of his Cambridge school days that had stood beside him through the three years he was there. The three years had not been easy for either of them although Sebastian, because of his family ties had it far easier. Percy had struggled both with the demanding lessons and the almost constant bullying; that was until he had had enough and turned on his tormenters.

"Well it was mainly due to my Captain at the time. He said I would need a good education if I wanted to make something of myself. It was through his many and varied contacts that he got me into the school and, even when I was at my lowest he would have a few words and keep me on track. I'm glad now that he did even though I hated every day in the damn place; well all except for our friendship."

"Well it seems to have paid off for you Percy if what I hear is correct. It's a damn shame that they expelled you from Cambridge as they did; still the others now carry your mark for the rest of their lives and will not ever forget their meeting with you. You know Percy; in the three years we roomed together I never knew you carried that knife with you. Unfortunately had you not carved your initials in their foreheads there was a good chance you could have stayed. Everyone including the Head knew about their bullying ways but they could not countenance you carving them up after you knocked them unconscious with that broom handle. "

"Well old friend, that's water under the bridge and to be truthful, three years was more than enough of that place for my liking. So tell me what have you heard old friend?"

"Oh this and that, you know how it is in the House of Lords; we get to hear everything sooner or later."

"Come on old friend, now is not the time to play coy; especially with me."

"Well I did have a paper come across my desk which stated that a certain Colonel Percy Cruikshank was to take over command of the spy division at the War Office. Now being as the name is not a common one it did raise my interest at the time."

"Ah so I have been caught out at last. Well Sebastian you are of course quite right although I think they wanted me for the job because it was beneath anyone else. Still I have tried to do the best I can for the country and that was always my one concern."

"Is it true you had something to do with that young drummer boy who took the newspapers by storm on the Peninsular?"

"Ah yes young Thomas; quite a boy that one, I may even introduce you if I get the chance one day. I think you will find him very entertaining and quite the surprise."

"Well if all the reports are correct that will never happen but I think I would have liked to have met him before he met his fate."

"Oh he didn't meet the fate they are portraying. I can tell you he is quite fit and well and causing all sorts of trouble for the French although he no longer fights for England but the powers that be have only themselves to blame for that event."

"Really! He is still alive and still fighting?"

"Oh yes, you don't kill off a boy like that."

"But who is he fighting for if not for England?"

"For the same people that truly believed in him. The Spanish and Portuguese; they even gave him a title as well as lands of his own and he is now one of their Generals. It's a shame really but I can see him not wanting to return after the war except to visit with his family. If that happens Sebastian then the King will lose not only a good man but one that could even be great in time."

"If you have such confidence in him, what then would it take to get him back to England?"

"To be honest, I don't think there is anything we could do if he wished not to return. You would have to meet the boy to understand that. Perhaps if he comes to England I can arrange for him to meet with you if you wished it."

"I think I would like that Percy; he sounds much like a certain young sailor who took Cambridge by storm."

"Personally I think he is far more at his age than I ever was but I will certainly make sure he makes your acquaintance if at all possible."

"Good I would like that immensely. Now what have you planned for the rest of the night?"

"Just a quiet dinner and then to bed; I have a lot to do tomorrow so an early night is in order."

"Well I shall leave you to your quiet night and get back to my other friends but I want you to remember something."

"What would that be Sebastian?"

"If there is ever anything you need or want done I expect you to call me and I don't give a damn who likes it or not. I still owe you and your savage my life and that can never be repaid."

"Thank you Sebastian, that means a great deal to me."

Sebastian Belmont rose from his chair and offered his hand to Percy as he got ready to leave. Old friendships never waned and Sebastian still had a debt to pay the sailor boy who had upset the status quo at Cambridge and given Sebastian a chance to experience something of the real world outside his normally protected life.

Percy finished the last of his Brandy and then went to find his solitary table for dinner. Percy sat at the back of the dining room at a small reserved table; very few were ever invited to the table and only those in the know could understand why. Percy finished his second glass of claret and pushed his empty plate aside just as Lord Belmont and his friends walked into the dining room.

Percy was just about to stand up when they arrived and he got a smile and nod from Sebastian as he and his friends were shown to a larger table at the centre of the room. Percy acknowledged the smile with one of his own and then left for his rooms; he still had a report to finish before his important meeting the next day.

Percy left his damp cloak at the attendant's desk as he entered Whitehall for his meeting; it was a long climb up the stairs to his own private office at the top of the building. It had been later than he thought by the time he had finalised his report and now there was only the meeting to take care of; he hoped his guest was already there and waiting, he wanted to be away from London as soon as he could.

Percy was not disappointed when he arrived at his small office; his guest was sitting in the only comfortable chair in the room except for the large leather one behind the old desk.

"Ah Colonel, right on time as usual. How was your trip home?"

"Good thank you Sir."

Percy made it to his chair behind the desk and settled his handful of papers on the desk in front of him before continuing with the meeting.

"Now then Colonel, what do we have?"

"It's much as we thought Sir. Marshal Beresford seems to have embellished his report a little. I think his objective was to promote himself in the eyes of others and retain his position at the cost of the young man."

"Aha, so what do you advise Colonel?"

"Personally Sir I think he should at the very least be censured for his claims and perhaps given a lesser place under Wellington."

"Good then I will accept your recommendation and I will attend to it as soon as I return to my office. Now then what about our young experiment?"

"Young Thomas is lost to us I'm afraid. The report from Marshal Beresford has done far more damage than we can repair and young Thomas is not a very happy lad with it at all."

"Is there nothing we can do to get him back on side?"

"I doubt it very much Sir. The Spanish and Portuguese saw his value very early on and have given him a title and a large estate as well as complete command of his forces so unless we can at the very least match that then I am afraid he is theirs."

"But what about his loyalty and patriotism to England Colonel?"

"I think that after the way he was treated by Marshal Beresford's report his patriotism may be less than we can rely on. On the other hand Sir, he would never actually turn against us and his hatred of the French is what drives him. I think Sir the only thing we can do is continue to support his efforts anyway we can and hope that sometime in the future he may change his stance."

"I shall think it over Colonel but I do tend to agree with you. Now what of the Morgans? Are they still with us?"

"Most definitely Sir, as you well know they would never turn their backs on England but they also have a very soft spot for our young man and have even registered a new shipping company in his name with Lloyds."

"A shipping company? Why the devil would they do a thing like that? Is old Henry finally losing his marbles?"

"Far from it Sir. I have heard that young Thomas has come into a ship that was declared lost at sea and it will now be used to supply his men when needed but you would have to ask old Henry for any further information on that subject Sir."

"Come now Colonel, after all these years I damn well know you are not telling me everything you know."

"That's as may be Sir but truly I am not at liberty to say more; perhaps if you contact Henry he may tell you more."

"You know damn well Colonel that I will get even less out of that old scoundrel than I get out of you. So then what do we do now?"

"The only thing I can think of would be to ask their Lordships in the house to award an open contract for anything the young man needs and hope he can continue to make life hell for Napoleon and his armies. If we leave him out on his own then we may have more problems than if we support his efforts."

"A novel thought Colonel but what about the services, they are going to kick up one hell of a stink if they see us sending much needed supplies to a Spanish force?"

Percy smiled as he watched the face of the man in front of him; he could almost see the man's brain working on how he could circumvent the military to get aid to Thomas.

"Well Sir perhaps a little deception would be in order when the time came?"

"Colonel I am inclined to agree with you even though I know damn well you are a devious man and have planned this all out a long time ago. Very well Colonel I shall approach their Lordships in the house and see what can be done. I don't suppose you have anyone in mind that could aid us in this endeavour?"

"Well Sir, there is one that comes to mind. I know he is often seen as a bit of a wastrel and not really of a desire to become involved in the machinations of politics, but I swear if there was a man who could really sway things in our favour it would possibly be him."

"And his name Colonel?'

"Lord Sebastian Belmont Sir."

"Belmont? You have to be joking Colonel. Lord Belmont is well known for his disinterest in the workings of Government. I doubt there would be a single Lord in the house who would listen to him."

"Do not underestimate Lord Belmont Sir, many have done that in the past and paid a high price for their ignorance. I would suggest you make him the offer but it would be better if you did not mention my name although you may mention the young man's name if it makes it any better."

"Well Colonel I don't really have the same confidence in Lord Belmont as you seem to have but I shall try; and if he says no?"

"Then Sir it would remain only for yourself to stand for what we want but as you well know that could create complications."

"Complications Colonel; it would bloody well bring down the Government. You know the King would not countenance the Prime Minister becoming involved with military matters."

"Yes Sir I well understand that but then again you have been involved from the very beginning so the least we can do is try to carry our original plan for the boy to the end and protect him as best we can."

"I know Colonel; I can only hope that this stays hidden as we first agreed."

"I am the only one who knows Sir so you can rest assured your reputation is safe but we also have to keep the promise to protect the young man as well as we can."

"Yes I agree Colonel. There is one thing that has always puzzled me though."

"And that is Sir?"

"How did you know he would be the one we needed?"

"I knew of his father and what he did and so could only hope the young man was made of the same fibre. He proved that and more at Rolica as we all now know."

"Well he has certainly proved his worth over and above what we hoped. How old is he now? It must be close to four years he has been out there?"

"Almost four years Sir, I believe he has just enjoyed his fifteenth birthday but has a head on his shoulders of one far older and wiser for such tender years."

"Indeed Colonel. Well if that is all I had better get back to Downing Street before they wonder where their Prime Minister has got to. I will expect you to keep me informed Colonel."

"As always Sir."

Percy watched the Prime Minister leave the office and breathed a sigh of relief. What had to be done was now done and he could soon return to Portugal to watch over his best kept secret. If the French only knew half of what was to come their way Percy was sure Napoleon would pull all his troops out of the blighted Peninsular. With the rumblings he had heard about Napoleons plans for Russia in the next few months came true then it would only bode well for the campaign in the long run.

The importance of Thomas on the Peninsular was to become even more real and needed if the American colony did manage to break away. The reports he had seen from there had already told him that England may not be able to hold the American colony for much longer; but that was out of his hands and his own responsibilities were to his young friend in Portugal.

Snot was surprised when he was asked to stay with Thomas's family for as long as he liked. It was something he was not used to and he soon fitted in well with Cromwell and even helped as much as he could on the small five acre farm. Watching the antics of Thomas's baby brother also gave him an immense sense of joy and fun; he had never been around children as young as the boy and it delighted him at every turn.

After a full week and more with the kindly people, Snot realised he had better make his way back to London. His father would not be too worried about him but time was running short and he needed to get back and make his report to the General.

Snot arrived back in London the next day and went straight to his father's tavern; he was just in time to find out that the Avante was at the dock and almost ready to leave with the cargo for Thomas. Snot would travel on the ship and land in the small private bay with the needed supplies; it was the first days of February and he was already late for his return.

It would take five or six days to get back as long as everything went well and this he knew would make him late to report. Snot could only hope that the news he carried about his General's family would make his lateness acceptable.

With the new masts, sails and shiny guns as well as being lengthened and the hull cleaned; the Avante glided through the slightly choppy sea with ease. A small fenced area had been hastily erected for Snot's horse aft of the main deck and Snot was allowed to stand on the quarterdeck with the new Captain. It was when they were less than a full day and night from the small bay that the topman called out that there was a sail sighted.

It was less than an hour to dark when she was sighted and as the smaller ship which was flying French colours was a tempting target for the newly armed and larger Avante, Captain O'Grady called for the new guns to be run out and the decks cleared for action. Snot wasted no time in checking his personal weapons after going below to reclaim his double barrelled musket.

Snot rejoined Captain O'Grady on the after deck and watched as the Avante ploughed ahead at speed to quickly overhaul the slower French sloop. With only a single lanteen sail and a smaller mizzen, the French sloop had little chance against the faster and well armed Ship that was now only a hundred yards away and showing a formidable number of guns along its main deck. The French Captain knew he was well and truly beaten and after being hailed, dropped his sails and surrendered his ship.

Captain O'Grady had little to no interest in the French crew and allowed them to take to the boats while he sent some of his own men onto the sloop to sail her back to the hidden cove with the Avante close on her stern for protection. It did not take long for the French boats to disappear into the darkness as the two ships turned back on course for the bay that had now been named on their charts as Toro Bay in honour of Thomas and also to confuse any who may have the bay marked in another name on their own charts.

It was late in the afternoon of the next day that saw the two ships anchored in Toro Bay. The sloop and its cargo were standing out in deeper water while the Avante was tied up to the newly completed wharf at the far end of the bay to unload its precious cargo of supplies for Thomas's army. Snot and his horse were the first ones put ashore so he could ride for Vimeiro to get wagons to carry the cargo back to the valley.

Snot rode hard for the valley and only slowed or stopped when the horse needed rest or he himself was too tired to continue. It was late on the second day when he came in sight of the entrance to the valley and he breathed a sigh of relief.

A half hour later and Snot had reported to Major Jones about the ship and the arrival of the supplies. Jones wasted no time in organising all those he could use in the camp to get the wagons ready and it was just coming on dusk when the first of them left for the bay; the rest would follow as the wagons were made ready.

Snot went to look after his horse and finally get some rest. The camp seemed strangely silent and cold with just about everyone going to help with the supplies, only the young men; many of them were those who carried wounds that made it difficult for them to fight in a normal battle had stayed so that the entrance to the valley was under guard at all times.

Snot hoped his lateness would not cause Thomas to be angry with him; he was meant to have been back before the end of January; perhaps the capture of another ship for Marking Shipping Company would make his General a little happier and Snot would not get into too much trouble for his tardiness.

Once the wagons were all on the move, Jones mounted his horse and made the best speed he could towards Toro Bay. In his panniers were his ledgers and writing materials; everything that came off the ship would be recorded in his meticulous hand and a full report would be made for his General to see when he returned to Vimeiro.

Jones arrived at Toro Bay well ahead of the wagons less than four days after Snot had left. On the new dock were piles of cargo which had been well covered with canvas to keep the weather off them. Jones slowed his horse and looked around until he found a place for the poor animal to rest and eat; he had pushed hard and now the horse deserved a long rest before the return journey.

Major Jones walked the length of the new dock until he was at the gangplank of the ship where he was met by Captain O'Grady. It did not take long for the two men to go through the manifest of the cargo so that the wagons could be loaded as soon as they arrived. Once that was done then Captain O'Grady pointed out the second ship in the bay and asked Jones what was to be done with it.

As Jones knew just about everything that concerned Thomas it was not difficult to know what to do with the sudden arrival of a new ship.

"Can the same people that rebuilt the Avante also rework that one Captain O'Grady?"

"I can make inquiries Major, it would be better if we could have the ship under the companies command. The more the merrier they do say Major."

"Do you know what her cargo is Captain?"

"No Major, we haven't had time to open hatches as yet; would you like it done while you are here Major?"

"If it were not too much trouble Captain; at least then we would have some idea of what to do with her."

"Right you are Major, I'll send one of the men in the dory and they can raise hatches for a look-see."

"Thank you Captain, now I better get back ashore and see to the wagons as it appears the first one is almost here."

Captain O'Grady nodded and turned back to the last of the unloading; he still had his hold three parts full of other cargo destined for Oporto where the new Company now had its own warehouse and a small dock. For Captain O'Grady it was not going to be as fast as he at first thought.

An hour later and the boatswain returned in the dory to give his report on the sloop's cargo; it turned out to be more unloading at the dock.

"So Boatswain, what have we got?"

"Mostly war supplies Captain; appears the French are having trouble with their overland supply lines and are sending most by sea now."

"Well if that's the case we might be able to pick up a few more on the way to Oporto if luck is on our side. Is there anything apart from war supplies?"

"Aye Sir, appears to be about a half hold of general cargo, mostly cloth and other such goods. Could be a pretty penny all told Sir."

"Right then Boatswain, it is your duty to get the war supplies ashore once we have finished with the Avante and then batten hatches and follow us to Oporto. We will wait for you to cast off then keep her close to our stern as we make way. Tell First Mate Bowden to come back here and you can take over for the run to Oporto. It looks like we will be on the hunt for more crew."

The Boatswain bowed his head with the usual touch of a nonexistent forelock and went see to his duties. Captain O'Grady watched over the final part of his own unloading and then prepared to leave the dock for anchorage while the sloop was attended to.

As the wagons arrived in ones and twos, they were quickly loaded and sent on their way. Jones held back six of the scullery lads so they had cooks on site as there were at least four days of cargo to move and they would need to feed the men. Jones invited Captain O'Grady to dinner that night so they could discuss the extra cargo from the newly captured sloop. It had raised a few problems of what to do with it and especially the war supplies.

"So Captain, do you have an accounting of the cargo?"

"Aye Major, I had the carpenter go through the hold and take stock."

"So what do we have?"

"There be twenty kegs of course powder for the guns, ten kegs of fine powder for musket and pistol, five chests of flints, ten crates of French muskets, four crates of Infantry Bayonets. That's all of the weaponry but there are also ten crates of French uniforms and other sundry items of war. Most of the hold is filled with bolts of cloth, casks of Brandy and wine as well as bales of wool and crates of china plates and other things for the table. In some of the other barrels there is a quantity of grain."

"Sounds like a good mix and should make good coin in Oporto or Lisbon. I think the muskets should be kept by us and I am sure the General would prefer you to have all of your men armed when at sea so I would suggest you make an arms locker and keep as many of the muskets and as much of the powder as you need. Now that we have a second ship it may also be best to keep all captured weapons for our own use when the need arises."

"Very good Major, I'll see to it just as soon as we make Oporto. Is there anything else I should be aware of Major?"

"No Captain, I believe we now have a Chandler at the new dock so he will arrange everything else for you."

"Very good Major, we will get the rest unloaded and be on our way as soon as you have the course powder unloaded off the capture."

"Thank you Captain O'Grady, now if there is nothing more perhaps we can settle down and have this fine dinner the boys have cooked for us."

The two settled at the small table and began to eat and drink as the unloading continued into the evening. Just before midnight the Avante cleared the small dock and anchored further away so the captured sloop could tie up and its cargo of gunpowder for the heavy guns be unloaded.

By sunrise the next morning, both ships were leaving the hidden bay and Jones was writing down his last entry into one of his ever-present ledgers. It remained now only for the rest of the dock to be cleared of cargo and a final return to Vimeiro where everything would be sorted and Surgeon Jervis would at last have his supplies. Jones had noted that the amount of supplies was far greater than he thought they had asked for; perhaps there had been an error in London but it was still welcome and would stock Mister Jervis's infirmary to the brim.

Jones had been back in Vimeiro for more than two weeks when he received a message that the General was returning with his men to replenish his supplies before returning to the attack. As yet Jones had not received any reports of the fighting to the north and east but he surmised it must have been successful if Thomas was returning to rearm and re-equip.

Estaban stood with his youngest cousin at his side just inside the tree line that overlooked the small town of Toro. From here they would have a long hard ride to make the rendezvous with his eldest cousin Pablo outside Tudela. The three pronged attack had been worked out between the four cousins. Estaban would take the youngest Diego and attack Toro, Pablo being the eldest would hopefully be able to attack Aranda at much the same time and then both would ride hard towards Tudela where they hoped to meet up with Thomasino and attack Tudela in force altogether.

Once the attack on Tudela was complete they would then all make for the meeting place in the hills near Somosiera with the Patron. Estaban and Diego had been keeping watch on the town below for the last two days as had others of their small force. Each evening the watchers had gathered to make their reports and the plans were set in motion.

The one overriding factor had been the spring weather; for Estaban and his musket cavalry there was little problem but for the French Company below it was an ever present burden and Estaban planned to take advantage of it as best he could.

Estaban and Pablo would time their attacks at approximately the same time and then both ride to Tudela to help Thomasino in a combined raid as the town was the largest of the three; they would then all turn south east and make for Somosiera before the French could mount any form of counter attack.

Estaban watched the four man guard at the end of the town of Toro. He had seen that most of the French garrison was made up of old soldiers and the very young recruits. It appeared to Estaban that the garrison thought they were well out of the fighting and their attitude and seeming sense of security had made them a little lax in their guard duties.

At both ends of the town the four soldiers on guard had a small table and chairs that they used for rest unless there were people coming into the town; they would then stop the visitors briefly and then let them enter the town for the day or to conduct their business. Even though there were reports of minor rebel activity all over Spain the guards did not seem to take it too seriously.

Estaban had planned that the best time for his attack was just at dusk; it was then that the full French garrison was gathered all in one place for the lowering of the French flag and the issuing or orders for the night pickets. The parade took about twenty minutes from when the garrison was all present before the flag staff so it gave Estaban and his Cavalry plenty of time to quickly cross the five hundred yards in the fading light and enter the town at a gallop.

There was to be no delay in the attack. The riders would pour through the town and into the central square where they would open fire on the hapless French while still at the gallop and then continue right through the town and out the other side without slowing. The French would only have moving targets in the dim dusk light and Estaban hoped that would be their best form of safety.

There was one other thing that Estaban was relying on and as yet he had not seen anything to disprove his theory. The hardest thing for any soldier, but especially during winter and spring, was to keep his powder dry and to this end most never loaded their muskets until needed. Many times a musket was ruined because the soldier could not clear the wadded shot and damp powder from his loaded musket and so the normal practice was to leave the weapon unloaded until it was needed.

For Estaban this was to be his saving grace; he hoped that with his men's speed and the suddenness of the attack, the French garrison would not have time to load their muskets to return fire and his men would be well out of the town before the French could do so.

As dusk drew in Estaban watched the day time guards leave their little table and chairs and move back into the town leaving the roadway wide open and unguarded for the time it would take to lower the French flag; Estaban whistled into the dimming light under the thick trees and was rewarded by the creaking sound of men stepping into their saddles and the many clicks of muskets being put on half cock.

The men were ready and the time was now right; Estaban gave the signal for the riders to move out from under the cover of the trees and form up in a three abreast column; it was time to put fear into the French invaders and it took only a glance to either side for Estaban to see the grim looks on the faces of those closest to him to know the French were going to pay dearly this evening.

The French flag was at half mast when the garrison realised they had a large number of riders approaching very fast. The faces of the Officers showed a range of emotions as they heard the riders coming closer. At first it was a look of wonder which soon changed to one of inquiry; that look was soon changed to one of fear as the first riders appeared at the edge of the square dressed all in black and standing in their saddles with aimed muskets.

The French garrison of one hundred and thirteen men had been caught flat footed and with empty muskets. Estaban could not believe his eyes in the dim light as he saw the entire garrison lined up neatly in three ranks before the half lowered flag; a second later and the loud sound of multiple muskets sounded over the quiet town.

The French garrison had no time to react as they were cut down by the withering fire of the mounted musketeers; while the French had their bayonets mounted they were no match for fast riding musket wielding riders who appeared from the darkness in a never ending stream; fired two shots from their standing position in their saddles and rode off into the fast dimming darkness of early evening.

The fast attack and resulting mayhem among the practically unarmed garrison left many dead and seriously wounded soldiers lying in the square and not a single answering shot had been made; those French soldiers still alive and able were still trying to load their muskets when the last rider disappeared into the darkness at the eastern end of the town.

The whole raid had taken less than two minutes and the French were to count their losses at forty six dead and thirty eight wounded, most severely and some of those would not see out the night.

The chaos created by the sudden and deadly attack had left the only Officer to survive with the problem of trying to organise some sort of defence against an enemy that had already disappeared into the darkness. Once again the French had reacted too late and with too little, the threat could now be heard riding away to the east and as the sound of the massed hooves disappeared the French were left wondering just what had happened in those few minutes and even though the groans and cries of the wounded proved they had just been hit and beaten by a rebel group it still seemed an impossibility.

Estaban led his men eastward; they had a long hard ride to make the rendezvous at Tudela and he hoped that Pablo had had as much success. Estaban was well aware that the Patron was going to attack the French at Medina del Campo later that same evening and they had all planned for the simultaneous attacks on the same day to cause as much disruption for the French as possible.

Estaban had little to worry about with Pablo; he had chosen to attack the garrison at Aranda a little later in the night and make best use of the darkness by attacking on foot with only a few of his men holding the horses just outside of the town in readiness. The night pickets at each end of the town of Aranda had been silently disposed of and the fact the French garrison was encamped in their own tents just outside of the town and not billeted in the town itself as in Toro made it even easier for Pablo and his men.

Any guard or soldier found outside his tent or walking around in the open was quickly disposed of with a quick slash of a very sharp knife from the shadows; Pablo then had his men take up a station outside each tent with their muskets. At Pablo's signal all hell broke loose as one hundred muskets fired into the sleeping men trapped inside their tents. The firing lasted only long enough for everyman in Pablo's force to fire both barrels and then they disappeared into the darkness before the French even had time to realise they were under attack; the results for Pablo and his men were even more devastating than his cousin Estaban had achieved.

By the time those who remained of the French garrison could get their wits about them, all they heard was the sound of a large number of horses disappearing into the night; no one had even seen the attackers let alone had time to load or fire off a shot in anger.

Pablo urged his men westward to make the meeting outside Tudela and rejoin with his two brothers and his older cousin Estaban; the planned attack on Tudela was to take place in the very early hours of the morning when hopefully the larger and better organised garrison of Tudela would be at their lowest. There would have to be a quick discussion on what information Thomasino had been able gather for them before they all took part in the final attack before turning south east for Somosiera.

The attack on Tudela proved to be just as successful as the previous two if not even better. Tudela was garrisoned by a force of two hundred French but the extra numbers counted for little when you have empty muskets and are attacked by musket wielding cavalry from three sides and in total darkness; the fact most of the garrison was settled in their beds and had little to no warning gave all the advantage to the attackers and Estaban made sure his men took full advantage of the situation.

As Estaban led his men to the south after the attack, they left behind only the cries and screams of the wounded and lines of burning tents; of the two hundred men in the garrison, only ninety six would survive to tell of the terrible night raid on their defenceless bivouac; of the attackers not one was found but a number of small red and gold flags lying on the ground at the centre of the camp soon told the French who was responsible.

After leaving the chaos of Tudela behind them, Estaban led the three troops of his cavalry across the River Douro and into the wide open plains of Castile which would lead them right on to Somosiera. Estaban had to find a good hiding place for the coming daylight hours as he did not want to be caught in the open by any roving French Cavalry patrols.

During the day the three troops hid in a long and deep ravine until the sun was only an hour from setting in the west. With visibility now low in the early dusk light, Estaban led his men once again to the south; he hoped to meet up with the Patron before morning and with luck they would all be together once again and prepare for their pending attack on Somosiera before moving further east.

The coming attack on Somosiera was planned for three days after the initial attacks on the other outlying towns and they were hoping that the wide distances between each attack would make the French expend even more troops into looking for them.

Late in the afternoon Estaban noticed the three observers watching them from a slight ridge at the foot of the mountains leading to Somosiera. As the distant figures were dressed in black he had little doubt they were the Patron's outer guards.

Estaban lifted his hand to the watchers and was a little relieved when he saw the answering signal; it was time to rejoin the others and get down to planning. Estaban led his three troops into the ravine that was the new camp of the Patron; while his men unsaddled and looked to the horses he went in search of the Patron to make his report.

That night the plans were changed once they saw what supplies they still had. There was enough for the attack on Somosiera but Molina and Villaviciosa would have to wait until they had resupplied back at Vimeiro. It was decided that the guns would expend as much of their munitions as they need at Somosiera and then break off and make haste for their home valley while the Cavalry and Infantry would continue with the attack until its end then act as rear guard for the guns as they tracked back home.

Estaban was welcomed back with smiles and open arms as he led his men into the camp; the celebration that night was a welcome relief for everyone now that they were all back together and everyone was safe even though they did have sixteen wounded but fortunately none were serious and the two young men trained and sent by Jervis were able to take care of them with ease.

Over dinner that night the Officers sat and talked about the upcoming attack. They all agreed that they would need at least six days of hard travel to get back to Vimeiro so the attack had to be within the next three days so they could leave the area before the 10th of February and be back at the home valley before the 16th or 17th. Once everything had been decided, Thomas sent a rider off to Vimeiro with the news of their pending move back home and the approximate date of their arrival. It would give those who had stayed behind a better idea of what was going on way out in Spain.

As Thomas and his men had only been in the ravine for little less than four hours before Estaban and the Cavalry had shown up, no one had yet been to spy on Somosiera; that was to be the first thing to be done next morning and hopefully they would be able to form a plan and attack within the limited time they had left before their return home.

It took two days for Thomas to get a good overall picture of the town and garrison at Somosiera and he smiled as he heard the final report of the garrison's habits and parade times; it all went to prefect the plan.

The final plan was ready and the whole small army would move into place during the night time hours of the 9th, the attack was planned for the first hours of dawn when the French would still be groggy from their beds but before they got to their breakfast. It was well known that a hungry man could not fight as well as a fed one and Thomas was banking on that and the early morning surprise for the best advantage over his enemy.

The last report they got was that most of the men of Somosiera were closely allied with the French garrison so Thomas and his men would get little if no help from them and to that end it was going to be full scale attack.

An hour before dawn on the 10th of the month the last gun was set in place and the gunners got ready for their opening salvo. The Infantry had crept close to the town and would enter after the guns had had their way with the defenders. Estaban had all of his men formed up behind the single Infantry Corps just short of the western end of the town and would also attack once the guns started to do their work. With Oliver Perrin and the second Infantry Corps at the eastern end of the town it was hoped that the French garrison would have to try to defend on two fronts at the same time.

The report told of not more than one hundred and fifty French in the garrison but Thomas also felt he could not count on the men of Somosiera either and would have to take them into consideration as well. Thomas gave the order that regardless of who it was, any man carrying a weapon was to be seen as an enemy and shown no mercy; his losses at Olivenca had now made him want every Frenchman or those who sided with them to be killed to the last man if necessary.

Thomas took his spy glass out and began to look into the gloom of dawn; while it was still dark there was just the smallest hint of dawn light in the east; it was time to wake up the French.

Thomas looked behind where he was hidden with the other men that were part of his guard detail and raised his hand above his head; Major Craven Morgan swore he would see the signal and it was only seconds later when the first rank of the guns opened up with the first barrage of the attack. Thomas at the time hoped his other men would be able to push hard and fast just as soon as the guns started the new firing orders. There would be little room for mistakes if they wanted to win and not end up firing into their own men.

The battle for Somosiera had started.

CHAPTER 9

.

Thomas and those around him knew that Somosiera would not be an easy nut to crack. As an Andalucian Estaban knew most of its previous record and did not hesitate to relate to Thomas what had happened only a few years earlier when Napoleon desired to take Madrid for the second time.

It was late in November of 1808 and the Spanish army was then only a shadow of its former self. The then Cortes had sent General Benito de San Juan with twenty thousand men to try to stop the forty five thousand that Napoleon had. Most of the remnants of the Spanish force were made up of what remained of their standing army and the rest were hastily recruited Irregulars, most of them coming from Andalucia; it was for this reason that Estaban especially wanted some revenge.

After a hard fought holding action at the gateway to Somosiera called Sepulveda where only three thousand irregulars managed to push back some of Napoleons best and oldest brigades; the Spanish then used the night to retreat back to Somosiera for what they hoped would be a final attempt to stem the flow of the French to take Madrid.

It was believed by Benito de San Juan that his sixteen heavy guns would hold the French in the narrow and steep sided pass and therefore save Madrid from the invading French. This belief in his own ability led Benito de San Juan to not only lose the pass but also many lives of the defenders and some three thousand of his last troops were to be captured.

Benito de San Juan's demise had come through what was to be called one of the most valiant attacks of the peninsular war by the enemy. It was later revealed that on the first attack, only a total of some 125 Polish Cavalry charged the waiting guns which were set in four batteries and believed by San Juan to be devastating in the narrow pass; it was only the determined charge of the Polish Chevau-Legers that managed to take the first two batteries and they were then joined by other Cavalry units to take the other gun batteries one after the other and open the way for the Infantry.

With the four batteries overrun it was then much easier for Napoleon to send in his Infantry under the command of Marshal Ruffin for the final stage and to mop up those few left in the pass.

It was for this reason that the men and boys from Andalucia wanted to at least cause as much damage to Somosiera and the French forces holding it as they could even though they could not really retake the town or pass and hold them.

For twenty four hours Thomas and his scouts watched the pass and carried out small scouting missions to see what they had to work with. The use of the heights for his guns looked to be out of the question as their sides were steep and rock strewn as well as large clumps of juniper and small oaks that made it difficult for the guns to be positioned with any hope of being effective.

It did not take long for the watchers to see they would have to come up with something new if they wished to carry through their attack and not turn it into another Olivenca.

Major Oliver Perrin came up with an idea which was soon taken up by Major Craven Morgan. As the other Officers listened to the two men discussing the situation it soon became apparent that they may just have created a new plan for future use as well as what they needed immediately.

The idea was discussed in detail and the more they heard the better the outlandish idea seemed possible. Carven Morgan would set his twenty guns in two ranks on the flat area at the bottom of the pass and some seven hundred yards from the town. They would have to be set during the hours of darkness and in silence so any French night pickets would not see or hear them.

Oliver Perrin was going to take one of the Infantry corps up the steep sides of the pass during the night and they would then make use of ropes in the darkness to swing down from above the town and take a position close to the eastern edge of the town. Craven and his gunners, when given the signal by Thomas, would begin to fire salvos by rank.

After each shot the guns would be raised a quarter turn in elevation so the next fall of shot would be about ten to fifteen paces ahead of the last. Craven mentioned, with a small smile that they could call it a creeping shot fall and the remaining Infantry Corps would follow closely behind the barrage as it crept into the sleeping town.

Estaban's Cavalry units would wait until the fall of shot was right inside the town before he would bring all three of his troops into play and then use them as a backup for the advancing Infantry as they would have to work their way through the narrow lanes and streets with care.

It would be the responsibility of Oliver Perrin to decided when or if he should bring his other corps of Infantry into the battle once he could see the plan of defence of the French garrison or if they were going to try to escape past where Oliver would have his men set at the eastern end of the pass.

Lorenco would set his sharpshooters low on the ridge just above the town and use their skill to pick off any targets they could see both during the barrage and afterwards as the Infantry and Cavalry entered and worked their way through the town.

It was quickly decided that Thomas would stay back with the guns and not take any chances in entering the town until everything was over; his six close guards would stay by his side at all times and were also under orders from Carmelo to not let Thomas enter into the fight at any cost. Thomas was not happy about it but at the same time could see the reasoning behind it after what had happened at Olivenca.

The loud crash of the first rank of ten guns filled the early morning stillness like a clap of thunder and continued to roll in an echo down the narrow pass as though it was a live entity. Close behind the first barrage the fifth battery of rockets sent their own salvo of sixteen rockets into the dim light of dawn.

The force now only had four rockets per launcher and so would try to make as best use of them as they could, once all were fired the rocketeers would join those at the guns and help where they could. It was acknowledged that the rockets would probably not do a lot of damage but they all hoped it would add to the confusion in the dim light of dawn.

Ten seconds after the first rank had fired the second rank followed suit while Craven Morgan watched in the dim light for the fall of the first shots. Craven knew his aiming had to be correct to the inch if he did not want to kill any of their own who were waiting in the dim light close to the edge of the town.

The first ten rounds fell well within the margin Craven had expected and his order for the second salvo a few seconds later would become his fire order for the rest of the barrage as the gunners raised their elevation a quarter turn at a time.

For all of those watching from the darkness it was like watching a field being ploughed. The huge geysers of stone and earth flew high into the air only yards from the edge of the town; the four sleepy sentries that were sitting around a small table at the entrance to the town never stood a chance as the heavy shot rained down on them. The next salvo dropped five yards inside the town and was the signal for those waiting outside the town to start to move forward.

In the lightening sky of dawn the bright flashes and the loud bangs of the exploding rockets above the town added to the surprise. Thomas watched through the dawn light as his 2nd Corps of Infantry under the command of Major Bently Trent began their advance with the three troops of Cavalry close behind; one troop ranked behind the other in a massed front.

The stillness of the dawn was now a raging echo of crashing guns and even louder explosions of the rockets above. The fall of the shot was wrecking havoc inside the town and Thomas could only try to imagine what the sleeping French thought of the rude awakening. The Barrage continued to creep forward as the Infantry and Cavalry followed as closely behind the line of shot as they dared; at this early stage there was little for them to do but keep a sharp watch for any French who wanted to make a stand in the chaos.

With the fourth salvo fired and followed by the last of the rockets there was now only time for one more salvo each from the guns before they would have to cease fire; the Infantry and Cavalry were now inside the town and taking care of any French soldiers still standing or trying to fight after the ravages of the heavy guns.

There turned out to be very little resistance from the terrified French garrison; they had been caught completely by surprise and their numbers were soon decimated by the rolling barrage of heavy shot as it tore into the buildings and down on the narrow streets of the town. For the French Garrison there seemed to be nowhere that was safe from the unexpected attack.

Collapsing walls of shops and houses were doing as much damage as the shot itself and it soon became apparent for the French that they had only one thing they could do. An escape to the east was now the only thing most of the garrison could think to do and any thought of staying to defend the town was thrown into disarray as salvo after accurate salvo tore into the unsuspecting and sleepy garrison.

The hopeful escape was soon cut short as the first panicked troops broke through the eastern end of the town and looked out into the lightening sky of dawn; what they saw waiting for them only brought cold shivers down the spines of those close enough to make out what was waiting.

Across the narrow road that led east stood three solid ranks of well armed troops; each carrying what looked like a double barrelled musket. Suddenly from both sides of the road came the sharp sound of sharpshooters already picking off the early morning targets from well concealed positions above the road; the three solid ranks in front of the escaping French did not open fire but their intent was obvious. Come within range and they would open fire; unfortunately for the hapless French escapees they had never met troops who had made a habit of double charging their muskets for extra range.

A Junior French Officer saw what was waiting for them less than sixty paces away and began to call his troops to form ranks and prepare to attack the waiting ranks of black clothed soldiers as more and more of the garrison arrived in the hope of escape; they were to find they had far less time to form lines than they thought.

Oliver Perrin had brought all his men safely over and then down the steep side of the valley which many would have thought impossible in that day and age. The loud order went out to fire by rank.

The French could not quite believe their eyes or ears when they heard the order to fire; surely the troops in black had made a mistake, perhaps the dim light had deceived them as to the range that the French were at; the first volley of the strange muskets soon put paid to that thought. The front rank of fifty fired their first barrel and then only seconds later the other barrel. One hundred lead balls flew with unerring accuracy into the forming lines of the French; the result was devastating but the French had little time to think as the second rank of black clad troops took their place at the front and fired while the first rank stepped back to reload.

The third rank never had to fire a shot as those French troops left standing or those sitting and lying in the road with wounds, suddenly dropped their muskets and raised their hands. Those French still trying to exit the town were at first confused with what they saw in front of them but the sudden sound of massed cavalry coming from their rear and the shouts of more musket wielding black clothed soldiers advancing on them soon had them also dropping their weapons.

The reprisal battle for Somosiera had lasted less than twenty minutes and the French losses were out of all proportion to the shortness of the fighting. The smouldering and burning town of Somosiera looked as though it would never rise again as the first strong rays of the early morning sun finally shone down to reveal the true cost to the French.

Homes and shops were now not much more than piles of broken rubble with fires and smoke filling the air. The cries of the wounded; many buried under the rubble by the heavy barrage of shot could also be heard as a strange silence descended over the town. Of the French Garrison there remained only four Officers and the unwounded numbered less than eighty.

Thomas saw the raising of the red and gold banner above the town and got ready to enter along with his six man guard; he gave orders to Craven to make his guns ready for the march and to start back to Vimeiro. The guns now had less than four shots each left and no rockets; they would have to rearm before they could once again go out after the French.

With Craven taking care of his guns for the return march; Thomas set off on his horse towards the waiting town where his men were keeping a sharp watch not only on their prisoners but also into every nook and cranny that may hide a possible threat from the French allies within the town.

Thomas rode slowly through the rubble strewn main street of the town; his ever alert guards close by the side of the horse with their sharp eyes watching in every direction for any possible threat. The French prisoners had been herded into the centre of the town and sat in a huddle under the barrels of both the Infantry and Cavalry; it was plainly obvious there was no escape and now the French forces had to worry about their own future.

Estaban sat on his horse with his eyes swivelling back and forth; he had detailed ten of his men to keep the French Officers separate from the men and under a direct threat from the muskets. Estaban among other Andalucian's now felt a new sense of satisfaction; the defeat of 1808 had been repaid in full and it now remained only for their Patron to decide the fate of the many prisoners.

Thomas had taken his time in wending his way through the damaged town; the heavy smell of burnt gun powder and lost blood was still heavy in the air and occasionally he could hear a whimper or cry from some of the wounded still buried inside the rubble. Thomas had grown hard over the last four years and had he even thought about it at the time; he was also becoming inured to the suffering of the French. The losses of Olivenca were still too fresh in his mind to have pity for their enemy.

When Thomas arrived in front of the small group of Officers he did not miss the surprised looks on their faces. While none of the Officers had ever seen the face of the rebel El Toro they did not need much thought to realise who their early morning attacker might be. The black uniform and youth of the newly arrived Officer told its own story of the means to their present defeat.

In his rough French, Thomas asked.

"Who is your Senior Officer?"

A Major stood up carefully and with one eye on the muskets trained on him and replied to Thomas.

"I am Major Languard and am now the Senior Officer and you Monsieur I presume are the notorious rebel El Toro or are my assumptions incorrect?"

"They are correct Major Languard, you and your men are now prisoners of Spain and it will be your actions that decide your fate."

"How do you mean Monsieur?"

"I am going to give you and your men one hour to find and tend to any wounded and then leave Somosiera but first you will order your men to dispose themselves of all weapons and equipment as well as their jackets; they may keep their boots. Any

Frenchman we find within the town after the one hour is up will be put to death. The time is running Major so I suggest you move quickly."

"You cannot do that! You say we are prisoners of war and yet you make threats. This is the actions and words of a barbarian."

"Yes Major just like the French at Abrantes; your time is running Major so I suggest you start quickly, many of my men are from Andalucia and have little patience and will not hesitate to shoot those still here when the time is up."

Thomas sat on his horse and looked down at the Major with what appeared to be little concern or even the faintest of empathy for those still trapped under the rubble of the town.

Major Languard had little option but to do as the young Rebel asked; his men were under the massed muskets of a far superior force and there was no other way out of his dilemma. Major Languard turned to his troops still sitting in the rising sun and gave the order to disarm completely and disrobe their jackets; it then became a rush for those who could to try to find and give aid to the trapped and wounded.

For every French soldier that went to find their comrades there were four of Thomas's men armed and watching closely. The French had been given no time to see to their dead and had barely enough time to watch over the living as the hour ran down. It was a sad and sorry looking force of Frenchmen that began to wend their way out of the town of Somosiera as the time passed; they were closely escorted by Estaban's Cavalry as they set their direction towards the nearest French held town for relief.

The nearest town to Somosiera was on the other side of the mountains at the eastern end of the pass. Thomas estimated that in the conditions the French would have to face it would take them a long two or three days to make it to Tamajon and he knew that he and his men would be well on the way back to Vimeiro long before the alarm could be raised and their attack known of.

As the last of the French left the town, Thomas signalled for the men to make ready to leave the town and turn towards Vimeiro; Estaban and his men would shadow the French retreat until they were certain the enemy would not turn back and then follow after Thomas. With their horses they would soon make up the distance and rejoin the small army to retire to Vimeiro; it would be a welcome break once they were back in their home valley to rest before once again going out after their hated enemy.

Once again the small army had to move with stealth and care; they were deep in enemy territory and could not take the chance of being found out now that their supplies were low. The days were once again spent in hiding and the nights were filled with fast travel. Everyone pushed themselves to their utmost during the hours of darkness and avoided every town or village along their route of march. Rations were now at their lowest but the men and boys did not stop their way west.

The chances of running into a French patrol in the hours of darkness were very slim but it still did not mean the men could take chances; there were still French sympathisers among the general populace and it would take only one accidental meeting for them to be found out and the French given the time to create a trap for them.

The order of march was very similar to other times. Lorenco sent out his Sharpshooters to act as a van guard and to watch the trail ahead an hour before the guns left. Next came the guns at a fast trot. The guns would be followed by the two Infantry Corps once the French had been sent off and would travel at double time until they caught up with the guns.

Estaban and the three Cavalry troops would follow along after the enemy had been set well on their way and would then catch up to Thomas and the Infantry Corps and take station on either side with one troop at the rear guard position. By midday the small army had come together near San Ildefonso and Thomas thought they had pushed themselves enough in the daylight hours; it was time to find a hiding place until dark.

Ahead of the retiring small army there were possible heavy French patrols. The attacks to their north and ahead at Medina del Campo would have the countryside in an uproar and the last thing he needed was for them to walk right into a large French force unprepared.

During the rest of the daylight hours, Thomas and his men lay in hiding in a long narrow and easily defended ravine; while he waited for nightfall he planned out the next nights march. It would not be long before they came to a river crossing on the Carrion, normally they would have used a common ford but with the country on full alert they would have to find another means of crossing.

Thomas and his friends made the plan for the crossing of the Carrion to take place in the last hours of the next day. It would be west of Segovia and in an area with little or no population; only a stray Patrol could or would see them if they were unlucky. As they would need some daylight to make the crossing it was timed to make the river bank just before dusk; once over they would immediately have the long hours of darkness to make their escape without being seen.

Their final hurdle would be the crossing of the River Tormes; this would have to take place at the narrow section between Alba de Tormes and Salamanca, not a place to make and error with a large French force close at hand in both towns. Once across the Tormes they would push hard through the night and try to make the River Agueda and then cross into Portugal and safety just east of Almeida.

For the rest of the travel to Vimeiro they could then take the day light hours and be able to move faster and far more safely; if their luck held out they should be back in Vimeiro within eight to ten days.

Thomas's force had not got away completely unscathed. During the entry into the rubble strewn town, the men of the Infantry Corps had needed to take precautions as they leap frogged from one pile of debris to another in their search for the French. The results of their advance had left them with three musket ball wounds, one sprained ankle, two dislocated fingers and other sundry scrapes, bruises and cuts.

It was fortunate that the three musket ball wounds were not too serious but it did mean that the young man with the thigh wound had to be given a place on one of the caissons as he would not have been able to keep up the pace; the same was done for the lad with the sprained ankle.

The other two musket wounds were far luckier, one had been grazed just above the ear where he would now have trouble growing any hair and the wide scar would be with him for life and the other was a flesh wound in the upper arm; Thomas and his men had been very lucky in their attack and the French losses more than made up for the few wounds he had suffered amongst his own men.

The next night they had skirted Segovia to the south and then force marched through the open plain to the banks of the River Carrion where they found a camp well before day light; they would cross the river in the dim light of dusk later that day.

Once across the River Carrion it was two more nights of travel before they came to the banks of the River Tormes and had to thread the needle between Alba de Tormes and Salamanca; another day was passed in hiding to wait for dusk before they could cross the river.

For the duration of their march they had the need to be as silent as they could. Daylight observations had shown the marked increase in French patrols all over the region; one slip and they would more than have their hands full of angry French troops.

The biggest worry was over the guns. Twenty guns and caissons made a lot of noise and the pace had to be kept at a slow trot to keep the rattle of fittings and the creaking of leather to a minimum as everyone knew that sound travelled twice as far at night than it did during the day. By the time they were at the banks of the River Tormes the guns had no grease left for the axels and they would now have to hope for the best and pray that none of the axels would need greasing before they made it across the River Agueda.

Although every precaution was taken to keep his men and equipment safe; Thomas still worried every inch of the way west. Just one slip up and they could very easily be sacrificial lambs to the slaughter of French patrols or worse yet, a full Brigade of French troops.

Nine days after the sudden and devastating attack on Somosiera, Thomas led his small army across the River Agueda and into Portugal; he was sure he could hear the sigh of relief from every man in his army as they climbed the western bank of the Agueda. The safety of Vimeiro was now only four or five days away and they could now return to travelling during the day.

With his whole army across the river Agueda and after they had travelled a little more than two miles; Thomas called a halt for the rest of the night. They could now rest after their harrowing escape and would begin the march for Vimeiro the next day with the full light of the sun to guide them.

The date was the 4th of March; little did Thomas know that in only a few weeks Viscount Wellington would attack in force at Badajoz and that Thomas's disruptions to the north would allow the Viscount to have a decisive victory before turning back north to meet Marshal Marmont at Salamanca in June of that year.

On the 9th of March a very tired, dusty and hungry army came into sight of the town of Vimeiro. It was noticeable that even the horses seemed to be happy to be in familiar territory and their ears perked up and heads raised as the terrain became more and more familiar.

The guns were now in bad need of greasing and there could be heard many squeaks as almost dry axels heated under the strain and dust of the long journey. It was decided that the army would stop in Vimeiro so the wheels could be greased and the men rested before they made the last two hour trek into the home valley; they were all safe now and there was no need for haste any longer.

With the dry axels finally greased by the time late afternoon arrived, Thomas called his men to get ready to head for home; they should arrive just before dark and were all now looking forward to hot meals and soft beds although most of them; especially the Infantry would forego the meals if they had to decide between one or the other.

Dusk was falling just as the long, dusty and tired column entered their home valley. Those who had stayed behind had already been warned of their approach by the sentinel on guard at the head of the passage into the valley.

It was a relief for everyone of the column to not only smell the fresh food cooking but also to see that the four large cauldrons used for heating water were sitting atop well built fires and there was steam rising from within. A hot bath was as much needed as a hot meal and the pace unconsciously increased as the new arrivals saw what was waiting for them.

It was as though the weary troops had silently agreed that the troops who had had the hardest time during the march to the valley could have first use of the hot water. The three brothers led their Cavalry towards the far end of the valley where their horse lines had been set up. There were long pole stands built there for them so they could tie their horses up and unsaddle and groom them before releasing them to roam free and to drink from the stream and eat from the large piles of freshly cut grass.

The gunners were turned towards what was now considered the Armoury so they could set to work on the much needed maintenance of the guns and carriages and unhook the harnesses of their own horses.

The Infantry wasted no time in going to their barracks to gather their personal wooden pails after divesting themselves of their equipment which would be cleaned after their ablutions. The pails would be half filled with hot water and the troops would use them for bathing. Most times the men would share one pail between two of them and then use the second pail for clothes washing; especially their underclothes, shirts and hose.

Thomas and his Officers turned towards their own houses where they knew a hot bath would be ready and waiting for them. While Sergeant Fairley watched over Thomas it would be those scullery boys not needed in the kitchens at that moment that would attend to the others.

It was not long before the sounds of laughter filled the valley as those taking their ablutions also turned it into something of a game as they splashed each other in between trying to wash the grime and dust from their bodies. In the distance there were the sounds of harnesses being taken off the tired and sweating horses along with light hearted banter among the men as the final realisation that they were safe at home began to take effect from the long tension that had been built up during the march.

Thomas got down from Santana and the horse was quickly taken away by one of the scullery boys to be unsaddled and groomed. Thomas looked tired and worn as he limped towards the door of his house; his limp had increased with his tiredness and it was quickly noted by the ever waiting Fairley. Thomas did not miss the frown on Fairley's face but ignored it as he walked inside and headed for the first chair he saw.

To one side of the front room was a large tin bath with steam rising from its depths; had Thomas not needed to relieve himself of his weapons he would have been tempted to just drop into the inviting bath and go to sleep; he had not realised how much the forced march had taken out of him until the moment of walking in the door.

Thomas glanced up at the worried look on Fairley's face and sighed; he almost knew what was coming as he asked his batman.

"Ok Sergeant, say your piece and then I can get on with a bath."

"Nothing to say Sir; if you don't know what you're doing to yourself then there is little I can do about it Sir."

"Fine, then there is no need for you to say anything later. Don't say I didn't give you a chance to nag at me. Now then help me get this stuff off so I can make use of that hot water. A good drink would also be nice if you can see your way to finding one for me while I soak."

Fairley gave a thin smile before he left the room after helping Thomas to undress and then Fairley carried away the dirty underclothes, shirt and hose; they would be washed while Thomas soaked in the tin tub.

Fairley did not return with Thomas's drink for another ten minutes but when he did, the first thing he saw was Thomas lying in the hot water with his eyes closed; the soft sound of snoring coming from Thomas told Fairley that it had all been a little too much for his General. Fairley did not hesitate to lightly shake Thomas on his naked shoulder but the reply was a mumbled grunt and Thomas only seemed to settle further into the welcoming embrace of the warm water.

Fairley gave himself a small smile as he took up the wash cloth and began to use it to clean Thomas as best he could; the heavy smell of the lye soap soon filled the small front room as Fairley worked away. It was during the washing of Thomas's hair that he suddenly came awake and realised where he was. Fairley stopped his washing when he saw Thomas open his eyes and become aware of what was around him and what was going on.

"You can take over now Sir, your drink is beside the tub. I shall go and get some more hot water; by the look of the dirt that has come off you so far you will need more."

Thomas was just too tired to bother making a remark about Fairley's lack of respect but he knew also that the young Sergeant had only his best interests at heart. Thomas reached for the glass of brandy beside the tub and took a deep swallow before taking up the wash cloth and began to clean off the rest of the dirt accumulated during the forced march.

Half an hour later and Thomas was ready to get out of the cooling water; Fairley was close by with clean clothes ready for him as he towelled himself dry; his glass of brandy had long since been emptied and now all he wanted was a good hot meal before looking for his bed, any business for the army would wait until the next morning.

Thomas was not alone in his need for rest as the valley began to quieten as the troops found food and then their beds; everything that could be done for that day was completed and now it was time for their bodies to rest before any more plans could be made.

When Thomas awoke the next morning, the sun was higher in the sky than he thought it would be; with a soft groan he tested his tired body and then swivelled around so he could get out of the bed. As expected his clean uniform was laid out for him and his boots had been cleaned and shone with a new coat of polish while his weapons were laid out on top of the cabinet.

The fresh smell of his normal early morning cafe filled his nostrils as he pulled his boots on; Thomas wondered if Fairley ever actually slept as his batman always seemed to be about when needed and Thomas could not think of the last time he had seen the young Sergeant resting.

Thomas went outside to the small round table that was always set up for him on the narrow patio outside his front door; Fairley had his cafe ready and waiting and was just in the process of setting out the cutlery for his breakfast which was sitting on the table in a steaming platter.

"Morning Sergeant! Do I have to test this for poison?"

"Not today Sir but perhaps tomorrow it might be a good idea."

"You are full of joy Sergeant. Now is there anything I should know about for today?"

"Yes Sir, the three Colonels would like to see you when you are ready and Major Jones has news for you about the young Lieutenant Morgan. Also Sir, Major Smithson would like to see you when you have time."

"Thank you Sergeant, can you let them all know I will be available just as soon as I have eaten."

"Yes Sir."

Fairley turned and left Thomas in peace so he could at least get one good hot meal into him before the problems of running a small army filled his days. Thomas could not understand how he could be so hungry as he almost shovelled the large platter of food into his mouth; the only thing that somewhat spoilt the breakfast was the odd twinge in his left shoulder as he lifted his arm.

When Thomas had finished eating, he looked down at the almost empty platter; he had eaten enough for two men and his stomach now felt boated and he burped loudly as he loosened his jacket and sat back to ease the fullness. A small smile came over his young face as he suddenly remembered what his father used to say about his eating habits.

"Son, your eyes are bigger than your stomach; you need to slow down before you look like a bloated sow."

Thomas suddenly felt a little homesick as the stray thought came to him; he would need to let his family know that he was alright and still fighting; with so much going on the last few months it had slipped his mind and now he had time to think it had come to the fore. Thomas put the thought aside as he got ready for the upcoming meetings with his Officers.

Fairley had brought him his second mug of cafe and he was just starting to sip it when Carmelo, Estaban and Lorenco arrived with broad smiles on their faces; it was time to get down to business. Thomas noted that Estaban now had the sleeve of his jacket folded back over to cover the place where he had lost his hand. During battle Estaban had worn a thick leather cuff made with a metal spike attached which he wore.

Due to the loss of his hand, Estaban had found it difficult to reload his musket and pistols and so now carried not only his musket but also a pair of heavy Dragoon pistols mounted on his saddle, his double barrelled Purdy under his arm and another brace of medium pistols in his sash. With his sword now hung on the opposite side for ease of use and the new extra spike in place of his hand; Estaban often looked like a walking armoury all on his own.

The three colonels sat down and were soon served with hot cafe's by Fairley, once they had taken the first sip they all got down to business. Thomas began the meeting.

"Carmelo, how are the men?"

"Many are in need of rest and I think they should have two days for themselves, Patron."

"Yes I agree Carmelo, they have done well and we will need them well rested before our next attack. Make a note of it and we'll tell them at the meeting later today. Estaban, what of your Cavalry?"

"Patron, they are now working on their equipment but also I think like my brother Carmelo, the men need rest and so do the horses if we want to get the best out of them."

"Agreed so we will tell them later today that there is to be no work for two days and the next five are only to have light work. Lorenco what about your Scouts?"

"As always Patron, they are ready when needed."

"Good then we will take a couple of weeks to make sure everyone is well rested before we move on Molina and Villaviciosa. We will have to ask Major Smithson what he has for maps of the area; hopefully he had time to get the details he needed while we were further north. Do any of you have concerns we should know about?"

All three shook their heads in the negative as they sipped their cafe's; for now it was a time of rest and for the three Colonels that also meant their Patron would also rest even if he was not aware of their plans for him.

"Well let's call for Major Smithson and see what he has for us."

Thomas turned his head to see where Fairley was and, as usual the young Sergeant was close by but not too close to make his Superior Officers think he was intruding or trying to overhear their plans.

"Fairley! Can you go and find Major Smithson, ask him to bring his latest maps of the Molina area. When you have found him then go and ask Major Jones to come and see us."

Fairley saluted and left the veranda to find the men his General wanted. Thomas and the three Colonels finished their cafe's as they waited for Smithson to arrive; it did not take long before they saw the Major approaching with a number of leather rolls under his arm.

As he waited for Smithson to get to them Thomas looked out on the valley. In the distance he could make out the men of the Cavalry working on their riding tack, the two corps of Infantry looked to be setting out their freshly washed clothes to dry or were cleaning their muskets and other equipment. On the right hand side of the valley, the gunners were already sweating over the guns as they stripped them down for maintenance and the horse handlers were working on the leather traces and metal fittings for the guns.

The long mess barracks were a hive of activity as the many young scullery boys set about cleaning and making the mess ready for the midday meal; the fires in the kitchen behind the mess were sending faint trails of smoke into the fresh morning air as the cooks worked in the open air on the large meat pits with what appeared to be a full sized Ox on a long thick metal spit; two younger boys were on one end and turning it slowly over the glowing coals.

Thomas turned back to his meeting as Major Smithson arrived with his newest maps.

"Good morning Major, what do you have for us?"

"Good morning Sir, these are the maps we made as you asked. We have made some changes and I hope you like them, it should make for easier identification of the various ground conditions."

"What are they Major?"

"Captain Marking has added colour washes to various parts which denote the type of ground in that area. If you can give me a second I will show you what I mean Sir."

Thomas sat looking at Smithson as he unrolled the first map of Molina; it was not the revelation that they would now have coloured maps but the name of the person who was making them. Thomas coughed before he asked.

"Ahh...Major, who is this Captain Marking?"

"Oh don't you know Sir?"

"No I don't Major."

Before Smithson could continue Carmelo interrupted and began to explain as he smiled widely at Thomas.

"I am sorry Patron; I am the one at fault. Sergio and Carlito asked me when you were so ill, they had no family and wanted to carry your name so if you did not get well there would be someone that carried your name onward. I should have mentioned it earlier but with everything going on it had slipped my mind. I am sure that they would give the name back if you are not happy with what they have done."

"No...no it's just that I never thought about such a thing, tell them I am very proud they would think it of such importance and that I am honoured to have them as my family members. Now then Major Smithson, let's see what you have there?"

The four Senior Officers waited as Major Smithson unrolled his maps and then set small stones on the edges to keep them flat. Thomas saw immediately how good they were, even had they not been colour washed they would have been better than anything he had seen before.

"These four are of Molina, in the other roll I have five I had to make of the area around Villaviciosa. If you will allow me I will explain the colour code that Captain Marking used."

"Thank you Major, please continue."

"It is very simple Sir. The green is grasslands, the brown is for open or bare ground, the grey is for stone and we have used white for houses and streets inside the town."

Thomas pointed to an area of brown that had minute spikes of black ink in the shape of three prongs.

"What are these Major?"

"Ah yes Sir, those are another creation of Captain Marking. His knowledge of the area was a great help and that area is brown for the time of summer when it is dry and very firm; Captain Marking though knew that the area during the winter can turn into a very heavy bog so he put those indicators there so you would know what it was when the rains came."

"I think it will be a lot easier if you just call the Captain Sergio, it's beginning to confuse me and will until I get used to having them use my name. Now then Major, what of these rings and numbers you have spread over the map?"

"Those indicate the elevations Sir."

"Elevations Major?"

"Yes Sir. If you will look at this one Sir, you will see that it has three circles inside each other. The general shape shows the outline of the knoll and the three circles show if it is a gentle slope if they are wide apart and if it is very steep the lines will be closer together. The number at the centre shows the height of the knoll and the number at the base tells us how big the knoll is. If you look over here Sir you can see how the lines run for some distance and are far closer together, my calculations tells us this ridge is approximately one mile long and some three hundred yards high with very steep sides. This small black line that wends back and forth indicates there is a small goat track that leads up to the top; no good for guns but men could scale it if needed."

Thomas stood in awe of the detail of the four maps laid out before him; it was almost like looking at the actual land itself; he would have to spend a lot of time with Smithson so he could fully understand the new ideas so he could make best use of them.

"I would like you to pass on my congratulations to the Captain for his attention to detail as well as your own Major. I must confess I have never seen maps like them before; it should make our job much easier when it comes to our planning."

"Thank you Sir I shall pass on your thanks to the Captain as soon as I get back to the map room."

"Map Room?"

"The war room in your house Sir, we call it the map room now as you will see if you have not already looked at it."

"I haven't been inside it yet; too much to do but I will look it over just as soon as I get done here. Thank you Major for everything you have done so far; these maps are going to be a great help. Now then I have something more for you to do when you and your unit have had a chance to rest up."

"We are ready when you need us Sir, what is it you want?"

"It's the Guadarrama pass, we are going to need as much fine detail as you can get for us; there have been a lot of armies that have failed to take it due to its difficulty; I'm hoping you can find us something new that we can use for our attack after Molina."

"How much time do I have Sir?"

"I would like something before the middle of July; we should have returned from Molina and Villaviciosa by then and I have information that the English have got plans for around that time to enter Madrid if all goes well for them after Badajoz."

"Very good Sir that gives us plenty of time to get your details correct; we won't let you down Sir, of that you can be sure."

"Thank you Major I know you won't. Now then can you ask Major Jones to come over while you go and see to your men?"

Major Smithson stood and saluted before he turned and left the four Officers to look over the new maps; there was going to be much for the four to learn on how to read them correctly and he was going to give them all the time they needed.

Major Jones arrived with his perennial ledgers under one arm and a file of papers in his other hand.

"Good morning Major Jones, what have you got for us?"

"Good Morning Sir. I have the pay ledgers for you to look over and the accounts for the stock purchases by Lieutenant De Silva. There are also some messages for you to read that Lieutenant Morgan brought back with him and another from His Highness as well as another from the Cortes which is more of a report than orders as far as I can make out Sir."

"Thank you Major, anything else we should be made aware of?"

"Just the arrival of more powder for the stores, we may have to ask Major Carterton to design a new armoury and powder store for us; we have had to use two of the houses as extra powder stores after the last ship delivery."

"We had a ship delivery Major?"

"Yes Sir, Lieutenant Morgan arrived back on the Avante and they had captured a small French sloop on their way here; it was filled with French supplies of powder, shot and weapons. I gave orders to the Captain of the Avante to make use of the extra muskets for the ship's crew. I hope I did not overstep my orders Sir?"

"You were the Officer that was there Major and I will back any orders you gave; besides we have more than enough weapons for our own use as it is. What are they going to do with the French sloop?"

"The Captain is going to try to have it refitted and use it as part of the fleet of merchantmen for Marking Shipping Company Sir."

"Well you can get with Major Carterton and see about the new armoury; I don't have any plans to move against Molina until I have seen the results of the English attack on Badajoz so the men may like a change from training; you can tell Major Carterton he can have as many men as he needs until that time."

"Yes Sir, I will pass that on to him. Is there anything else you need Sir?"

"Not at this time thank you Major. Good work on keeping the valley safe and well situated while we were away; it's good to know our home is in safe hands while we are away."

"Thank you Sir, if you will excuse me I will get back to other things."

Thomas nodded and then turned back to the new pile of ledgers and papers on the table; it was really the last thing he wanted to do but he also realised it was a necessary part of having a small army and trying to keep everything together and in order.

Thomas heard a soft cough behind him and turned to see the ever present Fairley waiting to be told to speak.

"Yes Fairley, how are you going to spoil my day now?"

Fairley seemed to either not hear or decided to completely ignore Thomas's comment.

"Sir it is after midday and the Kitchen has sent over lunch for you and your Officers; it is time for you to take a break and rest Sir."

"Fairley, if I did not know better I would think you had been speaking to my mother; I'm quite alright now you know and I'm certainly not a bloody invalid for you to order around when you like."

Fairley stood at attention and seemed to completely ignore Thomas's words as he replied.

"Yes Sir, but lunch has been served and it is time for your rest; I'm sure your mother would agree Sir."

"Damn it Fairley I'm not a baby for you to molly coddle."

"Yes Sir. Shall I send the lunch back to the kitchen Sir?"

"Do I really have to answer that Sergeant?"

"No Sir, if you wish I can serve it out here for you gentlemen Sir."

"Yes do that Sergeant; I want to look over these maps while we eat."

"And then you will rest Sir?"

"Fairley, you are stretching my patience."

"Yes Sir, I shall go and get the curtains drawn for your rest while you eat Sir."

Had anyone seen the smile on Fairley's face they would have known he had won again and even the acerbic words of their Commander could not shake the care that Fairley took of his General. Thomas turned back to his three friends and could only raise his eyes to the heavens; they all knew that Fairley had been right and that Thomas still needed a rest after the last campaign. While his wounds looked to be healed his body still needed the extra rest until it was fully back to health and the stresses of the last outing had taken more out of their General than the young man would let on.

An hour later and the four Officers broke up their meeting and lunch to go their own way, they had duties of their own to attend to and Thomas was once again under the caring but stern eyes of Sergeant Fairley. The heat of the day would be spent in the coolness of his bedroom for Thomas and Fairley would see to it that he was not disturbed until the day had cooled a little.

CHAPTER 10

When Thomas awoke a little later in the afternoon, the heat had eased although the humidity was still high. Fairley had placed a cooling drink on his bedside table for him and was waiting patiently with his clean clothes as well as a message.

Thomas stifled a small groan as his shoulder ached a little from him sleeping on it. Thomas knew that if Fairley heard him he would be given a sharp look of censure from his batman. Thomas rolled off the bed and began to re-button his shirt while Fairley lifted his jacket off the wooden coat hook for him.

"Lieutenant Morgan wishes to talk with you Sir, when would you like to see him?"

"Give me a few minutes please Fairley then call for him."

"Yes Sir, there is also Major Carterton waiting to see you as well."

"OK; tell Mister Carterton he can have some time after the Lieutenant. Do you know what it's all about?"

"I'm only a Sergeant Sir that would be above my station."

"Fairley!"

"Yes Sir?"

"Stop the crap, now what do they want?"

"I believe that the Lieutenant has some news of your family from home Sir and that the Major has a plan for the new armoury for you to look over Sir."

"You could have just told me that to start with Fairley; I should make you an Officer just so you have more to keep you busy."

"Thank you Sir but it would be unseemly for an Officer to be a batman; it would create too much talk amongst the ranks Sir."

"And I suppose you would be the one to start the talk Fairley?"

"I would never do that Sir, after all it may put me in line for promotion and that could be very upsetting Sir."

"Go and call Mister Morgan before I make you a Captain."

"Yes Sir, right away Sir."

Thomas hid his smile as he pulled his jacket on; he wondered what his days would have been like without the young teen watching over him. It was a thought he quickly pushed aside as he got ready for his visitors, once that was done it would be time for the general meeting with all the troops in their meeting place at the side of the valley.

Thomas carried the half full glass of cool fruit drink with him; he had come to like the tart taste of the limes and water and it was refreshing just when he needed it most. Thomas sat at the small round table under the awning of the veranda and out of the direct sunlight while he watched Snot Morgan come towards him with a wide smile on his young face.

"Good Afternoon Lieutenant, what do you have for me?"

"Good afternoon Sir, I have brought messages from home Sir and wish to apologise for my tardiness in returning."

"Think nothing of it Lieutenant; I really had little idea how long your assignment would take. Now what have you got in that pouch?"

Snot Morgan laid the leather message pouch on the small table and untied the strap before taking out the first of the written messages and laying it on the table for Thomas to see.

"This one is from the Captain of the Avante Sir; I presume it is to do with his last cargo and capture."

"Thank you Lieutenant, now the next?"

"This one is from me Da Sir, tells all about the Shipping Company and what he is doing with the new ship."

"New ship Lieutenant?"

"Message tells it all Sir but me Da has signed on a new ship to your company; the message explains it all Sir."

"Well then what's left?"

"Just one more Sir, a letter from your own Da, wanted me to carry it to you personal like Sir, right pleased he was when I went to visit and found out you were back on your feet again."

"Sit down Snot and tell all about your visit. Are they all well and what of my new little brother?"

"Thank you Sir."

Snot took the small chair opposite Thomas and began to tell him of his trip back to England and his visit with Thomas's family. He told Thomas of his ride to Lisbon and how he had found the ship to take him to England and what had transpired on the docks and during the voyage. Next he told the story of when he finally got to London and how he had been riding his horse one day when he got the idea of going in search of Thomas's family.

Snots story ended after he told Thomas about staying to help his father with the farm work and having time to play with his little brother; it was this that had kept him away later than intended but he felt the journey well worth it to have news to bring back for Thomas.

When Snot had finished his report, Thomas thanked him for his thoughtfulness in visiting his family and taking the time to wait for his father to write a letter to him. With everything complete Snot stood back up and saluted Thomas before saying one last thing; the twinkle in his eye did not go unseen by Thomas, even though he had a small tear in his eye.

"That brother of yours Sir, little though he be he walks right funny at times; just like a Jack Tar he is Sir."

Thomas could not help the laughter that burst from his lips as Snot turned about and left Thomas alone just as Major Carterton appeared in the distance and making his way towards where Thomas sat in the shade.

When Carterton had arrived at the table, Thomas told him to sit and show his plans so they could discuss it and see if there were anything needed.

"So what have you got for me Major?"

"Here we are Sir, thought this might do us nicely if we can get a few things not found here."

Thomas watched as the large roll was unfurled and laid open for him to see the design of the new powder store. To Thomas it looked quite impressive and the detail of the drawing left nothing to chance; Major Carterton must have spent many long hours working on it.

"So explain to me what I'm looking at Major?"

"Well Sir, I propose we put the new store down yonder at the far end of the valley and well out of the way of the rest of the camp. The walls will be built double thickness with rocks and mortar and I am told there is a plentiful supply of tiles at the works in Vimeiro for us to roof it. Inside it will be divided into stalls with the fine pistol and musket powder to the front and the course powder for the guns at the rear. I suggest Sir we put a single large wooden door with a heavy padlock on it facing into the valley; it can be made by the carpenter in the village I am told. If we use this just for the powder then the extra weapons we have can stay in the original store along with your coin chests. If anything happens and the powder store goes up then the rest of the valley should stay safe."

Thomas looked at the fine detail of the plan and thought for a few minutes before saying.

"How long to put it all together Major?"

"If you let most of the men work on it then not long at all Sir. Six to seven hundred men carrying a rock each doesn't take long to have good strong walls built, the only concern for me is the supply of mortar; it will take a good supply to complete the work Sir."

"What's mortar Major?"

"It's a mixture of sand and quick lime Sir, the sand is easy to get but the quick lime may be a little more difficult but it is needed for a good tight seal and to hold the stones tight."

"What do you suggest Major?"

"I was thinking perhaps that young Lieutenant you have purchasing the cattle and sheep; he may know where to get the lime from as it is used quite frequently in the construction of their own homes and buildings."

"A good idea Major. When you leave here send word for Lieutenant De Silva and ask him to keep watch for you, when you are ready to build then you can have all the men you need, it will keep them busy until we go out against the French once again in May, I want to have a go at them again after Wellington begins his push towards Salamanca in April."

"Yes Sir, I will personally guarantee that it will be well completed long before then Sir."

"Thank you Major, now if there is nothing more I have some very important letters to get to; please tell the men there will be a general meeting in two hours."

"Yes Sir."

Thomas waited until Major Carterton was on his way before turning back to the leather pouch with his mail inside; he barely noticed the slight shake in his hand as he searched for the one from his father. Once he had the letter in his hand, Thomas hesitated before breaking the seal and opening the single page, the unsteady scrawl of his father's hand was easily discerned and Thomas had to sniff to stop the sudden need for tears as the symbol of his far off home and family sat in his hand.

Thomas reached into his sleeve and took out one of his knives to break the simple candle wax seal. Next he slowly unfolded the cheap paper and laid it flat on the table before starting to read. The familiar unsteady scrawl now seemed almost foreign as he had got used to the precise and explicit messages of the army Officers but the personality of his father was undeniable in the roughly written and worded letter.

Cromwell Marking Sgt.

27th Feb 1812

Sun.

Both yor mutha and me is rite prowd that yoo is ower sun and am better off nown you is back on yoor feat agin after wot them frencheys don to ye. I is also rite prowd wot you don to save colors of the King and savd the repatashun of all them toff ofisas but to sea wot they don to yoo afta batal at that plase in Spanish land wos not rite atal. I got no blaim for yoo goin to Spanish army ware they seems to laik yoo mor. Yung snot don told me you now had lands aplenty an ar no longa party to nob ofisas of British army, I says gud for yoo and stik to yor guns and maik us prowd wuns mor. Tom yoo been a gud sun and no mistaik an I kan walk with hed hye nown yoo will do rite by all. Mutha has tiars for you but i says for she to stop as yoo is not a lital lad no mor. Yoor brutha be in gud helth an is rite chip of old blok, wen he nows of his brathas advejur i be sur he wil be rite prowd also.

Sun be of gud helth and woch over sholder for we wants you bak in gud order.

Yoor Da

Cromwell Marking Sgt.

Thomas felt another tear slip down his cheek as he finished his Fathers letter; there were times he did not think he would ever see them again but this single sheet of roughly written words gave him more hope than ever before. Thomas grunted as he determined that there was not a Frenchman in Spain that would stop him from going home once the war was done with; the fact of him staying there was another matter as he now also had other duties to the people of Spain and Portugal but that was for another time and place.

For the next few weeks Thomas watched as the new powder store grew quickly under the directions of Major Carterton. It seemed to Thomas, that every time he looked out into the valley there was a long line of men carrying large stones towards the building site as well as a number of wagons coming from further afield with more stones and two had been covered to keep the quick lime from blowing away while not in use.

The new powder store had double thick stone walls and was forty feet long and twenty feet wide, there was a large opening left for the single solid wooden door to be fitted into once the Vimeiro carpenter had it made. All the heavy beams and rafters had been hewed from trees outside of Vimeiro and carried back to the valley in a number of wagons.

Off to one side lay long piles of red clay tiles for the roof; it had taken almost every tile that had been made in Vimeiro at that time to fulfil the needs of the high roof. Everyone Thomas saw seemed pleased with the work and the break from normal military duties as they worked day after day on their new addition but it would soon be time to get back to what they were there for and the French waited them at Molina.

On the 8th of April, Thomas got a message that Wellington had beaten the French at Badajoz only days before and was even now turning his army back north to attack Salamanca. It was almost time for Thomas to once again lead his men against the French even though the way forward would be even more dangerous now the French knew that El Toro was again in the field.

On the 10th of April the last tile was laid on the roof and the men now turned to the onerous task of man handling each and every keg of powder from the old store to the new one, with the knowledge that they would soon be going out against the French at Molina, the men set to work with a new will and the powder was finally stored in only two days in its new home; it was time for Thomas and his men to make plans for the coming attacks in May.

The problem that arose for Thomas was being able to get so far inland to Molina. The French would still be on full alert for any large movement of troops and he did not want to take the chance of once again losing his guns to the French. Molina was a large town and had a heavy French presence; he would not be able to attack them without his guns. There had to be another way to get there without crossing so much of Spain and leaving open an opportunity for the French patrols to not only find them but to form up a large counter attack.

Thomas and his Colonels were standing around the large table with the map of Spain open upon it. It was not one of the finely detailed maps of Major Smithson but it did show all of Spain with most rivers and land masses shown; it also showed the major tracks and roads on the Peninsular.

The four men studied the map for over an hour before Estaban pointed to an area of coast between Almenara and San Carlos de la Rapita. The two centres were widely spread apart and there looked to be very little in between them.

"Here Patron, we could land the full army here on the beaches, there are many small coves along this coast. I know it well as my family often travelled to Valencia; all we need is the ships to carry the men, guns and horses. If we timed our landing for the hours of darkness we could be well inland before anyone was aware of us. From there it is only a matter of days and we can come on Molina from the east and south. It would be the last place the French would be watching for us."

The four friends looked at the map for a long time and considered Estaban's plan; it was both daring and dangerous but the first thought that came into Thomas's mind was if they could find enough ships for the daring attempt; there was only one thing for it; he had to make contact with Mister Percy to see what help was available.

The four friends stayed and planned in the hope they could somehow make it work, if it came off it would be a real feather in their cap and add even more confusion to the French forces. The biggest problem they could immediately see was the need for their ships to go into French held waters to unload and that was the main stumbling block to the plan; it would all depend on what and if Mister Percy could help them.

An hour later and Thomas was at his small table writing letters, one would have to go to his agent in Oporto to make contact with his own ships to clear their holds and meet him at Toro Bay and the other was to be sent to Colonel Lewis by one of his boys and then be delivered on to Mister Percy. It was the only way Thomas had to contact his old friend. He would send Sergio as his messenger as he had been advised not to show his face too often in Lisbon while English Officers were still there in numbers.

With Sergio on his way to find Colonel Lewis, Thomas and his friends settled back to working out their proposed plan for the future. It took another week before he had his replies from Oporto and Mister Percy but the results were very favourable. .The agent in Oporto reported that all of his four ships would be made available when he wanted them; Thomas did not miss the reference to four ships instead of the three he thought he had.

Mister Percy had done even better; it would remain only for Thomas to tell him the date of his departure from Vimeiro and Mister Percy would see that he had a naval escort for the ships when they entered French waters, He did not mention how or with what but the result was more than Thomas could have expected.

On the 25th of April Thomas had decided it was time to make their move towards Molina. The four ships of the Marking Shipping Company had reported that they were at anchor on the 23rd and awaiting his orders. With the final decision made, Thomas sent off a message for Mister Percy to tell him when they expected to be sailing into French waters west of Cartagena.

Thomas had not been told what sort of escort they would get but he hoped it would be enough to discourage any French ships in the area from attacking his small convoy carrying his troops and guns. On the arrival of his small army on the shores of Toro bay, Thomas saw what he had to deal with.

While Thomas knew he had an extra ship under contract and another small Sloop captured from the French, he was surprised to see a large Brigantine also anchored there with the others. Both the Brig and the Sloop had obvious evidence of new repairs as well as a number of gun ports not normally seen on this type of ship; it appeared the Council had once again come to his aide.

Once Thomas had met with all four Captains, he set about getting his men and guns loaded. With the extra space on the Brig it was decided that the guns and caissons would be carried by her which left the Sloop to act as powder ship for their munitions and a full Corps of Infantry. The Avante and the Beatrice Graves would carry the horses for the Officers and the balance of the personnel; it would be a tight squeeze but they were prepared to make any sacrifices needed to get a jump on the French.

As there was limited space on the four ships, Pablo had volunteered to use his Cavalry troop to take most of the horses overland and meet the convoy in the agreed landing place. While the trip was long it was still far easier and safer now the French had been pushed back by Wellington's latest victory and they should be able to make the landing place in good time with safety.

The small convoy left Toro bay on the 28th of April and turned their bows towards the French held waters off Cartagena; it would be a trip of four days as long as the wind stayed in their favour. It was in the very early hours of the 5th of May when the topman spied the faint outline of ships masts in the slowly brightening light of the morning.

Thomas and his Officers were soon on deck to watch the approach of what was quickly becoming three large English forty gun Frigates; it appeared Mister Percy still had a lot of pull in naval circles.

The sun was just breaking in the east when the three towering Frigates took station around the four smaller ships; a signal was run up the mainmast of the leading Frigate to ask permission to send an Officer to meet with General Thomasino de Toro. Permission was granted quickly and Thomas and his friends watched as a long boat was lowered over the side and six heavily built seaman and one Officer quickly scrambled into it and began to pull towards the Avante.

All of the ships had furled sails to the minimum and they were barely making two knots as the long boat drew closer to the Avante. When the long boat was alongside, Thomas stepped close to the gunnel to wait for the Officer to climb the rope ladder and step onto the deck.

It was plainly obvious to Thomas that the Officer; a man in his mid twenties; was not expecting such a young man to be the General he was seeking. The youngish Officer stepped onto the deck and was astute enough to note that Thomas was the Senior Officer by the fact that the others on deck were apparently deferring to him. The Officer stood to attention and; after introducing himself, asked Thomas.

"Lieutenant Bellamy Sir, are you General Thomasino de Toro Sir?"

The surprised look on the Lieutenants face when Thomas replied with a heavy London accent nearly caused Thomas to giggle.

"Yes Lieutenant, what can I do for you?"

The surprise was still on the Lieutenants face as he almost spluttered as he tried to relay his message.

"Captain Selkirk's compliments Sir; he would like to know your final destination so he can organise the escort. I am told he has orders to stand off the beach to guard you while your ships unload; all he needs now is for your course and final destination Sir."

"Thank you Lieutenant, please pass on my thanks to Captain Selkirk and if you would follow me below to the Captain's cabin I will show you what we have in mind."

"Thank you Sir."

Less than thirty minutes later and Thomas was watching the Lieutenant rowing back towards the waiting Frigate; it was not long before the signals went up on the lead Frigate and all the ships unfurled all their sails to take advantage of the favourable wind. Thomas's little convoy was now under the protection of the three heavily armed English Frigates; how Mister Percy had pulled it off he would never know but he was very thankful as they entered into French waters.

Captain Selkirk led the convoy out into deeper water so they would be less likely to meet too many other ships; the course he set was to take them through the narrow channel between Iviza and Majorca and then make a direct run into the beaches and bays of their intended landing place. Once Thomas's ships had been unloaded they would then return to English protected waters with the escort and return to their normal business while Thomas had the men of the Regiment prepare for their attack on Molina.

It was a further two days for the small convoy to finally reach the selected bay. The beach was a coarse shingle and the landing of the army and its equipment would not be without its difficulties. Thomas's biggest fears were for the guns and caissons; with only four long boats and three dory's it looked as though it was going to take a long time to unload, it was time for a meeting with the Captains.

The final decision for the equipment surprised Thomas when Captain Bowden suggested they run the sloop ashore at high tide and unload the powder and shot stores. Being the smallest of the four ships it was deemed that the other three could assist in pulling it off the beach on the next high tide, they would then do the same with the brig although it was suggested they ask for help from one of the Frigates as the brig was larger and heavier.

Lorenco would take his sharpshooter scouts ashore first and set a perimeter about a half mile inland, as yet there was no sign of Pablo and the horses so the guns would have to be manhandled up the shingle beach in pieces. The barrels would be removed and carried by the gunners once the ship was beached and then the carriages would be followed by the empty caissons which would be filled with the ammunition once they were high and dry.

The Officer's horses would be swum ashore behind the dory's with some of the men holding the lead ropes as they were rowed ashore. Thomas had time to take note that the three large Frigates had taken the station of line astern and began to patrol the seaward side of the bay about a half mile out and running from north east until just past the end of the bay before turning about and setting course south west where they would again turn about to follow the same pattern.

The last Frigate in line would just disappear as the first in line once again came into sight on its return track; Thomas found it a comforting thought to have the three forty gunners watching to seaward while they set to unloading. All Thomas now had to concern himself with was the whereabouts of the army's horses; he could only pray that Pablo had not run into any trouble before getting to them.

Inside the bay the water was calm and there was barely a ripple on the beach as the first long boats arrived with Lorenco and his men. Quickly jumping from the boats, Lorenco led his men outward to set his lines as the long boats returned for the next part of the unloading. They had just missed the high tide and so had twelve hours before they could beach the Sloop, the time was to be spent getting most of the army ashore in preparation for the heavier equipment to be unloaded.

The first bit of good news came in the middle of the afternoon, just as the Sloop was preparing to raise anchor and ready for high tide. At the far end of the bay Thomas saw the first signs of the awaited horses. Pablo had some of his men riding on the outer edges as guards while the main part of the troop were leading the horses on the end of a rope; there were about ten horses to a rope and all seemed to be in good condition after the long ride.

With the arrival of the horses it would now be easier to get the guns off the beach along with the three heavy wagons for the powder stores and other essentials. Thomas watched as the Captain on the Sloop lined his small ship up with the beach; as he neared the point where he would beach, the Captain dropped two stern anchors to assist in winching himself off the beach once unloaded. The other three ships would also act when the time came to pull the Sloop back into deeper water which should be a little easier as it would be riding high and empty.

From the high tide they would have twelve hours to unload their supplies before the tide would be good enough to refloat the Sloop. It had been decided that, should the Sloop prove to be easy to handle this way then they would also then beach the Brigantine and do the same for the guns, caissons and three wagons. It was an hour later and the Sloop was well beached and the unloading had begun; Thomas left the Avante and went in one the dory's to the beach, it was time to start to organise for the final move inland in a few days time.

With the Sloop clear of the beach, the Brigantine set itself on the beach at the same place; the unloading of its heavier equipment would take far longer than the supplies of the Sloop. As the Brigantine could only be unloaded from the bow until the water lowered further to low tide, it was decided to remove the barrels of the guns and manhandle them over the side four at a time.

On the beach below the bow stood most of the gunners, they had divided up into six man teams and had two long poles with canvas slings attached. The barrel would be placed on the sling and the men would carry them up the shingle beach; it was hoped they would be able to get all the barrels off the ship in short order, and so it proved.

Within an hour all the barrels were lined up neatly on the harder ground above the beach and now all they had to wait for were the gun carriages and the Caissons. It was decided to unload the empty Caissons first as they were lighter and would be easier to man handle; it was hoped they would be able to use the horses to pull the gun carriages up the beach so the men could rest before reassembling them.

As the ship now had to use its foremast for a winch, as they could only land one Caisson or gun carriage at a time it was going to take time. Once the equipment was ashore they would then have to rearm the Caissons and set the barrels, there was also the reloading of the wagons with their supplies that were now under canvas to protect them.

It took a further five days to finally finish unloading the ships and refloat the Brigantine while those ashore readied the wagons with all the stores and equipment so that the ships could now leave and Thomas's little army would be on their own. The two Infantry Corps had taken over the guard duties although they only worked one at a time with the other helping on the beach until their turn came to protect their friends.

Lorenco had taken his men deeper into the countryside to make sure the bay was well protected and they would not encounter any unwanted surprises. On the 14th of May the small army of El Toro was ready to make its move on Molina but before that happened they had to cover the distance without being seen by the French or any of their spies; it was going to be night moves once again.

Thomas would again send Lorenco and his men out ahead of them to not only keep them unseen and safe but also to look out for camping places for the daytime bivouacs; it was to be a trip of ten days and nights, mainly nights and they had the added need to skirt around the smaller towns along their route and stay close to the mountains. If all went well they would come in on Molina from the east; what they hoped would be the last direction the French would expect them to come from.

Thomas's biggest concern was how close they would come to the smaller towns of Tortosa, Fleix, and Alcaniz; one mistake and they could easily be discovered. From Alcaniz they would cut into the mountains and work their way west through the passes until they came in sight of Molina on the plains below them. It was difficult at best to get the guns and wagons through the confines of the narrow pass but it was the only way they could hope to take the town of Molina totally by surprise.

As before, Thomas and his army would divide once through the mountains; he would lead the guns and two Corps of Infantry through to Molina while Estaban would take his three Cavalry troops on towards Villaviciosa where he would try to time his own attack to that of Thomas's. The attacks were timed for around the 26th of May and it was hoped that would give them both time to form a plan of attack before they had to take action.

Once again Major Smithson's maps came into their own; his detailed work and fine drawing had given Thomas and his men a great advantage on planning their route through the mountains and almost to the back door of Molina with two full days to spare.

It was to be a tough two days as they needed to keep a quiet bivouac so close to a well held French position and the need to keep any fires small and low only for cooking meant the nights were chilly as they were still in the mountains even though it was summer. During the next two days, Thomas and his men kept a sharp vigil on the town below as they worked on developing a plan of attack.

Molina was positioned at the northern end of the mountain range and close in to the foot of the high mountains, it would not be an easy nut to crack and Thomas also had the added problem of his own escape route out of the area once the fighting was done. To the east of Molina was a large open plain which Thomas hoped would be to their advantage.

The final plan was laid out and Thomas and his Infantry and guns would take position out on the plains to the east of Molina and let the guns do most of the work with the two Infantry Corps acting as close in protection with Lorenco further out as a screen. Thomas and his watchers had noticed one thing that may be too their advantage. The French in Molina had no Cavalry; it appeared to be an Infantry staging post and supply depot.

The town and nearby French encampment would be bombarded by the guns and when Thomas thought they had done enough damage he would lead the men north over the plain and through the narrow pass north of Villaviciosa which would once again lead them past the entrance to Somosiera. Once past the Somosiera pass they would continue towards their final destination of the Guadarrama pass for their final attack on Escorial.

Their largest problem once free of Molina would be getting past Segovia and San Ildefonso without alerting the French to their plans for the area. Estaban would meet up with them near the narrow pass to the north of Villaviciosa and from then on it would all be night marches along the foot of the mountains to their final destination of the Guadarrama pass and Escorial.

After their attacks it was decided to head south and bivouac in the high ranges near Batuecas where the French had been pushed out earlier by the English and the country side was safer than staying around to wait for the English advance later in the year.

To cover his withdrawal from Molina Thomas decided on a bold plan. Calling for Lieutenant Wright of the 5th battery, Thomas asked the young Lieutenant if he would be prepared to be their rearguard. Lieutenant Wright did not hesitate as he replied in the affirmative and then sat with Thomas to discuss how it would be done.

Thomas was glad the young Lieutenant was prepared to hold the line while the heavier guns and the Infantry made their escape. The 5th battery were now old hands at setting up their rockets and then breaking them down for transport; Lieutenant Wright almost boasted that he and his men could have the rocket battery ready to move in less than two minutes if needs be.

The sixteen launchers were carried four to a horse with another six horses carrying the actual rockets, the twenty man team of rocketeers were also mounted and Lieutenant Wright swore they would be well clear of any retaliation before the French could close with them and cause harm.

Thomas took the young Lieutenant at his word and began to lay out what he had in mind for their eventual withdrawal. The plan was again simple in its set up; during the initial bombardment, Lieutenant Wright would not make use of his rocket battery but stay back behind the line of guns and wait for the last salvo and the hooking up of the guns before he would ready his own battery.

It was assumed that the French would be in a turmoil from the bombardment and this should work to Lieutenant Wright's advantage. With the withdrawal of the guns and the two corps of Infantry running alongside as a protective screen, Lieutenant Wright would open fire on the already confused camp with what they hoped would be four more salvoes of rockets and then pack up and ride towards the pass and rejoin Thomas and the others.

With the French having no Cavalry close by they should easily make the far off pass well before anyone could come after them. The attack was timed for an hour before dawn on the 26th, Thomas guessed that they could make the pass by the evening of the 26th if they pushed hard and had no problems along the way.

On the night of the 25th Thomas went from gun to gun and checked that every piece of loose harness or metal had been bound in sacking to stop any squeaks or rattles as they moved into position for the morning bombardment; silence and stealth was more vital now than at any other time but Thomas had also prepared a rude wake up call for the French garrison.

Thomas called for the last seventy six Originals and told them his plan for the French; he was not surprised at the wide smiles that he saw on his longest serving men and boys, they were all ready and willing to carry out his cheeky plan.

As they had planned to move the guns into position only five miles from where they had been hiding; Thomas estimated they could easily make it in good time without having to make the horses and guns move at more than walking pace; it would keep any stray noise to a minimum and the chances of discovery were cut down considerably and so it proved.

With more than an hour of darkness to spare, Major Morgan had his twenty guns lined up in a single long line at nine hundred yards and ready to open fire on Thomas's command. Half of the 1st Corps of Infantry stood ready at each end of the long line of guns while the 2nd Corps was in a double line just behind.

At the front of the 2nd Corps stood the seventy six originals with their drums at the front and sticks at the ready. The drums had always been carried on the wagons, even if they were never used but it had just become habitual. Thomas would call the order for the drummers when he saw the first faint hint of the dawn light.

To the rear of the 2nd Corps of Infantry stood the 5th battery, once those in front had cleared the field they would open fire into the French lines in the hope of causing more than enough confusion for the others to make a clean escape. Beside each rocket stand were laid out eight rockets, once they were fired the 5th battery would also pack up and pull out after the others.

With their observations of the last two days Thomas knew that nearly all of the French Officers were billeted inside the town in various homes of the Spanish residents and only the NCO's and troops were bivouacked in the tent lines to the east of the town. With no Officers present in the tent lines to give orders, Thomas and his men had a distinct advantage.

Thomas stood alone in front of the Originals; his drum was at the ready as he watched the sky in the east; General he maybe but he was also still a drummer and he was not going to miss the opportunity to discourage the French whenever possible.

The first faint hint of greyness showed in the eastern sky when Thomas raised his drum sticks above his head in the signal for the drummers to stand ready. With the certainty of long practice, Thomas lowered his sticks and began the first drum roll of the De La Guerra; it was time to awaken the French.

The order for Major Morgan to open fire was the silence of the drums at the end of the last drum roll, his men stood ready at the lanyards and the order of fire would be a count of three between each gun just as they would have done with a full broadside at sea. The order of munitions was to be three solid shot followed next by two canister and then back to solid, the last salvo would be two of canister and then they would hitch the guns and retreat to the pass with the 5th battery holding the line for them.

As the first light of dawn showed in the east, the French picket guards rubbed bleary eyes and yawned widely; they would all be glad to get back to their beds when their replacements arrived in another hour. Molina was considered to be a backwater, all the reports they had received told of the English well to their west and south; even the knowledge that the rebel El Toro was believed to have resurfaced around Salamanca held little fear for them; it was a long way from their little part of Spain.

The Brigade of twelve hundred men, mostly old hands or new recruits were quite happy to spend their time in the peace and quiet of Molina; it was far better than facing an advancing English army that seemed to be finding victory with ease.

At first it was surprise but that was soon joined by concern as the sleepy picket guards heard the far off sound of a growing drum roll; while none of them had ever heard the sound of El Toro's drums, the rumours had told them all about it and the fear it could instil when heard for the first time. The rumour had also told of the meaning behind the drums; the guards could stand, fight and die or they could run and save their own lives; they were never given the chance to make the decision.

As Molina came awake to the echoing sound of the early morning drums; the still sleepy and tired guards began to make out dark shapes through the growing mist of early dawn, their fear now became a palpable thing as they realised what they were seeing in the distance. There was no sight of the drummers that had now caused concern among those who were trying to awaken from their nights slumber; the early morning mist was distorting everything in the grey light of dawn and only the dark outline of the long row of guns could be made out.

After almost three minutes of the terrible rattle of the early morning drums, they suddenly stopped just as quickly as they had started; it was then the picket guards realised it was too late to run as the sound of massed cannon began to open fire well out of range of anything the guards could do.

Major Morgan stood to the left of number one gun and waited for Thomas to play the final drum roll; on its completion he would give the fire order. Craven waited patiently as he looked at the town some nine hundred yards away, it would not be long before he would change its appearance on the landscape.

Craven watched as Thomas finished the last drum roll, with his voice almost echoing over the silent and empty plain outside Molina; Craven shouted his order.

"On my order all guns will fire at the count of three. Number one gun...FIRE."

Craven watched with the eyes of a hawk as the guns fired one after the other with a count of three between each gun; for those watching it was like a rolling broadside as the dark barrels belched out smoke and flame and the whistling sound of the twelve pound balls were sent flying towards the unsuspecting and vulnerable town ahead of them.

After the first shot, Craven watched as the gun Captain went about his duties for the next firing. As the gun crew swabbed out the hot barrel and then gave space for the young powder monkey to insert the cotton bag containing the powder charge into the barrel; the next man could ram it home tightly and then the man carrying the black cast iron ball would place it also in the mouth of the cannon to once again be rammed tightly home.

The gun Captain was at the breach, he had to wait for the powder monkey to lay the charge before he could take the primer pick, push it through the primer hole so that some of the powder fell through into the flash pan to charge the frisson. The gun Captain would then inspect the flint and pull the hammer to full cock before stepping back with the lanyard firmly grasped in his hand; he would wait there until his gun crew were standing just behind him while he waited for the order to fire.

Craven checked that his guns had been reloaded and then called the next order.

"All guns up a quarter; on my orders to the count of three, number one gun prepare to fire...FIRE."

While the gun Captains had been preparing the gun to fire, Craven Morgan had been watching the fall of shot; most times he could actually see the shot in the air as it flew towards its target. The results were pleasing to Craven's eye as he saw some of the shot send great gouts of earth, canvas and what could have been body parts high into the air and the first sounds of screams from the wounded echoed across the distance to where he stood.

Not all the shot landed the same; some hit solid pieces of buried rock and careened off at a tangent or bounced along the ground carrying all before it. The burning fagots of the breakfast fires were scattered like flaming brands and the first fires started to set alight the dry canvas tents; often with men still inside them. Craven was not a man to smile at such destruction but he did give a faint grunt of satisfaction as he turned to give the next firing order.

For the French Brigade in Molina it was as though the very end of the world had arrived; the drums had awoken most of them but they were still in the throes of trying to awaken when the first loud sounds of the massed guns opened fire, the resulting carnage only caused more panic and the call for Officers was almost drowned out by the thunder of the guns which seemed to be surrounding them.

Partially dressed Officers ran from their billets and began to shout orders to try to bring some order out of the chaos as ordinary soldiers looked around with stunned looks on their faces. The sudden attack by so many massed guns so early in the morning had caught everyone by total surprise; they also had little answer to the mayhem that was starting to appear around them.

The next fall of shot was even deeper into the camp and supply depot; as the targets of the guns were closer together the damage and mayhem was even higher than the first barrage. The French were now almost into a stage of panic as they could not find any answer to the sudden attack and were totally unprepared for the early morning disaster that was now raining down on them from the massed guns in the distance.

Before the Officers could command order and try to figure out a plan of defence they all heard the rumble in the distance as the third barrage was sent their way; again it landed deeper into their bivouac and once again caused death and destruction as the heavy hot balls of metal landed in great gouts of earth and other less recognisable things.

Slowly the Officers began to gain some semblance of order as they tried to yell above the sound of the screams and cries of the wounded. NCO's ran about physically pushing young troops into battle order, the older hands already knew what to do even though the fall of shot was almost continuous. Already the French had lost fifty men to the guns but that was little consequence where the total number of troops were concerned.

Many of the troops had not even had time to dress properly and only had time to grasp their muskets and powder and run to form ranks in preparation for an advance on the enemy; something they were not entirely happy to do over such open ground but if they wanted to live through the day they would have to stop the guns from destroying their encampment.

As the French formed ranks and prepared to advance; Craven Morgan held back the order to fire, he wanted them fully out in the open for the next two barrages; both of which were canister; his order was crisp and clear in the early morning silence.

"All guns load canister, lower guns by a half and prepare to fire on my order at the three count."

Craven waited and watched as the French brigade formed ranks and prepared to attack the guns over the open ground. The third salvo had caused even more terror and damage to the encampment and town but now the French were getting organised; he knew they may very well not get too many more salvos off once the French had advanced enough to get within range.

As he watched, Craven could hear Thomas giving orders for the two Infantry Corps to prepare to protect the guns; Craven also decided to change the fire order for the munitions.

"All guns will stay with canister, on the third salvo all guns will fire at will and lower a quarter at range."

With the ceasing of fire from the distant guns, the French suddenly felt they had a chance to take them; all they had to do was cover the nine hundred yards in good order and not falter in their endeavour; the loudly shouted orders of the Officers and NCO's had the troops ready and willing; their ranks stood straight and ready as the order was given to advance.

Craven held his fire order as he watched the French Brigade begin their advance; it appeared as though they were growing in confidence with each step they took closer to the waiting guns. The French did not even think it strange that the guns had stopped and were even now not making any attempt to withdraw while they had the chance. Had the Officers or men been front line troops they may have realised that it was not normal for guns to not fire at such a range advantage.

The French had now gained a hundred yards and still there had been no shots fired from the waiting guns. More experienced Officers would have immediately known something was wrong with the situation ahead of them but lacking that vital experience they continued to push their troops to advance. They were soon to learn the error of their ways as the troops stepped past the one hundred yard mark. They never heard the order from Major Morgan but they did feel the results.

"All guns on the three count...FIRE."

The loud blast of the salvo rang out over the open plain as the guns fired one after the other with only a three count between them. As the last gun fired the first was almost ready to continue as the loud voice of Major Morgan rang out over the noise of the last guns in the line.

"All guns down an eighth, fire on count...FIRE."

On the open plain ahead of them the first canisters began to explode above the massed ranks of French troops, the results were devastating as one after the other the canisters did their deadly work on the massed ranks. Great holes appeared in the ranks as the dead and wounded fell screaming to the ground while those around them broke step and began to look for a safer place; it was only the cajoling and threats from the NCO's and Officers that finally got the inexperienced troops moving forward once again.

The second salvo of canister again took a massive toll on the troops and once again they faltered in their advance. The ground was now becoming a charnel house as those troops behind the front rank stumbled on their fallen comrades; if they hoped for any relief it was short lived as they heard the sound of the guns once again but this time they were firing independently and the plain became a scene of chaos as Officers fell along with many NCO's and the orderly advance stumbled as the Canister continued its devastating savagery.

The French had pushed and stumbled another three hundred yards but the large holes in their ranks were now very noticeable and there was less heart in their advance, the guns however never seemed to cease and there were those that had already turned and run from the death plains.

Craven looked at the French troops now some five hundred yards away. Craven reached into his jacket pocket and withdrew a silver boatswain's whistle; giving a long loud blast on the whistle to attract the attention of the gunners he called out his next order.

"All guns cease fire and prepare to withdraw."

At that order the sound of fast moving horse were soon heard as the guns were made ready to retire; Thomas led his Infantry to the front of the guns to protect them while they were hitched up, it was time for Lieutenant Wright to make himself known to the confused and scared French out on the plain.

When Craven finally had all his guns hooked up he gave the order to move out at the trot, Thomas and his Infantry took up station on either side of the long train of guns and worked as close in protection while Lorenco had his men take station well out to either side and the van to make sure the way ahead was clear.

As they moved off Thomas heard the first salvo of rockets take to the air as Lieutenant Wright fulfilled his position as rear guard, the quieter whooshing of the rockets filled the morning air above the far off cries of the French; they were to be even more concerned when the rockets exploded above their head sending small flaming balls of fire into their ranks.

Thomas was never to know how much damage and death they caused that day but the French report that was sent back to their superiors had counted the dead at more than four hundred and the total destruction of the supply depot; Molina would never again be the same place that French had thought of as a back water. El Toro's raid had made it clear that there was no place in Spain that was safe from his attacks or reach.

CHAPTER 11

Estaban stood inside the line of trees with his three cousins as they watched the town of Villaviciosa below the ridge. What the four cousins saw below was not good and it gave them pause as they tried to think of a way to carry out their intended raid.

It appeared that Villaviciosa had become a major hub on the supply and replacement line to the west and south where the English army was threatening to make inroads into French held territories.

The road leading into and out of Villaviciosa was now full of Cavalry, Infantry and supply wagons which were all heading west towards the battle lines either around Madrid or further east to Salamanca but for Estaban and his cousins it made little difference; there was little they could do with their numbers to disrupt the mass of French moving along the roadway.

Estaban had left the three Cavalry troops behind the low ridge he and his cousins were now standing on; it would give his men a time to rest while he tried to develop some sort of attack plan. Estaban knew he had the rest of today and all of tomorrow to find a way to attack the French but he would have to leave the area by the time his General attacked at Molina whether he had a target here or not.

For the rest of the day the four cousins hid under the cover of the tree line and watched the continuous parade of French might moving west. It was late in the afternoon before Estaban began to notice that the French were moving their troops almost in exactly the same way each time.

The time between one Brigade and another was about an hour and so far all three that had passed their observation point had been made up exactly the same. At the head of the Brigade were a full company of French Lancers; next came company after company of Infantry followed closely by both the guns and supply wagons. Bringing up the rear was another company of French Chasseurs to protect the rear of the column; if he mounted an attack against such odds it would be doomed to failure. Estaban had to find another way; he had no intention of letting his General down on the overall master plan they had worked out together.

An hour before dusk Estaban and his cousins saw the fourth column appear on the road but, as they drew closer to Villaviciosa they slowed their advance. As the four watched from their hiding place, the massed column below them appeared to be making ready to make camp for the night. For as far as they could see to the rear of this latest column there was no further sign of other troops. Could this be something they could build on and still be able to mount an attack? Estaban called softly to his cousins and signalled for them to follow him back down the ridge and meet up with the waiting men, it was time to put his thinking cap on.

During the night Estaban had two men go back to watch the night camp and return after an hour to report before sending another pair to gather what information they could. Slowly a plan began to develop as the reports on the camp came in.

In the early hours of the morning and while most of his men were getting some sleep, Estaban suddenly realised how he could make a vital attack with a very high chance of getting away without a single injury. The last report had come in and it was this that gave him his idea. The French had camped out in the open but close enough to Villaviciosa to make use of their water supply, a vital necessity for their horses. What they had not done was set out night pickets as would have been normal for any army in hostile territory; it was then Estaban realised that the French must think the land around them was safely in their own hands and they had no need of night pickets.

Estaban's main worry was over the notorious reputation of the Chasseurs and the Lancers; if they were allowed to get mounted then he and his men would be in grave danger, he had to give more and deeper thought to the plan he was working on.

All of the next day was spent watching the troop's move past Villaviciosa, the makeup of the columns had not changed and Estaban began to feel more secure in the rough plan he and the others had come up with. Estaban waited for darkness to begin to come down on the camp below before he turned back to the back of the low ridge; it was time to complete the plan and set his men where they would do most good.

It was just before midnight when the last watchers returned to where the others waited for them. After a further discussion Estaban set his plan. Once again the French had not set pickets and only a very small guard stood around the horse lines; it was here he planned to cause most of the trouble.

Estaban looked over his waiting men, after careful consideration he selected the best men from three different areas of Spain. Estaban knew they were the best men for the job at hand and would make no mistakes in what he was about to ask them to do. The twenty men were from Castile, Andalucia and Seville and were not only excellent men with a knife but could also move without sound on even the most broken of ground, something they would not have to deal with on the grassland of the plain below them.

Estaban's plan was simple in its deviousness; the twenty men would make use of the darkness as the first thin sliver of the new moon shed very little light. The men were to creep into the horse lines, dispatch the few guards that were watching over the horses and then cut free the lines. Once the horses were scattered he would bring in the rest of the mounted men and create as much havoc for the French camp as they could as they rode through the middle of the bivouac.

Estaban was hoping that with the Cavalry set afoot he would have the advantage and they could cause a lot of damage and destruction before riding off into the dark and turning for the meeting place with their General.

As they waited for the signal from the twenty men; which was to be a bird call, Estaban told every man to recheck their musket and pistol loads and make ready to mount and charge the camp on his command.

The frontal charge would be made directly into the camp, once the men had used their muskets they would break to the left and right so that they made their escape to both the east and the west so they did not have to turn back and ride through lines they had just attacked; it gave them a better chance of not being trapped on the return journey to make their escape to the pass.

The signal came just as the first ten silent men appeared from the darkness and made for the own horses; the others would scatter the horses once the attack started in the hope it would create even more confusion. Estaban did not miss the occasional smile on some of the faces nor did he miss the dark, wet looking blotches on one or two of the men's jackets, their bloody work had been done in complete silence and now it was time to repay a little of the cost due from Olivenca.

In the silence of the night only the creaking of leather could be heard as the three hundred men mounted, once fully seated there was then only the loud clicking of hammers being pulled to full cock. Estaban looked into the dark for as far as he could see so that he could make sure his men were all in two ranks, one behind the other.

His two ranks would give him depth for the attack on a reasonably wide front and he hoped it would cause a lot of damage; had he not been able to rid the French of their mounts he would not have been able to charge with any possibility of success if the Cavalry got mounted.

Estaban could almost feel the tension in the chill night air as he readied himself for the upcoming fight; he was sure that even their own mounts knew what was too come as they also snorted and shuffled their hooves as the time drew closer. Estaban looked to both his right then left and raised his hand in readiness for the order to charge the camp.

They had quietly led their horses out of the tree line in the dark and were now assembled on the lower slope of the ridge with just a few yards to the flat plain, it would give them an added impetus at the start of the charge; Estaban dropped his hand and the two ranks immediately broke into a fast trot with only seconds passing before they were at a canter.

With the camp now only a hundred yards away, Estaban cried out as loud as he could so all his men would hear him.

"CHARGE."

Every rider rose in his saddle to the familiar stance they took when firing their muskets from horseback. At the same time the thunder of hooves was heard by the sleeping French, the ten men left at the horse lines cut the last ropes and began to shout and yell at the tops of their voices and added a few pistol shots to add to the effect.

For the French who were still trying to pull themselves from their deep sleep; it seemed as though they were under attack from two sides as the thunder of the charging men mixed with the chaos and running hooves of their own horses only added to the confusion. Estaban's men hit the camp at much the same time as most of the French

161

were just coming out of their tents to see what was going on; for many it would be the last thing they ever saw or heard.

At no more than twenty yards from the orderly line of Infantry tents, Estaban's front rank opened fire with their first barrel; they were ten yards into the lines before they fired their second barrel and then threw their muskets over the backs and took out their pistols for the closer work ahead of them. The second rank followed behind but not wanting to fire into their own friends ahead of them, used their horses to ride down many of the tents; a number of which still had Frenchmen inside them.

When the Front rank changed over to pistols they slowed a little to allow the second and faster moving rank to come through their line and use their muskets on those still ahead of them. The ten men who had freed the French Cavalry horses had not wasted any time in jumping to mount some of those same horses and use them to leave the now empty horse lines and to keep pushing the freed horse's well way from the camp and the cavalry.

The dark night became a scene of thundering horses and fast volleys of Muskets that were soon interspersed with the lighter pistol shots and screams of wounded and frightened men. The dark clad riders were hard to discern for the French and most looked like dark spectres as they rode their hard charging horses through the middle of the camp and laid waste to whatever appeared in front of them.

For the French it was like a nightmare that never ended, not only were they caught in their sleep with no warning but they all had empty muskets and no time to load so they could return fire; the raiders were well through the camp before even the first soldier had loaded his musket only to find he had only a dark, fast moving shadow as a target.

As Estaban led the first rank to the right with Pablo leading the second rank to the left, they left behind chaos and destruction. The thunder of their hooves did not drown out the screams of the wounded or the shouting of the French Officers as they tried to bring some semblance of order back into their troops.

With Pablo leading the second rank out wide to circle around and once again meet up with Estaban to the north of the camp, the noise and confusion behind them gave them a sense of accomplishment and some little way to repaying the losses at Olivenca. Estaban and his men would never know the cost of their raid to the French but the report that went off to Marshal Soult had details of seventy nine men killed and one hundred and eleven wounded; it failed to mention the number of tents lost or the fact their prize cavalry was now afoot.

All that was ever found of their attackers were the now familiar small gold and red flags with a bulls head at the centre; it did not take much imagination by the French to know who had caused them such trouble.

For Estaban it had been a great success, he and his men had escaped almost unharmed and only one of his men had been injured, not by French musketry but by a loose tent peg flying up as the rider rode down the tent and the men inside. The peg had flown through the air and struck the rider on the brow which opened a nice cut so that his right eye was blinded by the free flowing blood. The poor rider was to be the object of many a joke over the next few days.

It was only an hour before dawn when Estaban and his troops saw the long column of their General ahead of them and almost at the pass through to the eastern end of the mountain range that would take them into the southern plain of Castile. Once the two columns had rejoined it was time to find their hiding place for the daylight hours; fortunately Lorenco and his scouts had found them a good hiding place just the other side of the pass.

Once the army had set its camp for the day, Estaban reported to Thomas and told him all about his own attacks. The success of his Cavalry had Thomas smiling as he congratulated Estaban on a job well done; that he had got away without a single death was even better.

The day proved to be hot and humid and the men found places in any shadows that were available. The supply wagons distributed water from the barrels carried on the outside of the decks and food was made ready on small cook fires well hidden at the back of the ravine.

Well before midday and, if one listened carefully they would have heard a few soft snores coming from the shadows. Only those detailed for guard duty could be seen moving around the bivouac. Major Morgan had placed his guns in three ranks facing towards the entrance into the ravine; all his gunners had settled down close to the guns just in case they were ever needed in a hurry.

The first shadows of dusk were showing when the army began to stir for the next leg of their journey. The next leg would be used to get past Somosiera while still in the dark, they then hoped to find another hiding place just before San Ildefonso so they would not be caught travelling in the early dawn light when passing between that town and the nearby Segovia.

They planned to once again hide during the daylight hours and then pass between the two towns late in the night when there was less chance of discovery. Lorenco once again would take the van and seek out a daytime hiding place while the slower Infantry and wagons made their way through the dark.

The last campsite would be west of the Guadarrama pass with the River Carrion on one side and the mountains on the other. The final plan was for the wagons to cross the River Carrion along with all of the Infantry when the rest of the army turned back east to attack Escorial, they would need the extra time to make sure they were safely on their way towards Batuecas when the attack went forward as they were the slowest of all the army units.

Estaban had given Thomas a new idea on how they may be able to fool any night time watchers. To this end Estaban explained to Thomas what he had noticed when spying on the French reinforcements and supply trains. Each and every supply train that Estaban had watched was formed up the same way. In the vanguard were a company of Cavalry, next came the Infantry and supply wagons along with the guns and then as a read guard was another Cavalry unit.

Estaban suggested they set up their own line of advance in the same way and, hopefully in the dark of night they would be mistaken for a French army moving towards the west and a future battle with the English. Thomas thought over the idea and could find little in it that did not fulfil the needs for his army to stay safe behind the French lines; he quickly relayed orders for the new formations.

As the last light faded Lorenco left the day camp and set out to scout well ahead of the army as he was always wont to do; he would be ahead of them for most of the night and when he found their next camp site would send some of his men back to lead the army to it.

With the new orders of march it took a little more time than usual for the army to assemble but once formed they stepped out at their usual pace, they had a distance to go before being safe again in their new camp and had to pass the valley leading to Somosiera before they were seen.

The night march went well and there were no interruptions as they moved towards their new camp site. There were two more hours to dawn when four of Lorenco's men found the army on the move and reported where the next camp was to be. With the number of men and equipment moving in such a long train, Thomas realised they would be very close to dawn before they made the camp back in the hills.

With little thought Thomas sent word that the pace was to be increased to the maximum that the Infantry could travel at; he did not want any of his men caught out in the open when daylight arrived. In the east the first faint hint of dawn showed in the sky as the army finally gathered in the deep ravine. The Infantry were all breathless and sweating heavily as were all the horses and the rattle of the guns and wagons soon filled the ravine with their noise; it was a close run thing but at least now they were safely in hiding for another day.

There would be no cooking fires this time as both San Ildefonso and Segovia were far too close for comfort, they would have to last the day on the bread and cheese they had carried with them for just such an occasion. Before anyone settled down for the day all weapons and equipment were checked and inspected, now was not the time to let a small thing like tiredness make them sloppy and cause problems if they were found out during the day.

Once again Major Morgan had his guns lined up in three ranks and facing the entrance into the ravine; he would have little pity for any Frenchman that tried to attack them through the entrance of their temporary home.

The full heat of the day was tempered by the high walls of the ravine; it was only during the few hours either side of the middle of the day that the heat struck those hiding there. By late afternoon the shadows had lengthened and the army of El Toro was getting ready to once again move on towards their final camp site before attacking Escorial.

The nights march would take them past the Guadarrama pass and end on the banks of the River Carrion; it was here they hoped to spend the next day while scouts were sent out to look over Escorial. Escorial was tucked away in the narrow pass with high ridges on either side, not the most ideal place to attack but one that should put the fear of encirclement in the French that were holding Madrid.

The plan of attack would be finalised once Thomas had the reports of the scouts but his need to have his supplies and Infantry well away from the fighting took precedence at this stage. The road to Batuecas was not an easy one and the final climb into the mountains where the town was situated would be hard on all concerned and they would still have the crossing of the River Alagon to contend with before the climb up to the town and a hoped for haven while they waited for the English to take Salamanca.

With dusk descending quickly, Thomas set his formations just as the French were wont to do; it was the only disguise they would have during the hours of darkness. Two hours before dawn found Thomas and his army clearing the banks of the Carrion for their camp site. Less than a half hour away was a narrow ford that would be just large enough to get the wagons across during the dark hours of the next night.

The new camp was kept in a tight circle with the heavy guns in an outer circle around them; there were also the men of Lorenco's scouts further out as an early warning. It would be very difficult for an enemy to sneak up on them undetected. Lorenco had sent ten of his men high up on the mountain side so they would have a better view of their surroundings and to offer an added measure of protection from discovery.

With the new camp secure, Thomas sat in his small tent and looked over the detailed maps of the area; even with his lack of local knowledge he could see that Escorial was not going to be easy.

The rest of the day was spent resting and preparing the wagons to cross the river in the evening. It was a little deeper than they would have liked but now they had little option. Thomas did not want his supply wagons or his Infantry to be caught on the wrong side of the river if the French garrison at Escorial managed to break out and form a counter attack.

Late in the evening, every man in the camp helped to get the wagons across the River Carrion and on their way towards their eventual stopping place at Batuecas; they were put under the command of Major Perrin. Many who had to leave with the wagons were not happy but Thomas's reasoning could not be faulted as far as their safety went. For two days Thomas kept his remaining men in the camp while Lorenco's scouts surveyed Escorial and its environs.

On the morning of the third day, Lorenco's scouts returned with the news they had been waiting for. With little time wasted the five scouts began to give their reports and slowly a plan began to develop in the minds of Thomas's Officers. The narrowness of the pass would limit the numbers that could be used in a counter attack but the French were reported to have some six or seven hundred troops in their garrison, including Cavalry.

To Thomas's way of thinking it was obvious the French in Madrid well knew this pass was a vital part of their defences and had garrisoned it with sufficient numbers to make it difficult to make any sort of advance on Madrid.

The narrowness of the pass would not allow Major Morgan to use all his guns as they normally would have but he soon came up with a way to make the best use of what he had. As usual for such a well defended place, Thomas had no intent to charge into their midst; once again his guns would wreck havoc and then retire with the three troops of Cavalry protecting their rear.

Major Morgan would only be able to use fifteen of his guns in line in the narrow confines of the pass; even then he would only have little more than a yard and a half between each gun. His range would be at maximum of around eleven hundred yards which would give him plenty of time to fire a number of barrages before having to pull his guns back to safety. To make use of all his guns, Major Morgan proposed that the fourth battery would position themselves a further two hundred yards back and load only canister; two hundred yards behind them would be the fifth battery of rockets.

As the fifth battery could break down their rockets faster, they would be the last line of defence as the guns pulled out and Estaban's Cavalry would then act as the final rear guard against what they assumed would be French Cavalry once the pursuit happened; that there would be a pursuit there was little doubt, even if the French only had a few Cavalry left they would still come after the notorious El Toro.

The scouts had reported one thing that made Thomas sigh with relief, in the town of Escorial there were now no more civilians; it appeared that as the town was a vital link to protecting Madrid it had been cleared of all the civilians by the French forces. Thomas surmised that now he would not have to worry about killing any innocents, anything that moved in the town was the enemy.

It was two hours before dawn on the 12th of June when Thomas watched Major Morgan sight his guns on the faint outline of the town ahead of them; the distance was just under eleven hundred yards and each gun had been raised almost to its maximum and would stay that way during the entire barrage. Once again Major Morgan had his horses closer than normal as he wanted his guns on the retreat well before they could be attacked by the town's defenders.

Thomas sat his horse with Carmelo and Estaban beside him, his personal guard was standing close by and on full alert; they were not going to allow another Olivenca if they had anything to do with it. The small group of Officers was positioned back beside the fourth battery but still had a clear view of the sleeping town in the distance and were now only waiting for Major Morgan to give the first fire orders.

In the faint light Thomas and his friends could just barely make out the small picket fires of the night guards and he was well aware the French had at least six two gun batteries facing their way. Major Morgan was hoping to cut down the number of guns with his first two barrages; he did not fancy a contest with guns that may well have been sighted in for some time even though the range was at the extreme.

It was not long before Thomas and the others heard the loud voice of Major Morgan in the still morning air.

"All guns will fire broadside then fire independently...FIRE."

In the grey dawn light the sudden flash and loud rolling thunder of the fifteen guns filled the pass of Guadarrama as it echoed and bounced between the high cliff sides; for those in the town of Escorial it must have seemed like the end of the world had come as the roar of the guns woke them from their night's sleep.

While the gun crews went into action to reload their smoking guns with more powder and shot, Major Morgan watched for the fall of shot while his gunners worked furiously in front of him. After watching the fall of the first shots; Major Morgan called loudly before the independent fire took over.

"All guns down a quarter; two rounds and up full."

The first fall of shot had landed well inside the sleeping town and Major Morgan wanted a little more destruction on the outer limits to reduce any chance of the defensive guns returning fire once their crews had assembled.

From those last orders there was little time for more as the guns began to fire independently in what was to become an almost continuous barrage of shot. Thomas and his friends watched as the front of the town became nothing more than a scene of erupting earth mixed with what appeared to be metal gun parts. The haze of dust and smoke soon hid the outer environs of the town as the gunners tried valiantly to outdo each other in reloading faster than any others.

The fourth barrage had been sent on its way well before there was even the tiniest of movement from those holding the town; the surprise had been total and the defenders were battered by sound and shot mixed with a thick shroud of dust thrown high into the morning air.

The guns continued to fire at will and, with no answering fire from the town they continued to pound the undefended troops and buildings. For a good ten minutes the guns had it all their own way as the French tried to gather their wits and find a way to stop the slaughter and destruction.

It was a further five minutes of pounding fire before the French started to respond to the early morning attack. Somehow a few of the French gunners had managed to get to the remaining guns outside the town. Although only two French guns could be sighted, it was enough to cause some concern for Major Morgan. Amid the crashing of his own guns Major Morgan yelled at the top of his voice.

"Number one battery down a half and sight the guns. Fire at will."

The two remaining French guns had already fired their first shots but both landed some fifty yards short. As the dust settled and the French gunners worked furiously to reload, Major Morgans 1st Battery went into action; the five shots falling close enough to cause concern but did not disable the French guns. It was now a race by both gun crews to get their next and better aimed shots off before the other could take the advantage.

It had to be the years of working the guns on board a wallowing ship that gave Major Morgans gunners the slight edge as they fired their battery only seconds before the French could get theirs back into action. The five guns of the 1st Battery sent their shot screaming towards the French guns just as the French Officer was about to call the fire order. It was never to be as five great gouts of flying earth and rock flew into the air around and on the two solitary guns.

When the dust and smoke cleared there was little to see but the two broken chassis of the French guns; their barrels lying broken on what was left of their carriages and the ground around them was strewn with the bodies of the gunners; Major Morgan was quick to call orders.

"Number one Battery return to main target."

Thomas could now see the town clearly in the early morning light as the dawn brightened with the hint of the morning sun in the east. The town was now becoming hard to see as the dust and smoke filled the air above; Major Morgan's gunners were now almost firing blindly into the target, the narrowness of the pass had been to their advantage and they had used it well.

From his position at the rear of the main gun line Thomas could see more clearly than Major Morgan and it was this fact that gave him the first warning of the French beginning to organise. Through the thick and cloying dust and smoke of the town, Thomas could now make out the French Infantry beginning to assemble at the edge of the town for an advance on his guns; it was time to pull back.

Thomas reached for one of his pistols and aimed it into the morning air then pulled the trigger. Even Major Morgan heard the smaller sound of the Pistol above the heavy thunder of his guns; it was the prearranged signal for him to withdraw his guns.

Major Morgan quickly reached into his jacket pocket and withdrew his boatswains whistle; a long loud blast on the whistle soon caught the attention of the gunners and, those who were still in the act of reloading continued and then fired as the sound of horses was heard above the explosions.

Major Morgan looked through the heavy pall of gun smoke and could just make out the assembling Infantry but it was not them that he grew concerned over; it was the build up of Cavalry that lent urgency to the retirement of the guns.

Lieutenant Kent commanded the 4th Battery and had heard the high pitched whistle; it was now his time to take over. Lieutenant Kent went down the line of his five gun Battery and checked with each Master Gunner to make sure they were all loaded with canister. The maximum range for canister was nine hundred yards and he would have to wait until the Cavalry were within range before he could open fire; it was hoped by then that the first three Batteries would be well on their way to their rear.

Thomas and his friends watched as the Cavalry formed up behind the long ranks of French Infantry, Major Morgan now had his guns almost hooked up and ready to retire, they should be well away before the Cavalry could come close enough to cause any trouble.

The French Cavalry was made up of a mixture of heavy Chasseurs and the lighter Lancers; it was obvious they had been mashed together in urgency by the French command. Thomas estimated there were some one hundred and fifty or more of the Cavalry; it would be up to the 4th Battery to cut down those odds and then the 5th Battery to cause as much confusion in the Cavalry ranks while the 4th retired to safety.

Estaban left Thomas's side to return to his three troops of Cavalry, they would be the final line of defence should the French Cavalry break through and follow the retiring guns; it would all have to depended on timing as they could easily end up in a running fight if they also allowed the French Infantry to advance closely behind the Cavalry.

Five minutes after the long, loud blast on the boatswains whistle and the three Batteries were on the move rearward. In the distance the French Cavalry had now formed up in ranks for the charge and were even now beginning to advance at the walk towards the gun positions in close formation. At the front were the lighter Lancers with the heavier

168

Chasseurs close behind, they would be the main thrust into the gun positions once the Lancers had cleared any guards around the guns.

Major Morgan had used his gun sight to range nine hundred yards for Lieutenant Kent, all the young Lieutenant had to do now was wait for the French Cavalry to reach the pile of rocks that marked his maximum range and then open fire. He would lower his guns a half turn at each firing until ordered to retire himself and his guns. As he was placed two hundred yards behind the other three Batteries he had plenty of time to watch the French Cavalries formation and adjust his guns to suit.

Major Morgan's guns were now well behind the lines as the French Cavalry broke into a fast trot in preparation to building for the final charge; as they passed the pile of rocks that signified the nine hundred yards, Lieutenant Kent called his fire orders.

"4th Battery, by barrage...Fire."

The five guns opened up with a loud roar and sent their deadly canisters soaring into the morning air; as the projectiles flew towards the unsuspecting Cavalry, Lieutenant Kent's gunners worked at speed to reload and lower their guns a half turn. Thomas had been told to retire behind the fifth Battery by Carmelo and his personal guards made sure their charge did as was suggested. There was not going to be another Olivenca under their watch even though Thomas felt he was quite safe behind the Lieutenants guns.

As Thomas slowed near the 5th Battery so he could turn and watch the effects of the canister on the French Cavalry, he could just hear above the roar of the 4th Battery guns the first three Batteries riding off to safety; he could not resist the sigh of satisfaction as his main guns escaped; so far the plan was working.

The French Cavalry was not expecting the sound of bursts above their heads but the effects of the canister shot took immediate effect on their well ordered ranks; the order was passed to rise to the canter, they still had some distance to go before they could attack the five guns they could now see ahead of them; the sooner they covered that distance the better they would all be.

As the Cavalry rode through the first barrage of canister they broke into a fast canter with the Lancer's lowering their long lances in preparation for the final charge into the five guns in the distance. The second barrage of canister exploded with violence right above the fast moving Cavalry and tore holes in their smart ranks and caused many of the horses to rear back or try to escape from the thundering explosions above their heads along with the deadly rain of hot pellets of metal that showered down on them.

With the ranks broken it took the French Officers a little time to call the Cavalry back to order and continue with their advance; it also allowed Lieutenant Kent's gunners a few extra seconds to reload and re-sight their guns.

The Cavalry was now only five hundred yards away when the young Lieutenant ordered the last Barrage and then called for the guns to retire, it would be the signal for the 5th Battery to make ready their rockets which they had positioned some two hundred yards further back; the final line of defence were Estaban's three musket wielding Cavalry troops.

Once again Thomas was told to move back by Carmelo, again against his will but none of his friends would let him argue the point and his personal guards were all in full agreement. Thomas turned and rode his horse back to where Estaban had his first Troop waiting ready, their muskets now in hand as they sat their horses patiently waiting for their turn at the French.

The French Cavalry was now showing large holes in their broken ranks; there was now little order and the Lancers were mixed in among the Chasseurs as the few remaining Officers tried to get some semblance of order for a final charge at the five guns which they could now see were beginning to retire from their position.

As the five guns ran for safety, the Officer's called for a charge in the hope they could still catch the retreating guns on their faster horses even though the guns were retreating at what some might consider break neck speed.

As the broken ranks started to come to the gallop the air around them was suddenly filled with whooshing rockets that exploded and sent showers of small flaming pellets into their midst. There was little let up in the rockets as they could be reloaded far faster than the guns, for the French it was another worrisome act that they had not been prepared for but the Officers urged their men onward even though their numbers were now considerably reduced.

Thomas saw the broken ranks of Cavalry trying to reform their lines, their galloping charge had been temporarily broken but they were not about to give up on destroying the guns that had wrecked havoc in the early light of day.

Lieutenant Wright urged his men to work faster as they reset the rocket frames, there was just time enough for one more salvo of thirty two rockets before they would also pack up and run for safety; it would then be up to Estaban and his musket Cavalry to delay any pursuit for as long as possible. Once again Thomas was more or less ordered to retire with the 5th Battery while Estaban set his lines and once again Thomas was not happy about being sent away when his men were about to come into danger but he had to comply and turned his horse to follow the track left by the 4th Battery.

The French Cavalry had been cut to pieces by the devastating and continuous fire of the guns. Estaban now estimated their numbers to be less than ninety and there was little order in their ranks as the Officers tried to organise a final attempt to capture or destroy the fast retiring guns; as yet they had not seen the waiting Cavalry who had taken a position just around the last bend of the pass and out of full sight of the French.

Estaban had positioned himself close to the bend where he could keep an eye on the demoralised French Cavalry, there was no sign of the Infantry and for that he was thankful, he did not want to have to fight a combined force of Infantry and Cavalry in the narrow confines of the pass.

Estaban finally caught sight of the remains of the Cavalry; they had reformed their ranks and were now coming towards where Estaban and his 1st troop waited for them. At approximately one hundred yards, Estaban called his men of the 1st troop to form ranks across the road of the pass and prepare to fire in volleys. The 1st troop was in three ranks and would fire both barrels each before retiring behind the others and making a run for safety behind the other two troops that waited further back along the pass.

The other two troops were placed further back and would have their turn as each troop retired; Estaban was the only one that would stay to the last and retreat only when the last rank of number three troop had fired their muskets.

As the French Cavalry drew closer, Estaban made one final check on his weaponry especially the thick leather cuff with the sharp spike where his right hand had once been. All his pistols were loaded and ready as was his musket. It had take weeks of practice for Estaban to learn to fire with his left hand, the barrel of his musket was rested on top of his right forearm for ease of aiming and he had had to change to a shorter musket because he was unable to hold it in the conventional manner to stop the recoil.

Estaban could almost see the startled looks on the faces of the fast trotting Cavalry as they saw number 3 troop lined in ranks across the pass; as the Officer was about to call for the charge at less than sixty yards; the first rank of men dressed in black fired off their volleys from both barrels and then withdrew before the French could react; the second rank taking the place of the first and continued with more devastating volley fire.

The surprised French had little chance and men began to fall from their saddles with regularity as the mounted musketeers took their toll on their ranks. Once the third rank of the troops turned and rode off at haste the French tried to work out what had just happened, all they could do was look at their losses and wonder what or who they were meant to be fighting.

At every turn the French Cavalry had been beaten and now they were unsure if they should proceed to chase after the guns that had now long disappeared; it was decided by the last remaining Officer that the French Cavalry was not going to be humbled by such unorthodox tactics, they would continue to ride after the invaders regardless of how many of them were left.

The last Officer led his remaining men on a charge after the fast retiring riders; as they came around the final bend before the open plains at the head of the Guadarrama pass he was struck with sight that could make the blood run cold. Lined across the entrance to the valley was a mass of musket wielding Cavalry; waving his hand in urgency the Officer tried to turn the men back the way they had come.

What waited he and his men was a Cavalry force that must have outnumbered his last fifty odd men by at least five to one; ahead of them it was a like a solid black wall mounted on some of the finest horses the Officer had ever seen; and on the back of each horse was a rider with a musket aimed right at his few last survivors; it was once again a no win situation.

The Officer did his best to call off the charge but even at the last moment he knew it was all far too late; the resounding echo of hundreds of muskets was only diminished by the torrent of lead balls that flew unerringly into the charging Cavalry. Horses and men fell as though a scythe had cut through them in one devastating slice and his once proud troop of Lancers and Chasseurs seemed to disappear before his very eyes.

The second volley only went to cut his men down even further and, for those who survived there was little chance unless they turned their mounts and retreated as best they could. It was a sorry small column that retreated from the battle of Guadarrama pass; never had the French Cavalry been assaulted by such a force and their losses would be numbered at over a hundred and thirty. Only sixteen Cavalrymen and one wounded Officer made it back to Escorial to make their report; of the attackers they found no evidence of even wounding a single one but the fact of actually seeing the black uniforms soon told the French who they had been up against.

There was now little doubt that the infamous El Toro was alive and active once more. There were many disturbed sleeps that night as word went around about whom they had been trying to face off with; it would only go to grow the legend of the rebel that could not be killed and would set fear into many a young Frenchman when told the Rebel leader was in their area.

Estaban watched the remnants of the French charge struggling to retreat, it was not compassion that made him call for his men not to pursue the French but a need to return to their Patron; Olivenca had been somewhat avenged but there was still a long way to go before any of them would consider the debt paid in full.

Estaban led his men from the pass in pursuit of his Patron; there was now a need for the army of El Toro to rest well before they would once again go into the field against their hated enemy. Batuecas was nearly two days away with two river crossings and he did not want his Patron to be left without he and his men's services for too much longer.

Estaban caught up to Thomas and the fast moving guns within five hours of hard riding. It was as the last gun was forced across the River Tormes that Estaban and his tired and sweaty Cavalry came into sight of the others. It did not surprise Estaban that Thomas was still on the eastern bank of the River watching that his men crossed first in safety before he looked to his own welfare.

Thomas had turned as soon as he heard the sound of galloping hooves behind him; he smiled as he saw the torrent of black clad riders coming hard towards him, he had little doubt that Estaban would bring his men home without any pursuit from the French.

When all the army was once again together, Thomas called for the next leg of their journey to Batuecas to continue. They could now move at a slower pace and with a certain amount of security as they were almost within reach of the English lines to their west; it was time for rest and recovery while they set to work on what they could do next to help the war effort.

As there was no longer a need to move during the hours of darkness, Thomas pushed the men to the banks of the River Alagon and sent his scouts forward to find an easy crossing; it was estimated that within another day or so they should be making contact with the others that had gone on ahead and all of them could finally settle into a camp around the environs of Batuecas for a well earned rest.

By the 16th of June the army of El Toro was in camp just outside Batuecas; for the last full day they had had no trouble let alone even seen any sign of the French. Thomas had sent out fast mounted patrols of six men in the direction of Salamanca to keep watch for the English advance which he had been told would come soon; he did not have long to wait.

That same day one of the patrols returned with the news that the English were moving towards Salamanca in force and that there appeared to be only one French army in the vicinity, that of General Marmont. On the 17th of June, it appeared that Wellington entered Salamanca unopposed. The French seemed to have kept their distance and only shadowed the English army looking for an advantage before attacking the well drilled force.

While Thomas no longer felt much in the way of duty to the English army itself; he still had his duty to his new homeland and that meant he still had to take his war to the French whenever the chance arose, this was one of those times.

Thomas called his Officers to his small tent and they began to look for ways to slow the French and cause as much trouble behind their lines as they could; there was also the fact that Wellington also had both Spanish and Portuguese troops under his command.

At this stage Thomas was not aware that Marshal Beresford had been recalled to England under the pretext his skills with organisation were sorely needed and that now Wellington was in full command of all English forces on the Peninsular. Had Thomas been aware of this he just may have considered working closer with the Viscount.

Thomas never found out how much influence had been used in England to get Beresford out of the battle lines and that his old friend Percy had had far more to do with it than anybody would ever know. It was to be a few years before Thomas was to meet a member of the English House of Lords and get the full story over a few glasses of the finest Oporto wine that Thomas could produce.

The people of Batuecas were only too glad to have their hero El Toro in their midst and went to great lengths to help in any way they could. The goat-herders would take Thomas's small patrols over unknown tracks through the mountains to gain a better sight of what was going on down on the Salamanca plains while the town's hunters helped to keep the army supplied with fresh game and meats.

At any one time Thomas had more than ten patrols out watching the goings on of the two armies as he developed new plans to disrupt the French. It appeared that both armies were not yet ready to commit themselves to battle as Thomas and his men watched them shadow each other over the plains. There were small skirmishes between the French and English patrols but as yet the full armies had not been called to action on a larger scale.

When Thomas had a better understanding of what was going on, he began to lay plans for his own interventions. His final plans were to use the night and as much as possible disrupt the French sleeping hours; it was just the sort of fighting his men preferred.

As yet Thomas could see no way to use his guns so most of the night attacks were performed by his Infantry and mounted troops. As an added disruption, Thomas allowed Lorenco to use his sharpshooters during the hours of daylight; their ability to stay well hidden and snipe at the French troops almost with impunity went a long way to making for some very nervous soldiers in the French lines.

While the numbers of the French losses were not high overall; it was the continual small raids that caused the most concern in the French camps. That they were under attack by the infamous rebel El Toro there was little doubt; the small flags left behind by the raiders told the French all they needed to know. For the ordinary soldier in the French army it was almost a nightmare; none ever knew if their turn on guard picket would be their last.

It was not uncommon for a whole picket guard to be found lying dead in the morning or at the change of the guard and yet not a sound was ever heard or an alarm raised; only the bloody mess of slit throats told the story when the guard was eventually found. During the day as the French marched to shadow the English army they came under continual fire from well hidden positions by sharpshooters. For the French troops the shooters were very rarely seen and the chance to return fire and actually kill the hiding shooters was out of the question.

It was becoming a war of attrition and the French were losing on that front when it came to using conventional tactics against a small, fast and mobile force like the one Ell Toro used. The war on the peninsular had now become a war of nerves and cunning and the French were once again losing it.

Thomas had been watching the manoeuvrings of the two armies below on the plains from his position on the heights of Batuecas, he spent many days following almost hidden tracks led by the hunters of Batuecas so he could get a better overview; many times he was away from the camp for days which made his friends very nervous; especially as he would sometimes go out all on his own and without his personal guard.

For the following weeks Thomas kept up the small guerrilla attacks on the French and the effects could easily be seen whenever the time for bivouac arrived; at this time the French soldiers could be seen to become very nervous and extra alert.

Thomas was not really interested in what the English were doing but he was concerned at where and what the Portuguese and Spanish forces were doing; they were now his concern. When it came to the real battle as he knew it eventually would; Thomas wanted to be in a position to help them as much as he could.

Each day the movements of the two great armies were marked on Smithson's excellent maps and eventually Thomas was able to work out a form of pattern that could be to his advantage when the time for the real battle arrived.

Viscount Wellington was not surprised to learn through his patrols that his onetime Drummer Boy was in the field and close by even though he had had no contact with the boy. Many was the time when he was given a report from one of his many patrols that they had been rescued from a French ambush or sudden skirmish by the black clad forces of El Toro.

For Viscount Wellington it was even more of a wonder that the young General had not made any attempt to contact him so they could co-ordinate their attacks or harassments of the French army; he was never to learn the why of it but it did raise his ire to know the ex-drummer boy still preferred to do it all his own way without the supervision of far more experienced Officers.

On the 21st of July it appeared to Thomas that the French under Marshal Marmont were attempting to out flank the Viscount's forces; Thomas prepared his men for what he thought was too come. The 22nd of July was to prove to be one of the defining moments of the peninsular war and Thomas, along with his little army was to play a part that few expected.

CHAPTER 12

The 22nd of July dawned with clear skies and from where Thomas looked over the dry plains below, he could see the two great armies trying to outflank each other. To the south stood Marmont's divisions while those of Wellington were lined up to the north and east while Wellington observed his enemy from the high ground behind the town of Arapiles.

To Thomas it looked much like a board game as the armies worked to find a weakness in their enemy's lines. At this stage Thomas did not know if he should bring his own men into the action as this was not the sort of fighting they had trained for and Olivenca was still fresh in his mind.

At first he saw the two great army's probing the others defences and then pull back to adjust and look for another way to take the day. Thomas watched from his vantage point at the small skirmishing fights with interest. It was the first time he had been able to stand away and above a really big battle and not be involved, it also gave him the chance to see how each army manoeuvred for the best advantage; something he had not been able to watch before.

As the morning wore on and into the early afternoon it soon became apparent that the French Marshal, Marmont; had been able to get some of his divisions away from the main lines and was intent on attacking the English lines on the east flank. Thomas watched as the battle plan unfolded before his eyes, that the French now seemingly had a distinct advantage there was little doubt. It was not long before both Thomas and the French got a surprise.

Wellington had held back one of his most prized divisions for just such an occasion. With the French divisions fully extended on the eastern flank of the English lines, Wellington released his reserve 3rd division led by General Packenham along with D'Urbans Cavalry; they were to be followed a little later by General Leith's 5th Division and supported by General Bradford's Portuguese Brigade but it was General Packenham's Division and D'Urbans Cavalry that was the real undoing of the French attempt to outflank Wellington's army.

As Thomas watched the manoeuvring from his vantage point, he caught sight of one of the companies forcing its way deeper into the ranks of the French Infantry. Even from where he stood he could see the bitter fighting that was going on as the front ranks came together in vicious hand to hand battles. Something suddenly took hold of Thomas as he watched this particular company fight its way forward.

It was a little ahead of the other companies and appeared to be led by a younger Officer; perhaps a Second Lieutenant. The men with him were fighting with bayonet and musket butts, when they were no longer useful in the close hand to hand the men resorted to hand axes and wooden handled maces mounted with cast iron tops.

Thomas could easily see from his better position that the forward company could be in danger of being cut off at any moment as most of the other companies were a little behind and the usual close ranks no longer gave them as much protection on the flanks.

With total disregard for his previous decision to avoid any part of the confrontation, Thomas called Estaban and Carmelo to his side and gave them orders to ready Pablo's company of Cavalry. Without a thought, Thomas turned his horse towards the battling company and led the Cavalry charge with Estaban and Carmelo by his side, their advantage of height and the slope of the low ridge gave them an extra impetus as they charged towards the men below.

On the plain below a small ridge, Ensign Pratt of the 2/30th foot of General Leith's 5th Division tried to hold his position at the head of his company. This was his first major battle and he did not want to disappoint or fail in this his first command. The fighting was vicious and reminiscent of an ugly brawl as he and his men turned into something akin to feral animals.

The shouts and curses were interspersed with the cries of wounded men and the clashing of metal weapons or the heavy dull thud of musket butts. The smell of blood and dust filled the air as he and his men pushed forward and deeper into the French lines; his uniform was no longer neat and clean and even one shoulder of his once smart red jacket was torn by a close thrust of a French Bayonet.

It was one of those strange pauses that could occur during even the hardest of battles that drew Ensign Pratt's eyes forward and at first he could not believe what he was seeing; just one hundred yards ahead of where he and his men sweated and fell were the French Colours and Eagle of the French 22nd Regiment; Ensign Pratt had just seen something that would give him an inhuman strength to advance but would his remaining men be able to breach the stoic French guard around the famous colours.

From his vantage point on the heights of the Lesser Arapiles ridge, Wellington saw General Packenham's 3rd Division along with D'Urbans Cavalry slam heavily into the leading division of the French General Thomiere's army. The attack had been so effective and destructive which resulted in the death of General Thomieres and it was not long before Wellington sent orders for Leith's 5th Division along with Bradford's Portuguese Brigade to also attack General Maucune's Division. The results were the same as before as the well drilled red coated troops tore apart the French lines.

All over the plain where the French had thought they had gained an advantage now became a disaster of great magnitude as one after the other of the French Divisions began to crumble under the power of the English and Portuguese attacks. The final attack by Le Marchant's Heavy Cavalry which swept into and through General Brennier's Division and caused total havoc, finally broke the back of the French attempt to outflank Wellington's army.

For Ensign Pratt it was another part of the battle that he had little knowledge or interest in; his sole objective was now plainly in sight and this was the only part of the battle he was for the moment, interested in.

Ensign Pratt gripped the barrel of his empty pistol a little tighter in his left hand that he now used as a club as he swept his sword into the neck of a nearby French soldier as his men struggled around him.

Ensign Pratt had to spit twice to clear his throat from the dust and powder smoke that drifted over the battle so he could call his men to order; a plan had come to mind as he defended himself against the continuous attack by the French troops.

Ensign Pratt raised his bloody sword above his head as he yelled with all his might although it did come out a little croaky but the effect was what he wanted.

"Form a wedge on me."

Ensign Pratt had to yell twice to get the notice of his struggling men, or what was left of them but they were soon by his side in a wedge formation as he turned his eyes towards the French Colours. In a final all out effort, Ensign Pratt led his men on a mad rushing charge to break through the French ahead of him and then attempt to make for the Colours now surrounded and defended by a full company of hard bitten and stoic French troops.

The enemy seemed to suddenly disappear before his clubbing and slashing, many now retreating in total disorder but Ensign Pratt only had eyes for the greatest prize a soldier could covet.

As he and his men broke through the final line of troops, Ensign Pratt saw the Colours only fifty yards ahead but the guard was ready and waiting for him and his men, their reduced numbers were now facing charged muskets and willing defenders. Ensign Pratt called for his men to halt and charge muskets, that they may well be going to their deaths was evident on all their faces as they quickly loaded empty muskets and pistols.

The French Colour Guard had now formed three ranks facing the English Red Coats; they felt confident in their superior numbers and better position; the defence of the Colours was everything to these hard bitten men of France and they would not relinquish them easily.

Ensign Pratt was about to give the order to advance when he heard a thundering of hooves to his right; had he been caught out by French Cavalry? If this was so then he and his men could count their lives in seconds and not hours; against French Cavalry they had little hope of survival let alone a chance to take the Colours. Ensign Pratt could give only one order.

"Form Squares and prepare for Cavalry."

With a square of two ranks formed, Ensign Pratt; from his position at the centre, turned towards where he heard the Cavalry; what met his eyes raised considerable doubt and some concern. He had never seen Cavalry like that which was now coming at a gallop towards where he stood with his men; the French also seemed confused at the sudden appearance of the black uniformed Cavalry.

The Cavalry swept over the plain towards the seeming standoff of the two protagonists. When they were no more than a few hundred yards from the small tableau, the black clad Cavalry formed into two ranks and swept towards the French Colour Guard; one rank riding across the front of the French lines and the other to the rear.

The French were far too slow to react to the sudden new events and the Cavalry were standing in their stirrups and firing muskets as they swept past the shocked French troops. Being under attack from both the front and rear at the same time only caused more confusion in the French lines as the Officers tried to decide which way to send their fire orders.

Before the French could decide on which part of the Cavalry was the most dangerous it was already too late; the Cavalry had swept past firing both barrels of their strange muskets and leaving behind bleeding and dying ranks of French Guards. As the Cavalry swept past they rode only for a few more yards before swinging their horse around and taking a position of three ranks just out of musket range while they reloaded their unusual muskets.

Ensign Pratt, while overawed by the sudden turn of events did not lack in understanding as he saw the devastation of the French defenders; he also noticed the black clad Cavalry was not attempting to charge again but sat their horses just out of range to watch what Ensign Pratt wanted to do; he did not need to be told twice or to even think about his next actions.

Ensign Pratt raised his sword and yelled as loud as he could.

"Fix bayonets; CHARGE."

Ensign Pratt led by example, something his men could understand and followed with loud yells and curses as they surged forward towards the French defenders whose lines had been completely broken by the Cavalry charge; they did not even have time to form ranks for volley fire before the young Ensign and his men were amongst them with bayonet, knife, axe and mace.

The fight was over far faster than Ensign Pratt thought it would be and suddenly he was holding aloft a black staff with a golden Eagle at the top and the French Colours in his young hands; around him the last of his men stood in awe of what they had just done; in this day and age it was almost unheard of to carry off the Colours of the enemy.

As he stood with the French Colours in his hand Ensign Pratt heard the sound of massed hooves moving in his direction; was it to be that in his finest hour he would have to relinquish the Colours to a foreign power. He and his men were outnumbered and out gunned by the strange black clad Cavalry; there was little he could do if the newcomers insisted he hand over his trophy.

As the massed Cavalry drew closer Ensign Pratt noticed that at least three of the riders at the front wore fine gold braid on their shoulders and around the sleeves of their black jackets; it did not take a genius to recognise he was in the presence of Senior Officers even though their allegiances were in doubt or at best unknown.

Ensign Pratt did what any good young Officer would do; he drew himself to attention and stood waiting to be told by a superior what he had to do. The Cavalry stopped only yards from where Ensign Pratt and his remaining men stood at attention, the three Senior Officers rode closer while the others stayed back with their muskets resting on their thighs as though prepared for anything untoward.

Ensign Pratt saluted as the three Officers stopped nearby and looked down at him from their saddles; he was momentarily surprised at how young they all looked but a bigger shock soon hit him as he heard the younger of the three address him with the accent of a London dock worker.

"I wish to know whom I am addressing Sir?"

"Ahh...err... Ensign Pratt of the 2/30th Foot Sir."

"Well met Mister Pratt, you and your men fought well and deserve your victory; I hope your valour will not go unnoticed by your superiors."

"Uhm...Thank you Sir, do you wish to carry off the colours Sir?"

"Not at all Mister Pratt, we just wanted to even the odds a little, the victory is entirely yours and well deserved it was."

"Thank you Sir, and to whom do I owe our lives Sir?"

"Ah yes, well Mister Pratt it is perhaps in your best interest not to know that at this time; perhaps some time in the future we may meet again and I can pass that information on to you. For now I would suggest you take your well earned trophy and enjoy your victory. It was a very brave charge Mister Pratt; I only hope you live long enough to benefit from it. I will say my farewell Ensign, perhaps we will meet again."

"Uhm...thank you Sir and thank you for your timely intervention; I am sure I would have lost many more men if you had not intervened on our behalf."

"Think nothing of it Mister Pratt; we are all here to see the last of the French in these lands."

With a smile and something of a half salute from the speaker, Ensign Pratt watched the strange Officers and black clad Cavalry turn about and ride in the direction they had originally come from. Although it was a strange event, it was something he never mentioned to a living soul. It was sometime later he did overhear some talk in the mess about a small army known as the Spanish Guerrillas who were said to be led by a young Englishman who had once been known as the Hero of Rolica.

The coincidence did not go unnoticed by the young Ensign but the young Officer had said to keep his involvement silent; Ensign Pratt was not about to break his word on the matter.

Thomas rode at the head of the Cavalry unit as he led them back to his vantage point above the battle ground; he felt good that he and the others had been able to help the young Lieutenant to take the French colours; as he had said to the young man he truly hoped it would do some good to the young man's future.

He had just stopped on the ridge above the battle field when he heard a loud cursing close by; turn his head he saw Pablo holding his left thigh with blood oozing out between his fingers. Pablo had been hit on the top of the thigh by one of the few French soldiers who had managed to get off a shot; the boy was not happy and proceeded to invent a few extra curse words as another of the riders dismounted from his horse and rushed to help place a rough bandage on the wound.

Estaban looked at his cousin with a thin smile on his face; the words that were on the tip of his tongue were never said but the twinkle in his eyes relayed his thoughts to those who were watching. With his cousin being looked after Estaban just raised his eyes to the heavens and the faint sound of a chuckle could be heard by the others. The hour was late and the battle looked to have been a resounding success for Wellington. The French were in full and hasty retreat and their losses were far greater than the English and their allies. The evidence of that fact could be seen strewn all over the battle field and the cries of the wounded could be heard by those still high on the ridge.

Thomas called his men to retire to their camp; there was little for them to do now and he wanted his men to get some rest before he continued with his plans for the French. Thomas turned his men towards their camp at Batuecas and marched them back to rest, there was still a lot of work for them once the battle field had been cleared and there were still the main armies of Marshal Soult, Joseph and Suchet to think about.

Later that evening, as Thomas sat with his Officers around the large central fire; he began to talk about what they should do next. With Wellington winning a decisive battle against Marmont there was now little for them to do until they found out where the rest of the French armies might be. It was concluded that Wellington would now probably march right into Madrid as there were no armies in the immediate area which could contest his advance.

Thomas and the others talked over their present situation and after an hour they came to the only conclusion that made them all feel right. It was time to once again return to Vimeiro while their back trail was well protected by the English advance. There would be no need for the continual night marches and they would be able to make far better time than when first coming out into the field; it was time to go home.

The return to Vimeiro was taken a little more casually than previous hurried retreats were and it was not until the 7th of August before Thomas and his army saw the entrance to their special home; an hour later and they were beginning the hard work of looking to their arms and horses. It was to be another two days before all was returned to normal but then they would have more than enough time for rest before going out again.

On the 10th of August, Thomas was notified by the guard detail at the entrance that there was a small carriage approaching; it had only a driver and one single passenger. Thomas sent word to allow the carriage through and that one single visitor would offer them no harm; and so it proved to be right.

When the small carriage pulled to a halt close to where Thomas was waiting he felt the smile on his face widen as he recognised the short and portly figure sitting at the rear; the large frame of the driver was also very familiar. Thomas stepped forward as Mister Percy stepped from the carriage also with a smile on his face; his rough, plain cloth suit was dust covered and there were smudges of the same road dust on Mister Percy's face and cotton gloves.

Thomas was the first to speak as the shorter man strode towards him.

"Mister Percy! I didn't know you were coming, would you like a cold drink or something to eat?"

"Hello Thomas and, Yes to both questions; it's been a long journey from Oporto and not much time to stop for the good things in life. Now how are you my lad; enjoying your fame and fortune?"

"Come and sit here in the shade Mister Percy. Uhm...what fame and fortune? I have no idea what you're talking about?"

"Oh well most of it can wait until later, first I have what I hope is some interesting news for you."

Thomas stopped as he saw Fairley arrive with two glasses and a bottle of French brandy on a small silver tray; once the two drinks were poured Fairley left to find some food for the two friends as it was now close to lunch time. Thomas took note that his other friends were keeping their distance as he and Mister Percy talked; they knew Thomas would tell them all about the meeting when the time was right but for now they respected the privacy that the two may need.

With his drink in hand, Thomas turned back to Mister Percy.

"So what is your news Mister Percy?"

"Well Thomas, it would appear that Viscount Wellington carried out an inquiry into certain aspects of the battle of Albuera; he reported his findings to the powers that be and a short time ago Marshal Beresford was asked to return to England to take up a post more suited to his abilities; it would appear we will not see him on the battle field again."

Thomas kept his silence, but he felt a twinge of justice deep inside that the man responsible for his men's deaths had at last been sent away and he could now forget him and get back to doing what he did best. Thomas just nodded to Mister Percy as he waited for the rotund man to sip his brandy before continuing.

"Now Thomas, the next news is very secret and I must ask you to keep this information close to your chest; no one at any time must know this or we could both be in deep trouble."

Thomas nodded that he understood his friend perfectly. Percy continued after another small sip of brandy.

"For the last four years we have had the assistance of Prime Minister Perceval, unfortunately he passed away last May and we now have to deal with the new Prime Minister Robert Jenkinson the 2nd Earl of Liverpool. As yet we are not quite sure of his commitment to your cause but I am doing all I can to make sure you continue to be supplied with everything you may need. There is however one bright point; we have the full and total support of a friend in the House of Lords and his influence is far beyond what some may think so I feel we are still in the good graces of the Government. We have our ways of bypassing the Prime Minister if it is needed."

"You never told me about the Government involvement Mister Percy; is that why our supplies are arriving regularly?"

"It is a part of it Thomas but we also have other means at our disposal; there are those of us that want you to have the chance to succeed and there is little we won't do to make sure that happens. Now then the next thing is Wellington has entered Madrid and is on his way towards Burgos but we have heard rumblings that the French are massing and they are going to try to push him back before the winter arrives so we will have to wait and see how that part goes."

"So it appears that the tide has turned for the French Mister Percy?"

"Yes Thomas but that is not all. Napoleon foolishly made a push into Russia; his advances have been great but he is starting to suffer some losses and I feel his chances of taking Moscow are not great, especially if the winter moves in and he gets caught out on the steppes; we shall have to wait and see what happens in time but it does solve one of the problems that could have reared its ugly head for us. If he continues into Russia and meets the same sort of resistance he has had so far then he will not have the reinforcements for the Peninsular war; that can only be too our advantage. If this all happens as we are hoping it will, then you may have a chance to really make some inroads in the not too distant future."

Thomas nodded his head to let Mister Percy know he understood what he was hearing and then waited while the smaller man sipped his brandy before continuing.

"Now I did hear that you had a certain influence in helping a young Ensign take some French colours at Salamanca although it is not generally known by those in high office, it was well done and I thank you for that. I know you did not need to put your lives at risk for Wellington's men but it was a good thing you did; it totally demoralised the French. Now the next thing I would like to suggest may not be too your liking but I feel it is necessary for your continued assaults on the French lines. We feel that it would be too your advantage to move your base closer to the action; perhaps around Moncorvo or Braganza. Both locations will give you less distance to travel in your efforts against the French but still keep you safely behind the English lines of advance. I know you may not like the idea of leaving Vimeiro but I thought we may suggest you keep some of your men here as a staging post for your supplies as your ships can land close by and then you can have your supplies carried to you in the north. What do you think?"

"It would seem a better option now that the French lines are being pushed so far back and it would make our task a little easier even though I don't like the idea of leaving here, the people of Vimeiro have been like family to my men and I don't want them to think we have just used them and then forgotten how they took us into their homes and families."

"Well the final decision as always is yours but it would make things better for you and your men on the travel front and we are sure the French will eventually have to move northward to escape back into France; you would be in an ideal place to cause them considerable discomfort when they start their retreat. Now the next thing I have to ask you is rather delicate if I may say so; it is to do with what your plans are after the war. There has been talk about your attitude to returning to England after the war and what you may have planned. I don't need your word right now but if you have some feelings about your plans sometime in the future, we would really appreciate hearing from you."

Thomas looked at Mister Percy as though he had not heard the older man. The war ending had been the very last thing on his mind and he had not even given the possibility any thought at all let alone his returning to England once it was all over. Thomas sat and took a small sip of his brandy; he had barely touched it since they had started talking; was it now time to start to think of his future? There was still a war to fight and win before he could give any serious though to what was to be done after it was all over.

Percy Cruikshank could see the indecision on Thomas's face and decided to put his young charges mind at rest; there was no real immediate need for an answer and there was still a lot of fighting yet to do.

"Thomas, there is no need for a reply right now but in time, when you have had a chance to think things through I would like you to let me know what you wanted; whatever you decide is right by me. It is your life and future and only you can decide what is to be done so for now let it rest. Have you given thought to my suggestion about moving your headquarters further north?"

"It's not much time Mister Percy; I will have to discuss it with my Officers and men first. It's not a decision I want to make on my own so perhaps you will stay for dinner and leave in the morning; I will organise a general meeting later today and we will have an answer for you before you leave us. Will that be satisfactory?"

"Yes Thomas, that will be fine by me and thank you I would love to stay until tomorrow; I have missed your fine table and good drink; it has been some time since I could sit back and relax for a little while."

"Good then I will get Fairley to prepare a room for you and have your carriage taken down by the barracks. Will your drive be alright in the barracks for the night?"

"That man can sleep on rocks if needs be Thomas, have no fear for him. Tell me, where is your own carriage? I don't see it in the valley."

"I keep it in Vimeiro, the people have put a barn at my disposal and the driver stays there to watch over the horses and carriage. I very rarely use it now."

"Well look after it, you never know when it will come in handy and after all you are a Don, can you think of what the Prince might say if he thought you were not living up to your title?"

Thomas chuckled at the thought that crossed his mind; he was pretty sure the Prince would laugh out loud at any though of Thomas sticking to the rules of etiquette as far as his title went. Thomas smiled at Mister Percy just as Fairley came back from showing the Carriage driver where he could stay.

"General. Is there anything else you gentlemen will need?"

"Yes, would you go and find the Colonels and ask them to join us; once that's done can you set a room for Mister Percy; he will be staying the night and also ask Major Jones to come and see me as soon as he can get away from his ledgers."

Fairley saluted and left, he knew Mister Percy was a very important man and had decided to behave himself for the moment. Fairley moved off to follow his orders as the two men poured a little more brandy in their glasses while they waited for the three Colonels to join them.

With the arrival of Carmelo, Estaban and Lorenco the discussion soon turned to the news that Mister Percy had brought. Within a few minutes after being told the news the three Colonels began to give their ideas on what they could do in the immediate future. Mister Percy had one last piece of news for Thomas and his friends.

"Thomas, Prince Pimentel will arrive back in Lisbon around the 20th of September; he has asked me to invite you to meet with him on or close to that date so you can discuss the needs of next season's advances against the French. It would mean that you still have plenty of time before you have to consider moving your army north and you never know; he may have a few ideas for you on that front as well."

"Thank you Mister Percy, it would give us some breathing space even though I have my doubts about returning to Lisbon just when the English may be returning there for the winter months."

"Well they may not retire that far for winter; if they have to hold their lines during those months I would think they may be further north and east. Are you not wanting to greet your fellow countrymen?"

Thomas could see the small smile on Mister Percy's face as he watched Thomas's reaction to the news.

"In all truth Mister Percy, the more I can avoid them the better I will feel but if there is something I have to do then I will carry out my duties if that's what the Cortes or the Prince asks of me."

"Very courtly words young Thomas and I don't believe a bloody word of it; however even the most onerous of tasks must be done if we want to win this war as I'm sure you understand. Now the last thing the Prince has asked is that you and your Officers once again carry your dress uniforms with you; he is hoping that you will muster your full Officer corps and present them when the time comes."

"Damn not another ball is it?"

"To be honest Thomas, I don't have a clue what he is up to so it's going to be as much a surprise for you as it will be for me."

"Oh you will be there as well?"

"Yes, he has asked for my presence this time. Shall we meet...say on the 19th of that month; I may have a better idea of what he plans for us."

"Very good Mister Percy the 19th it is. Now then let's go and see about the men and what they think of the idea of moving north."

The meeting lasted until a little before the evening meal was due to be served; the final decision was agreed on by everyone and concluded that most of the army would move north in December. They could make a new camp near Braganza as they would then have the safety of the Asturian and Cantabrian mountains at their back with most of the northern roads that the French may use for their eventual retreat close by.

With the final decisions made and agreed upon everyone's mind turned, as all youngsters know; to food. The heavy smell of cooking meat wafted in the air of the valley as the three pits with their whole sheep turning on them came to the ready; it was not long before hungry bellies were rumbling and mouths watering as the scullery boys set about carving the meat from the spits.

As he had always done, Thomas led his Officers to one of the long trestle tables among the men. As before Thomas just picked any one of the tables and sat with his men with the other Officers taking places at other tables although Thomas made sure that Mister Percy joined him.

Mister Percy was at first surprised at what Thomas and his Senior Officers were doing as he saw them find places amongst the men for dinner; it took Percy a little time to reconcile his thoughts with what he was seeing and comparing it to the distant relationship that the English Officer's had with their own men.

Percy felt a new respect for Thomas and settled back to watch and listen as the troops; both young and old around them began to treat Thomas just like one of them and drew Thomas into many discussion that had very little to do with military matters.

Percy was impressed as he saw and heard Thomas talk and join in the joking with his men; it was obvious the young Officer had not forgotten his own humble roots as a drummer boy more than four years ago. It was a refreshing view point for Percy and he sat quietly and watched the interplay between the young Officer and his men. All thoughts of rank seemed to have been put aside when it came to meal times and Percy was beginning to see why Thomas could call on the loyalty of his men and boys so easily.

As he sat eating and watching what was going on around him, Mister Percy began to get a new grasp on how this most unconventional army worked. The food was not only good but could be called excellent and there was plenty of it. Mister Percy let his mind wander back to what the English troops were given and had little trouble in recognising the difference between the mostly rotting canned beef and hard tack biscuits that the English troops got and the marvellously fine spread and good Spanish wine that this army of misfits had; even their soup was fresh and well made whereas the English were wont to serve something akin to soup that could also have been used for washing plates and dishes.

Another thing that attracted Percy's attention was the mixture of the different Corps; it appeared that when it came to meal time there was little difference between a onetime naval gunner and a small street urchin from somewhere in Portugal, they all sat together and chatted like old and close friends; it was at this point that Mister Percy realised that every conversation was held in the Spanish language with only the occasional word or two of Portuguese used.

It was fortunate for Percy that he had a good grasp on both languages as he never heard a single word of English spoken during the whole meal or, when he thought about it; had he heard English used during the normal time of day except when he was speaking with Thomas earlier.

For Mister Percy it was a revelation and he could only sit back and enjoy the atmosphere that pervaded the large mess and those around him. Mister Percy was brought out of his reverie by the sound of a young voice speaking to him from his left; Thomas sat on his right. Once Mister Percy turned to look at the owner of the young voice he saw it was a young lad, his accent was almost pure Billingsgate and he had a cheeky grin on his young face; although he did speak English to Mister Percy.

"Wotcha Guvna, you one o them toffs wot helps our boss then?"

Mister Percy smiled at the cheeky grinning boy and smiled as he replied.

"Yes young man, one of them."

"Right Guvna, then you betta know we don' take kindly to no ossifa wot does im wrong; yous unnerstand right?"

"Officer."

"Wot?"

"It's pronounced Officer, not ossifa."

"You takin the micky Guvna? Just you mind wot I says; anyone does wrong with the boss and you got all of us to watch your back for. Don't like our boss bein taken for no fool like."

"Don't worry young man I'm the last one you have to worry about doing that to him."

"Well you mind my words Guvna, you do right by him and we be alright with you; if not!"

Mister Percy quite understood the unsaid threat and could only smile at the boy who was no longer smiling; his own memories of saying something similar to a rough and dangerous boatswain when he first took George in was very much the same. The smile on Percy's face almost slipped as he thought back all those long years ago to his strange meeting in that far off Pacific hell hole. Percy shook his head to rid himself of the long ago memory and turned back to the young boy beside him.

"Tell you what young man, you watch over him and keep him safe and I will have no reason to come looking for you in the dark of night and spoil your dreams with my knife...agreed?"

Percy watched the startled look on the boy's face as the youngster tried to think of an answer; suddenly the boy's face broke into an even wider grin as he held out his rather greasy right hand after placing the sheep's knuckle on his tin plate.

"Right you are Guvna, you got yourself a deal. Course Guvna you wouldn't get within feet of me afore I heard you but that's never no mind, you do good by the boss and I will watch his back."

Percy took the greasy hand without blinking and shook; the grip was far firmer than he thought it would be for someone so young.

"Then you have a deal young man."

Percy raised his mug of Spanish wine and said to the boy.

"A toast to our boss to seal the deal."

Percy smiled as the boy grabbed for a mug half filled with wine and raised it up before taking a rather large mouthful and swallowing with a little exaggeration.

"The Boss."

The rest of the meal went without any further suggestions about Mister Percy's motives and it was later in the evening when the mess started to clear as the troops went in search of their beds or to go out on guard.

The next morning dawned overcast; it appeared the first hint of the coming winter was making itself known. The camp was already alive by the time Mister Percy made it to the table outside the home of his friend Thomas. The fresh smell of the early morning cafe hung in the slightly damp air as he took a chair on the other side of the table from Thomas.

There were no words spoken as the two old friends sat and enjoyed their early morning cafe; everything that needed to be said had been said and it was now time to let their brains work on any upcoming problems. For Thomas there was the need to think about the move north and how they would keep their home valley guarded and their sea-born supply line open.

Once the early breakfast had been eaten, Mister Percy called for his carriage and said his farewells to Thomas and the other Officers that had arrived to see him off. Mister Percy told Thomas he would probably not see him before he appeared for the Prince in Lisbon. Thomas stood and watched Mister Percy ride in his carriage out of the valley; it was time to get back to thinking about how they were going to move their army and supplies north.

Thomas called for Major Smithson, the young Officer and his small patrol of map makers were just what he needed for a reconnaissance to the north to find a suitable new campsite. Thomas along with his three most senior friends gave Major Smithson the details he would be looking for and what he wanted as far as safety went; he did not want his men put into danger unnecessarily.

The days passed as Thomas and his army prepared for the move north to Braganza, they were waiting only for the return of Major Smithson to tell them where the new camp should be placed. As the time passed the camp began to get a feeling of nervousness as the time to move drew closer. Wellington had been forced to retreat back west when the three armies of Soult, Joseph and Suchet combined and outnumbered Wellingtons force; it appeared there would be something of a stalemate during the coming winter as the armies kept their distance from each other.

Major Smithson arrived back at the camp on the 12th of September with his new maps and the report Thomas had been waiting for. It was not long before the orders were given that the army would move early so they were well encamped at Braganza before the worst of the winter storms hit the area. Thomas set the date of moving to the first week of November as he hoped to be back from Lisbon by that time and it would give his men plenty of time to ready everything for the mass move north.

On the morning of the 17th of September, Thomas assembled all his Officers for the journey to Lisbon; that he was not looking forward to the visit could be easily seen by the way he moved or talked but he had his duty to perform and he would not refuse an order from Prince Pimentel or the Cortes. When they left the valley, Thomas rode his horse down as far as Vimeiro and then made sure his new carriage was ready to follow along until they were within a few hours march of Lisbon before using it. If he had to obey the rules then he would, even under protest; Thomas's Officers were often seen with smiles on their faces when they glanced at the empty carriage.

Late in the afternoon of the 18th the small army of Officers rode into the city of Lisbon; the sultry look on Thomas's face as he sat angrily in the back of the carriage said it all and the occasional ribald remark from his friends did not help his attitude or what he thought about having to ride in the carriage. Carmelo had ridden ahead to find lodgings for them all and was waiting just inside the city limits as the small army of Officers arrived. Taking note of Thomas's angry look, Carmelo smiled at him and then just turned and led the men into the city and eventually to the closed in yard of a large tavern; he had booked the entire tavern for their use.

With the number of black clothed and mounted Officers in a single group it did not go unnoticed and there were many calls of pleasure and welcome from the cities populace as they recognised them. Thomas tried to keep his head down and his black flat crowned hat well over his features as the column rode through the town.

When they reached the tavern, Thomas was quickly out of the carriage and heading towards the open door; he still felt like an invalid when riding in the carriage whereas when riding his own horse he had a certain amount of anonymity being mixed in with the other riders all in black.

As the large group of Officers were sitting to dinner later in the evening it did not surprise Thomas when a young soldier dressed in the uniform of red jacket and silver and brass buttons of the English delivered a letter to him. The message was from Mister Percy and stated he would meet with them for breakfast the next day. Thomas dismissed the young messenger without a reply and went back to his dinner; tomorrow would tell him all he would need to know so for now all he wanted to do was enjoy his meal.

CHAPTER 13

Thomas awoke in the morning to a slightly overcast day; winter was closing in and the fine hot and sunny days would soon be a thing of the past. Thomas was not really surprised to see Mister Percy sitting at table when he came down for breakfast; it was times like these that Thomas truly appreciated his own cooks as he smelt the weak cafe and saw the sparse spread of food on the waiting table.

Thomas sat opposite Mister Percy and poured his first cup of cafe, he started a little when Mister Percy reached across the table with a silver flask and poured what appeared to be a good dash of brandy into Thomas's cup.

"It will make up for the lack of flavour." Mister Percy was almost chuckling as he saw the look on his young friends face as the brandy topped up the cup.

"So mister Percy, what brings you here at this hour?"

"Just a chat to bring you up to date with what's been happening and perhaps an idea of what is to come in the next campaign season."

Thomas took another sip of the weak cafe and squinted a little as the brandy hit the back of his throat.

"So what are we to do?'

"Well Wellington has been pushed back to Ciudad Rodrigo so he will encamp there for the winter; I think he has ideas of pushing forward to the east once the new season starts. His first objective will probably be towards Burgos, I think he is hoping to catch the French before they can consolidate their forces to stop him. During winter he will be receiving more reinforcements, something the French cannot do while Napoleon is tied up in Russia. The way things are going for him in the north I doubt Napoleon will win out and that will only mean he will have nothing to reinforce his Generals down here. Wellington's plans at this stage are to divide the French army's and then pursue them one at a time until he has them where he can send them all packing back to France."

"So you think that by us going to the north and raiding behind their lines we can help to once again pull much needed troops from Wellington's front?"

"Yes that's the basic idea but we also want you to do what you do best, take every advantage you can to disrupt them not only for Wellington but for the Spanish advance as well. I know you will be seeing the Prince tomorrow but just be careful; there is some dissention in the Cortes and the return of the King may well upset people in some quarters."

"The Spanish King is back?"

"Not yet but Ferdinand is making noises about returning once the French are on the move out of Spain. The Cortes are not very happy about it and have signed a document they claim to be the new Constitution of Spain. Ferdinand is still being held at the Chateau of Valencay but there are murmurs that this will not last long if Napoleon has to retreat from Russia in disarray."

"So if the King returns to the Spanish throne, what will happen to my men and army?"

"At this point I don't know; most of what I have told you is just speculation on my part but the signs are pointing towards him returning. Something you should know and be made aware of is that he is not the same type of man that your friend the Prince is. Ferdinand is a greedy and self indulgent man and is only concerned with his own welfare; when, or if he returns I would be inclined to watch what is going on very closely. You have a lot of supporters in the Cortes as well as having the Prince on your side and I don't think the King would really want to go against the people if it came to your titles and land but, with that man you can never tell."

"So you suggest that for now I continue doing what I am doing and that's to keep the French on their toes?"

"Yes, your way of warfare is not only making the French try to rethink their strategies but it is adding a lot of fear into their new troops. Do you think you will be able to continue into the winter with your attacks?"

"Once we get to the north that should be little problem, with less distances to travel we can cover a large part of Spain in very quick time."

"What of your supply lines, have you thought them out yet?"

"We are thinking of using our usual cove to unload and then transporting it all by wagon to where we will be; it will add time to the delivery but it's the only thing I can think of."

"Why don't you move it all to your warehouse and docks in Oporto? You have everything you need there and the travel north will be cut drastically as well as your ships not having to cover such distances?"

"Oh yes I had forgotten all about that, I'll have to tell Major Jones to remake his plans and we will probably have to have a large party to thank the people of Vimeiro for all they have done for us over the last four years. Thank you Mister Percy, I knew there had to be another way but could not think of anything."

"Well I wouldn't worry too much young Thomas, you have a lot of things to think on now you are a General and this is only a minor thing. Now then what do you have on your lap for the rest of the day?"

"I have to let the Prince know I am here and find out when he wants to meet but after that I think it will be back to Vimeiro and get ready for our move north."

"Well young man I would not put all my coin on that happening in the next few days; the Prince probably already knows you are here so I would not be surprised to get a call from him sometime today."

"Yes you are probably right; nothing seems to get past him especially this close to his headquarters."

The two friends sat in companionable silence as they both sipped their luke warm cafe; the brandy only making it drinkable as it cooled. As the two sat opposite each other, Thomas's friends began to arrive for their own breakfast; the comments they made at what they saw would not have made the tavern keeper happy if he had heard them.

Carmelo, Estaban and Lorenco joined the two friends and began to eat the sparse fare on the table and attempt to drink the thin weak cafe; their faces saying everything they thought about their first meal of the day. Thomas could see the gears in Carmelo's head turning as he tried to force another piece of greasy lamb down his throat along with a somewhat old tomato that had seen better days.

With the sparse breakfast now pushed aside, Mister Percy gained his feet in preparation to leave; Thomas eased his own chair back and was about to stand when he heard a disturbance near the tavern door, Thomas looked in the direction of the tavern entrance.

Thomas saw that three of his Lieutenants, Snot Morgan, Simon Kent and Peter Wright were holding their pistols on a young Officer while behind him he felt the presence of Fairley standing close by. Sergeant Fairley was the only non Officer in his group as he was expected to go wherever Thomas went.

"Lieutenant Morgan! What's going on?"

"Stranger in the room Sir."

"Lieutenant Morgan you should know what the uniform of His Highnesses Cavalry Officers looks like. For god's sake let the poor man through before you scare the hell out of him."

"Yes Sir, sorry Sir."

"That's alright Lieutenant, just next time give the man a chance before you poke a pistol in his face."

"Yes Sir."

Snot sat back down at the table with his face flushed but his attitude said he felt he was right to stop any stranger that may be a threat to his General and some of the whispers also agreed as the others also sat down. The newly arrived young Officer made his way to Thomas's table where he came smartly to attention and saluted before handing Thomas a sealed message.

Thomas quickly cut the missive open with one of his boot knives; much to the shock of the young Officer standing in front of him. With the message open, Thomas quickly read the short order.

To General Don Thomasino de Toro

From H.H. Prince Pedro Pimentel

Don Thomasino,

It would be my pleasure to offer you and your Senior Officers an appointment at my Hacienda where we last met to discuss the future of your forces and the future of Spain. I hope that 10 of the clock on the morrow is suitable and fits within your own needs. Please inform my Officer if this time agrees with you.

Prince Pedro Pimentel

C.C. Caballeria Espanola

Thomas looked up at the young Officer and told him that he accepted the kind invitation from the Prince. The young man smartly saluted, turned about and left quickly to relay the message. Thomas turned back to his friends just as Mister Percy took his leave. For the rest of the day, Thomas and his Officers could rest up and take time to relax; the months to come were going to be busy and it was a good chance to rest before action had to be taken once more to free the peninsula of the French.

The rest of the day was spent taking their ease; there was little discussion about what they may be asked to do the next day at the meeting and more about the low quality of the food in the tavern. Even after Carmelo took the tavern keeper aside and told him a few home truths about who his special guest was it seemed to make little difference to the man; he just shrugged his shoulders and mumbled something about food costs in the city then walked away.

The next morning the breakfast spread had not improved nor had the quality of the cafe; Carmelo got a look on his face that could only bode ill for the tavern keeper at some time in the future.

Thomas and his most Senior Officers left for the meeting with a good hour to spare, the city of Lisbon was now the central hub of the war effort and the population had grown dramatically in the four plus years of the war. Thomas let Estaban take the lead in front of the coach he was obliged to sit in; it was fortunate that he had allowed as much time as he did as the crowds slowed the progress of the coach as it tried to make its way to the Hacienda on the outskirts of the city.

Once they had arrived at the gates of the Hacienda, Thomas saw that it had changed little since the last visit and that there were still a large number of troops guarding the property. They were quickly let through the large solid gates and the coach was driven up to the main door where the Prince stood waiting for them.

Prince Pedro Pimentel smiled at Thomas as the coach drew to a halt at the bottom of the stone steps and Thomas descended to stand alone while his three Senior Officers dismounted their own horses and let them be led away by the Hacienda hostlers.

Thomas walked up the steps with his three friend's just behind as the Prince stepped forward with his hand out to greet them. Thomas shook hands with the Prince and then followed the man inside the cool shade of the building where they were once again led to the room used for planning.

There were no other Officers present this time and Thomas and his friends were directed to four empty chairs while the Prince took one at the head of the map covered table. It was not long before the Prince got down to business and explained why he wanted to meet Thomas without other Officers present.

"First of all Don Thomasino, I would like to congratulate you on the plans you set in motion prior to the taking of Salamanca; everything you said would happen not only succeeded but even surpassed what I was expecting. There are those among my own Officers who still cannot grasp how you managed to make it work so well. The landing of your forces on the beach was really a master stroke and obviously caught the French totally by surprise. Now then I am sure that Colonel Cruickshank has already met with you and informed you of what may happen during the next campaign season and I would like to know what your thoughts are on the matter."

"Your Highness, at this stage we have no definite plans except for moving our camp north to Braganza. We will run our supplies through Oporto and then we plan to attack the French rear and supply lines throughout the winter but at this stage that is as far as we have gotten in our planning."

"Well it certainly sounds as though you may cause even more problems for the French if you are able to attack at will during the worst months of the year. Did Colonel Cruickshank inform you about Napoleons coming problems in Russia?"

"Yes Your Highness but he did mention that it was not a certainty but it may hold promise if the Russians are able to hold him and force him to retreat during the winter."

"Yes I am sure you're quite right, if it all comes to pass then the French army here in Spain will be at a disadvantage and if you are able to limit their supplies then we may see the beginning of the end of their rule here."

"My men and I will try to do our best Your Highness."

"I'm sure you will Don Thomasino, now to other things. Did the Colonel mention that we may see the return of the King?"

"Yes Your Highness, it was mentioned."

"Do you have any thoughts on the matter Don Thomasino?"

"No Your Highness, I have no knowledge of things to do with politics or royalty and I'm not sure how it would make any difference to us."

"I see well there are many plans afoot and some of them would not be in your best interest; however, I still have some little sway over what may or may not happen at this stage so I can tell you that Spain will honour its debt to you and your men; on this you have my personal word. There are those within the Cortes that are against the return of the King and this could create a few problems for some but you can be assured that your lands and title will be made safe regardless of what the eventual outcome is. There may come a time when I will have to recall you from Braganza, I hope you will be able to leave there in time for a meeting if it is called for."

"As always Your Highness we are at your disposal whenever you need us; if you send a messenger I will come as soon as I can get away. It may take a little extra time if I am away from camp but I promise to attend as soon as I can Your Highness."

"You do not stay in camp when your men go out to fight Don Thomasino?"

"No Your Highness, we all fight together." Thomas paused as he looked at his three friends before continuing. "Although there are some who would like to stop me Your Highness but I feel I need to be with my men."

"A most unusual attitude for a General Don Thomasino; I do hope you are taking all needed precautions when in the field with your men?"

"Yes Your Highness, my men make sure I do not get into too much trouble even if I want to."

"Good, I don't know what we would do without your unconventional way of battle; it has been most effective and saved many lives when battle is finally joined with the French. Now the last thing I wanted to ask you, do you have everything you need for the upcoming winter?"

"At this stage Your Highness yes, but until we are back in the north I will not know for sure; however with my supply line so close we should be able to manage what we want to do until summer is once again here and the new campaign season is underway."

"Well Don Thomasino I can only wish you luck and hope that we meet again in good health once the winter is over. There is one last thing I wish to ask."

"Yes Your Highness?"

"Tomorrow night there is to be another ball which will be hosted by Viscount Wellington to celebrate his victory at Salamanca earlier in the year; he has asked if you would put in an appearance as he wishes to thank you for your efforts prior to the battle and, I believe that during some stage of the battle you also intervened to assist in a victory."

"So this is why you have asked for all my Officers to be present with their full dress uniforms, Your Highness?"

"Exactly Don Thomasino, there is always safety in numbers. The ball will be held at the Resident here in the city, I am sure you are now familiar with it."

"Yes Your Highness, very familiar."

"Good then shall we say at seven of the clock tomorrow evening; I will meet you inside once you have entered, perhaps another small show of force."

Thomas smiled along with the Prince as they all stood up to shake hands once more before leaving; the thought of another ball did not go down well with Thomas but then his duty as a Spanish Officer meant he could not avoid the evening.

The rest of the day was spent relaxing; that evening Thomas noted that there had been a remarkable change in the quality of the food. When he asked about it, Thomas was told that the tavern keeper had had a change of heart and sold his tavern to others; the improvements in the food were welcomed as their table was filled with some of the best the city could provide.

Thomas knew better than to inquire about the sudden change and a single quick glance in Carmelo's direction went a long way to explaining it all. Carmelo sat in his chair with the air of a man who was comfortable with his life and the wide smile he was wearing told Thomas of his friends involvement with the new changes; it was all he needed to satisfy his curiosity and he left well enough alone.

It was six thirty of the PM when Thomas and his Officers left the tavern for the Residence. Thomas had insisted that Carmelo, Estaban and Lorenco all sit in the carriage with him; if he had to ride in the damn thing then they could bloody well suffer along with him. The rest of the Officers were all mounted on their fine horses and dressed in their best uniforms; it was a stirring sight for the city folk to observe as they rode past in formation.

When the troop of Officers in black arrived at the gates of the residence, Thomas saw that the front courtyard was being used by a large gathering of troops which formed an honour guard that stretched from the gateway to the wide steps of the main house. Thomas's carriage stopped in front of the gate and his Officers formed up behind and dismounted, their horse were led away by a small army of hostlers as the men formed up around the carriage and stood at attention as Thomas and the others dismounted.

With everyone ready, Thomas led his men through the open gates and along the wide stretch of the courtyard; the honour guard stood on either side of the marching Officers at attention and with their muskets at the position of salute. It took a few steps before Thomas recognised the honour guard. To his left were men of the 33rd, his old Regiment; and to his right were those of the 2/30th Foot, the same Regiment of the young Ensign he had helped at Salamanca.

As he neared the steps, Thomas saw the larger than life figure of a familiar face although it was now marred by a new scar that ran from the right corner of the man's face and disappeared into his large mutton chop whiskers; Thomas stopped in front of the man and smiled up at the same stern face.

"I see you are still standing Sergeant Major, did you forget to duck?"

"Aye Sir still standing I be. Duck Sir, a Sergeant Major does not duck Sir as those damn Frenchies found out."

Thomas let a small chuckle break through as he looked at the sparkle in the Sergeant Major's eye. Thomas completely ignored the fact he was holding up the line of new arrivals in his pleasure to see an old and familiar face after so many years had passed.

"And how did you manage to get such a cosy duty Sergeant Major; I would have thought an old soldier such as you would rather be in a tavern somewhere."

"That I would Sir but seems there is some young General expected that the powers decided should have honours; Mind you Sir, they do say he is really just a young ranker in disguise but I wouldn't know nothing about such Sir."

"Then I will have to keep an eye out for him Sergeant Major; perhaps I can learn something from him."

"That you may Sir, they does tell me he can be right devil given half a chance Sir."

"Then it is all the better I keep my eyes open. It was good to see you Sergeant Major but I better get inside or there may be words said about my lack of manners."

The Sergeant Major straightened up just a fraction more as he let the faintest of smiles show on his rough features as Thomas touched the tip of his bicorn hat and led his men up the steps towards the open doors of the Residence. Waiting just inside the foyer and partially seen by Thomas was the very erect and formidable figure of Viscount Wellington; he was surrounded by his most Senior Officers all of which were quite familiar with their young black clad guest.

The Residence was on a very large and select piece of ground, it was easily capable of having four hundred guests at one time. Thomas led his Officers up the steps until they reached the patio before the foyer where they came to a halt in front of a youngish Captain of the Cavalry. The Captain came to attention and saluted before he asked Thomas.

"Sir, whom may I introduce to the gathering?" It was apparent by the look on the Captain's face that he was not sure if the strange Officers would understand him and the further fact that the one who seemed to be the senior most of them looked to be no more than about eighteen or nineteen years old. The youngish Captain did not find out the true age of the General until much later in the night. Carmelo stepped forward as they had all arranged before hand and took over the introductions for the Captain.

"Captain, you may introduce General Don Thomasino de Toro, Commander of the 1r Regimiento Guerrillas Espana and his Officers."

The Captain smartly about turned and led Thomas and the others through the large doors and into the main foyer, from there he took them to a huge pair of open wooden doors where the Viscount stood with a line of Senior Officers as they waited to greet their guests.

The Captain came to attention and, in a clear and loud voice introduced Thomas and his Officers to the large crowd already gathered inside.

"My Lord, Ladies and Gentlemen Officers, General Don Thomasino de Toro, Commander of the 1r Regimiento Guerrillas Espana and Officers."

The Captain stepped to the side as Viscount Wellington stepped forward and held his hand out to Thomas.

"Welcome to the Residence General Thomasino de Toro, I hope you and your Officers will enjoy your evening and perhaps at some time you could spare a few minutes of your time to meet with me in private."

Thomas was at first a little surprised at the invitation but did not let it show on his face; instead he shook hands with the Viscount and said.

"Thank you My Lord Viscount, I would like that very much and am at your convenience."

Thomas took note of the Prince standing further inside the large ball room surrounded by another large contingent of Officers. Viscount Wellington released Thomas's hand and indicated for him to go on through into the ball room proper as he had other guests to greet.

Thomas led his men into the ball room where he was quick to join the Prince as they watched the dancers move to the modern music of the time. Thomas noted that there were a lot of old familiar faces amongst the Senior Officers but there were also a large number of new young faces amongst the Junior Officers. Campaigns such as had just passed in the last season took a huge toll on young Officers so he was not really surprised at the many new faces.

Thomas and his men joined those of the Prince, they now had quite a little army of Officers in one section of the ballroom and it was noted by a number of the guests. Thomas and his men stayed amongst the Spanish and Portuguese contingent, they all felt comfortable with men they knew well and, now that there was no longer a language barrier, many of the conversations were of things outside military matters.

It was another hour before Thomas saw a young English Officer coming in his direction obviously with the intent of speaking to him; little did Thomas know that the arriving young Officer had been given very explicit instructions from his superior; to whit, Viscount Wellington.

"Captain Miles, would you please take a message to General de Toro for me and ask him if he would care to meet with me in my office. I would stress that you are to show all due respect and honour to his rank and then accompany him so that he does not have to prevaricate in finding my office."

Captain Miles snapped to attention and saluted before leaving in the direction of the young General; he was well aware of the young man's reputation as well as knowing that the Viscount would brook no deviation from his orders. Captain Miles drew close to the large group of foreign Officers and came to attention as he looked at the young General.

Thomas waited for the young Captain to speak as his other friends drew silent and watched the Captain with uncertain eyes.

"The Viscount Wellingtons compliments General de Toro; he asks if you would do him the honour of joining him in his office and that if you agree then I am to escort you to him Sir."

Thomas looked at the very correct Captain and let the faintest of smiles lift the corner of his mouth as he replied.

"Thank you Captain, if you would please lead the way."

The Captain was at first surprised by the Generals accent but then remembered his orders from the Viscount; with a salute to the young General he turned about and led Thomas towards the private office where the Viscount awaited him.

The Captain knocked on the closed door and it was immediately opened by Colonel Lewis to whom Thomas gave a big smile of welcome. Once inside Thomas saw the Viscount had loosened his jacket and was seated not at his desk, but in a large softly padded chair off to one side, there was another vacant chair opposite the Viscount. With a single gesture, Viscount Wellington indicated for Thomas to take the other chair while Colonel Lewis left them to their own devices. Thomas waited for the Viscount to speak first.

"General, may I call you General Marking? It may save me some confusion."

Thomas nodded that he didn't mind and waited for the Viscount to continue.

"General Marking I find myself at something of a quandary and at the same time a little disconcerted. I am sure you are by now well aware that General Beresford has been recalled to England for his unconscionable actions and his report. This is a new position for me to be in and I am sure you are well aware that I am not in the habit of offering apologies for any of my actions. However if there is one occasion where I find myself in the need to change my attitude it is now. General Marking, I would like to offer my sincerest apologies for the events that took place after the battle of Albuera and in the way you were personally treated. My views and those of the War Office are that you were indeed treated appallingly and for that we are eternally sorry."

"Thank you My Lord Viscount, I am only sorry that the event ever came to this point and I accept your apology without reservation; I am well aware that it was not the fault of either yourself or the War Office."

"Thank you for your understanding General Marking. There is one thing I would like to discuss with you but first I must congratulate you on assisting a certain young Ensign at Salamanca; I am sure your actions have secured the young man a good future with his Regiment and for that we are all grateful. The last thing I would like to discuss with you General Marking is your position at this present time. I know that we cannot offer you all that the Spanish have done but we would sincerely like to ask if you would reconsider your position and return to our forces. Napoleon's armies are on the back foot and I'm sure we will have him out of the Peninsula within the next two years even though there is still a lot of hard fighting to do before that time arrives."

Thomas nodded his understanding as the Viscount paused to get his reaction.

"Thank you My Lord but I am sure you can understand that at this stage I must in all conscience stay with my present command, there are those who rely on me and I cannot let them down. However, I will as always try to relieve your army when I can by continuing my attacks on the French behind their lines and also assist in any battle where I do not have to put my men at unnecessary risk."

"Well I can only thank you for your honesty and hope that some time in the future we can repair the rift that has developed between our forces; that you would be willing to continue to assist us is taken as a sign that all is not lost. Have you thought about what you will do when this war is over; perhaps where you would decide to reside when peace arrives?"

"No My Lord, at this stage all my thoughts must be for my men and what is occurring at the present. When the time comes I will have the time to consider my future but they will also include my men's future; they have stood by me even at the worst of times and I cannot throw them aside for my own personal endeavours."

"A truly magnanimous attitude General Marking, we can only hope you have the chance to put it all in effect and that once the fighting is done you will find a peaceful place to live out your life; you truly have my respect and the respect of many of my Officers."

"Thank you My lord but it is my people who have made it all possible, I could not have done what I have so far without their valued help."
"I can appreciate your concern for your people General and how much you value them. Now then I think I have taken up more of your time than I should, perhaps we should return to the ball and I hope we can look forward to a better relationship in the future."

"Thank you My Lord, I also hope that things will improve for both our sakes, as you know I still have my family in England so there are times when I am torn between them and the need for me to watch out for my friends."

"I can fully understand that General Marking, I think we should leave it as said and then see what the future holds for us both. Again my thanks for your understanding."

Thomas stood at the same time as the Viscount and; with a shake of hands the two onetime adversaries called a truce, re-buttoned their jackets and left the office for the ballroom and the rest of the night's entertainment.

With his meeting over, Thomas rejoined his friends and the Prince to watch the festivities of the ball; it was as he stood beside the Prince that Thomas saw some of his younger Officers beginning to relax and enjoy the occasion although most of it also included a few glasses of very good wine and brandy. Thomas smiled as an evil and fleeting thought crossed his mind.

With his younger Officers drinking a little more than was good for them, Thomas decided to start back to Vimeiro before first light; he whispered his nefarious idea to his three closest friends and they quickly agreed with wide grins on their faces. The thought of many sick faces and rumbling stomachs and hung-over heads gave the four friends something to look forward to.

As the evening progressed Thomas was called aside by the Prince for a private discussion; as they stood close in one of the small alcoves at the side of the ballroom,

Prince Pimentel told Thomas about his worries for his young friend and his move to the north.

"Don Thomasino, I have to give you a small warning, if you are going to set your new base at Braganza you will be close to Leon and there are still those who live there that are not yet friendly to Spain; you will also have a number of men coming and going from further east in Navarre; if I were you I would watch any newcomers closely. There are many diverse small armies of guerrillas and not all of them are lead by good men so I would try to keep your wits about you. In the north I do not have as much sway as here in the south so there may be little I can do if trouble occurs."

"Thank you Your Highness for the warning; we have run into similar types before so I will keep a sharp eye out for any that look untrustworthy."

"Good Don Thomasino, that's all I can ask, none of us here in the south want you to be put into a situation that you cannot control. Well my young friend, that's all for now, I am sure you more than have your hands full with your upcoming move north so we can leave it there for now. Again you have the thanks of the Cortes and the people of Spain."

"Thank you Your Highness, as always we shall try to do our best in expelling the French."

"I'm sure you all will Don Thomasino, now then let's get back to the others; there is still fun to be had for those who seek it."

The two friends returned to the others and settled in to see the ball out. It was late in the evening when Thomas called his men to him and gave the order for everyone to return to the tavern; he did not tell the younger Officers that they would be leaving before sunrise as most were too far into their cups to have taken notice as they staggered out of the Residence and called for their horses.

There were a few ribald remarks for the three youngest Officers when they fell from their horses on their ride back to the tavern; it was nothing when compared to how they would feel within a few hours when they had to start the return to Vimeiro.

On arrival back at Vimeiro the first thing for Thomas to do was check the organisation of his wagons and mules for the move north. The long journey back to the valley had not been without incident; much to the merriment of the older and wiser Officers. The younger ones who had over indulged now paid the price for their bravado and many were still looking a little unsteady when they entered their home valley with many a ribald remark thrown their way by wiser heads.

Once everyone had settled back into the routine of the valley and the need for preparation for the move; Thomas was not surprised to learn that much of it had already been planned by the ever resourceful Major Jones. All the wagons had been checked for any defects and their now large herd of mules were also ready for the long march. As Thomas looked around the valley that had been their home for more than four years, he felt a small lump in his throat at the thought of leaving it all behind.

On the afternoon of the 27th of September, Thomas decided to begin the move north early so his wagons and guns had a chance to make up time. The Infantry would go along with the wagons and mules not only as an escort but it would be easier for the men than trying to stay with the mounted cavalry. Thomas had decided to stay behind with his two Friends Carmelo and Estaban; Lorenco was given full charge of the wagons, mules and Infantry for the move as he and his men would as normal take the vanguard even though there was little chance of any French troops attacking the strong supply train so far to the west.

The supply train would take the road directly through the pass of the Estrella Mountains to Guarda, from there they would move straight north to the River Douro which they would cross at the town of Moncorvo, it would then be a long straight run to Braganza across the wide open plains. With winter so close they could get caught out by early or sudden storms so all precautions that could be taken were looked into.

Thomas and the mounted troops would take a different route, one that led them through to Oporto first and then on to the new camp site that Major Smithson had marked on one of his very detailed maps for Thomas. By the time the wagons and mules were fully loaded it was the 29th of September so there was little else to do but get them on their way north.

As he watched the supply train move out of the valley he could not help but notice the four armed guards that marched alongside the small donkey cart of Lieutenant De Silva; Thomas turned to Carmelo and was about to ask why the small cart had such a large escort but Carmelo beat him to it by lifting one eyebrow and smiling; for Thomas it meant it was better not too ask so he turned away and watched as the mules filed in behind the wagons; the heavy guns were last in line.

By early evening the valley seemed deathly quiet as Thomas looked around at the home of four years. Without the noise and voices of his men he was beginning to feel a little lost even though he still had three hundred Cavalry nearby but the valley just felt deserted and empty. With the leaving of his main body of troops the valley had partially died, it was as though some of its life force had been taken from it and now there were only the bones left for those still left behind.

On the morning of the 30th September, Thomas led his Cavalry out of the valley and down into the town of Vimeiro; it was time to pay homage to the people who had become, in many cases, the second family for many of his men and boys and to thank them for the steadfast support at even the worst of times. The rest of the 30th was spent in Vimeiro where a large fiesta had been organised for Thomas and his men which continued well into the late hours of the night and was enjoyed by everyone present.

At dawn on the 1st of October Thomas and his men said their farewells to the people who had been their second families but left them with the promise that Thomas would at some time return to see them all once more just as soon as the French had been pushed from the lands of Spain. Thomas led his men onto the coastal road that led directly to Oporto, they would traverse the coastal road where it was mainly low lying plains where they could make good time and hopefully be in Oporto in just a few days or at most a week.

Thomas had underestimated the distance even though he had travelled it before; it was fully ten days before he saw the outskirts of Oporto in the distance after he crossed the Douro at Gramido but it was still a pleasure to see the end of the journey now so close. Thomas had been given instructions by Mister Percy on how to find his dock and warehouse; it was right on the outskirts of Oporto and almost the last dock on the waterfront.

When Thomas saw the dock that was now considered a part of his holdings along with the shipping company, he could plainly see that it was quite old although not run down as would be expected by a place of such age. The dock itself was well made and extended along the river front for some distance, there was enough space for two smaller ships to tie up at the same time. Behind the dock was a large warehouse; its red tiled roof was in good repair and the white-washed walls had been freshly coated. There were three large double wooden doors along the front of the warehouse that faced the open dock.

Thomas almost had a small smile on his face when he saw a very familiar banner flying above the warehouse; there would be little mistake in knowing who was the owner; the black bulls head at the centre of the banner made sure of that. Above the central door was a freshly painted sign saying that the warehouse belonged to the "MARKING SHIPPING COMPANY" Thomas felt a small shudder run through him as he saw the brazen sign; it was time to look for the chandler and see what had been going on and what new arrangements would have to be made.

As Thomas led his three hundred men through Oporto he did not see the looks they gathered as they passed by the people. While it was not unusual for the People of the port to see troops in their town it was unusual to see the ones now riding in formation with the loud clatter of hooves on the cobble stones; everyone in both Spain and Portugal knew who the black clad riders were but they had never seen them so far inside the town or with such a large contingent of Cavalry. That evening in Oporto there was much speculation as to why their famous young Patron was in their town with such a large force; the rumours were never answered.

As Thomas led his men along the open dock he spied an older man standing outside the first double doorway. He looked to be in his middle years and was of a thinnish build, his once dark hair was now tinged with grey and he wore a pair on rimless spectacles. As the man saw Thomas lead his men towards him he immediately straightened up and prepared to meet his famous owner for the first time.

Thomas stopped his horse near the waiting man, before he dismounted he asked Estaban to take the rest of the men and find somewhere they could make camp for a few days while he talked with the waiting man; Carmelo would stay with Thomas and it was no surprise for anyone that Sergeant Fairley also wanted to stay along with ten others. Thomas frowned as he saw the ten men sit their horses while Estaban rode way with the rest but he knew there was little he could really do about it. Carmelo and Estaban had made it standing orders that Thomas was to have a guard detail at all times; even in the safety of Oporto.

Thomas cleared the frown from his face at what he considered unnecessary caution on the part of his two friends but also knew he would not be able to really do much about it; he would just have to accept it and move on. Thomas dismounted in front of the waiting man and then stepped towards him with his hand out.

The man stood erect and grasped Thomas hand with a surprisingly firm grip for one who Thomas though looked more like an office bound book keeper.

"Welcome Don Thomasino to your warehouse and docks, I am Eduardo Forsca and have the honour of being the chandler and manager of your company here in Portugal. Mister Cruickshank told me you may come to visit at some stage so this is indeed a great honour for us all and I hope I can be of some service to you while you are here. If there is anything you wish to know I would be happy to answer all of your questions."

"Thank you Senor Forsca, I am happy that at last I can get to see what has been arranged here. Is there somewhere we can talk so I can find out what is going on; I must confess I am not familiar with business matters and need all the help you can offer to understand it all."

"It will be my greatest pleasure Don Thomasino. I am at your disposal any time, day or night; you have only to ask and I will see that it is done."

"Thank you again Senor Forsca, would you have an office we can go to? There are things I wish to ask you and I don't think the dock is the right place to discuss these matters."

"Certainly Don Thomasino, if you would like to follow me I will take you to the office immediately."

Thomas followed Senor Forsca back into the first warehouse with Carmelo, Fairly and his ten man guard close by. Thomas almost had to stop as he entered the large warehouse, the smells and sights were totally knew to him and he did not know where all the goods could have come from. From what Mister Percy had said this was just for the supplying of his army but in the warehouse there were many things that had little to do with the war effort; Thomas now had many more questions than first thought as he looked at the towering rows and stacks of produce and goods.

Senor Forsca led Thomas and his friends through the narrow lanes between the goods until they came to a small walled off section of the warehouse; inside were two younger men working over high desks and making entries into large ledgers. Thomas almost smiled as he thought of Major Jones sitting at one of the desks; the young Welshman would be right in his element.

Senor Forsca led Thomas into another smaller room that had a solid looking desk with wall to wall shelves filled with ledgers, there were only two straight backed wooden chairs in the room and one was behind the desk. Senor Forsca indicated for Thomas to take the chair behind the desk while the man stood in front and waited for his owner to speak.

Sergeant Fairley and his ten men stood outside the office but close to the second door on guard while Carmelo stood by the door but inside the office. Thomas indicated for Senor Forsca to take the other chair and then waited until the older man was comfortable before asking any questions. While he waited for the man to get comfortable, Thomas looked around the rest of the office. On the wall closest to the door was a large chalk board; on it were the names of five ships and beside each name was a date and place name; it all looked very organised but Thomas did not really know what it all meant.

"Senor Forsca perhaps you could begin by explaining the workings of the company to me; as I said earlier I am somewhat ignorant of business matters."

"Certainly Don Thomasino. Well firstly you now own five ships as you can see on that board by the door. They are made up of two captured Sloops and one Brigantine and then you also have your original ship, the Avante along with the ship Beatrice Graves which is under contract for a two year period. The Sloops and the Brigantine have been renamed once they underwent work to make them more seaworthy and safe by means of adding cannon to their decks. The first sloop has been named the Pipito, the second is now the Bernado and the Brigantine has been called the Sea Nymph. The three smaller ships travel in convoy to England for your supplies but they also carry goods we purchase from here and other places so they are fully loaded both ways. The Beatrice Graves crosses the sea to the new world and does trade with the new colonies taking our goods and products and returning with cotton and tobacco. The Avante has travelled to the Islands of the Indies with both French and local goods and exchanges them for Rum and Sugar. The Rum is unloaded at your London agents and is then sold on to the Royal Navy; the Sugar is carried back here where she then reloads our products to return once again to the Islands for more trade."

"You mentioned French goods, where do they come from and how did you manage to get them?"

"Ah yes, well Don Thomasino, perhaps it is time to tell you more about myself. I am from a small village in a place called Fuenterrabia; it is on the border with France and is positioned right on the coast. I am sure you may be able to guess what our main business is! being it is so close to France and yet part of Spain. In that place I have many relatives, all of which are involved with the local pastime of buying and selling at a certain profit. My family has four coastal Luggers with a very shallow draft and are able to go right in close to certain beaches on the French coast where they buy wine and cognac. Once loaded they make their way back to Fuenterrabia and store the goods until the three smaller ships put in there on their way back from England they then load it and deliver it back here. Your agent in England always makes sure there is space enough for the goods that are being held for you. With France now in the throes of war there are many who have little problem in selling their goods to us as well as we have contacts in France that have dealt with my family for generations."

"It sounds like a very lucrative business Senor Forsca and I am sure your family is doing well. Now then what of our supplies, do you have enough to keep us supplied if I was to send twenty wagons a month to you?"

"Yes Don Thomasino we can accommodate them easily although there is one thing I must ask."

"What is that Senor Forsca?"

"We seem to have a large store of English food supplies that are never asked for; what should I do with them or do you wish to have them transported to your camp?"

"What type of food are they Senor Forsca?"

"It is that peculiar canned meat the English love so much and there are many boxes of the small hard bread they make; are they of use to you and your men Don Thomasino?"

Thomas sat and thought for a few seconds, the last thing he wanted for his men was corned beef and hard tack. Thomas smiled at Senor Forsca before answering.

"No Senor Forsca, we have no need of it but if I may suggest that you find a good agent and perhaps he can sell it on to the English army, my men and I have the full use of fresh foods so have no need of any of it."

"Would you prefer that I ask your London agent to stop sending any of it; it would make more space on the ships for the goods from Fuenterrabia?"

"Yes that sounds like a good idea Senor Forsca; as long as we keep getting a good supply of powder and shot there is little else we need."

"Very good Don Thomasino I shall make the arrangements. Now then is there anything else I can do for you during your stay in Oporto?"

"Yes Senor Forsca, I am in need of accommodations for my Officers and I, my men will camp just outside the city until we are ready to leave; can you recommend a tavern for us to use?"

"Perhaps you would prefer a small Hacienda that is vacant at this moment. I have an acquaintance that has just recently been forced to vacate his home; it is on the outside of the city so perhaps your troops could also find quarters there."

"That sounds ideal Senor Forsca, I will send word to Colonel Estaban to reroute the troops there if you will tell me where it is?"

"Certainly Don Thomasino and there is one more thing I would like to suggest. Would you and your Senior Officers consider dining with me and my family this evening; there is one more thing I wish to show you but it is at my home."

"Thank you Senor Forsca, it would be our pleasure to join you; I have only to send word to my other men to set camp at the Hacienda and then we can join you at the time you desire."

Over the next few minutes Thomas noted the address of the vacant Hacienda and then called for one of the guards outside to carry the message to Estaban; Thomas and the others would join Estaban shortly after they had completed any more business at the dock. At six of the clock Thomas rode with his three Senior Officers to the address Senor Forsca had given him. The house was not far from the docks but far enough back from the sea front that it was away from the centre of trade and gave his manager and family some peace from the rigors and noise of the docks.

Thomas found the house with little trouble and he was pleasantly surprised by its size and good condition; it was a home built for a large family and looked as though it had been well lived in by its occupants. Senor Forsca met Thomas and his friends at the small gate where a young boy took their horses and led them away to another gate further down the lane where he disappeared inside to look after the mounts.

Thomas was greeted by Senor Forsca who had a broad smile on his face as he held the gate open for his guests.

"Welcome to my home Don Thomasino, if you would like to follow me inside I will introduce my family, they have been waiting with great expectation to meet the young man who has turned out to be our saviour from the horrors of the French."

"Thank you Senor Forsca, my men and I have been looking forward to this evening."

"Good then I hope you will enjoy yourselves. Is the Hacienda sufficient for your men's needs?"

"Yes it's perfect; you will have to tell me how much it costs so we can make some recompense to the owners."

"There is no need for any recompense Don Thomasino; the Hacienda has been vacant for some time and it is good that it can be of use. Now then if you will follow me I will introduce my family."

"Do you have many children Senor Forsca?"

"Yes Don Thomasino, I have seven sons and one daughter although my daughter is now married and lives with her husband but all of my sons still live with us; it is a way for me to keep watch over them as they are all employed in one way or the other by the company."

Thomas followed Senor Forsca into the house where he saw a line of five boys ranging from the youngest who was the same boy that had led their horses away and looked to be about ten years of age, up to a young man who looked to be in his early twenties. Senor Forsca introduced the boy's one after the other until he came to a heavy set woman who could only be his wife.

"And lastly Don Thomasino, my Wife; Donna Maria."

Thomas bowed slightly to the smiling woman and then asked Senor Forsca.

"Senor Forsca, I though you mentioned you have seven sons, are the others away working?"

"No Don Thomasino, they are out on guard, they will join us when their time is up and two others will take over for them."

"On Guard Senor Forsca? I don't think you have many Frenchmen to worry about now their lines are deep in Spain."

"Oh Don Thomasino it is not the French I worry about, it is the local brigands. You see Don Thomasino in our business and for over two hundred years my family has dealt only with cash, I know the banks like to deal with nothing but paper in the form of letters of credit but the people we deal with will only take coin for all transactions so I keep it all here under lock and key. I do not trust the banks Don Thomasino and why should I pay someone else to do what I can do for myself."

"That's true senor Forsca but how do you keep it all and know what you have?"

"Ah, there is where my eldest comes in." Senor Forsca pointed to the twenty something young man and said. "Hernandez is very good with numbers and books; he keeps a very accurate tally of every coin that passes through our hands. If you wish he can show you his efforts and tell you to the last sou what is owed to you and the company. It is all held here in our family vault for your inspection and is available to you on demand at any time. When I sold the company to Mister Cruickshank I told him of our ways of doing business and he agreed we should continue in the same vein. Should you desire it we can change it to suit your own demands."

"The matter of monies has never been easy for me to understand Senor Forsca but if Mister Cruickshank thinks it is the way to go then I am willing to abide by his decision. Perhaps you can show me your vault after dinner so I can understand it further."

"If will be my pleasure Don Thomasino but first let us have a drink while my wife finishes the preparations for dinner."

Thomas nodded his agreement and followed senor Forsca into a side room that was obviously set up for the reception of guests, only the oldest of the boys followed them in and took a chair off to the side when the drinks had been poured and given out. The conversation was now relaxed as Senor Forsca told Thomas of his family history and how he had come to sell his dock business to Percy Cruickshank.

It appeared Senor Forsca was having a little trouble with the dock due to the great influx of English traders who were taking over so many parts of the waterfront for the war effort; when he was offered the chance and a great deal of cash to sell his dock and warehouses as well as take over as manager of it all for the hero El Toro he was only too glad to comply and worked hard to make sure it was all a success. His family ties and contacts went a long way to helping the fledgling company of Marking Shipping to slowly gain a good market in many different arenas.

Dinner was as normal for this part of the country; very, very good and had Thomas and his friends laughing along with the many family jokes while they ate. That Donna Maria was an excellent cook went without saying, with such a large family to feed she would have had a lot of practice and young men's bellies were not always easy to fill. As the diners sat at the end of the fine dinner and while sipping some excellent Oporto wine, two of the younger boys rose and left the room; they were soon replaced by two of their brothers who had been the ones on guard. The two newcomers were quickly introduced to Thomas and the wide smiles of greeting indicated they were happy to meet the great El Toro in their own home.

Thomas felt a real familiarity with the family setting, it was something he had not had before and he wondered how things might have been if he had had so many brothers around him when he was younger. The feeling gave him a sudden pang of nostalgia as he thought of the little brother he had not yet met; he determined he would do everything in his power to make sure his brother would know the true meaning of family.

CHAPTER 14

Thomas enjoyed the family atmosphere of the dinner, there was fun and laughter among the boys and adults and for Thomas there seemed to be a closeness he had not seen before; perhaps due to the pressure his father had tried to raise him under.

At the end of the meal Thomas once again asked about Senor Forsca's determination to stay away from banks and hold what Thomas assumed could be a large amount of solid coin in his own house or grounds.

Senor Forsca soon invited Thomas to join him in seeing his family's small vault. It was built out in the courtyard at the back of the house. Senor Forsca led Thomas and the others outside to see his specially built vault. It was of solid stone blocks and appeared to be about twenty years old. The roof was made from thick slabs of slate instead of the normal tiles; Senor Forsca told Thomas that the roof was made of slate to combat anyone from trying to break in through the roof as it was tougher than fired tiles.

The small building hidden at the back of the courtyard was about six feet wide and eight feet long with a strong looking metal door at the front, there were no windows and the small building looked solid and impenetrable.

Sitting outside the locked door was one of Senor Forsca's sons. Tucked into his waist sash were a brace of large pistols and across his knees lay an old style blunderbuss the barrel of which must have measured three inches across; of the second son there was no sign. Senor Forsca smiled at his son and then stepped to the metal door and gave a strange knock that was obviously some type of signal. Thomas could just barely hear movement from inside the small building and within a few seconds, the sound of a heavy bolt could be heard as another son unlocked the door for his father.

Thomas was led inside the small building and shown how it was set up; the son inside was also armed with an ancient blunderbuss and brace of pistols; anyone trying to get inside this building was in for a deadly reception from the two sons. The interior of the building was again plain unfinished stone but three walls were lined with heavy wooden shelving and a small desk sat alone at the far end.

On the shelves were a number of wooden boxes, except for the top shelf on the left wall; it held a large number of thick ledgers, again each one was titled. All of the small wooden chests had good solid metal bands around them and each had a paper tag with a name written clearly on each one. Thomas looked at the orderly rows of shelves and marvelled at the organisation. Senor Forsca began to explain it all to Thomas as he looked around in the dim light of two small lamps.

"Don Thomasino, as you can see each box carries the name of the person or company that it belongs to. The chests on the second shelf belong to myself and my sons; as each one collects his wages for the month it is put into his chest and he can withdraw from it at his leisure. On the lower shelf to the left side are the chests that are your share of the profits from your ships as well as the Captain and crews share. On the right side are the shares that go to your agent in London and on the lower shelf are the chests we use for new purchases of cargo; each of which is named for the ship that carries those goods. My eldest is the one who organised it all and to be quite frank, he is really the only one that fully understands how it all works but I can assure you he will be able to account for every single sou that has passed through his hands."

Thomas could only nod as he looked at what must be a full time job just to keep track of everything; he also wondered what Major Jones would think of the workings of this new vault. Thomas was truly impressed but was hesitant to ask how much coin was held in the name of his Shipping Company; he was saved the embarrassment of having to ask by Senor Forsca asking him if he was interested in seeing his own chests.

Thomas nodded at the question but was not really expecting anything too much as the company had only been going for a short time if measured against long established companies that had been sailing the seas for more than a hundred years.

Senor Forsca turned to his son and nodded towards a number of chests and then held out his hand. The son reached into his thick warm coat and produced a metal ring that held a number of thick heavy keys; handing it to his father he went a pulled out four of the larger chests on the bottom shelf on the left. For the first time, Thomas noted that the front of each chest held the simple outline of a bulls head in black paint along with a number from 1 to 4.

As Senor Forsca unlocked the first chest his son reached up and took down four ledgers from the top shelf. As chest number 1 was unlocked, the son gave one of the ledgers to his father who turned to Thomas and indicated for him to look inside. The chest was three parts filled with small canvas bags; each was tied firmly and placed neatly in rows; there were a lot of small bags in the chest.

Senor Forsca then opened the ledger and showed Thomas all of the very correct entries; each was dated and a ships name was marked in one of the many columns that went across the page; there were a lot of pages that had entries on them.

"Now Don Thomasino, this chest is the one for silver coins; each bag has one hundred silver coins in it and here on the right hand column is the running total of the chest. Chest number 2 is also silver but it is full so we had to start with a second chest. Chest number 3 is gold coins and number 4 is for the precious stones that are sometimes used for trade instead of coin; we have some traders that prefer to use the stones instead of coin. Do you wish to have the totals read for you?"

"No Thank you Senor Forsca, I am sure that everything is in order but it does seem to be a lot of money for such a small company to have earned in such a short time."

"Perhaps Don Thomasino but then your ships are carrying cargos that few others have the ability or contacts to purchase; as I explained previously, my family is very large and we do have certain advantages over others when it comes to obtaining valuable cargo."

"I see, well then why was it you sold your Docks and warehouses, with those sorts of contacts you should have been able to make a very good living without having to sell?"

"Ah yes Don Thomasino, it may appear so but without the needed ships to carry it then there is no use having any cargo in the first place and for us to obtain ships was almost impossible and that is where you and your good friend Senor Cruickshank came in. To be honest Don Thomasino, I am relieved that the dock is sold; it now allows me more freedom and time with my family. When Senor Cruickshank asked me to take over as manager it was really a blessing in disguise. When the time comes for me to return to my home in the north then I will have good sons to carry on your work here for you."

"Then you hold no hard feelings for the loss of your docks?"

"Certainly not Don Thomasino; if there was a man worthy of taking possession of the dock then it is yourself. When Senor Cruickshank told me it was for the saviour of Portugal I found I could not resist his generous offer; besides I must admit I am now making more coin than ever before as I don't have the costs of victualling ships at my own cost nor am I responsible for ship repairs if they are carrying my cargo. Do not fear Don Thomasino, I will watch over your docks as though they were my own and my sons I swear will follow on after I am gone. Now Don Thomasino, there is only one last thing I would like to ask of you."

Thomas nodded as he watched the son relock the chests and push them back into their places on the lower shelf.

"What would you like us to do with your share of the profits; if you wish I can have them placed under guard and carried to your Hacienda or continue to hold them here until you decide what should be done with them."

"I think for now Senor Forsca that it should all stay under your care; the situation in Spain is still a little volatile and the French are not yet beaten. If I may I will inform you about it all at a later date. Now then Senor Forsca, I think it is time for my men and I to return to our beds; tomorrow we will start our move north once again. I would like to pass on our thanks to your kind wife and sons for all they have done for us and hope that not too far in the future we can spend some more time with your kind family."

"Thank you Don Thomasino, it is little compared to what you and your men have done for Portugal."

Senor Forsca led Thomas from the vault and towards the gate where their horses were miraculously waiting for them; the youngest son was holding them all while he smiled at the important visitors. Thomas thanked the youngest son and the once again thanked Senor Forsca for his hospitality before turning his horse and leading his friends back to the Hacienda where the rest of the troops waited for them; there was still a long way to go before they would be in their new camp in the north and it was time to get moving.

Once out of the environs of Oporto, Thomas turned his troops to the east and set the horses to a trot; he hoped to make Moncorvo before the following night closed in on them. It would be a long ride and may even have to continue into the dark of the night if he wanted to make the distance in the two days he had planned. From Moncorvo he would lead his men northward through the plains of the Traz os Montes and continue the ride until they had the new camp site in view.

It was at times like these that Thomas truly began to appreciate the talents of Major Smithson; his detailed maps made it easy to know where he was at any one time and knowing the distance to the next objective could be better planned and timed almost to the hour. As guessed Thomas and his troops arrived at the outskirts of Moncorvo just before sun set on the second day.

It had been a long and hard ride and both the horses and men would need an extra day of rest to recuperate but for now time was not a problem but the need to avoid being pulled into unwanted situations with the people of Moncorvo had to be avoided at all costs.

There was a need for a good solid guard to be kept around the camp site as there was a soon a large number of the residents of Moncorvo that wanted to meet or just stand and watch the men of El Toro the Patron and saviour of Spain as they were wont to believe. Thomas only allowed a small number of his men to venture into the town itself for the purpose of buying supplies for the camp. In the early hours of the second morning Thomas once again led his men away from the town and directed their steps towards the north; the plains of Traz os Montes now beckoned them forward.

As they travelled the wide open plains, Thomas was surprised at the lack of people that they saw; there were a few small groups of farmers tending sheep or goats but little else; it was as though the whole countryside was setting in for the coming winter which Thomas and his men noticed more at night than during the day. The troops moved at a steadily but not too fast a pace; they had plenty of time and knew they were now close enough to the new camp site to not need to push themselves or their horses.

Their new camp site was a good day's ride from Braganza and to the north in a large open canyon. They had the mountains behind them which were almost impassable where they were situated and the open plains to their front gave them a good uninterrupted view for miles around. Thomas led his troops to the east of Braganza close to the border line with Leon and then turned a little west and north and made for the final stop on their long journey.

In the middle of the afternoon of the 25th of October, Thomas saw the tidy lines of tents in the distance and the small runnels of smoke drifting skyward from the early cooking fires. Spread across the front of the wide canyon mouth were the twenty guns of Major Morgan's Artillery and Thomas could just make out the smaller figures of his Infantry and gunners working hard to build small redoubt walls in front of each gun for protection.

It did not take long for the encamped army to make out the dust raised by the hooves of the horses which quickly became the familiar sight of dark uniforms and well drilled ranks coming towards them. From somewhere inside the tent camp came the sudden sound of the drums of the Originals as they struck up the Del La Guerra in honour of the arrival of their commander.

As Thomas and the mounted troops rode into the camp he saw that they had already resurrected their original old canvas tents and had them all erected in a neat and tidy order. At the centre of the camp was once again the central kitchen and mess hall and a separate six man tent had been erected for Thomas to use as his command tent close by; just outside the command tent flew the army's colours on a freshly cut flag pole.

As Thomas led the troops into the camp he saw Lorenco waiting near his command tent for him. Carmelo went with Thomas and dismounted while Estaban led the others to the rear of the campsite where the horse lines had already been prepared for them.

Fairley took Thomas and Carmelo's horses towards the rear of the camp and followed along with the others while Thomas greeted Lorenco and congratulated him on bringing all his men through unscathed; they had been at the new site for only four days but had worked hard to make it ready in time for Thomas's arrival.

For the next two days the army settled into their new home; the most important thing they would need with the soon arrival of winter was a huge amount of firewood; it was to this end that most of the men went out to begin gathering everything they could find; winter under canvas was not for the faint hearted.

While the men worked at gathering firewood, Thomas set about working on plans for their raids into French held territory and at the same time waiting for the return of Major Smithson and his small corps of map makers; they had gone off into the province of Leon to investigate what and where the French may be as well as make more maps for the new places they would see.

Over the next week the camp became more and more secure and as yet there had still not been any sign of Major Smithson's return; it was time for Thomas to take other actions. After discussions with Estaban, Lorenco and Carmelo, it was decided to send out two of the mounted Company's to scout out the land over the border and see what they could find in the way of French supply trains.

It was decided to send Pablo and Thomasino's Company's as they were the two oldest and Estaban preferred to keep the younger Diego close by. The two Companies' of Cavalry were to break up into ten man sections once they were inside French held territory. Each ten man troop would carry supplies for ten days and, once they were gone they were to make their own way back to the camp and report to Thomas and the others on what they had or had not seen.

There were strict orders that none of the smaller troops were to take any actions against the French unless they were attacked first; even then they were to fight only to escape and not stand just for the sake of revenge or glory. With the orders given, the two Companies' left the camp the following morning and once past the outer limits of Braganza they turned their faces towards the province of Leon and into Spain.

It was fully thirteen days before the first ten man troop rode into the new camp; it took Thomas only a second to see one of the riders was injured but still upright in his saddle. The rider had a rough and dirty sling holding his left arm and there was a blotch of blood near his shoulder; Thomas immediately called for Mister Jervis to look at the injured rider before he called the young Sergeant who had led the small troop to come and make his report.

Thomas led the way back to his command tent and then waited as the dust covered young Sergeant began his report.

"Don General, we were sent north towards Astorga around the base of the mountain range. We had been travelling for about four days and west of the River Elsa when we saw a supply train travelling south on the east bank so we decided to follow it. We kept our distance just as ordered and had been following for only a day when we saw a large force of guerrillas attack it from the north. As ordered we stayed well back and did not interfere but it seems the guerrilla's had another smaller force that I did not see until too late. As we had been ordered to avoid any fighting I tried to tell them that we were on the same side but the leader wanted to take our weapons and horses for himself; when I refused one of his men opened fire and wounded trooper Belas. Under fire I immediately order my men to return fire and escape back the way we had come from. Once clear of the other force I determined that we should make our way back here without delay and make my report."

"Thank you Sergeant, you did exactly the right thing; our men's lives are far more important than trying to make friends at this stage. Did the leader give you his name or anything we can use to identify him?"

"No Don General; as I said he just demanded our horses and equipment; I don't know if he was going to let us go or not but I could not take that chance."

"Very good Sergeant, take your men and get something to eat and tell them to rest; we will have to wait for the other units to return and make their report. Did you by any chance note how large the supply train was or where it may be headed?"

"I did try to make a guess at their final stop Don General but it is only my guess and the direction they were facing."

"Then tell me what you think, anything you can add may help us at some time."

"Well Don General they appeared to come from the direction of Leon and the way they were going I would say they were heading for the ford across the Elsa and then through possibly to Sahagun or even further south to as far as Medina de Rio Seca. If I was to make another guess Don General and taking into account the small number of escort they were going to some type of depot."

"Thank you again Sergeant, now go and get some well deserved rest. We can now wait to see what some of the other troops have seen or taken note of."

Thomas looked up from the table he used for the maps Major Smithson had so far made of the general area but there was none that had any detail of the area the Sergeant had talked about; once again he would have to wait for his map makers to return so he had better details. Thomas began to talk to the other three as they went over the details they so far had from the Sergeant. If there really was a large depot only a few days hard marching from where they now were then it held some hope of hitting the French hard and well behind their lines of supply, just as they had always tried to do.

The next morning provided another of the ten man patrols; they had been working in the Sahagun area which bordered the River Carrion. Their report was similar to the first in that they had also seen most of the supply trains travelling further south. From this it was assumed that the Sergeants observations of a large supply depot in the area near

Medina de Rio Seco could in fact be right, now they only had to wait for more confirmation.

The next arrivals were Major Smithson and his little gang of map makers; Thomas did not miss the bloody bandages that some of them wore, especially the one around Maketja's brow but they all seemed to be at least one or two days old. Thomas decided to wait for their report until the wounded had been seen to. Over the next two days the last of the patrols arrived back with their reports and it was only two days after the last arrival that the plans were begun.

Thomas, once he heard about the small fight that Major Smithson's men had got into was not happy about what was going on; his men were not being attacked by the French patrols but evidently by another group of Guerrillas from the north; who they may be aligned with was any bodies guess but Thomas was not happy about it. It was not long before Thomas found out why he was having trouble from another group and it was not too his liking.

Two days after the last patrol arrived back, Thomas suddenly heard a loud piercing whistle from high above the camp; it was one of Lorenco's Sharpshooters who had been placed above as a guard. The four Senior Officers looked up to where the man had been hidden among the rocks of the steep slope. It did not take long for the hand signals from the guard to indicate they had a large party riding towards the camp.

When asked by the same means, the guard indicated the group was a good three miles away but approaching fast. Lorenco signalled for the guard to come down quickly and tell everything he had seen. Thomas and the others watched as the young guard almost threw caution to the winds and came charging down the steep slope without a care for his own safety.

It was only a minute before the young guard was standing in front of them breathless but still trying to speak through his panting breath.

"Sir, riders; a large group about three miles out and coming this way. They don't look like French but they also look as though they mean business."

"Major Morgan, stand your men to the guns. Estaban take your Cavalry to just behind the guns and get them ready. Carmelo get both Companies' of Infantry ready but go to ground so you can't be seen. Lorenco can you get your Sharpshooters up high on both flanks them come back here with me; we will go out and meet them before the guns, if they try anything then we turn and run back here and let the guns do their work.

Thomas did not even flinch as he called out orders and the camp suddenly became a place of running men and boys as they got ready for whatever might come. Thomas called for the colours to be raised and flown while he waited for his horse and checked his own weapons out of habit. As soon as Lorenco had returned from giving his orders, he and Thomas mounted the waiting horses and; accompanied by a ten man guard, rode two hundred yards to the front of the guns but on the very edge of the left flank to await the oncoming riders.

Thomas glanced behind him to look at the camp; it was pleasing to see the twenty guns all manned and ready and the three hundred men of the Cavalry sitting patiently behind them. As yet Thomas did not have a full count of the men approaching his camp but he was not going to take any chances with being suddenly overrun.

It was not long before Thomas could at first hear the approaching riders and start to see the first of them begin to appear up over the gentle rise of the land. Thomas tried to do a quick count but; as more and more riders appeared he gave up but was sure there had to be more than a hundred; the numbers still favoured him at this point.

Thomas led his small party a little forward so that whoever was leading this group could see he was there to talk or was the leader of these men and wanted to speak first. The large group of newcomers first saw the small mounted group but then only seconds later spied the semi circle of heavy guns aimed in their direction. Thomas let a small smile form on his lips as he saw the riders suddenly start to slow their horses as they saw the guns for the first time.

Thomas took note of the heavy set man at the head of the group as he raised a hand and stopped the group some one hundred yards from where Thomas sat waiting; even the French would not have attempted to take the camp with so many heavy guns looking right down their throats and with a large mass of Cavalry armed and ready to charge it would have not only been foolish but deadly.

The two groups sat looking at each other; Thomas waited patiently for the other man to move first, he was not about to give up his ground or advantage by moving even further out into the open.

It took another two minutes before Thomas saw the man he assumed was the leader shrug his shoulders and call ten others to his side; once the others had joined the man they began to ride slowly towards Thomas but kept their hands well away from any weapons.

Thomas examined the man as he drew closer. He was a solidly built man with a rough beard and looked to be in his middle years, the men with him looked to be cut from the same cloth and it was evident that none of them were happy just at the moment but they seemed to acknowledge that they had little choice if they wanted to find out more about this small army that had camped near Braganza.

As the leader drew to a stop just a matter of ten yards from where Thomas and his friends waited and his own men took up a position close behind; he looked at the party now close in front. Slowly a gap toothed smile spread over the man's face as he looked at the men he had to deal with. When the man began to speak he immediately noticed the northern Castile accent which was different from his own High Catalan.

The man edged his horse a few steps closer and watched the young man as he looked Thomas up and down before speaking.

"It would seem the ghost stories might be true after all. Am I right in thinking you are the infamous Patron El Toro?"

Thomas looked the man straight in the eye as he casually placed his right hand on his hip and only inches from one of his Manton's as he just nodded without speaking.

"Then El Toro I would ask you what you and your men are doing on my lands?"

"Your Lands?"

"Yes my Lands. I am the famous Stephano Samosa; all of Castile belongs to me."

Thomas did not miss the name or the subtle hint of trouble in the man's eye as he said his name. With little reaction from Thomas, Stephano Samosa continued but this time with a little more steel in his voice.

"You do not recognise the name? I am surprised El Toro; after all it was you or some of your men that murdered my cousin but that is something we can discuss at a later time, for now I have something else to ask you about."

Again Thomas stayed silent as Stephano looked at what lay in front of him; he did not miss the fact that the gunners seemed to be holding canister shot ready at the barrels of the guns nor that the Cavalry were all holding their muskets at the ready on their thighs. The hidden Infantry was totally missed by Stephano.

"You do understand my words do you not El Toro? I was told you speak our language and yet you have no words of greeting for me; it would seem most unfriendly for one of your reputation."

"What is it you want Senor Samosa?"

"Why compensation of course. Your men made a number of attacks on my own men and I am here to collect what is owed for their deaths."

"What makes you think you are owed anything Senor?"

"As I have already said, Castile is mine; you shot some of my men and you owe us the taxes for their deaths. I will make it easy for you El Toro; you will give me ten of your guns and fifty of your horses and then we can speak more of what you owe for my cousins death at your hands."

"The reports I have had are that your men fired on mine, even after they made an offer of friendship; perhaps it would be better for you to pay me so we do not leave your bones on this valley floor."

"Ahh...El Toro, you must be gravely mistaken, my men would not fire on anyone without my say so. Perhaps it was just a stray warning shot and your men misinterpreted it."

"I have a total of seven men injured by your muskets Senor; there was no mistake on your part. Now if you have nothing further I would suggest you leave before my gunners become impatient and decide to fire a few warning shots."

"Are you making with a threat El Toro; I am here only to see justice done and am being most friendly even though I personally have lost family blood to those street urchins you call an army."

"Senor Samosa, what your brother did cost innocent lives, many of which he and his men took; his ending was a result of his own savagery. If you wish to cause a fight here then we will happily fulfil your wishes but you will get nothing from us. We are here to fight the French if you want to side with them then you also will be on our list as those who work against Spain and will be treated like any traitor."

"El Toro, I came here in friendship and all I get is hostility; I must warn you that you do not know what you are facing. If you persist in your hostile ways I will have to bring my whole army down upon your heads and that you will not survive. You may not know but I can call on two hundred and fifty of the toughest men in Spain and against your little boys it would be nothing but an hour of entertainment for them."

"Is that all you have to say Senor Samosa? If so then I would ask you to leave while you still can."

"Very good El Toro, if that is what you want then so be it; I only hope you have enough coffins to bury you all when I return. I know the French may not have been able to settle your ways but I and my men are a far different basket of fish. Until we meet again Patron El Toro, I hope you can enjoy the rest of your short life."

Thomas did not relax as he watched Samosa turn about and lead the men back to the main throng; it was not until they had disappeared totally that Thomas turned his horse back towards the camp. No one heard him swear under his breath, now he had one more enemy to watch his back for; he would have to now deal with Samosa as well as the French.

As the men stood down from the visit of the man known as Stephano Samosa, Thomas called for his three friends; they would now have to make plans to fix the new problem with the bandit. Thomas asked for the advice of all three as they sat under the small leaf of his tent. The sun was just a glimmer in the overcast sky but there was still humidity in the air.

"Patron!" Asked Carmelo. "I think it would be good idea to have someone follow Samosa and see if we can find his camp or where he holds the bulk of his army if he has such a thing."

"Yes Carmelo, I think you are right but who would be best for such a dangerous task, we need someone who knows the lay of the land but is also cunning enough to stay out of Samosa's clutches so he can get back to us and report."

"If Maketja was not injured I would suggest he go." Estaban said. "But they would only have to see his bandage or injury to know who he was; however there are two others who may be what we are looking for and have the cunning and ability to not be caught."

"And who are they Estaban?"

"Why Sergio and Carlito Patron, they are still the best we have at disappearing in plain sight and can follow any trail at any time. With Samosa having so many men with him today the trail will be easy to follow from a distance and your two sons should be safe as long as they do not close the distance during daylight hours."

Thomas thought about the suggestion and truth be told he could not think of any other way if he wanted to find Samosa's camp. Thomas looked at his three friends just in case they had anything else to say; when they stayed silent he sent word for his two young Captains to come and see him.

With the arrival of Sergio and Carlito Thomas set out what he was wanting and asked the two smiling youngsters what they thought, their answer was almost immediate.

"When shall we leave Papa; it would be best not to let them get too far in advance of us?"

"I only ask that you both take all the care you can, the man is dangerous and I want you both back here in good health. Just try to see where he is camped and how long he may stay there; winter is almost on us and he may be making plans to settle in for some time but; at the first sign of trouble you ride back here at top speed and do not wait for anything."

Both youngsters nodded and left in a hurry to get ready; Thomas sent word to the kitchen to ready same food for the pair to take with them, there was also an extra issue of powder and shot for each of the youngsters. Less than thirty minutes had passed before Sergio and Carlito were disappearing into the vastness of the plains on the trail of Stephano Samosa.

As the afternoon passed without incident, Thomas and his army used the time to get better settled for the coming winter; there was still much to be done before they could see out the bad weather in some little comfort. The plans for the large supply depot at somewhere around Medina de Rio Seco were now well underway; there was only the need to make sure of its position before they took direct action.

Three days after the two boys had left to track Samosa, Thomas sent a troop of twenty Cavalry towards the south; they were to look for the presumed depot and report back when they had something more positive, until then Thomas and his men could only sit in the camp and wait until they got word.

It was fourteen days before they finally saw two lonely, dirty and hungry youngsters riding towards the camp. They were still both dressed in peasant rags but they had their weapons at the ready as they rode closer and Thomas could see the tiredness on both faces; they had been pushing themselves hard but Thomas was glad to see them both safe once more.

During the time the two boys had been away Thomas had worried every minute and, even though he tried to hide it from the others; usually without success. He wasted no time in calling for the kitchen hands to cook something hot for the duo.

Sergio and Carlito sighed as they dismounted in front of Thomas's tent; he could immediately see how worn out they were but there was a sparkle in their eyes as they made a wide bright smile for their adopted Papa.

"We are home Papa and we have good news for you."

"Come on you two sit down here and tell me what you got up to and what you found. I have the kitchen cooking food for you now so there is a little time for you to tell all."

The two boys almost groaned as they sat on the waiting chairs; as they did so there were suddenly a large number of others beginning to surround the tent to listen to the boy's escapades.

"We have found him and his camp Papa, it was not difficult as we stayed well back so they would not see us. Samosa was in a hurry and did not watch his back trail as he should have so it was easier. Papa he is an evil man, just like his cousin was. He would raid any farm on his way for supplies and animals and leave nothing for the people; if they resisted he would kill them, it was a bad time for some." Carlito told him; it was then Sergio's turn to report some of what they had seen.

"We tracked him all the way to Miranda on the Navarre border; it is there he has his main camp and has taken over the town for his own use. On the second day after he got there we changed our clothes for some of the boys in the town and went to look closer. His powder store is in a large barn close to the only tavern but he may now have more trouble than he thought."

Thomas only had to take a glance at the smiling face of Carlito to know the two boys had been up to something they were not meant to do.

"And?" Thomas asked with a raised eyebrow.

Carlito again took up the story.

"It would seem Papa that during the fourth night a great storm came and somehow the tiles on the barn were very loose and many fell from the roof; it was such a waste to see all those barrels of powder get wet and useless, I don't know how they were all open to the rain but it would appear that the tops of the barrels had all been split open at some time and the rain wet the powder badly."

Sergio took over once again with the same wide smile as Carlito.

"The next morning the rain was still heavy and the Senor Samosa got very angry with his men when he saw the tiles lying on the ground all broken so he went into the barn and saw how all his powder was now lost; were his men of good character we may have felt sadness for the five he shot for letting the powder be destroyed; it was a very sad thing to see Papa."

Thomas did his best to keep a stern look on his face as he looked the two up and down before saying.

"I thought your orders were to only watch then come back and report; if Samosa had caught you inside his town you may even now be in small pieces to feed his pigs."

Thomas did his best to keep the forming smile off his face as the two boys looked up at him with total innocence before Sergio spoke again.

"Us Papa, what did we do but follow your very good orders; although I must admit that it was careless of us to slip on those tiles that caused the powder to be ruined but, had the rain not come then he may still have enough powder to fight you but now he will have to find some more and it would give a good Officer with many men time to destroy his badness while he has little to fire back with."

Thomas had to relent as the two boys refused to back down from their devious plan. Before Thomas could say more two of the scullery boys arrived with two plates piled high with hot food. Carlito and Sergio were eating even before the plates landed on the small table in front of them.

Thomas stood to the side as the two hungry boys shovelled the food into their mouths; most of the time swallowing without chewing first, Thomas had no idea how long it had been since the boys had last eaten but it had to be a number of days.

Thomas called for his three friends; he felt sure that he had to stop Samosa well before taking on the French Depot or he may have an enemy behind his back and his winter camp would be in danger while his other men were away. As the two boys began to slow their eating, Thomas asked them.

"So how many men do you think he has with him?"

"When we first found him he had many; we think about three hundred but it was hard to count the exact number as some went and others came. When we left there were many who looked to have left for the winter to return to their own homes until next year but he still has a large number with him; perhaps two hundred and fifty. He does not have any big guns and many of his men only have pistolas and no muskets; we counted perhaps one hundred muskets but some exchanged with others so it was hard to tell the right number."

"You both did good even if you did forget my orders for a short time but even then it is a good result, I am proud of you both so when you have finished your food you had better get some rest and change into warm clothes; tonight feels like we might have snow up in the mountains."

Thomas turned back to his three friends to ask what they thought about going after Samosa very soon and before he could get new dry powder but, before any final plans could be made they had to look over Major Smithson's maps and see what he had on that area.

It was two days before they finally had a workable plan. The plan would now depend on their ability to move quickly and unobserved as much as they could but at the same time they needed to leave their winter camp as well protected as possible; Thomas was not about to let Stephano Samosa come and attack his men while he and the others were out hunting him in Miranda.

Knowing that the man was now low on powder might just be enough reason for him to try to take everything Thomas and his army had. Thomas was not about to give him the chance.

The plan called for two Companies of Cavalry and ten of the guns to go after Samosa while the two Infantry Companies and the other Cavalry Company stayed with the last ten guns as well as the rockets of the 5th Battery. Lorenco's men would be split between the two forces, those staying at the camp would be watching from the heights while the others did what they do best and work at the van of the main body that was going to Miranda.

For the last three days the sky had been overcast and the visibility had been low even in the middle of the day. It was almost a good time to get going; for Thomas and the others, the worse the weather the less chance of being seen or caught out by anyone who might report to Samosa. There would be no wagons for supplies, everything they would need would have to be carried by the men or mules and that could mean there were going to be some hungry men by the time they wanted to return home but Thomas could see no other way around the problem.

Next day was spent preparing to move against Stephano Samosa; they would leave the camp the very next morning and ride hard to make the distance hopefully before Samosa knew they were coming. Thomas at this stage was not aware that they were in for one of the worst winters for fifty years but it would all mean his plans went far better than he thought it would.

It was still dark when the men began to form for the move to the east; every member of the troops moving east had rechecked their weapons to make sure their muskets had their leather caps on the barrels to stop the rain from making the barrels too wet to use, the covers for the hammers were also checked. The ten heavy guns were also checked and covered and the mules they were going to use to carry the extra powder and supplies were already starting to move out right behind the vanguard of Lorenco's men.

The weather had not decided to be kind and the rain swept over the ground in wavering sheets as the long column disappeared from the view of those still in the camp where Carmelo had been put in charge to make sure the camp stayed safe.

The ten guns going with Thomas had been given an extra pair of horses to pull them as the ground was going to be a thick quagmire in very short time and they had little time to wait for bogged guns to be freed.

To avoid the rough road between their camp and the outskirts of Braganza from being too badly cut up for the guns; Thomas set them at the head of the march and directly behind Lorenco's vanguard. With the mules and Cavalry following behind the guns, the column moved faster than they would have had the guns been in their usual place at the rear.

Even though the road was narrow and soon cut up badly they were able to move around Braganza under the shadow of the sweeping rain storm without being seen; their next challenge would be crossing the Esla which they hoped to get to sometime in the night hours; there were no plans to stop for nightfall as long as they had the cover of the storm.

Midnight found the column sheltering as best they could on the banks of the Esla River; with the storm still blowing it was too dangerous to attempt a crossing in the dark. The one surprise for Thomas and his men was the good condition of the road from Braganza to the banks of the Esla; it had made for easy travelling for the guns as it was well built and quite solid.

In the first light of dawn the storm had lessened and was now only a light misty drizzle. The ford was a little high but as yet was still passable by the guns. Thomas sent half of one Company of Cavalry across first as a guard and then had the guns cross as fast as they could; the extra pair of horses making the job of beating the faster flow of the current much safer and easier.

At the first sign of a somewhat watery sun poked its head above the distant mountains; Thomas turned the column further to the east and north as the dark clouds over the far off mountains threatened more rain in the not too distant future. Thomas tried not to worry too much at the bad signs; they still had the River Carrion and another tributary of the River Douro to master before they could turn even further north for the final push to Miranda and what awaited them there.

Having to scout south of Sahagun to avoid any chance of being seen; Thomas and his column now became slowed by the absence of any form of solid roadway, the small tracks were soon turned into quagmires by the fast moving guns and the hundreds of hooves; their chances of making their daily estimated distance of 70 miles a day were now cut down and so they had little option but to continue to move through most of the night hours.

Each day ended a little before midnight and, without the time to prepare hot food the camps were at best miserable but the thought of the bandit Samosa being able to take advantage of their weapons and guns drove them onward even under these trying conditions.

Two more days after crossing the Douro Thomas had turned the column even further north; he planned to cross the tributary north of Miranda and under the heights of the Asturian and Cantabrian Mountains which would then act as a safe zone on their left flank as they worked their way south and east towards their final goal.

Miranda was protected from the east by the mountains which cut down where Thomas could place his attack; during the whole trip he had had his thinking cap on as he tried to find the best way to make the man pay; one of the first things he could not do was mount a frontal assault, it would be far too dangerous and held the possibility of high losses even if Samosa was short of powder.

A further day and a night of travel in what had now become a very cold and chilling wind found Thomas and his men on the banks of the Tributary; if the measurements of Major Smithson were correct; and Thomas had little doubt that they were, then Miranda was now only two days and a full nights travel away; it was time to send an advance scout out to find a place to hide and recoup their strength before the attack.

Once a place of safety could be found to rest, Thomas and his Officers would make a final scout of the town and make the final plans for the attack once they had seen the actual ground they would be fighting on; for now they still had two days and a cold wet night of travel to get close enough for their burgeoning plans.

CHAPTER 15

It was midmorning when Thomas and the others of the column spied the advance scout waiting for them just across a small stream. The column was now as close to Miranda as they wanted to be without being noticed by any guards that Samosa may have set.

By midday it was a tired, wet and cramped column that finally stopped in a deep ravine where they would make their final camp; from here they would try to attack the home base of Senor Samosa but first they had more scouting to do on the town.

As dark approached the last of the canvas shelters was raised and the men settled down for the first hot meal in two days. The ravine was deep and narrow and afforded them good cover and an easy defence should it be needed. Miranda town was less than three hours away but with the winter weather being so contrary Thomas felt they were safe for the short time they planned to be there.

As the Senior Officers sat over the warming food they discussed what to do next; it was imperative that they had more detailed information on the town now that winter had closed in. Although Sergio and Carlito quickly volunteered for that duty, Thomas felt they had done enough and it was decided that six of Lorenco's scouts would go out to watch the town for the next two days; with luck on their side Thomas hoped to make his attack in the early hours of the third day.

For the next two days and nights, the weather stayed settled and it was only the cold wind off the mountains that caused any discomfort. Thomas was sitting in his heavy winter cloak when the six scouts returned with their final report.

From what the scouts had seen, Senor Samosa did not think he needed much of a guard at this time of year and so there were only ever two men at the southern end of town to watch the road that went from south to north. Behind the town on the northern side the road disappeared into a narrow pass that was just wide enough for two wagons to pass but was bounded by high steep sides.

Two of the scouts had ventured into the pass to look it over; it appeared to be the only way for Samosa and his men to escape if Thomas attacked from the south. To the east and west were low ridges that gave the town an appearance of being nestled in a shallow bowl. For Thomas and his men there was only one problem that they had to work on; if Samosa and most of his men escaped to the north then Thomas's army would still be under the threat of attack at a later date.

The men's report told Thomas that it appeared that Samosa and his men had full control over the town; most of the outer homes seemed to be empty of any life and only the very centre around the church and the municipal building were in use along with some of the closer houses and shops. All appeared to be used for accommodation for Samosa's men.

In the evenings the central square was where they all congregated to eat and party into the late hours of every night; the general feeling seemed to be that they were safe from any form of attack and especially more now that winter had moved in. It was the northern escape route that worried Thomas the most; after listening to a detailed and vivid description by the two scouts that had looked the pass over; Thomas decided on a bold move.

Thomas called for Major Carterton who was both Colour Commander as well as Engineer; he had something special for him to do. After a short discussion the plan to stop the escape of Samosa and his men was finalised and the preparations were begun. In the early hours of the evening, Thomas went over the plan for a last time.

Craven Morgan would set two batteries of five guns, one on top of the rise to the east and the other on the rise to the west and they would open fire in the early hours of the morning while the men below were still in their beds. Major Carterton and his men along with six extra scouts would lead two mules with four kegs of powder into the pass while it was still dark and find a place where they could blow the steep sides of the pass to cause a blockage so there could be no escape for the men in the town when the guns opened up.

Thomas and Estaban would form up the two companies of Cavalry in four ranks one behind the other across the road to the south, when Samosa and his men came out of the town they would be met by a force of two hundred mounted and well armed Cavalry; with the double barrelled muskets the Cavalry would present four hundred loaded barrels at the towns force.

Thomas now knew that a number of men had left the town for the winter; the scouts had said there appeared to be about thirty men that left with large packs and they turned to the north. The guns would open up on Thomas's command in the very early hours and the signal would be the explosion from the pass to the north. The guns would have to be set up in the dark of night and as quietly as possible; Craven Morgan would have to judge his range as best he could through Thomas's spy glass and his own dead reckoning.

Craven had decided to set his guns only six hundred yards from the edge of town; in the darkness they would remain unseen but he had his men cover anything that may rattle or squeak so that they could not be heard in the night. Every man's powder was checked as was that of the guns; the wax paper they used for their cartridges made it far easier than the old fashioned idea of powder horn and separate shot. For those few that found damp powder they soon set about replacing it as the night moved in and the camp made ready to move slowly and quietly into position.

The first to leave were the small party of men that made up the force under Major Carterton. It was barely dark when they left and they hoped to have their charges laid before the middle hours of the night. Two hours after Major Carterton had left; Major Craven Morgan left with his guns. While Craven Morgan had to move much slower than he liked, it was the only way to keep any stray noise to a minimum in the silence of the night. Thomas and Estaban followed only minutes later and they kept their horses off the road and on the softer ground along the verges.

Midnight found Craven and Thomas's forces settled into their positions; the heavy guns had had to be manhandled up the small rises in the dark as the horses only slipped on the wet sloping ground. Thomas and Estaban sat their horses huddled in their heavy winter cloaks as they waited for the signal from the north; there was little doubt in anyone's mind that they would hear the explosion; four kegs of powder made a lot of noise in the silence of the night and the narrow pass would channel the sound directly towards them.

Major Carterton and his small force were forced to swing wide of Miranda and tuck in close to the mountains so they could pass by without being seen. While it added a little more mileage to their mission it also gave them far better footing than travelling further out on the softer plains and with only two mules there was little chance of cutting up the ground until it was impassable.

As they moved through the darkness, Major Carterton and his small party could hear the sounds of revelry from the far off town; it was almost comforting as they knew it meant there was little chance of being seen as they moved towards and then into the pass.

Major Carterton led his party deeper into the dark pass as he looked for a suitable place to set his charges. They had travelled about a half mile into the pass and just turned a bend in the rough road when Major Carterton saw what he was looking for. The bend had caused the road to narrow and the sides were steep and covered in what appeared to be scree and small scrub trees. There were a large number of big rocks that appeared to be finely balanced and it was only their size and weight that kept them in place; this was the place he had been looking for.

It did not take many words to get the men working as he pointed out where he wanted the four charges laid and where they would be most advantageous for what they had planned. Three of the men were sent back around the bend to keep watch as the others set to work with spades and bars to create a hole large enough to set the four kegs in.

Two were set on the east side of the pass where it was hoped they would cause a major fall of loose scree and larger rocks. The other two kegs were to be set under a large overhang that protruded out over the road; if he managed to blow the overhang then the pass would be blocked for a long time to come. The digging and setting of the charges took three hours before Major Carterton was happy with the results and the last keg was pushed into place and covered with the loose stones and gravel that had been removed to make the hole.

Major Carterton sent all but one of the men back around the bend; he and the other man would lay the fuse and set it alight before running for cover with the others; they would not wait to see if the charges did their job but instead make a hasty retreat into the night and head back towards where the rest of the army waited.

Thomas sat his horse beside that of Estaban and waited for the sound that would tell them Major Carterton had been successful. The revelry in the town had died down and now there were only the occasional flickering torch in the square to indicate that there had been people around earlier. Craven Morgan had welcomed the party in the town as it gave him plenty of light to range all his guns; he was confident that he could now wreck havoc even when darkness shrouded the centre and square.

Thomas raised his spy glass and took another look into the gloom; he could just barely make out the two huddled figures in their cloaks as they tried to keep the chill of the night off them while they stood on guard in a doorway on the edge of the town.

Thomas thought it was about two hours until dawn when he heard the rumbling sound of the explosions in the pass to the north of Miranda. Had no one known what had caused it the rumbling could easily be mistaken for the sound of thunder off in the distant mountains; for Thomas and the others it was the sound they had been waiting for and it was less than a minute before another rumbling sound filled the early morning air.

Thomas was still watching the hunched men at the edge of town when Craven's guns opened up with the first salvo of the five guns from the eastern rise; it was only seconds later when the five on the west also opened up. The darkness of the night was split asunder as the bright flashes and whistling cannon balls filled the morning air. Thomas watched as the two man guard jumped to their feet and looked to the east only to be surprised once again as the five guns were answered in kind from the west.

As Thomas knew it would, Craven Morgan's shot landed in the centre of the town and began to wreck havoc as the balls crashed and careened in to and along the cobble stone streets; the small fountain at the centre of the square was the first thing to succumb to the hot cannon balls and was soon followed by the walls of buildings and showers of roof tiles.

Craven's guns kept up a steady barrage of shot as the sleeping men in the town tried to find cover from the sudden and deadly attack; those who had over-indulged the night before paid with their lives as they were trapped inside the houses they had taken over as their own. The two men on guard had stood in shock as the second salvo crashed into the town before they both took to their heels to find cover.

Thomas and Estaban led their four ranks of waiting Cavalry forward under the guns above them and then took up a station about three hundred yards from the southern exit of the town, the front rank taking the extra time to once again check their muskets and pistols, all of which had been double charged for what was soon to come.

From inside the town Thomas and his Cavalry could hear the sounds of fear and the even louder sound of someone trying to restore some sort of order as more shot landed in amongst them and the town now began to take on a look of a major battle site as more houses and buildings crumbled under the force of the cannon balls that seemed endless for those still inside the town.

Many fires had been started and the town was now lit as though in daylight; shadowy figures could be seen running for their lives as the buildings crumbled around them and the screams of the wounded filled the air. Thomas was startled when Estaban called for him to look ahead, Thomas had been sweeping his spy glass to the west when the call came.

As he looked back to the southern exit of the town, Thomas saw a large group of men trying to form some sort of ranks and were definitely turned in their direction; they were close enough to be seen from the burning town and it appeared that they would be set on a course of revenge for the sudden and bloody attack.

The man at the head of the enemy riders was not hard to guess; his large bulk and distant angry words left little to guess work; it was Stephano Samosa himself. Thomas and Estaban called their men to the ready even as the guns of Craven Morgan continued to pound the town below them, the many fires now making it easier to range their guns in the now dawning light.

Thomas did not see the sudden arrival of Major Carterton and his small party as they had moved to take a position behind the guns on the western rise and had been covered by the last of the darkness before Stephano appeared and tried to organise his men for an attack on Thomas's four ranks of waiting Cavalry. Thomas had to guess at the numbers that faced him but he knew it could not be more than a hundred men; most of which were on foot and many of them seemed to be without muskets as he looked them over with his spy glass.

Estaban took over the ranks and, in no uncertain terms; told Thomas to stand by the fourth rank and not in the front line as he so desperately wanted to do. Estaban's look brooked no argument and Thomas had to pull his horse back to the fourth rank; his swear words did not go unnoticed by those close to him and many broke out into smiles as he rode back grumbling about his place in the line.

The unruly gang of men led by Stephano Samosa looked to be exactly what they were; disorganised, unruly and thinking only of escape from the continuous pounding of the guns on the two hill tops. Stephano Samosa did his best to get a little order in his men and had not as yet seen the full extent of the numbers he was facing in the dim grey light of dawn.

Estaban gave the order to move forward as the rabble in front of them tried to find and escape route away from the guns. It was not until a pause in the cannon fire that Samosa heard the approaching sound of many hooves coming from the dimness and the vague dark shapes of well drilled Cavalry moving in four straight ranks towards him and his men.

The intent of the oncoming Cavalry was plainly obvious as he saw them break into a trot and the now more visible front rank rise in their saddles and lift a musket to their chests in readiness to lift them further to their shoulders as they broke into a canter. The black clothed Cavalry was now less than one hundred and fifty yards away and Samosa was trying his best to call his men to some sort of order.

Samosa and about thirty of his men were the only ones mounted on horses but they were no competition for the well drilled ranks coming towards them at a fast pace. Before the Cavalry even got within firing range a large number of Samosa's men on foot began to break back towards the town in something of a panic, they had never faced such a well drilled force before and to stay and try to fight two hundred well drilled and mounted troops was almost certain death.

Stephano Samosa knew that he was in a hopeless position as the first rank of charging Cavalry raised their muskets to their shoulders and fired the first volley as they galloped closer; it was only a few seconds later when the second barrel was fired again in volley and Stephano knew he could not stay and hold his ground. As the first rank divided at the centre and rode to the east and west, the second rank which was only fifty yards behind now came into full view.

Stephano did not wait to see what had happened after the first two volleys and spun his horse back towards the town even though the guns above were still firing down on them; there was only one way out of the killing flied and that was to ride as hard and fast as he could for the northern pass and escape back into Navarre, around him the ground was already showing the dark patches of blood and the writhing bodies of the wounded and yet the riders still came on without pause.

Even in his haste to get away, Stephano Samosa had to begrudgingly admire the discipline and well drilled ranks that thundered down on him and his men. Every horse somehow kept its place in the straight line even though they were no longer under the control of the reins and only the leg pressure of the riders was being used to direct them. A sudden flash of insight caught Stephano by surprise as the thought of what he could have achieved with such a well drilled force but for now his own life was paramount.

Stephano spun his horse and kicked it into a gallop; he was quickly joined by what was left of his mounted men which number about twenty five. For those on foot there was little escape and the second rank of Cavalry opened fire on those trying to run for their lives back into the town.

From his place beside Diego on the end of the fourth rank, Thomas saw the whole debacle of Stephano's men running for cover, many of those who had tried to return fire found that there muskets either misfired because of damp powder or fired wide of the moving targets that were galloping down on them. The first rank under the orders of Estaban, had now ridden wide on both sides of the town, the second rank under Pablo's orders spun left and right to join his cousin as they reloaded and Thomasino led the third rank forward.

By the time Thomasino had taken his place as the front rank there were no targets left for him, those of Samosa's men that had escaped the vicious volleys of the first two ranks were now running for their lives through the town even as more cannon shot landed among them.

From his high point above the town, Craven Morgan saw the broken lines of Samosa's men take to their heels in an attempt to escape the early morning mayhem; it was time to stop firing and get his guns off the rise and rejoin his General down on the plain for more orders. Craven lifted a small red flag and waved it back and forth as a signal for the other battery to also cease fire and hook up their guns and return to the plain in front of the town.

It was plainly obvious in the stronger morning light that Stephano Samosa and his men were trying to make a break for the pass and there was no attempt to defend the town; their only concern was for their own safety and that meant immediate escape to the north.

Thomas pulled his sweating horse to a halt just inside the now empty town; the air was full of dense smoke both from the burning shops and houses as well as the heavy sharp tang of powder. The air was filled with dust and he could still hear cries from the wounded and trapped inside the town. Thomas was quickly surrounded by Thomasino and Diego's men as they stopped on the very outskirts of the now broken town; Estaban and Pablo were covering the east and western sides but made no attempt to follow the fast retreating men towards the pass.

The first dim streaks of the dawn light found the town silent except for the sound of crackling fires and moans of those wounded in the cannon salvoes or crushed under the walls or roofs of the buildings that had been devastated by the continuous barrage.

Thomas waited for the Officers to join him just inside the town; once the guns had come down from the rise to the east and west he would formulate the last of his plan to rid the country of Stephano Samosa. There was no feeling of guilt for his actions as he was sure in his own mind that the man Samosa would have done even worse to him and his men had he had the chance to attack Thomas's camp first.

Thomas called for Major Carterton to join him so he could get a report on the conditions in the pass; as yet he had not heard whether the blocking of the pass had been successful or not or if it would contain Stephano Samosa while Thomas and his men got ready for the final fight.

Once Thomas had heard what Major Carterton had to say and the probably result of the explosion, Thomas called the others for ideas before finally giving the orders to make for the entrance to the pass. Once there he would have his men stop at the entrance and call for Stephano Samos to surrender; Craven Morgan would arrange his ten guns at the entrance and wait to see what happened.

Lorenco offered to take his men into the town and look for any that remained and then rejoin Thomas at the pass; they did not want anyone to their rear that could cause problems while trying to get Samosa out of the pass.

An hour later and Thomas's men were ready; his Cavalry had remained mounted but about one hundred yards back from the entrance into the pass. Carven Morgan had arranged his guns less than fifty yards from the opening and was being instructed by Major Carterton where the best place to aim them for maximum effect should Samosa refuse to surrender.

The plan was simple, Thomas would call for Samosa's surrender and if it was refused he would let Craven use his guns to fire as high up into the walls of the pass in the hope of causing even more slips; as a last resort he would use canister above the narrow road of the pass to rain down on any who thought they could hide away in the rocks and scrub that abounded the sides of the pass.

Thomas used his spy glass to look down the length of the pass before he went a little close to call out to Stephano; ten of the Cavalry riders were close by his side as he stopped his horse just fifty yards from the entrance and less than fifty yards in front of Craven's guns. There was little sign of Samosa or his men in the pass but that did not mean he was not watching what was going on from some place of hiding.

As he sat watching the pass, Thomas could occasionally hear the faint echo of a shot from the town behind him; he pushed any thoughts of what it might mean to the back of his mind, what lay ahead at the moment was far more important.

"Stephano Samosa, I am calling for you to surrender to us; if you do so then I will guarantee that you will be heard and then your fate decided; if you refuse to come out now then I will take all and any actions I see fit to end your bandit raids on the innocents of Spain."

Thomas sat and waited for a reply; he just knew the man had to be hiding in the pass and could not escape; or hopefully not escape. Thomas waited for another few minutes without a reply from the pass; as a last effort he called one more time.

"Time is running out Samosa; come out or I will open fire."

Thomas had barely finished when he saw several puffs of powder smoke from further along the pass; it was a reflex action that made him duck just as something whistled by above his head; he had his answer.

Thomas turned his horse and led his guard back behind Craven's guns before turning his horse and calling out.

"Mister Morgan, your guns can open fire. When you are satisfied with solid shot then change to canister; I want that pass to look like a tilled field when you are done."

Craven saluted and then called for his gunners to prepare to fire. Within a minute the sound of ten guns opening fire crashed and reverberated down the pass and out into the open plain. When the first of the powder smoke cleared and while the gunners were reloading for the next salvo, Thomas looked into the pass to see large gouts of stones and rocks erupt skyward as the heavy shot drove into the walls of the pass less than five hundred yards away.

As stones and rocks rained down into the pass and clouds of dust rose in the sky; Thomas saw a small part of the left bank of the pass begin to crumble and then slide down onto the road; he was also sure he saw at least one body amongst the rubble as it slid downward.

The second shattering salvo filled the pass with more sound, smoke and dust as the ten reports echoed in the early morning stillness; Thomas was sure there would be little to survive the pounding that Craven Morgan was sending into the confines of the pass. The third salvo did even more damage to the pass and then Craven called for a change to canister.

While his first three salvoes had been aimed to where the bend in the road disappeared down the pass, his canister was going to be fired as high as he could raise his guns; the extra height would see some of the canisters fly past the bend and explode high in the air; anyone below was in for a torrid time. Just as the first salvo of canister was fired into the pass; those watching saw a mass of horses come galloping towards them in what appeared to be utter fear; there were no riders and the horses were running wild as they swept past the line of heavy guns and out into the freedom of the plains.

Thomas was watching the effects of the bombardment standing beside Craven Morgan; he had his spy glass to his eye as the first salvo of canister exploded high above the road of the pass. Even from his place a good five hundred yards from the explosions he could still hear the whistling balls of the canister as they ricocheted off rocks and blasted down on anyone that could be hiding below.

Before the second barrage of canister could be fired, Thomas saw what looked to be a white rag or shirt tied to the barrel of a musket being waved back and forth from behind a large boulder near the bend in the road. Thomas called for a halt to the barrage and then, along with his ten man guard rode forward and called out to the flag waver.

"Come out now or I will continue to fire."
Thomas waited and watched and it did not take long before a number of very frightened men began to appear through the settling dust; some walked under their own steam but others were being held by their friends as they had received wounds from the canister and shot. Thomas watched as fifteen broken men struggled towards him through the large boulders and masses of small stones and rocks that now littered the bottom of the pass. There was no sign of Stephano Samosa.

Estaban moved one rank of Cavalry closer to the opening to cover the approaching men and keep his General safe just in case one of the men had ideas of taking advantage of the situation. Slowly the small group of men struggled and limped their way forward until they were standing only yards away from the black clad forces waiting for them. Thomas looked down at what appeared to be thoroughly demoralised and beaten men; looking at the man carrying the musket with the white rag flag, he asked.

"Where is Samosa?"

"He is dying further back in the pass; he tried to escape by climbing the blockage but was caught when those last shots exploded. I don't think he will last much longer. What do you want of us Senor El Toro?"

"Give up all of your weapons and wait here under guard until I return, if you cause no trouble while I look for Samosa then you will be released to return to your homes but, if I catch any of you anytime in the future you will not walk away. Now give up any weapons you have, including knives and wait here until I return."

Thomas watched as the few survivors removed all of their weapons and then sat off to the side with Pablo and his men watching them like hawks. Thomas and his ten guards rode on towards the pass to try and find Samosa and make sure the man was not just trying to escape over the blockage in the pass while his men surrendered.

Thomas and his guard slowly made their way through the rubble that now covered the road and occasionally had to ride around a particularly large boulder that had been loosened from the side of the pass. After riding around the bend in the road, Thomas and his guards saw the devastation that Major Carterton's powder kegs had created.

The pass would not be used for a long time to come as a large part of the walls had collapsed and completely blocked the pass from top to bottom; it was a loose dam rising almost sixty feet in the air and contained boulders that must have almost been the size of a small house and interspersed with the larger boulders were huge rocks and a mass or finer rubble.

Thomas estimated that the pass would not be used for any trade for some time to come and that any thought the French may have had to transport their supplies via this pass were now long over. As they pulled their horses to a halt, Thomas saw three figures lying only yards above the bottom of the pass; two were obviously dead as there was little left of them after what must have been a very close, if not direct hit by the canister shot.

Below the two bodies was the bloody figure of Stephano Samosa; his chest was covered in fresh blood, his left arm hung uselessly and his left leg was almost unrecognisable as a limb. Stephano Samosa was just barely conscious as Thomas dismounted and slowly worked his way up to the dying man; his right hand always close to the Manton pistol at his back.

Thomas stood above the dying man and looked into the pain filled eyes; even though Samosa must have known he was dying he still held Thomas's look with a glare of what could only be called, hatred. Even as Thomas watched Samosa tried to lift the pistol in his right hand and aim it at his nemesis El Toro; the foreign boy who had somehow become the Hero of Spain.

Thomas stood unflinching as he watched Stephano Samosa try to lift the pistol but his serious injuries had taken all the strength from his one remaining hand and he coughed as blood formed on his spittle covered lips when he tried to speak.

"Is this what you wanted, to see the end of our family line. Does your revenge reach so far that you must kill all of the Samosa family?"

"Senor Samosa, had you not made your demands when we first met there would have been no today. This is what you brought down upon your own head and was not my wish, just as your cousin made his own decisions and had to pay the price for his demands. My men and I are here to try to defeat the French; we never wanted to fight those who could have helped to rid Spain and Portugal of the French."

"Your words are nothing more than platitudes; I know you foreigners, you just want what is ours and you think you can do it by killing off anyone who opposes you." Stephano coughed up more blood as he made his accusations but Thomas found he could hold little pity for the man, regardless of the words Samosa spoke his actions had already told Thomas the true nature of the man's heart.

Thomas stood and watched as Samosa was again wracked by a heavy coughing fit and then it was only seconds before the blood covered man's head dropped back onto the stones and a last sigh escaped his bloody lips. Stephano Samosa was dead and somehow Thomas felt little for the man that had chosen to take the path of a bandit when he could have had the people of Spain behind him had he chosen to stand against their enemies.

Thomas took a last look before turning around and making his careful way back to his waiting guards; there was work to do and the French were waiting for his personal attention.

On returning to where the fifteen prisoners were waiting, Thomas issued orders for the survivors to leave for other parts of the country; his final warning about seeing any of them again was reinforced and then he sat with his men as they watched the remnants of Stephano Samosa's band limp and stumble their way towards some unknown place. What their fate was did not concern Thomas or his men, they had much more important things to think of; the least of them the possibility of a new French Supply Depot somewhere in the south.

The long road back to their camp was a little more leisurely although everyone still kept their eye and senses alert for any possible danger. The weather was now into full winter and where they had once been able to make good time now became an almost daily battle to make headway. After leaving Miranda to the vagaries of the war and battling fourteen days of bad roads, weather and conditions, Thomas and his tired and dirty column finally came in sight of their camp.

It was almost as though the whole column sighed with relief all at the same time as those who had stayed in camp came out to greet them back to their temporary home. In all the time he had been away from the camp, Thomas had not thought except in passing about his scouts that were sent to the south; as he stepped from his horse he saw one of the young men waiting for him so he could report their observations.

The young man took one look at the condition of the new arrivals and called out that he would tend his report in the morning. For that small gesture Thomas could only smile; he and the returnees were in no real condition to listen or make plans until they had rested and eaten a decent meal which would have been the first full hot meal in over six days.

Thomas awoke the next morning to not only find he was still fully dressed but to the sound of heavy hail on his tent. As Thomas tried to move so he could get redressed in fresh clothes he suddenly felt the pull in his left shoulder. His wound while healed, still reminded him that when the weather was cold and damp he should take better care of himself.

Thomas rubbed his shoulder as he swung his legs over the side of the bed, the thought of having to strip down while outside the wind blew the cold mountain air through the flap of the tent took away any chance of him smiling to greet the new day.

Somehow Fairley seemed to know that Thomas was awake and up as he pushed aside the flapping tent flap and came in with a large bowl of steaming water for Thomas to wash in. Thomas could still smell the old sweat and dirt that covered his body as Fairley placed the bowl of hot water on the small table at the centre of the tent; Fairley then stood back and waited for his General to strip off the worn and dirty clothes so he could take them away to somehow clean them.

Thomas almost groaned as he stripped the filthy clothes from his still aching body until he was standing in the cold air only in his underclothes; they too would have to be replaced by clean ones once Fairley had found them in the only clothes chest that Thomas had brought with him.

Thomas did not think of the embarrassment as he slipped off the dirty underclothes, the goose bumps quickly forming on his skin from the cold only made him move faster as Fairley quietly left the tent so Thomas could get clean and change into fresh clothes in peace.

A half hour later and Thomas was starting to feel more like his old self, the fresh smell of soap and clean clothes brought a smile to his lips as he placed his battered old black hat on his head and made ready to greet a new day. The hail had finally stopped and now there was just the cold wind to contend with but it was easily solved with the use of his heavy winter cloak; it was time to get back to business.

The camp was slowly coming to life as Thomas stepped from his tent to see all the cooking fires doing their best to throw out heat in the cold wind and cook the large amount of food needed to keep his small army moving. It was a welcome relief when he finally sat at the table as his other Officers began to show up for breakfast, there were plans to make and reports to listen to.

With breakfast over and most of the men and boys looking to their equipment, Thomas asked for the scout to report what he had seen to the south.

"So what did you find for us Sergeant?"

"We found their depot Sir but I think it's a lost cause if you wanted to try to attack them. It's very well defended by some thirty heavy guns and well constructed barricades, there are also three companies of Chasseurs and at least a full Regiment of Infantry camped close by but it does look like one of their largest depots that we have ever seen."

"Where is it exactly?"

"It's placed south of Lerma and bordered on two sides by the mountains, the plain to the north is wide open and I would say almost impossible for us to attack without having large losses. I'm afraid Sir that this is one we can't get at, not without huge losses."

"Did you happen to notice where their supplies were coming from or have we closed off their supplies with closing the pass at Miranda?"

"We watched for any supply trains and those we saw all seemed to come through the mountain passes to the north east via Burgos or possibly even further east. I think the closing of the pass at Miranda will make the French have to use the roads across the Ebro and through Logrono. We ventured into Navarre for a short distance and most of their roads were carrying supplies but they were having trouble with the weather and conditions so I think it will be slow going until the summer is here."

"Thank you Sergeant, you and your men go and get some more rest while I think this one over."

The young Sergeant saluted and left the Officers to their planning, there was still his equipment and horse to tend to. Thomas turned to the others and raised an eyebrow in inquiry for some suggestions as to what they should now do. With the depot so well defended it was obviously a foolhardy gesture to try to attack it, there had to be something else they could do to harry the French over the winter months.

The time seemed to pass quickly as the men discussed and then rejected plan after plan until it was time for lunch, again it was the kitchen boys that lifted the spirits of the small army with their efforts to keep them all well fed during the cold damp months of winter.

During lunch Thomas decided to call a general meeting of all the men; he wanted new ideas on how to attack the French and thought, as he had previously, that his men often came up with ways and ideas the Officers had not thought of.

Thomas sent word that there would be a general meeting before dinner that evening and that he wanted all the men to put their thinking caps on to see what they could come up with to make the French pay.

It had already been noticed and decided that the biggest burden the army had was movement. With the winter storms and bad road conditions it was at times almost impossible to move in any numbers and the distances they were capable of moving were now cut down to less than half in a day's journey and that was not always an easy journey.

The mainstay for Thomas's army was its mobility and the wet and often muddy roads lost them that advantage and so now they had to be twice as careful about what and where they formed and attack. There was no denying that the large depot posed a tempting target but Thomas was not about to make his men stand as they had in the valley before Albuera and suffer as they all had that day.

Late in the afternoon as the sun tried to push its watery light through the thinning cloud cover; Thomas stood and watched as all his men began to assemble for the meeting, he was thankful that the wind had eased and at the moment there was little sign of more rain. The men found semi dry rocks or just squatted as best they could in some dry place as they formed a large circle around Thomas and his Officers.

At times like these, when it was a General meeting there were no ranks; each and every man could have his say no matter what it was and all were accorded the respect of being heard fully before others raised questions or gave their own opinions. Once they all knew the full reason for the general meeting the ideas started to form and be made known to those listening.

It was almost dusk before the meeting came to an end and the general consensus was for more patrols to go out and see what could be found that did not entail a large force to be moved through the winter conditions. Thomas had divulged to the men that the opinion of Prince Pimentel was that the English would probably attack towards Burgos in the spring and it was then agreed they should perhaps look more to the north than the south for their targets.

By the end of the meeting it was finally decided that the idea of more patrols to the north would be more to their advantage and to this end new plans were going to be drawn up as there were still several more passes leading through the Asturian and Cantabrian mountains that they may be able to use for their raids on the French.

Leaving the heavily defended south to the vagaries of winter and the possibility of an English attack in the spring seemed a better and safer idea for the small army; it was now time for more detailed plans and patrols to be made and then any final decisions would be taken. The meeting adjourned just as the evening cooking fires sent out their smells of fresh food and the men went off to look for their plates; even the weather seemed to have decided to play nice as the once overcast sky suddenly cleared and the first stars of the night began to show in the darkening sky.

CHAPTER 16

Thomas awoke to a feeling of something being not quite right; as he sat on the edge of his cot it suddenly dawned on him what it was, there was no sound of the wind that had blown almost continuously ever since they had arrived at the new camp. The previous night he had felt the cold more than normal and; as he stepped outside his tent he felt the crisp crunch of frost under his boots.

Above the sky was cloudless for the first time since arriving and the morning stillness was almost unsettling. As he looked around the camp he saw his men starting to emerge from their own tents and look around in wonder at the clean clear skies above. It was now mid December and the last two months of continuous storms, rain and wind had taken their toll on the camp and the men in it.

For the first time in months Thomas heard the trilling of birds in the hills behind them, it was almost as though spring had arrived early. For the men of El Toro's army the clear sky and bright sunlight which was becoming stronger by the minute; gave them some hope of getting laundry done and drying out the muddy ground that had become the norm for the camp.

From the camp kitchens came laughter as even the scullery boys seemed to take a fresh heart from the bright new day. The large marquee that was the camp mess had taken a hard beating in the last storm and they had to strip down one of the smaller tents and cut it where needed to make patches for repairs and to replace three of the heavy poles with branches cut from trees further up the sides of the ridge above them.

The last of the scouts had returned the previous evening and there was now hope that they could work on some plans for the return to upsetting the French in one form or another. To the north the reports had told them that they had seen smaller French supply trains trying to get through the smaller and less well known passes; it was these Thomas and his men thought of attacking.

In supply quantity it would be small but any disruption was to their advantage and would cause the French to use more troops to guard them. With the pass at Miranda now shut off completely and a coming threat of English attacks in the north, the French did not have a lot of options to use; anything that caused them problems would be in the allies' best interests.

For four more days the weather stayed calm and even warm during the middle part of the day although the nights were cold and crisp. Long ropes were strung all over the camp and the sight of washed clothes drying in the bright sun made the camp look more like a laundry than a military camp. Weapons and equipment were checked and then double checked, the blustery storms that had swept the camp over the last two months had made it difficult to keep personal items and equipment in good order.

On the fifth day of fine calm weather, one of the outer guards came running towards where Thomas sat with Estaban, Carmelo and Lorenco as they sipped their early morning cafe in the first warming rays of the rising sun.

The young Portuguese teen slid to a halt and; after saluting and with a panting voice said.

"Patron, there are men approaching in force, they are yet some way off but they are definitely coming this way."

"Did you see who they might be?"

"I am not sure Patron; the distance is yet a little too great but soon we will know more."

"How many do you think they are?"

"Perhaps fifty Patron."

Thomas reached behind him and took up his large spy glass from where it lay on top of a trunk.

"Here take this and see what you can then come back and tell me."

The young teen saluted once more and ran off with the spy glass grasped firmly in his hand, Thomas turned to Carmelo.

"I think you had better call out the first company and form them up in ranks; also ask Major Morgan to have his guns readied for canister shot just in case we need him."

Carmelo nodded as he rose and trotted off towards the Infantry tents to call the 1st Company to ranks. Thomas and the other two rose and went off to their tents to arm themselves so they were ready for anything that may occur. The rest of the camp did not need much time at all to realise something untoward was going on and the rest of the men could soon be seen also donning their weapons and looking for orders.

Finally, as Thomas moved quickly towards the inner ring of guns, he saw the young teen guard returning at a run with Thomas's spy glass held firmly in one hand while the other was wrapped around the butt of his shouldered musket. The teen stopped and saluted once again as he breathlessly began to give his report.

"Patron, the men I have not seen before but they move very much like we do on a long march. Through your fine glass I could see they wore uniforms of a strange colour that again I have not seen. We are not sure if they are French Patron, what should we do?"

"What colour are their uniforms?"

"It is a dark colour but they are very dirty and some of the men do not wear uniforms but the clothes of farmers and villagers."

"Very good, go back and call the picket guards to come back into the camp, we will wait for them behind the guns."

The teen saluted and, after giving Thomas the spy glass back; once again took off running to call in the guards from the outer ring. Thomas was not sure who he was about to face but the fact that these newcomers seemed to be aware of their location did raise some doubts in his mind as to whom they may be.

Thomas looked out onto the plain for the first sight of the oncoming force; before he lifted his spy glass for a closer look he decided to call all of the men to station. Carmelo took over and gave the order for the 2nd Company of Infantry to form up beside the three ranks already standing at the ready behind the guns. Estaban had already called all his Cavalry to mount and take a position at either end of the Infantry ranks.

As Thomas lifted the spy glass to his eye he heard Major Morgan call out the range for his guns and for the gunners to ready canister. Thomas moved his spy glass back and forth until he had the far off black dots centred in his glass. As he watched the far off shapes move towards his position they began to appear larger and he could now see how they were moving; it did not take long for him to smile as he removed the spy glass from his eye and turned to Carmelo.

"Where is Lieutenant Morgan?"

"He's just bringing up his men from the kitchen to stand in the line with the Infantry Patron."

"When he gets closer call for him to come and see me; you can tell the men to stand at ease and send word to Estaban to take his men back to the horse lines, they won't be needed today."

"So you know who they are Patron?"

"Yes Carmelo, there's only one other force that moves like us; it would appear Mister Grey and O'Rourke have found us; how they knew we were here we will have to wait to find out."

Carmelo left Thomas and began to shout orders for the men to stand down, Thomas waited until Snot Morgan was standing before him before issuing his orders.

"Lieutenant Morgan I want you to organise your men to set all the cauldrons on the fires with water for heating, next get the kitchen working and set two of the lambs and two of the goats on the spits for roasting; I'll leave the rest up to you but you will need food and drink for at least fifty visitors but I'm sure they will enjoy some hot water before they eat."

Snot Morgan snapped to attention with a cheeky smile on his face as he saluted and then ran off back towards his private domain of the kitchens; his men and boys had work to do. Thomas stood and watched as the rapidly closing force came nearer, he could now see them plainly and, as his own men had gone through the winter under the same conditions he felt for them as he saw their condition.

It seemed to take forever for the force to come closer; Thomas could now easily make out the two prominent figures of Mister Grey and O'Rourke as they chivvied the men along with the usual rough words used by the leaders of such forces.

Thomas stood immobile as he heard the loud rough voice of O'Rourke swearing at the efforts of the tired and dirty men in his charge; his broad Irish accent getting thicker as he swore louder with each command as he ran on the left of the column with Mister Grey on the right.

As the tired men drew closer to where Thomas and the others stood waiting; Thomas heard Mister Grey order the men to straighten up and better form their column; they were to show the waiting Officers that they were fighting men of Grey's Rangers.

Finally the column had made it to within yards of where Thomas stood waiting with a wide smile of greeting on his face; the return smile of O'Rourke and a thinner smile from Mister Grey said it all as the Column was ordered to halt and stand at attention.

The men were panting and the black rings around their eyes told of the strain they had been under. The dirty uniforms that had once been dark green now looked not much better than rough rags as they tried their best to hold their places. Colonel Grey and the newly promoted Sergeant Major O'Rourke left the men to step closer to Thomas as they also snapped to attention but both had a smile on their faces as Colonel Grey spoke first.

"General Toro, the men of Grey's Rangers request permission to encamp with your forces and I carry messages for your perusal Sir."

Thomas did the best he could to stop from laughing out loud as he heard the request from one of his oldest friends and to hear it put in such a formal manner almost had him giggling out loud but he pulled himself together and took on a serious look as he replied.

"Colonel Grey it would be my pleasure to offer you and your men assistance and the run of our camp. I have the men preparing hot water for you and your men and a lunch will be served in two hours. I would ask that you and Sergeant Major O'Rourke join me at this time if it be your pleasure."

"Thank you Sir, it would indeed be our pleasure to join you."

"If there is nothing else Colonel then I will ask Colonel Carmelo Grey to take your men to the camp kitchen where the water is heating while we adjourn to my own tent so you can rest and change; perhaps the Sergeant Major would like to join us as well?"

For the first time, Sergeant Major O'Rourke spoke and, just as Thomas thought it would be; it was the O'Rourke of old.

"Of course I'm coming Lad, now if you two have finished with the bloody blarney then you can find me a bloody drink. Have you any idea what you are doing to an Irishman standing out here blathering all bloody day long when he could be drinking?"

Thomas immediately let his face relax and smiled widely as he replied.

"You're the one that's standing around blathering O'Rourke, come on let's go find something to wet your whistle. Some of my scouts returned with a dozen bottles of fine French brandy just a couple of days ago, they said they found it lying on the side of the road and, of course I believed them, just as you would."

"Fat bloody chance lad, now where the hell is it?"

"Come on you misbegotten son of a drunkard, the bottles are in my tent. Are you going to join us Mister Grey?"

"Do you think I would let that bloody Irishman anywhere near a bottle without my watching over him?"

The three old friends left the site as Carmelo led the others away towards the kitchens; for the moment all was calm in the camp and there were a number of Thomas's men that were looking forward to some new faces to have around and to ask question about where and what the new men had been doing in the north.

The three old friends went to sit outside Thomas's tent; as Thomas sat and was about to call for Fairley, the young man appeared as though by magic as he always did.

'Fairley can you get one of those bottles of brandy and some glasses please; then I would like you to get the bath tub ready for Mister Grey and afterwards for Mister O'Rourke."

Fairley saluted without saying a word and disappeared only to return a few seconds later with the bottle and glasses on a tray; it appeared he had them ready long before they were needed. Thomas thanked him and began to pour out a good measure in each glass.

"So Mister Grey, how did you know we were here and manage to find us?"

"Our old friend Percy; he sent me a message and told me where you may be camped and if the chance arose to look out for you on our way back from the north; of course it was O'Rourke's nose for booze that finally led us here. Well that and we also heard about the town of Miranda being almost raised to the ground because of some bandits; that led me to only one conclusion of who it may be."

"Well Miranda is a long way from here so how did you know we would be here?"

Mister Grey took a hefty sip of his brandy and raised an eyebrow before nodding to Thomas that it was indeed a good brandy before continuing.

"Well at first we were just trying to get back to the lines when Cooper thought he saw one of your patrols heading in this direction from somewhere in the north east; there is only one force we know of that wears all black uniforms and so we just followed the trail left by the horses and here were are."

"Well I'm only glad that it was you and not the French."

"I don't think you will have much trouble with the French for a while as long as you stay well away from the south. They've been massing in readiness for the new season so you would be well advised to keep your distance."

"Yes we thought that as well, we did look at their supply depot but it was too well defended to even try. So what have you been up to; it's been some time since we heard from you?"

"Oh we've been across the border and into France, bloody nasty place that is lad; full of bloody Frenchies. We had to be on our toes all the time but at least the Viscount will be pleased with the news we carry. So how long do you plan to stay way up here and what are you up to?"

Before Thomas replied he noticed O'Rourke fill his glass for the third time and smile widely at something only he was privy too.

"Well after we had to leave the supply depot we had to look for something else so we are looking to the north east in the hope of causing more trouble for the French. If they think they are not even safe so far behind their lines to the north then we hope they will pull much needed troops up here and away from the Viscounts front."

"Well there are certainly plenty of targets for you up north but you need to keep a watch on your back trail, they are bringing men across to replace their front lines as well as guarded supply trains."

"Can you tell me much about the passes they use to get through?"

"If you have a half decent map we can show you just about every trail and pass they could possibly use but first I need that bath and then O'Rourke will need one as well before he drinks your supply of brandy dry."

Thomas nodded and then looked for Fairley; again his batman was standing only a few feet away and waiting for orders. Thomas, even after all the time Fairley had been watching over him, could still not get used to how the young man seemed to know when he was wanted. Thomas smiled at Fairley and just nodded. Fairley looked at Mister Grey and then said.

"Your bath tub is ready Sir; if you would follow me I will take you to it. Is there anything else you need General?"

"No thank you Fairley; if you could ask the kitchen to have extra water heated for Mister O'Rourke once Mister Grey is finished then that will be all."

"Yes General."

Fairley led Mister Grey away to where the small canvas bathing area had been set up and then left for the kitchens to get more hot water. Thomas turned back to the smiling O'Rourke.

"OK O'Rourke, what has you so happy?"

"That's easy lad, good company, good brandy and a hot bath what more could a man ask for. Now then how has it been for you? I see the camp is quite impressive. Dry floors in the tents and little mud around the camp lanes; how did you manage it all in this filthy weather?"

"I have a very good engineer; it was all his idea and it kept the men busy when the weather got too much to do anything else. Firewood is our biggest bugbear but we now have a good supply coming in regularly when our supplies arrive from Oporto; it's the same with the feed for the horses."

"Well you certainly seem to have it all sorted, not bad for a scallywag from Limehouse. Now then one more brandy and then I'm ready for some of that hot water; as much as I think water is the drink of the devil I will put up with it this time."

"You are still a stubborn cuss O'Rourke but for some reason I like you and am glad you are on our side."

"Jeesus for a General you are right kind but I wouldn't make a habit of it lad, people might think you are going soft now that you are one of the toffs and we can't have that sort of thing going around the army now can we?"

Thomas chuckled as he looked at the wide open and smiling face sitting opposite.

"Come on O'Rourke, you know bloody well that won't happen, besides I don't think my men would put up with it for long without telling me to pull my head in."

"That's true lad but then you is only a drummer boy and we all know what sort of trouble they get up to."

Thomas laughed as he then took a sip from his glass; as he replaced the glass on the table he looked around to see what the rest of the camp was doing. The two old friends sat in companionable silence as they waited for Mister Grey to finish his ablutions; the rest of the camp went about its normal duties. A half hour later and Mister Grey rejoined them; he looked a lot better as well as cleaner although his clothes still had smudges and a few threads loose but had been brushed by Fairley into something resembling clean.

O'Rourke moved off as Mister Grey took his seat and refilled his glass before speaking.

'So Lad do you have those maps I was talking about so I can then show you where and what we saw that may help you with your nefarious plots for the French?"

"Yes Mister Grey, I'll call Major Smithson; he has spent nearly all of his time making new maps of all the places we have been to in Spain and a lot of places we have not been yet; if there is a map of the north he will have it somewhere."

Thomas turned in his chair and was not really surprised to see Fairley standing just a short way off and waiting for any orders from his General.

"Can you find Mister Smithson for me please Fairley, when you do ask him to bring any maps he has of the north east that may contain the passes through the mountains from France?"

Fairley turned and silently left to follow his orders. It was only minutes later when Major Smithson arrived with a bundle of his hand made maps tucked under his arm. After being directed to the third chair, he placed his pile of maps on the table and looked to Thomas for further instructions.

"What do you have on any of the north eastern passes; you and your men were out there for over a month so I hope you have something we can use?"

Major Smithson laid out four of his maps for the two to look over; the look on Mister Grey's face as he saw the detail on each and every one of the maps showed he was impressed with the details and precision that had been used to make them. After looking over each map he finally straightened up and turned to Thomas.

"Firstly I have to congratulate the Major on his fine maps; I don't think I have ever seen anything like it before. Does the Viscount know you have these?"

"He has never asked so I never told him Mister Grey; it just never crossed my mind."

"Well my advice is to not tell him and to keep the Major well away from his own map makers or he will try to steal him away from you. Now then back to business."

Mister Grey laid the first map on top of the others and began to trace with his finger across the surface of the map.

"You are here just north of Braganza. If you follow this line here until you come to just south of Astorga then turn east to the tributary of the Esla you will come to a rough road that leads to Leon; bypass the turn into Leon and follow the ridge to the next gorge that is running along the banks of the Esla true. The French are using this gorge to bring a large quantity of their supplies through from further north and it should be easy for a cunning Officer to set up a number of ambushes deeper in the gorge. Next there are the passes further to the east."

Mister Grey paused as he looked for another map and then once found he laid it over the top of the others.

"If you hold back from attacking them in the gorge you can follow it to the end and it will bring you to their main road that they use through the mountains. At the end of the gorge turn to the east and make for Espinosa you will have their main route right under your guns. Everything they bring across the border goes through that pass; if you can do damage there you will cause all sorts of trouble for them but; be warned, it is often heavily guarded and would mean a real fight. There is one thing that may be in your favour and that's that most of the men guarding the supply trains are conscripts and old men that are no longer of any use on the front lines. If you use all your cunning you could do some real damage to them and their lines of supply."

Thomas looked over the long way he and his men were from Espinosa; it would not be an easy trip and danger would be all around them if they got trapped in the narrow gorge leading to the east. After a few minutes of thinking he asked Mister Grey.

"Is there any other way into the main pass apart from the Esla gorge?"

"Well there are the goat tracks that run all over the mountains but I don't know if you would get your guns over them at this time of year; perhaps in summer they might make it but it would be hard work and add days to your travel time. I personally think it would be best for you to use the winter weather to make your way through the gorge and close off any chance they had of resupply by that road."

"Are there any other ways to attack them?"

"Well if what I've heard about you closing off the pass at Miranda is true then they have only one other choice of passes."

Again Mister Grey paused to find the map he wanted; he was still in awe of the maps and could not work out how the young Major had got all the way through French held country to make them. He guessed there was far more to the young Major than he first thought as he found the last map he was looking for.

"Now this is the only other way they have to bring in supplies with any ease."

Mister Grey pointed to the map and began to trace the roadway with his finger once again so that Thomas could follow him more easily.

"You will need to go back in the direction of Miranda until you get to the northern end of the River Ebro; once across the river there is a main road that leads into the mountains and through to Biscay; it would perhaps be an easier route and would close off their main routes without having to battle through to the east and Espinosa. The other thing it would accomplish would be to also limit how much they can get through to Espinosa as Biscay is the hub of the supply route. However it will also be one of the most heavily defended places on either route."

"Thank you Mister Grey, it gives me quite a lot to think on."

"Not a problem lad but just remember that you may be going into a hornet's nest; the French will not give up their supply lines very easily although again you have the inexperience of their guards that may go a long way to helping you if you decide to go ahead with your plans."

"Thank you again Mister Grey, I'll take it all into consideration before I make a move but we do have to do something while their main troops are tied down by the weather."

"Well it may just be the weather that's on your side if you can move your guns into position to take advantage of their lack of desire to move in bad weather."

Before Thomas could reply they were once again joined by a much cleaner O'Rourke who wasted little time in filling his glass with brandy once again.

"So what have the big wigs been talking about behind me back?"

"Don't you start O'Rourke, the lad and I have been working on his future plans and they have little to do with your drinking." Mister Grey replied with a faint smile on his lips.

"Now you hear that lad, you see how he treats me? Damn slum toff is all about his self nowadays. Do yee have a place for a good fighting Irishman in your little group of misfits?"

"There's always a place for you O'Rourke but I wouldn't want to take you away from your cushy little job with Mister Grey." Thomas chuckled as he watched the look of disappointment on O'Rourke's face even though it was patently artificial.

"Cushy you say lad, do you have any idea what he puts me through every day? O'Rourke do this, O'Rourke do that; why lad it's enough to make a man take up the drink to drown his sorrows and far be it for me to do such a thing." O'Rourke reached for the bottle once again to top up his glass as he smirked at Thomas.

"Yes O'Rourke I can see that you would hate to take up drinking to take your mind off your woes."

"Aye lad that would be the truth of it. Oh well I suppose I will have to just be the plaything of this here slum toff until I get me self killed off or find a good brewery to sleep in."

As Thomas chuckled at the outlandish claims, Major Smithson got ready to leave the small group of friends to continue their day. As he was about to leave, Thomas asked him.

"How is Maketja doing Major?"

"The Captain is fighting fit and as mad as hell Sir; god help any Frenchman that crosses his path any time soon and the scar will be with him for life if he happens to forget."

"Well you can tell him we are working on something to give him the satisfaction he wants but he will have to wait for a little while yet."

"I'll pass it on to him Sir, I'm sure it will make him feel better."

"Thank you Major, I may need to call on you and your men again before long."

Major Smithson saluted and left the three to finish their day together; Thomas turned back to his friends and refilled his own glass as he saw Fairley standing nearby.

"Yes Fairley?"

"Lieutenant Morgan says dinner will be ready in an hour Sir, is there anything else you will need in the mean time?"

"Aye Sergeant, another bottle of this fine brandy if you please." O'Rourke replied before Thomas could. Fairley smiled and went into the tent to gather another bottle; it still amazed the young man how much the Sergeant Major could drink and yet not show the slightest hint of drunkenness.

The dinner that evening was much like old times; there were ribald remarks along with loud laughter as old friends among both the Officers and men once again had time to exchange stories. As the wine and brandy flowed in copious amounts, tongues grew looser and the laughter even louder while outside the first flurries on this year's snow began to make itself felt.

For those in the confines of the warm marquee used as the mess tent, the change in the weather outside went unnoticed until very late when the time came for the revellers to find their beds. The next morning found many men shivering in their cold beds. Over the ground outside their tents lay a white wonderland although for those who were shivering under their blankets they could have thought of another name for the white shroud that was nearly a foot deep.

Colonel Grey's men had been a little better off as they had been given the use of the mess tent to bed down in; the continuous heat from the cooking fires had kept a large amount of warmth around them for the rest of the night.

Thomas shivered as he eased his body from his cot; with shaking hands from the cold he tried to dress as quickly as possible. It was the arrival of Fairley that gave Thomas a little hope of getting some warmth back into his body as his batman rummaged around in Thomas's trunk until he found the heavy woollen items made by the mothers of Vimeiro for all of the boys a number of years ago.

The woollen goods were comprised of two pairs of black fingerless gloves and a long red and gold striped scarf as well as three pairs of thick black hose. Thomas was glad of the new clothes as he had not found a need to wear them before now. The thick hose made his boots a little tight but his feet were almost instantly warm; the gloves, once slipped on his hands gave him better control over his chilled fingers and the addition of the long scarf wrapped around his neck a number of times and pulled high enough to cover his nose now left only his black hat to be placed on his head.

When Thomas went outside to see the white frozen landscape; he saw that he was not the only one to look for their woollen clothes. Colonel Grey's men were slowly forming ranks in their thick cloaks as they prepared to move out and head south. Thomas spent a few more minutes with Mister Grey and Sergeant Major O'Rourke before the order was given for his visitors to turn south and leave for slightly warmer climes.

For the rest of the day, Thomas had the men preparing for what looked to be a cold and hard winter. Around the camp there was a lot of work to do as the twenty guns needed to be cleared of the built up snow and then greased and covered with canvas for protection. The final pieces of the long open lean-to for the mass of horses had to be completed for their protection.

All stores were checked for any damage and then it was all hands to gathering firewood; if the snow stayed around for too long then they could be in trouble and so they had to prepare as best they could. With the snow thick on the ground, their supply wagons may have trouble getting through to them on a regular basis although Thomas knew they had a good supply of everything they would need if the wagons could not make it.

As he looked around the camp a sudden thought came to him; if he would be difficult to supply by wagon then the French would also have the same problem. Thomas called for his Officers as his thoughts began to develop further in his mind.

With the extra knowledge he now had thanks to Colonel Grey and O'Rourke he saw a possibility to get at the French supply lines with little danger to his men. If his own camp was now under a foot of snow then the passes further north would be closed by even deeper drifts. While it seemed that his guns would be of little use as there would be far too much difficulty in moving them, his Cavalry should have an easier time of it and they could be just as effective against supply trains in such weather.

Thomas and his Officers sat and discussed what they might be able to accomplish if they took the chance to move on the French supply lines while the snow worked in their favour. It was almost lunch time before the meeting adjourned and the decisions had been made; the three Cavalry companies would move against any French they found while the camp was guarded by the guns and Infantry with Carmelo left in command.

For the rest of the day, Thomas had his Cavalry prepare to move out and go north; the target he had finally decided on was to be the two passes that led from Balboa; one to the east and the other to the south. There would be no major attack on Balboa but they would harry any supply trains they found in either pass. After some discussion with his men he thought they would be able to successfully attack any supply trains they were fortunate enough to come across.

With snow on the ground, the French wagons would be lucky to make ten miles a day and this left Thomas and his Cavalry with many opportunities with their more mobile force and better firearms to take advantage of any situation they came across.

As the day moved into evening; Thomas and Estaban went from one horse and rider to the next to check that they would have everything they would need both for the long journey and for their own safety both with the weather and any fighting they may get into.

The mobile force would also have twenty mules to carry all they would need but even then they would be moving with only the bare minimum of equipment and supplies; it would be up to themselves to make use of any supplies they could garner from their attacks on the French.

As the darkness clothed the camp in deep shadows, Thomas and his army watched the beginnings of more snow start to fall; the only saving grace they could think of was that there was very little wind to make their night even more miserable. In the kitchens the fires had been stoked up high to help warm the large marquee the side of which now carried their canvas sides to block out the cold night while the men ate and talked about what was yet to come.

The night was again cold but the air was clear and sharp when one breathed in. Every cot now had an extra blanket taken from their small supply but somehow there were still small drafts of cold that found their way into the cots even after the men tried their best to make a small tight nest out of their blankets.

Morning found the camp now under nearly two feet of snow and the kitchen fires glowing as hot as they had ever been in an attempt to bring more warmth into the marquee as the men filed in from their tents; all wearing their woollen scarves pulled tightly around their faces and their wool mittens on their cold hands.

Breakfast was hot and there was plenty of food for all, the kitchen boys had also made extra large cauldrons of cafe so the men could help themselves as often as they wanted. At the end of breakfast and with the snow finally stopped, Thomas called for the men of the Cavalry Companies to make ready to move out just as soon as the last of the mules had been loaded.

As Thomas and Estaban led the long column out of the camp they kept a watch on the mountains above them; there were heavy grey clouds still sitting almost motionless over the top of the peaks even though a weak sun was trying to push its light through in an attempt to bathe the camp in its weak heat.

 Thomas and Estaban rode at the head of the three companies as they turned east towards the area around Braganza where they would then turn towards the plains and more open country of Leon and the wide open spaces they would need to cross before the upcoming river crossings. Thomas had allowed ten days to cover the distance through to the banks of the River Carrion; he would then have another six days to make the start of the pass just north of Miranda and work their way through the pass to their final destination south of Balboa.

The journey was not made any easier when they came to the wide open plains of Leon and the wind grew as it came off the mountains and swept over the plains in sharp cold gusts. It almost became a battle on its own just to make thirty miles a day and those roads that were passable were slippery and sometimes turned to a cold mush as the number of horses and mules broke through the covering of ice and snow.

When the long column finally made the banks of the River Carrion Thomas realised it had taken them and extra three days to push through the snow and over the slushy roads. The river in front of them also did not look appetising or easy to cross. Both banks were deep in snow and the River itself was flowing faster than one would think. The maps of the area that Major Smithson had made showed only one possible crossing point and that meant they still had another full day to make it to the ford; there was no safe way they could cross at their present position.

An hour before the sun disappeared in the west, Thomas and the three Companies arrived at the ford. The river was shallower even though the water still seemed to be flowing fast. Estaban suggested the mules should cross first as they were well known for their stable footing in difficult places and it would then show the Cavalry riders what they were up against.

Thankfully for Thomas and the others, the crossing went well and there were no difficulties in getting through the ford. As it was near dark Thomas called a halt for the night when they had got a little over a mile from the ford. It was going to be a cold night and the fires would only be small cooking fires that were made from the surrounding scrub pines.

As the troops had no tents they had to make use of their heavy winter cloaks as bedding and also keep their warm winter woollies on. The next morning there were a large number of groans as the men tried to fight the cold as they unrolled from their temporary beds. Thomas had not set guards that night as he felt they would be safe while the weather was the way it was.

A rough breakfast was put together with the mainstay being very hot cafe that was swallowed almost before the mug was clear of the small cauldron. The mules were once again loaded with what remained of their supplies and the troops mounted and ready to go well before mid-morning. Once again Thomas and Estaban led the Companies eastward towards Miranda; with luck they would find the turn off into the pass that led to Balboa before too much longer.

It was a further three days before they came to the banks of the River Ebro and the feeling of the men grew more positive, they were now only a hard riding day away from turning off into the pass north west of Miranda and towards the passes of Balboa.

So far the flurries of snow had stayed away and the column was making better time than they thought they would. After finding the opening into the pass they were searching for, Thomas sent out a ten man troop to search ahead; they were now in the lands where the French could still hold sway and their need for supplies could mean his small party could run across supply trains at any time.

From Major Smithson's maps Thomas knew there were at least four small villages or towns further in the mountains and he wanted to avoid them if he could; being so close to the French border could mean they were all in favour of French rule and he wanted to stay hidden for as long as he could.

Once across the River Ebro Thomas had the ten man patrol look for a ravine where they could establish a small camp well out of the sight of any casual passerby; he wanted somewhere that was not too close to Agueda Lador which was the first town in the pass.

It was in the early afternoon of the second day when they found an ideal place for their small camp; it was a well hidden and small ravine that would be easily defended should they need it yet was well within striking distance of the main road used by the supply trains and gave them a quick escape if needed.

Their first night in the narrow ravine proved to be better than they thought it would be; while there was snow on the ground, the wind flowing down the ravine had pushed much of it to the sides leaving the central area almost clear. Thomas's most concern now was for the horses; the mules had carried bags of oats for feed but that was now almost finished so he would have to find more feed before the week was out, it was just one more thing he had to ponder on.

The first night in their temporary camp went without incident and now it was time for Thomas to send out patrols to try and discover any French movements on the supply line; it was to be sooner than he thought it would be.

CHAPTER 17

Thomas watched as his first patrol left the ravine; around him he could hear the groans of those who had spent most of the night huddled in their thick capes around small fires, the ground was still cold in these early hours but the faint hint of sunlight began to send slow warmth into aching bones.

As the fires were built up for the breakfast cooking Thomas called for his Officers; it was time to make what plans they could and await for the return of the patrol. It was only two hours later when the patrol came back hurriedly with their report. A convoy of ten fully laden wagons were making their way south through the pass and it appeared to be heavy going for the four horse teams.

The wagon guards were lighter than Thomas thought the French would provide in that there was only a single soldier sitting alongside the driver with two more sitting on top of the load on each of the wagons; there appeared to be no Cavalry escort.

Thomas thought over these facts and could only surmise that the French felt very safe so far behind the front lines and felt they had no need for mounted escorts for such a small convoy. The Officers pulled out Major Smithson's maps of the area and looked at what they may have to work with; in less than an hour they had a plan made and ready to put into action.

The plan called for all three Companies of Cavalry to take part. Pablo would lead his Company to the left of the muddy road and dismount his men to take up positions among the snow covered rocks and scrub. Thomasino would lead his Company to the right of the road and do the same while Estaban and Thomas would lead the third Company and block the road ahead with the other Company; they would not dismount but remain on their horses in a full show of force.

It took only a half hour to find the place for their ambush; in the distance they could hear the sound of swearing drivers and the heavy tread of horses under strain; they had made their ambush point just in time to set up and then have to wait only minutes for the first heavy wagon to make an appearance.

For the French drivers and escort it came as a huge surprise to see their way forward blocked by more than one hundred black clothed riders that formed three ranks; all of which were armed with what appeared to be double barrelled muskets and all of them pointed directly at the wagons.

Even though they were facing insurmountable odds, or maybe it was the ignorance and fear of inexperienced guards that made the first Soldier stand and bring his musket to bear on the massed Cavalry ahead of him. He never got the chance to pull the trigger as, from each side of the roadway and for most of the length of the small column; there came the shattering fire of two hundred hidden muskets from the bushes and rocks bordering the muddy road.

The heavy smell of burnt powder, the neighing of scared horses and the echo of the shots in the still morning air shattered the peace as both Pablo and Thomasino took the initiative and opened fire before a word could be said. It took only the single concentrated volley of the two Companies to almost wipe out any resistance, the five that survived the devastating volley could only sit with mouths agape and wonder what had just happened.

Before the five survivors could do more than blink as the results of the massed volley tried to imprint on their minds eye, they were immediately surrounded by large numbers of the black clad soldiers, the muskets pointed unwaveringly at their heads.

While Thomas had little thought for the trials of the French, even he was almost stunned at the ferocity of the two brothers and the results of their surprise volley of shots. Thomas, accompanied by Estaban and Diego, rode forward until they came to the five men. Thomas spoke in his rather stilted French but the message was abundantly clear even though his accent was not of the best.

"Drop your weapons and step down; if you do as I say you will be released and escorted to the nearest village without further harm, refuse and you die here and now."

The three guardsmen quickly dropped their muskets and leapt from the wagon top while the two remaining drivers also stepped down and then all five stood silent but fearfully waiting for what might come next. Estaban sent Diego off to call the other two Companies to mount and return to where Thomas sat with the third Company watching over their captives. Thomas wasted little time in detailing Diego and twenty men to escort the survivors towards the nearest village of Vittoria which would be about two days walk for the five men.

Thomas instructed Diego to escort them only until the late afternoon and then turn around and make their way to their temporary camp at the ravine while Thomas and the others set about taking over the ten wagons and driving them also to the camp, they now had a free resupply of goods thanks to the French.

With the five captives on their way back to freedom, Thomas asked for the wagons to be given a quick inspection and then for those who had some experience of wagon driving to turn the wagons towards their camp and then see what they fully had to work with.

On the first quick inspection, it appeared five of the wagons carried grain and the others were loaded with a mixture of food stuffs, a quantity of powder and other needed equipment any army needed. With the quick inspection complete and the canvas covers once again tied down to protect the goods from the weather, Thomas gave the order to return to camp; it would be three more hours before they finally drove the last wagon deep into the ravine where they could begin to see what they had to work with.

There was little to the camp and now that they had ten captured wagons, the ravine almost felt too full although there was still a lot of empty space left further along the length of the ravine until it came to a halt against high towering cliffs at the end.

The first business of the day was to see what exactly they had captured. The five wagons of grain would be used to feed the many horses and it was from a suggestion by one of the young men who had joined them from the navy that a good use could be found for the horses used to pull the wagons. As the grain was needed for their own horses, the young ex-navy man suggested they kill off the wagon horses as needed to feed themselves, or; as he put it.

"Well Sir, aint nothing better than a good thick horse stew to fill ones ribs and would save the grain for our own horses. Three hundred men would soon make use of the meat Sir and two horses a day just might be good enough for all to eat well and fight harder if it please you Sir?"

"A good idea Trooper, see if you can get some of the men that have worked on the land and know about butchery to make a start; we'll get the wagons unhitched and you can take your pick as soon as you're ready. There's another thing you can do while you are working on getting us some fresh meat."

"Yes Sir?"

"Ask around and see who can do the cooking, with luck there might be some pots and pans in the wagons for them to use."

"Yes Sir, I will get to it right away Sir."

Thomas let the Trooper leave and then called for his four Officers. It was time to think how they could improve the camp for what they hoped would be a successful stay and enable them to raid almost at will along the French supply line.

By the end of the day Thomas could look over his temporary camp with some satisfaction; the wagons were already being formed up to be used as cover from the elements. The wagons were stripped of their wheels and then tipped on their sides to make an effective windbreak, the canvas tarpaulins were also put to use as they were stretched over between two wagons and then tied down as a light roof.

One wagon was set aside for Thomas's use and again, it was one of the ex-navy men that came up with the idea of making better use of any spare canvas so they could start to get some of the men off the ground when sleeping; Thomas liked the idea immediately as he listened to the older man.

"Well Sir I was thinking that we could make use of the extra canvas by making hammocks. With a little work we can stretch them between the wagons and mayhap raise a dozen men off the cold ground in each of the ones we've tipped."

"How would you go about it? As I see it you would need someone with a good strong needle and the knowledge of sewing and then there is the fact of hanging them?"

"Easier than it would seem like Sir. We got us at least ten men from the ships with us, now you may not know it Sir but us Jack Tars has always carried the makings around with us Sir."

The man paused as he reached under his jacket and then lifted it so Thomas could see that around the man's waist was a thick black leather belt. On the belt was one of the usual knife sheaths worn by most Sailors; it was something he had rarely taken the time to notice. The man shifted his sheath around until Thomas could see it more clearly.

'Well Sir, its common for all Jack Tars to carry his knife when on board ship as you might know Sir, tradition being as it is Sir. Now there is also one other thing all jack Tars carry with them."

The man reached down to the sheath and from a small pocket at the front of the knife sheath pulled out a long thick needle with a slightly curved tip which was shaped a little like a spear head but looked very sharp.

"This here is what we calls a sacking needle Sir; uses it for repairing the sails when they gets torn and ripped in storms or battle. I noticed there is plenty of tackle from the horse traces that we may be able to make use of. Now then Sir, if'n we Jack Tars cut up the extra canvas into size and then strip the tack from the wagon horses we can make up a good number of Hammocks, wouldn't take much then to fix them good and solid inside the wagons now they laying on their side like Sir."

"Well if you think it will work then go and find your other Sailors and see what you can do; we may not get a hammock for every man right now but if we get more supply wagons we might get them all off the ground before long. Thank you Trooper a good suggestion, now all we have to do is find a way to protect what we have taken from the French; if we get another storm we could lose it all in one night."

"If I may suggest Sir?"

"Go ahead."

"You got close to three hundred good men here Sir, what if they was to spend some time building a store house out of all these stones we got laying about. Three hundred men will make right quick work of it and we can still use some of the canvas to make a roof if they make the walls high enough. It might not be good looking but may protect our goods Sir."

"Sounds like a good idea to me, do what you can with the hammocks and I will get Colonel Estaban to set the men to work on the store. Thank you Trooper, I won't forget your good ideas and I'm sure you can go back to the men and then use that bloody big needle to sew on a Corporal's strip."

"Thank you Sir, I'll see it all gets done Sir."

"Thank you Corporal."

Thomas sat back as the newly promoted Corporal left him to see to his new duties. Thomas was soon joined by Estaban and the two sat back as the men got busy with resetting their small camp. After a short rest, Thomas called for the maps that Fairley had packed for him and then set about looking over them with the help of Estaban.

Thomas's idea was to give the French as little time as possible to recover from their first sudden attack. The Frenchmen he had released would still be on their way to Vittoria and he did not want to let word of his attack get out before he could take advantage of both the weather and road conditions to make more trouble for them.

With hard work and the men labouring late into the night, the roughly made store was soon finished; it would not win any prizes for building but would serve its purpose for the time they planned to be there and the eight wagons set in pairs with canvas roofs soon had roughly made hammocks slung inside that would allow up to twelve troopers to sleep a little more comfortably.

The men without Hammocks had to find other ways to sleep for the time being but, Thomas decided, for as long as they were in this camp he would use any more wagons to make shelters for those who still had to find a dry spot near the small fires for sleeping.

The sun had barely made itself known the next morning before Thomas had the 1st and 2nd Companies ready to ride out in search of more wagon trains, the need to keep the French on the back foot was imperative if he wanted his overall plan to work. Within two hours the two Companies were well into the gorge that had been the scene of yesterdays attack.

Thomas had a small troop of Cavalry consisting of only six men ride well ahead of the main force, they were to mark any supply trains that were trying to make their way through the gorge and then return to form up for an attack. It was only a half hour later when the six man troop returned with the news that a train of twenty wagons was forcing its way through the slush and snow towards them; it was time to set their trap.

Making use of the natural surrounds, Thomas set his two Companies much as he had the day before except this time he had only one Company to hide in the rough terrain on both sides. Once again they had kept Diego back at their camp for protection as Thomas assumed any trains they came across would still be guarded only by the same low standards of the first one.

When he caught the first sight of the supply train he was not surprised to see it much as he thought it would be, a single guard beside the driver and two young soldiers sitting on top, there was still no sign of any Cavalry escorts.

Unlike the previous day, Thomas and the Company did not sit squarely across the roadway but divided into two ranks and held station on each side of the gorge; from there they could attack down both side of the wagon train if needs be while Pablo held the high ground on both side with his dismounted troopers, the extra horses were being held back by some of the riders and out of sight of the oncoming wagon train.

Thomas watched as the first of the wagons suddenly took notice of the road ahead, the driver and guards had their heads down and their shoulders hunched as they tried to keep some warmth in their bodies as they rode through the morning chill deep in the gorge; it was to Thomas's advantage that the drivers did not see him until too late and were almost upon his two ranks before they saw what was ahead, by then it was already too late.

As the front guard suddenly stood up and raised his musket even though it was a hopeless gesture in the face of such odds, a single shot rang out from just to Thomas's left; Estaban had intervened before the guard could fire; it then became a valley of death as Pablo's men joined in with devastating volley fire at those further down the wagon train while the other men with Thomas also opened fire and urged their horse forward so as to ride down the length of the stalled wagons.

The sudden battle was over almost before it had begun; many of the young and inexperienced guards never even got the chance to use their muskets as they fell under the withering fire of the hidden men above them and the fast riding double ranks on the roadway.

The gorge was suddenly silent as the last few shots echoed down the gorge in the still morning air; the powder smoke hung heavy above the scene of the ambush as Thomas and his men looked at their handiwork. Of the eighty or so men that had been either drivers or guards there were now less the twenty able to stand unassisted and three of those were showing wounds either in an arm or leg.

While to some the battle may have seemed to have been rather short and sharp, Thomas's men did not get away unscathed. While he had not lost anyone he did have wounded although none too seriously. Thomas decided to send the wounded back as wagon drivers after they had been quickly attended to by the young man sent by Major Jervis for just such occasions.

There were two of the younger troopers that had heavy bruising and small cuts from jumping on one of the wagons to use their boot knives when they had fired both barrels. A little later Thomas reminded the young men to make use of their pistols next time. Next were three older troopers and one Corporal that had been hit by the badly aimed musket balls in the upper arm with one carrying a thigh wound from another errant musket ball.

Thomas rode up to the guards and drivers who were even now trying to work out what had happened in those few terrible minutes when the morning had started out just like any other day for them and now it had turned into one of their worst nightmares. The survivors were quickly pushed together and those further back were pushed forward under heavy guard until they had joined what was left of their compatriots standing in front of Thomas and his men.

It did not take Thomas much time to decide to send the survivors off in the same manner as those of the day before. With the captives directed back towards Vittoria and away from close help; he hoped it would once again delay any French reprisal against he and his men for some little time yet to come. Pablo had twenty men detailed immediately to escort the survivors out and away towards Vittoria while the remainder of his men saw to the wagons.

What was on the wagons was not really of great concern, just the fact of denying the French with anything to do with the war effort was a win and anything that his men could get from the wagons was seen as a boost to his own supplies and the efforts of his men.

As the survivors left under guard to set their faces towards Vittoria, Thomas took out his map of the gorge and used some time to look at it closely.

He guessed they were well into the gorge and possibly only a day or so from the main road leading to Balboa. He had no intention of getting much closer if he could avoid it but it did not mean he was going to make it any easier for the French to hold the pass if he had a choice in the matter. In a rough estimate, Thomas thought they would be able to continue to raid the gorge for at least five more days before he would have to move his base of operations.

From what he had so far seen, the French were sending only one wagon train a day at any one time; this could only be to Thomas's favour and the lack of Cavalry escort made his job that much easier and safer.

It was still a surprise for Thomas that as yet they had seen no reinforcements travelling south. As Thomas was not aware of the problems Napoleon was having far to the north in Russia, the lack of replacements for those in the south would have been easily explained and he may have been able to step up his deadly intrusions.

With the days fighting being over, Thomas sent the twenty wagons back towards his camp with only the drivers aboard; it would mean twenty less troopers in his small force but he wanted the wagons and their contents well out of the way so they could not be taken back if things went wrong.

During the rest of the daylight hours Thomas and his men ventured deeper into the gorge to investigate any and all places that would be a possible ambush point. They would spend the night once again out in the cold but with luck they could find a small ravine to keep the worst of the wind and chill out of their bones. The promise of more action the next day leant a little light hearted joking amongst those who stayed, the escort for the captives would once again return after the Frenchmen were well on their way towards Vittoria and could not turn back to cause trouble.

After a cold night and some discomfort, Thomas took his men further through the gorge in search of another supply train. It was as they came close to where the main roads joined just south of Balboa and then branched off towards the west that Thomas's vanguard saw a larger supply train making its way through the towering pass in the direction of Espinosa.

With one of the riders returning to Thomas to report the supply train, the others shadowed the large column from a distance and tried as best they could to stay out of sight of the well guarded train. Once Thomas had all the details of the column he set about making his plans; this time there would be no frontal assault and he told all his men to stay well out of sight until the supply train stopped for the night.

According to his fine maps, Thomas knew the column would have to stop for the night as the distance would prohibit them from making the journey to Espinosa in one single day. It was a long day of playing cat and mouse as Thomas's force shadowed the unsuspecting French. As the day drew on the weather once again turned in Thomas's favour; the first flurry of snow almost caught him and his men by surprise considering the day had been clear and cloudless.

The first hint of problems to come was the sudden cold gust of wind that ran through the pass; Thomas sent word ahead for the vanguard to retire back to the main force and consolidate their force. The French would soon have to stop because of the now fast moving front of grey clouds that were rolling over the top of the pass and the increase in the thickness of the falling snow.

Although it was still early in the afternoon, the oncoming snow storm darkened the depths of the pass as though night had already fallen. For Thomas and his men the sudden appearance of the storm gave them some hope of not only catching the long column but having the near darkness to aid them in their planned assault.

It was now time to move forward with great care, Thomas did not want to stumble onto the column unprepared or to give any warning of what they were about to do. As Thomas and Estaban led the men forward with care and on foot, as they had left their horses behind where some of the younger troopers were set to watch over them; the first dull glimmer of fire light was seen not too far ahead.

It looked as though Thomas's summation had been correct and the supply column had decided to stop and wait out the sudden storm; it was now time for Thomas and his men to make final plans to either delay or totally disrupt the long column.

As his men waited patiently for the French to become cold and tired from the incessant snow and wind, Thomas set out his bold plan as the men huddled around him with their thick cloaks pulled tightly around them and their red and gold striped scarves wrapped around their throats and faces so that only their eyes showed below the black hats.

This fight was going to be far more personal than any other they had fought as Thomas had decided to use only pistols and knives for the assault; it would mean they would have to enter the wagon lines and deal with any French they came across on a very personal basis. The one overriding fact that would help Thomas and his men was the fact the storm would cover much of their activities as long as the snow fell and the wind blew.

The plan was to take the men of one wagon at a time and then slowly work their way deeper into the column without being seen; most of the killing would be done with their large boot knives and the pistols were only as a last resort. Once a single shot was fired, Thomas knew that all hell would break loose as the French came to realise they were under attack.

The attack was to be in a relay. Each wagon was guarded much as the others they had taken although there was an extra man on each one. The first wagon would be attacked by six of Thomas's men just to make sure the driver and guards were quickly and hopefully silenced before any alarm could be made. Once the first wagon was out of action, the next six man team would venture forward and take the next in line.

The attack would continue in the same fashion until they were either discovered or had actually taken the whole column; again it was the weather and dim light that would aid them. In the dim light ahead, Thomas could just make out the first wagon with the horses still in their traces and no more than ten yards ahead of that he could just barely make out the faint outline of the second one with its small fire lit just off to one side of where the front driver's seat was.

For those who stayed back it was ordered that they keep their muskets in hand in case they were needed; for the six man team going into the attack they would sling their musket over their back and carry the large boot knife in one hand and their double barrelled pistol in the other. The pistol could, if needed, be used as a club with the knife doing the real damage.

Pablo asked to be allowed to take the first six man team; if he was successful then the next team would be led by Thomasino while Pablo stayed back to rummage through the wagon to see what it carried. From then on a team would leap frog from wagon to wagon with those who were holding back as cover guard moving forward only when the next wagon was taken.

Pablo's attack was fast and silent, the wind covering any stray sounds from the sudden scuffle that developed with the men sitting huddled over the small fire. The fight was over in less than twenty seconds as Pablo's men used their large sharp knives to the most effect and silenced the five men around the fire without raising any alarms. As Pablo's men began to silently release the canvas tarpaulin from the back of the wagon, Thomasino moved his six men forward in silence.

Once within striking range, Thomasino led his men with venom against the huddled men at the second wagon. The second wagon was taken just as quickly and silently as the first and Thomas and Estaban silently led the rest of the men forward to where Thomasino was even now loosening the ties on the tarpaulin. The next six were led by one of the Sergeants to the next wagon in line and the same silent attack was made to great success.

The slow creeping of the troopers went unnoticed in the snow storm and Thomas's men were well into the long column with nothing but death in their wake. Thomas's men had now managed to take twelve wagons without the French guards even knowing there was an enemy in the vicinity although it was the weather that aided Thomas and his men the most.

As it would happen, wagon number thirteen did not go as well; while the team had little trouble in dealing with the men huddled around the fire, they did not notice that there were only four men and not the usual five. Unfortunately for the team the fifth man had taken time to walk around the other side of the wagon to relieve his bladder and stepped back into the firelight just as the team stood up from their grisly work.

The guard and the men of the team seemed to stand staring at each other with total surprise until one of the team took the initiative and jumped forward with his bloody knife to finish off the last man. In his fear and lack of understanding, the sole guard opened his mouth and began to yell loudly just as the sharp knife pierced his chest and drove with force into his heart.

The French guard's voice choked and gasped as the cold steel sent him to his death but his loud shout had now attracted some attention from the vague outline of the wagon ahead. As the men of the next wagon could just be seen getting to their feet as though they were shadows in the heavy snow; Thomas gave the sign for the men with him to raise muskets in preparation for any attack that may come.

The six men of the forward team suddenly took things into their own hands and the Sergeant that led them got the men to sit down by the fire as though they were the guards and hoped the men of the next wagon would not stop to count how many sat by the fire.

From the next wagon came a call asking what the yelling was all about; thinking quickly and using his knowledge of French, Thomas called back from his place behind the thirteenth wagon and hidden by the swirling snow which also helped to disguise his bad accent.

"Do not worry, this idiot just pissed on my boots and I gave him something to think about for next time."

The reply that came back was mixed with what could only be a chuckle.

"You're lucky he was not taking a shit, now let us get some rest, this damn storm is making me feel the need for a warm woman and we won't be seeing that until we get through to Espinosa."

Thomas and his men sighed with relief as they watched the dim outline of the men ahead return to huddling around their small fire. Thomas knew they would now have to wait in silence for those ahead to settle back and ignore what was around them before he could continue with his attack. As far as Thomas could tell there were still more than a dozen wagons still left in the column and he wanted to try to get them all even though they would not be able to take many of them back to their camp.

Thomas and his troops waited patiently as the storm continued to rage around them; it was now even difficult to make out the next wagon and this could only bode well for the rest of the fast descending night. With the snow storm blanking out any movement and the night now only minutes away from full darkness; Thomas gave the signal for the leap frogging attack to once again continue.

The next team went forward and it was only a short time later that Thomas barely made out the sound of gurgling as another throat was cut cleanly by the large boot knives. There had been no decision on what they would take or if they would take anything from the supply column, they were a long way from their camp and the last thing they really needed was to be slowed by heavy wagons when so close to the French headquarters in Balboa.

By midnight the attack was over and the floor of the pass looked more like a charnel house than a means to travel from one town to the other. The French dead lay in their own blood as the small fires first spluttered and finally died without being tended.

For Thomas and his men it was now time to see what, if anything they wanted from the wagons. It was finally decided to only take the last wagon in line that was closest to their return road; anything that could not be put aboard would be destroyed before they left. There was no way they could leave the supplies for the French to be collected at a later date.

With the column and pass under his control, Thomas gave orders for the many wagons to be searched for anything they could make use of and for it to be carried back to the last wagon, everything else was to be prepared for destruction by using the gun powder carried by some of the wagons, they would leave nothing for the French to recover.

The last wagon was almost over full when Pablo and six others arrived back with four wooden crates, it was the last of the goods they would take with them but Thomas could not think of why the young Captain had insisted on talking the four plain looking crates. With a little grunting and moving of cargo already on the heavy wagon, Pablo managed to get the four crates on the wagon and then stood back with a wide smile on his face.

Two more horses were attached to the front of the last wagon and everything was ready for their return to their hidden camp. Thomas and Estaban stayed back with a few of the men as the wagon was turned with difficulty in the pass and then pushed forward towards the exit of the pass with the rest of the men in file on both sides, they would remount their horses once they had arrived at the point where they were being held near the entrance to the pass.

Thomas and his small group waited as the creaking wagon disappeared into the gloom, the snow was easing and the wind had dropped so that the flurries were now less and the snowflakes drifted down rather than being blown like a hail storm. With the final disappearance of the wagon and the last men being no more than faint outlines in the softly drifting snow; Thomas turned back to the remaining wagons.

After taking an hour to release the wagon horses from their traces and setting them on their way towards Espinosa with a few well timed pistol shots; Thomas set the others to work; there was to be nothing for the French to recover.

Where they could, Thomas and the others set a barrel of gun powder under the wagon and where they could not they made use of some of the still smouldering fires. With only eight of the wagons being set with gun powder, Thomas and his men waited to make sure the other wagons were well alight before each setting a long fuse of raw powder along the ground, lighting it and then running for their very lives as the bright trail of fire hurried towards the waiting kegs.

Thomas and his men just made it out of reach when the first keg exploded with a sound that seemed far louder than it should have for a single keg but it was soon followed by the others in a quick succession of blasts that echoed in the pass and the shock wave rolled along the length of the pass and even knocked Thomas and his men to their knees as it rolled by.

Raising themselves back to their feet, Thomas led the men out of the pass and quickly came to where one of the troopers had stayed behind to hold their horses, the pass behind them showed a bright glare of multiple fires reflecting off the high sides and heavy clouds above; there would be little left for the French to gain from that particular supply column.

Thomas led his small troop into the darkness as they followed the trail left by those already on their way back to their camp. It had been assumed the wagon would have great difficulty with the deep snow drifts along the way but Pablo had come up with a simple answer so they would not be slowed by its weight.

Pablo set his own Company in the van with three riders across the road to break a path; they would change over about every ten minutes to keep the lead horses fresh while they forced their way through the drifts. At the centre came the wagon with what was now a relatively clear road flattened by the nearly one hundred horses of the 1st Company. The remaining troopers of the 2nd Company followed the wagon turning the rest of the road to a state of thick wet mush as the many hooves scattered the now dirty snow even further; it was an easy trail for Thomas and his men to follow.

It was less than a half hour after leaving the destruction of the supply column when Thomas and his small troop finally caught up with the main army; from then on it was just a long hard ride through the darkness with the cold chill of winter trying to disrupt their way forward.

Thomas had no intention of stopping during the hours of darkness as they were far too close to the main road leading to Balboa for comfort or safety, they would push on into the dawning light for as long as they could so as to be as far away from their latest attack as possible before any French could take notice and then take their revenge.

It was a long hard ride and by the middle of the next day they finally came to the turn off that led back to their camp although they very nearly missed it as the road was still almost belly deep with snow and the three riders at the front were just barely awake after such a long night and hard day.

Seeing the condition and tiredness of his men, Thomas called for a halt so the men and horses could take a few hours rest before once again venturing onward. Thomas knew he was taking a chance in stopping while still on the main road but he felt he had little option if he did not want some of the men put into too much danger.

Thomas felt the risk of being found by any stray French Patrol in such bad conditions was at best minimal and the welfare of his men had to come first. The army of tired men dismounted and stretched tired and aching limbs as the many horses stamped their hooves on the frozen ground, possibly to show they were happy to at last be rid of their burden for a while.

Thomas thought it would far too dangerous to make fires for heat and so the men huddled close to each other wrapped tightly in their cloaks and tried to get a little sleep before being asked to once again mount and ride on. Thomas estimated that they may· make their camp site either in the last minutes of the dusk light or early in the night; he did not want to stay out in the open for much longer and his men and their mounts badly needed food and rest; it had been a long and hard patrol.

With only three hours past since stopping, Thomas and Estaban went around the cold dozing men and shook them awake; it was time to make a last full effort to make camp and the warmth of hot food and shelter.

With the men finally remounted and ready to once again move forward, the 2nd Company under Thomasino took the lead as his horses were now a little fresher than those of Pablo's Company, they would use the same system of three at the front and replace them every ten minutes or so as they broke the trail through the snow drifts. It was much later in the evening than Thomas thought it would be before they saw the faint light of many fires in the ravine off to their right.

They had again almost gone past their objective due to their tired condition; another hour and they were easing off their horses as those who had stayed in camp under Diego ran over to take care of the bone weary horses and let the returned men look for a place to rest while others stoked up the fires to cook hot food in the form of a thick horse meat stew.

It seemed to Thomas as though he had just closed his eyes when he felt his shoulder being shaken with some vigour. When he could force his eyes open he saw the familiar figure of Fairley standing over him with a large dish from which came a marvellous smell of cooked meat. Thomas struggled in his heavy cloak as he tried to sit up from where he had been laying; the cold chill of the night left his bones aching but the smell of the food soon had him greedily forcing the food into his mouth as though it was his last meal.

Around him Thomas could hear the sounds of others as they talked and joked while taking in the first hot food in days although there was a distinct sound of weariness in the forced laughter and loud jokes.

Thomas finished his hot stew in quick fashion and without another thought, lay back down and closed his eyes; he would not awaken until the faint glimmer of sunlight the following afternoon managed to flicker across his closed lids. With a long groan and a little shaking of stiff bones, Thomas opened his eyes and stretched his body which complained in uncertain ways about being laid out on the cold ground for so long.

Fairley was at his side within seconds, a hot steaming mug of Cafe held out for Thomas to help get his limbs moving more freely. It took Thomas another half hour before he felt like doing any business of the day; around d him the camp was slowly coming back to life while those who had stayed back from the patrol set about looking after those who had had the hardest of times.

The late afternoon saw most of the camp once again out and about, Thomas called for his Officers and then set about forming a plan for their future. It was with some surprise that Thomas managed to work out that the date was probably the first days of February, the fact he had once again missed his birthday, his sixteenth, did not get past him. It was a shock to learn that he and his men had been out on patrol for more than a month; it was this small fact that dictated his next move for his Cavalry. It was time to return home.

With his closest Officers sitting around him Thomas began to tell them what he had in mind; the organisation for their return to the main camp north of Braganza would take up the rest of the afternoon and into the early evening which then came to a halt as the call for dinner was heard. The preparations for their move would start early the next day once all the men had been told of the details during the evening meal.

As the plan was discussed by all present, any problems that may have arisen were soon found answers and, by the end of the meal everything was ready to put into action the very next day. When Thomas returned to his upturned wagon he used as his accommodations he set about going over the plan one last time.

To keep enough supplies for the travel back to their main camp they would make use of only five of the wagons, Pablo for some untold reason wanted to take the single wagon they had brought back from their attack near Espinosa although he did agree to removing a large part of its contents to make it light enough to keep up with the others. Of the horses they had left they would be able to set six horses to each wagon for easier travel.

For all the supplies they could not take with them and the remaining wagons there would be a large fire set and everything would be destroyed so the French could not at some time reclaim them in the future. Early the next morning the preparations began for their departure; it would take a full two days before they were all finally ready to leave.

What was to be left behind was now stacked high and it actually took three pyres to get it all piled up; it was mainly the broken down wagons that took up much of the space and the few remaining French wagon horses were set with leads so they could be taken with the troops for food on the road. They were still a long and difficult way from their main camp.

For the last three days the sun had forced itself through the cloud cover and begun to melt the snow on the ground; while it would still be a hard journey the melting of the snow would make it just a little easier on the horses.

The plan was much as they had used when retreating from the pass of Espinosa with Pablo taking the lead with the wagons close behind. Diego's Company was given the duty to ride alongside the wagons as flank protection while Thomasino would once again be the rear guard; Thomas and Estaban would place themselves just behind the last wagon.

With a wave of his arm Thomas had the men set the fires and return to their mounts; with the fires well underway it was time to leave. As the long Cavalry column began to leave the ravine that had been their temporary home, Thomas noticed that most of the riders were carrying the hammocks that had been made for many of them by the three ex-sailors; they were rolled up and tied to the back of their saddles.

Thomas thought back to the first time that the hammocks had been put to use. While there had been a number of derogatory remarks about the strange hanging beds and a lot of laughter at the results of those who tried to use them for the first time, they had now become a very sort after item and there was still a long list of those wanting them when the three men could find enough canvas to make them.

Nearly two thirds of the troopers had the hammocks and they were very particular about looking after them. Thomas turned back to face the front as Pablo led the first Company out of the ravine and onto the still frozen road. Behind the retreating column the fires increased in strength as they devoured the wooden wagons and all of the supplies that could not be taken back to their camp. Even after ten minutes of travel those in the rearguard could still hear the faint sounds of crackling wood and louder explosions of the powder kegs they could not fit on their own wagons.

As the column cleared the last knoll that led out onto the plains, Thomas for the first time in months felt what he thought was a light breeze coming from the south. If the southerly continued to blow or increased in strength, it would soon melt most of the snow and while this would be welcome news it also had its drawback. With the large drifts of snow melted the roads would turn into quagmires. Thomas could only hope that the frozen ground would stay firm until at least the wagons had passed.

CHAPTER 18

By the third day, Thomas knew that winter was finally giving ground as the bright sun continued to work on the frozen roadway. Although the warmth was welcome it did not make for any easier going and many times the wagons had to make use of some of the escort horses being used to help them continue to move forward.

The further they progressed onto the open plains, the more difficult it became to move at any speed. On the worst day they covered only ten miles until they finally came upon more secure ground and were once again able to make better time.

It took Thomas's army nearly fourteen days to make it all the way back to their camp north of Braganza and the sight of the rising smoke of the cooking fires was such a relief after the hard dogged slog that some of the tired men even raised a cheer. As each day passed Thomas was able to keep the column moving with good speed as the mules they had and had been used to carry the grain for their horses were able to be added slowly to the wagons which made it easier to make it through some very tough going.

The outer guards of the camp had seen the approaching column for some time and the cooking fires were well stoked and hot food cooking well before Thomas led the exhausted men into camp. It did not take much for those who had stayed behind to see the condition of both the men and the many horses; it had obviously been a torrid time for all.

Even though young Fairley looked just as beaten as any of the others; he did not hesitate to go looking for hot water for his General to wash with; that and a good helping of hot stew was his present priority. Thomas could almost not believe the improvements in the camp since he had left; everywhere he looked he could see the talents of Major Carterton and his engineering abilities.

There had been a lot of construction going on during the winter and what had only a month or so ago been a ramshackle collection of tents and very rough stone walls was now a well set out collection of small stone huts with canvas roofs and the main lane between the two long rows of huts was now covered in thin sheets of a slate like stone that kept most of the mud at bay.

Thomas could now see that as the weather improved Major Morgan had had his men uncover the guns and they were now set for action should they be needed. Those of Lorenco's men that had been left behind now had well protected positions in the outer ring to act as the early warning eyes and ears for the new camp while the rest of the Infantry Companies had worked long hours under the direct orders of Major Carterton.

Thomas was led to his new home at the centre of the new camp where he was ushered inside to see the two small rooms set aside for him. His bedroom was at the back with the main room acting as his dining room and war room all in one.

Carmelo joined Thomas as the tired young General began to strip out of his soiled and smelly clothes; there had been no time for bathing while they were on the road and the sight of the tin bath being even now filled with hot steaming water left Thomas with only one thing on his mind.

As Thomas stripped for his bath, Carmelo gave him all the news and relayed a message directly from Prince Pimentel which had arrived two weeks previous by rider. The Prince wanted to see Thomas at his earliest convenience when he had returned from the north; the Prince would be in Zamora during the month of March and would wait for Thomas's return so they could meet in that town.

Thomas looked at Carmelo and could only smile, the reply needed no answer; Thomas would make the journey to Zamora after he had recovered from the last escapade and not before. The Prince had waited this long and Thomas could not see where a few extra days would make any difference; besides, he did need the time to recover his strength after the last fourteen days.

For the next two days Thomas was brought up to date on the events in and around the camp since he had left with the Cavalry to harry the French. As much as Thomas hated the thought of having to do paper work, it was an essential part of his army and Major Jones had no intention of letting his book work slip. Thomas had orders to sign as well as copious amounts of papers to do with his shipping company, far more than he thought he would have to do.

There were also the men's wages to be gone over and what money they had available to pay them. It came as a surprise for Thomas that they had suddenly received a large injection of coin from the last raid; now he knew why Pablo had been smiling when he loaded the four plain looking wooden crates onto the wagon and insisted they take them with them on the journey home.

On the morning of the third day, Thomas decided it was time he showed his face to the Prince; he felt better rested now he had four warm walls between him the chill of the nights. The snow was even now being slowly melted on the lower slopes of the mountains and the southerly winds continued to melt away the drifts that had made travel so onerous.

Estaban was left in charge of the camp and Carmelo would go with Thomas for the meeting along with the usual guard which they now insisted would be made up of twenty men as well as the ever present Fairley.

After a hard riding two days, Thomas and his men entered the town of Zamora; after a few questions of some of the locals he found the house being used by the Prince, that and the large contingent of the Princes guards made it easier for him to find.

Thomas and Carmelo were very quickly taken into the presence of the Prince who looked as though the full weight of the world was upon his shoulders but it soon changed to a full smile when he saw his favourite General being ushered into his temporary office by his Adjutant.

"Don Thomasino, Don Carmelo, it's good to see you both in good health; I was starting to become concerned as the days passed and there was no sign of you."

"Good morning Your Highness; I'm sorry for the delay but we just got back from the north only a few days ago and needed some rest before coming. Is there something amiss that you needed me to attend to for you?"

"Yes Don Thomasino, there is a lot going on and I need to bring you up to date with what is to be expected this campaign season. I fear that I am going to ask you to once again put yourself and your men in danger and I'm not sure it is the wisest of choices on my behalf. Before I continue can I offer you and Don Carmelo some good hot cafe and little sustenance before getting to the point?"

"Thank you Your Highness, we would both like a cafe, we did not stop for anything this morning as I wanted to get to see you as soon as possible."

The Prince turned his head and told his Adjutant what was needed before turning back to the table before him where he had a range of maps spread out.

"There are a number of events taking place at the moment, the most vexing is that I have some of the Generals starting to make noises that could disrupt any chance of Spain coming under one government and now I have heard the King is going to return at the first opportunity which may or may not cause even more problems while the war is ongoing. Viscount Wellington has plans of taking the fight to the French just as soon as the ground is firm enough for him to move his army; I believe he has now amassed over 120,000 troops to his cause, so we now have a good chance of sending them back to France once and for all. The French forces have now been put under the command of Napoleon's brother Joseph who still believes he is our king. It now seems that Napoleon suffered an horrendous defeat in Russia and has taken every man that could be spared to bolster his own army now that the Austrians and Germans have re-entered the war effort as allies of the Russians. Joseph's forces here in Spain have been reduced drastically and your actions over the winter have made it almost impossible for them to receive re-enforcements and supplies. Your closing of the Miranda pass has left them with only one major pass to use now and that is where the Viscount is preparing to meet them and finally push them from our lands."

Thomas sat and sipped his hot cafe as he nodded that he understood the explanation so far.

"From the last meeting I had with the Viscount it would appear that he has plans to cross the northern mountains of Portugal with his main army and try to cut off the French retreat to France via the Balbao Pass. Marshal Jourdan has an army estimated at around 68,000 and is at present somewhere between the River Douro and the River Targus, Wellington is going to try and trap him there between the rivers with a three pronged attack. If Jourdan does escape there is only one place he can go and that is towards Busaco. What I have to ask you Don Thomasino, is do you think your force can cause as many problems for the French army if they were to withdraw to Busaco.

Anything you can do to delay any attempt of the French to use the pass of Balbao would be of assistance."

"I will look into it Your Highness, as you are well aware we are not the sort of force that can attack from fixed positions if we wish to take advantage of any situation. We will of course look into any possibilities and try to assist the Viscount and his forces where we can."

"Good, I knew I could rely on you to do your best. Now there remains my problem of the Generals in the Cortes. I would ask that you continue to maintain your separation from any political views or actions as you have so far done. If it comes to a fight, and I sincerely think it will, then the less you have to be involved the better for your future and that of your army. When the King returns I fear there may be even more problems and the less your name is used in the politics of Spain the less chance the King would have to censure you in any way after the war. Do you understand what I am saying Don Thomasino?"

"Yes Your Highness, it has never been my intent to become involved in any political events of Spain or Portugal, I am here only to fight and had never given any thought beyond that Your Highness. When the war is done all I want to do is have a good and safe home for my men and I."

"Well I am glad to hear it Don Thomasino but I do have a fear that circumstances may intervene whether we plan for it or not. I can tell you that one thing will be for certain and that is that Spain will be in for a torrid time once the French have been sent packing and I would not want our most valued General to become involved with what may eventuate after it is all over."

The Prince paused as he looked for map on his table, after finding what he was looking for he looked over at Thomas and Carmelo before continuing.

"The Viscount is already on the move with the bulk of his army taking to the mountains in the north while his second army is readying for the advance through the centre. The northern army under Sir Thomas Graham is going to try to cross the mountains and attack the French from the rear and right flank; if he succeeds with his ruse he could catch the French in a pincer and destroy them before they can retreat to France. If the plan fails due to the mountain crossing then it is there I am asking you to hold back the French. At this stage I think your best chance would be the Bilbao Pass; do you have any knowledge of it?"

"Yes Your Highness, we have made use of it before and have some knowledge of it; it was where we were when you called for me, there are many places we can delay any French withdrawal."

"Good then I will leave it all in your hands and hope that all will be as we wish when the time comes. Now we come to the last reason for asking you to meet me here. The Viscount has asked me to find some men that know the northern mountains and to act as guides for Sir Thomas's army as they make their way through what is believed to be impassable country. It came to mind that you have many young men from all over Portugal and Spain and I was wondering as to whether you had some from the northern regions that could take up that task for the Viscount. As I said earlier, the army is already on the move but I think that they would only be making about ten or fifteen miles a day so it should be easy for you to catch up with them well before the mountains."

"Yes Your Highness I think I have a number of young men that could fill that role for the Viscount but he will need interpreters, none of those I am thinking of speak English and I would not want mistakes happening due to incorrect interpretation."

"I see, well the Viscount has asked if you would meet with him at Ciudad Rodrigo within the next few days to make plans for that to happen."

"If I can leave for my camp toady then I can be there to meet the Viscount in perhaps six or seven days Your Highness."

"Then if you can do this for me I will once again be in your debt Don Thomasino. Now then enough of this morbid talk; it is time for lunch and I would like you to join me before you leave for your camp."

"Thank you Your Highness, it would be our pleasure and a good meal would see us on our way in good spirits."

"Good then it is done and once again Spain will owe you a great debt that I only hope she can repay at some future time."

Lunch went on for more than an hour before Thomas finally called a halt and made ready to leave for his camp, there was a lot of travelling to do and not much time to do it in. Two days later found the small hard riding group entering the camp with the look of those who had slept little over the last few days; as he dismounted from his horse and before he even took his own condition into consideration; Thomas called for Maketja and Estaban to join he and Carmelo in his small two room house.

The planning session took over an hour by which time Thomas was fully ready for a rest; it had been a hard and fast ride to get back to the camp and start to make plans for the guides he had been asked for. Maketja had volunteered to form a group of northerners to act as guides but Thomas still had the problem of finding an interpreter for the English.

As Thomas stepped from the house to take a few breaths of fresh air, the answer to his problem walked past whistling to himself. Thomas smiled as he saw the familiar figure and thought back to the last time he had asked the boy to carry out an important duty for him; The fact the same boy had become very close friends with Maketja also helped his decision. Thomas watched the familiar figure for a few more seconds before calling out.

"Lieutenant Morgan I would like to see you if you have nothing of importance to do at this time."

Snot Morgan straightened and sent a warm smile at Thomas before changing directions and smartly walking towards where Thomas waited. Snot came to attention and, with a rather cheeky salute said.

"Yes Sir, I am at your command Sir."

"Come inside Lieutenant, there is something important I have to ask of you."

Thomas led Snot inside the house before indicating a chair for the boy to sit in, once he was also seated he began.

"Lieutenant I have something important for you to do but it may be very dangerous so I have to ask you if you will take it on instead of just giving you a direct order. The last thing I want to do is have to tell your father that I was responsible for you losing your life on my orders."

"Yes Sir, I can see how me Da might get upset but if you need me then I am here for whatever is needed to end the French."

"I am going to meet with the Viscount Wellington soon and he has asked for some guides to lead one of his army's through the mountains, Maketja is selecting the men now but they will need an interpreter that speaks English or there could be some confusion with directions and language. I would like to ask you to go in that capacity so there can be no mistakes. The one order I will give you and the others is that under no circumstances are you or the others to join in any fighting under English Officers orders. You and the men are there only to act as guides and that is all. If the English get into a fight I want you and the others to get your heads down and stay safely out of it. Is that quite clear Lieutenant?"

"Yes Sir. When do we leave Sir?"

"Early tomorrow morning, make sure you have all your arms with you and anything else you deem fitting for a long journey; I'll Have Colonel Colosio find you a good horse and Captain Maketja will have a number of mules selected to carry anything else you will all need."

"Yes Sir, Thank you for the chance Sir."

"Just keep your head on your shoulders and return safely and don't take any chances or cause any trouble."

"Yes Sir."

Snot stood up and gave one of his best salutes before a wide smile crossed his face and he ran from the house as though he was going on a special Holliday and not into danger as was more than likely. Thomas returned to his final preparations to meet the Viscount before he decided it was time to get his head down. Tomorrow would be the start of another long, hard ride towards Ciudad Rodrigo.

Thomas had estimated it would be a very hard four days ride almost without stopping before he would make Ciudad Rodrigo and as tired as he presently was, he was not looking forward to it. While he had spent most of the last five years being under constant pressure and always seemed to be tired or just recovering from exhaustion it still did not make it any easier as time passed.

Thomas was fully aware that he and his men could at any stage out ride and out march any known army of the day but it still did little to ease any aches and pains that developed during such times. Thomas sighed as he forgot about dinner and almost fell onto his small bed to sleep; he would eat an extra large breakfast before leaving and make up for his hunger in the morning.

Thomas's eyes were closed almost before his head hit the pillow; he did not hear Fairley enter the room and felt nothing as the young teen quietly undressed his General and then left to get the clothes washed while Thomas slept the sleep of the dead.

The sun had just begun to show the faint pink of early morning when Thomas finally forced his still tired eyes open. The smell of fresh cafe had him reaching to the small side table before he even really knew what he was doing. Somewhere outside the room he could hear the ever present Fairley doing something but it was not until he had taken four good large sips of the hot cafe that his mind began to work properly.

After leaving his warm bed, Thomas saw that his black uniform was laid out and ready for him; he often wondered what his life would be like without the thoughtful and dedicated attention to detail that Fairley provided day after day without complaint.

Thomas was finally dressed and stepped into his solitary front room to see what was happening; Fairley had set the small table with a large hot breakfast and was waiting off to one side for his general to appear.

"Thank you Fairley, I think it's about time you placed another stripe on your arm. Go and find Major Jones later and tell him to place your new rank in the pay book. I want you to stay behind this time as I hope to be with the Viscount for as little time as possible and then return at speed. I have a feeling we don't have much time before the trouble starts with the French again."

"Yes Sir. Sir, do you wish me to ready a travelling trunk for you?"

"No thank you Fairley, I want to be in and out well before I will need anything. Whatever you can't get into my saddle panniers can stay behind; when you've finished here I want you to go and tell Colonel Estaban to relate to my escort to do the same and that I will be wanting Colonel Grey to accompany me as well."

"Yes Sir."

Fairley quickly finished what he had been doing and disappeared so he could carry out Thomas's orders. It took Thomas less than a half hour to finish the large breakfast and then look around for what he may need for his fast trip to talk with the Viscount. While the travel time may be four days or so, he had little intention of staying longer than to have the meeting and leave at the earliest moment.

The winter campaign had taken a huge toll on Thomas and most of his men; had he had a looking glass he would not have seen the same boyish face of five years ago nor would he have seen anything to indicate innocence in the face that would have looked back at him. It was at these momentary pauses between campaigns that Thomas's thoughts would wander and it took a great deal of inner strength to resist them taking over his persona.

As had already been proven by those looking at the young General, instead of looking like any other sixteen year old, Thomas would have seen the face of a teen much older. Amid a few faint facial scars and newly forming wrinkles that should have only been made by one far older than he was; he would have had to also agree he now looked to be almost at the start of his twenties and the young skinny drummer boy of the past was now only a distant memory.

Thomas stood in his doorway as he watched Fairley lead his horse Santana towards where he stood waiting. The two panniers looked to be full and the saddle had been well buffed and polished ready for his use. Behind Fairley Thomas could see Carmelo and his twenty man escort mounting, they also had a pair of well packed panniers tied on their saddles.

Ten minutes later and those staying in the camp watched as their General left quickly with his escort; it was obvious from the start that there would no time wasted during this trip. The ride was long and hard but Thomas led his men on almost at breakneck speed and stopping only for a few hours sleep when both the men and the horses were just too tired to continue.

Dawn was breaking just as Thomas and his exhausted escort rode into the quiet streets of Ciudad Rodrigo; all around there were signs of English troops, either those who were going out on guard or those returning from their posts. Thomas ignored the puzzled soldiers as he led his men through the still quiet streets of early morning; there was little now that he would let distract him from his objective. If all went as he hoped, he wanted to be back on the road for Braganza before the day was at an end.

After asking one of the early soldiers for directions, he found out that the Viscount had his headquarters on the other side of the large town. The soldier told him it would be easy to find once through the last street. Thomas almost smiled at the strange look the soldier was giving him when he heard the definite London accent on a young man that looked at first sight to be foreign; the look was replaced with disbelief once he heard Thomas speak but his was not to wonder why.

Thomas left the soldier with his unasked questions still without an answer and rode off to find the headquarters of the Viscount; the sooner the meeting was held the sooner he could leave and return to his own camp.

When they exited from the town, it was just as the soldier had said. On the eastern edge of the town was a sea of tents that stretched almost as far as the eye could see. Every tent was in a straight line with a narrow lane between each rank. Near the centre of the huge camp an area had been set aside for a large parade ground which at the moment looked to be nothing more than a large brown muddy quagmire but its intent was plain to see.

It took little for Thomas to spy the mass of Tents he was looking for. They were off to one side of the large parade ground and a little apart from those of the ordinary soldiers, the lanes around the large bell shaped tents were also of much better quality and there was little sign of mud underneath the mass of duck boards that were used to keep the boots of the Officers clean and free of the muck below.

The first rays of sunlight were tinting the tops of the tents as Thomas and his escort rode towards the largest of the group of tents; he was not really surprised to see the now very familiar figure of Colonel Lewis standing at the front of the largest of the tents; he was accompanied most surprisingly, by Colonel Grey. Thomas led his men forward until they stopped before the two waiting men. With a small hand signal, Thomas and Carmelo stepped from their hard ridden horses and handed the reins to one of the waiting escort; they would take the horses away and find somewhere to rest them while the Officers talked.

Thomas and Carmelo took the few steps to take them within a hands breadth of the two waiting men; it gave Thomas a little start as both men snapped to attention and saluted as he and Carmelo came up to them; Colonel Lewis was the first to speak.

"Good Morning General, The Viscount has been waiting for you, if you will follow me inside we can get down to business."

"Thank you Colonel Lewis; you know Colonel Grey I am sure?"

"Yes General. How are you Colonel Grey?"

"Well Sir." Carmelo replied before turning to his father and for the first time that he could ever remember, Thomas saw Carmelo blush as he held out his hand to his stern looking father in greeting. "Hello Papa."

It surprised all those present as the stern faced Colonel looked at Carmelo with a discerning eye before he stepped forward and took Carmelo in a hug and then stepped back and said something that Thomas thought Carmelo must have been waiting a lifetime for.

"I'm very proud of you Carmelo, just as your mother would have been. What you have done in helping the General is far more than I could have thought you capable of when you were young. Whatever happens in the future I want you to remember that there is nothing that will ever change my opinion of you and I will go to my grave just as proud as I am today."

Thomas watched with disbelief as two tears formed in Carmelo's eyes and ran slowly down his weather beaten cheeks; Thomas could only think that this was a time that should be remembered and that it had affected Carmelo like Thomas had never seen before. Before much else could be said, there came a deep sharp voice from inside the tent.

"Colonel Lewis! If you have finished with your chums I would appreciate their attendance as soon as possible. We have a war to fight and the French will soon be on the move."

"Yes My Lord, we are come right in Sir."

"Then bloody hurry up Colonel, I don't have all day to sit waiting around while you exchange pleasantries."

Thomas almost let a giggle escape his lips as Colonel Lewis raised his eyes to the sky before he smiled and indicated they should all go inside before the Viscount came out looking for them; not a good idea this early in the morning. Colonel Lewis led Thomas and Carmelo into the tent with Carmelo's father close behind. When he saw the Viscount sitting behind his desk, he was at first surprised the man was dressed as he was.

There had never been a time when Thomas had not seen the Viscount impeccably dressed in a smart uniform but this time he was in his shirt sleeves and looked as though he had just arisen from his bed; had Thomas known that the Viscount had yet to see his bed he may have understood the man's unkempt state.

"Good morning General Marking, thank you for coming; we have a lot to talk over and I do need your assistance if you would see your way to helping us."

"Good morning Sir; we will of course try to do what we can to help you but, I ask that you not have plans to have my men put in unnecessary danger so that your army is better able to take advantage. As you well know Sir, I am under the orders of the Cortes and my men are under my command."

Thomas watched the Viscounts face change as he stated his own limits, something that was not normally done to any superior Officer and especially not the Viscount; the sole commander of all English and allied forces.

Thomas waited patiently as the range of emotions ran quickly over the Viscounts face; it quickly went from shock to anger and then to resignation as he looked down his long nose at one of the very few Officers he considered to be competent and trustworthy for the upcoming campaign season.

"Point taken General Marking but I did not envision you being placed in a situation you did not control, but I will keep your words in mind. I assume that by now you have had words with His Highness Prince Pimentel so if you have no objections I will just continue under the assumption that you are now aware of our situation."

"Yes Sir, the Prince has made mention of some of your concerns and I and my men will do what we can to assist in any way we can."

"Thank you General, now then firstly we need the assistance of some of your men that have a good knowledge of northern Spain. I have sent one part of my army to try and cut off any thoughts of retreat that the French may have and am badly in need of a guide to taken them through the mountains. It has been said that it is impossible to move an army over the terrain but I am sure that with the right people there must be a way past without running into the French prematurely."

"I have already taken care of that Sir, my men are already on their way to intercept your army and lead them through the mountains."

"You have? Well I must say you do move very quickly General; it is easy to see why you are held in such high esteem by His Highness and the Cortes. Now my next problem is the main French army."

The Viscount turned to the large rough map lying on the table in front of him, Thomas covered his mouth with his hand as he tried to keep the small smile from being seen when he saw just how rough the maps were when compared to the finely drawn ones of Major Smithson. It had not really occurred to Thomas before just how rudimentary the English maps were until now.

As the Viscount traced his planned advance across the map Thomas stayed quiet and did not give any indication that he was already aware of much of what the Viscount was now trying to explain to him; he had already made some tentative plans of his own and had no intention of revealing them to the Viscount unless it was needed to keep his men safe.

"The main French forces are at present camped between the Douro and the Targus rivers and I plan to force them to move north towards Burgos where some of my armies will cut them off from the roads to France. If all goes as planned I hope to trap Jourdan inside the passes where he will not have freedom of movement and narrow his front so that Sir Thomas Graham can get at them from the right. I have been informed that you were responsible for the closing of the Miranda pass and that has made it easier for my forces as the French now only have one way open to them and that is through the narrower passes towards Balbao. My one concern is that the French will be able to escape through to France before I can get to grips with them and this is where I would like your assistance."

Thomas watched as the Viscount once again traced a possible road for his frontal attack which he explained to Thomas was mainly a feint in the hope the French would think it was the main attack and then turn their forces towards the little known town of Vittoria where they could be trapped and then beaten. There was one thing that had worried the Viscount and that was the need for a small force to limit the ability of the French to withdraw back into France with their army intact. To avoid this the Viscount asked if Thomas could once again make concentrated raids on the French supply lines and close as many roads as he could.

The main assault if all went well in the early stages of the campaign would be around the River Zadorra where it narrowed down into a hairpin bend, there were ample bridges across the river and the Viscount was certain the French would not be able to destroy all of them in time to stop his own forces from breaching the French lines by the use of the bridges.

The Viscount told Thomas that he had it on good authority that after the ravages Napoleon had suffered in his disastrous attempt to take Russia, he had pulled valuable men from the Spanish front to bolster his own depleted forces in Europe. The Viscount deemed that now was the right time to make his best advance and defeat the French once and for all while Jourdan's forces were so weakened by the men drafted back to France for the Emperors needs. Now that the Austrians had joined forces with the German armies and were intent on pushing Napoleon back to Paris and his final demise, the Emperor was in bad need of men to fill his lines.

As Thomas watched and listened to the Viscount's needs they were suddenly interrupted by a young Lieutenant as he carried a large tray of food into the tent. The Viscount looked up at the young man with a frown before sighing and looking at Thomas and the others.

"Gentlemen would you like to join me for breakfast, I'm sorry I had no idea of the time; perhaps we can pause here to catch our breath and eat before we continue."

The others present agreed and the young Lieutenant then had to reorganise a small side table so everyone could select what they wanted from the overfull tray; Thomas suddenly realised he had missed his early morning cafe and wondered if his slightly sullen mood had anything to do with that oversight.

The men all joined the Viscount in a hurried meal and as they ate it gave them the time to consider what the Viscount had so far imparted to them. For Thomas there was a lot to consider and paramount was the safety of his own men if they were going to be out on their own with the English and allied armies pushing the French towards them with little back up.

By late morning most of the planning had been completed and Thomas was hoping to get back on the road before lunch. With all the details he now carried in his head there was a lot to do before his men would be ready to face the French once more and at the same time try to assist the Viscount and the English with their own plans.

"Well General Marking, you can now see what I hope is my future plans and how I could do with your assistance in keeping the French held in the passes to the north, anything you can do that allows me to once and for all destroy their army will be greatly appreciated. My main concern is for the area around Vittoria and the passes leading to Balbao And on into France. What do you think you could do to help me hold them back from the passes?"

"Well Sir, we have already done a lot of raiding in the passes to the north and the French would now be very much aware of their vulnerability there now but I am sure we can still keep them on their toes and do a good amount of damage to their supply lines once you have started your advance. With your attacks in the south they should be more concerned with the problems in that direction and we may be able to cause considerable problems for them well behind their front lines."

"Do you have anything more positive for me General?"

"Not at this stage Sir, I will need my men to do reconnaissance before I can finalise any plans but I will guarantee that your attack to the north will be made as easy as I can make it."

"Thank you General Marking, it is all I can ask at this stage. Will you be staying in camp for this evening? We have a special celebration in the Officer's mess this evening and I would like you to join us if you had no other plans?"

"Thank you Sir, but I need to get back to Braganza; it's a full four days ride and I need to get my men ready and have the region scouted before your attack."

"Very good General Marking, I fully understand your concerns although it would have been nice to have you in the mess for the evening but as you are well aware as I am that duty must come first. My thanks again for your assistance and God speed for your endeavours."

"Thank you Sir, I can assure you we will do our best to slow the French for you."

It was with a little relief that Thomas made his way out of the tent along with Carmelo; before they could go looking for their escort, a familiar rough and course voice called out behind them.

"Just a moment General, if you have a few minutes I would like to talk with you and my son."

Stopping and turning to face Colonel Grey, Carmelo and Thomas stood waiting patiently as the older man caught up with them.

"Sorry for calling you back but I wanted to say a few things without other ears hearing."

"Certainly Mister Grey; did you have some other place in mind?"

"Well I did think we would be safer at my camp than out here in the open; at least there I have my own men watching our backs."

"Very good Mister Grey, lead the way and like little puppies we will follow."

"That's enough of your cheek lad, you may be a big General in others eyes but I can still see a grubby little drummer boy wandering around a battle field with nary a friend in sight."

"That you may Mister Grey, but I've learnt a few tricks since those days, least of which is to have a good friend at my side when confronted by the evil men of the Sharpshooters Company."

A thin grin crossed Colonel Grey's face as he led the two youngsters towards where his own men were camped. In his own mind he now had to agree with O'Rourke that the pairing of the two had been the best way forward. He himself had not been in a position to keep watch over his son during the start of the war and now he was glad that he had allowed O'Rourke to talk him into letting his boy go along with a very young Drummer Boy after the battle at Rolica.

On arrival at the site where Mister Grey and his men were set up, the first thing Thomas saw was the relaxing figure of Sergeant Major O'Rourke. The Sergeant was sitting on an old folding wooden chair with his booted feet resting on an old battered trunk. His plain jacket was fully open and it appeared the top button on his rough serge trousers had been undone and the black cravat around his neck hung open. In one hand was a half full glass of what could only be brandy and his old pipe was grasped in the other; on the table beside him was the nearly empty bottle of the same brandy.

"You look remarkably comfortable O'Rourke; are you taking advantage of your missing Colonel?" Thomas asked with a wide smile on his face.

"Enough of that lad, I can still put you across me knee should the occasion arise, General or not."

For the first time in a number of years, Thomas was taken totally by surprise; not only by O'Rourke's speed but the fact that he was nowhere near as drunk as he had made out. There was sudden laughter from those closest when they saw Thomas lifted bodily and placed over the Irishman's knee. Embarrassing as the act was it was nothing compared to the three hard whacks on his upturned backside before O'Rourke placed him back on his feet.

"Now there you go lad, I told you I could still do it."

Thomas rubbed his slightly tender behind but still let the smile break through as his right hand flashed inside his jacket and produced one of his double barrelled pistols and placed it squarely in the centre of O'Rourke's forehead.

"Good you are O'Rourke, but youth and speed will always win the day."

It was the dry chuckle from Colonel Grey that finally broke up the small tableau as he said.

"Well O'Rourke bested by a bloody drummer, you should have taken more care with that bloody bottle. Now you two if you have finished mucking about I have some things to pass on to you."

Thomas replaced his pistol as O'Rourke reached for the brandy bottle one more time; the rueful look on his face as he watched his young friend turn back to Colonel Grey said it all. O'Rourke was pleasantly surprised and a little proud how the lad had turned the tables and went to show he would never be an easy push over for any man.

"O'Rourke, go and get those other chairs so we can sit for a while so I can impart my wisdom on this young rebel General."

"Do I look like a servant? By the powers I'm reduced to fetch and carry for any bloody toff that has ideas above his station. Do yee see lad what this damn upstart ranker makes me do for him."

"Yes O'Rourke, now I can see with my own eyes how you are treated; I could almost feel sorry for you if it were not that you are Irish and we all know what that means in this man's army."

As O'Rourke moved away to get the extra chairs the three could hear him mumbling about fancy Officers taking advantage of lowly Sergeants, his mumbling was interspersed with the puffing of his pipe. O'Rourke returned with three more folding chairs under one arm and placed them in a semi circle around the small table before taking up his glass and emptying it with one gulp.

Colonel Grey began to speak as O'Rourke refilled his glass, although Thomas did notice it was not nearly as full as it had been before their arrival.

"I was watching your reaction to his nibs request; at a guess I would say you already have something in mind for the eventual battle plan. Do you mind telling me what you were thinking?"

"Not at all Mister Grey. I was thinking of taking all my men back to the camp site we used over winter; from there I can attack in a number of different directions and still have a good escape route if I need one."

"What of the men you sent after Sir Thomas and his divisions?"

"They have orders not to get mixed up in any fighting but to lead Sir Thomas to the northern crossing of the Esla and then break away and return to our camp before any battle is joined. With luck they should be able to rejoin us before the middle of May."

"Good for you lad, now then I want to tell you to stay well away from Balbao, I know you have done some real damage to some of their supply trains but what we saw up north in France could mean some real trouble for you. If I've read things properly then I would say you should sit back and wait for the main battles to be over and done with then use your skill to block or harry any Frenchies that will try to retreat back to France. With your attack on Miranda and Sir Thomas coming from the north east, the French will only have one road to escape and that's the one you will be sitting on."

Thomas nodded his head in understanding as he listened to the older and wiser man; the last thing he wanted to do was lead his men into a full scale battle and lose men he did not want to. Thomas stayed quiet as he watched Mister Grey get his thoughts together before continuing.

"Now the other thing I've heard is that Joseph Bonaparte the so called King of Spain is somewhere ahead, perhaps with Jourdan or he may be with Soult but he is trying to get back to France and his brother. If you see a chance or anything that even vaguely looks like him or his baggage train then I would set up somewhere and try to trap him. Personally I think the French will make a stand and then, if they have to, will retreat back to Burgos and try to hold Wellington there. If Wellington gives them a bloody nose there is only one place they can make for with any hope of holding Wellington back and that's Vittoria so stay well away from there as well unless you can see a safe way to use your ambush skills."

Once again Thomas nodded his understanding of the situation that Mister Grey was explaining to him.

"If Wellington gets the French running back towards France then I would say this war will be over before the next year is out so this is not the time for you to get careless lad. I would suggest that you make no attacks that you know you can't win or if there is even the smallest of doubt over. Do you understand what I'm saying?"

"Yes and thank you Mister Grey, some of what you've told me I had not thought of but I am determined to have all of my men finish this war in one piece if at all humanly possible."

"Good then we are on the same course. You've done far more than most during this damn war lad, and now it's almost over there's little need for you to stick your neck out just so others can make a name for themselves. Well that's all I have to say lad, just keep your head down and don't take any stupid chances. We've got the bloody French on the run so now it's up to you to get home safe."

"I'll do my best Mister Grey but as you know I still have men and boys that deserve a chance for final revenge on the French and if the chance arises I am not going to stop them. Most of my Spanish and Portuguese men have lost everything to them and I am determined to see they get their chance."

"I can understand that lad but don't let the need for revenge cloud your judgement when it comes to their lives and your's as well. Make it home safe and sound then you can sit back and look at what you have done. There's not many that could have accomplished what you have in the last five years lad, there's much for you to be proud of and to go looking for revenge at this stage could be the wrong thing to do."

"Thank you Mister Grey, I will keep your words in mind. Now I must get on, we have a long journey back to Braganza and a lot of planning to do. Thank you and O'Rourke for everything you've done for me, I don't think I would have lived through this without your help."

"Well then God speed lad, keep your head down and your powder dry; I don't know if or when we will meet again but I hope it's in better times."

Thomas stood as did Carmelo; it was almost heart warming to see Colonel Grey reach out to Carmelo and give him a quick hug before the two youngsters went in search of their escort so they could begin their return to Braganza, there was still a long road ahead and many French to face before the war would be done.

CHAPTER 19

It was late afternoon on the fourth day when Thomas, Carmelo and the escort finally made it into the camp at Braganza. For those watching the return of their General, it was obvious they had had a tough ride home. The horses were flecked with white foam from their heavy sweating and the riders were covered in days worth of dust and grime; the riders also looked as though they had slept little in the last four days as their eyes were dark rimmed and looked hollow on their grime laden faces.

Thomas was glad to once again finally be back with his many friends; the column had only stopped when needed and they had forced themselves onward regardless of how tired they felt. It was only the health of the horses that made them stop along the way. Thomas and his men had been riding almost nonstop since before dawn with only a pause at midday for a quick bite and to rest the horses.

As Thomas eased from his tired and foam flecked horse he felt the ache of his bones from the long hours of riding; he would need a good rest this night to try to get back to something approaching normal. While Thomas was well aware he had much to do, his present state of tiredness had other ideas for him and it was with relief he saw the ever present newly promoted Sergeant Fairley waiting patiently for him at the door to his small house.

Thomas let a soft groan escape his lips as he finally got to sit down in a stable chair and let Fairley ease off his hot and tight boots, a hot bath was waiting close by for him to slip into and soak away the aches of the last four days.

Without realising it, Thomas drifted off in the hot bath, the long days of travel had finally caught up with him and it was now up to Fairley to watch over him until it was time to leave the hot bath and look for his bed. Dinner was something that Thomas would ignore when he finally fell into his bed and the soft snoring of a tired body could be heard in the late afternoon heat.

When Thomas finally opened his eyes and tried to rub away the crusty goo from his eyes, he still felt as though he needed more sleep but the rumble in his stomach tried to urge him to find sustenance before much more time passed. The sound of Thomas groaning as he tried to sit up and then swing his legs over the side of the cot soon got Fairley's attention as he dozed in a chair close by the bedside.

"Anything to eat Fairley?" Thomas asked his batman.

"Yes Sir, I have some cold meat and bread ready for you. Do you want a cafe or something a little stronger?"

"Cafe would be fine thank you Fairley. Does Major Jones have all your details for your new pay and rank?"

"Yes Sir, he did opinion that it was about time, but that's not for me to say Sir."

"Cheeky bugger. Right Fairley I'll have that food and the cafe now if you please then I can dress and get the day underway; we have a lot to do."

"Yes Sir. There is one thing Sir."

"What is it Fairley?"

"It is only about two hours after midnight; do you want me to wake everyone now?"

"Oh damn, I thought it was far later. OK Fairley let me eat and drink then I can start to make a few plans before everyone else wakes; you had better get to your own bed when you have finished here, you may not get much rest from here on out."

"Yes Sir, thank you."

As Fairley walked out of the room Thomas suddenly realised that his batman was now almost fourteen; he had no idea where the time had gone but his batman had always seemed to be there and somehow know without being asked what Thomas's needs would be. It was times like these that Thomas realised how the others had watched over him without complaint; he owed so much too so many of his men and he had no idea how to repay them for their steadfastness.

With Fairley gone off to rest, Thomas sat at the small table and sipped his cafe while chewing on the meat, bread and cheese that Fairley had left for him. In front of him were a number of Major Smithson expert maps with each showing a part of the wide pass that led from the southern plains through to Balbao; some of the light pencil marks on the maps showed him where he had already been when raiding the French supply trains.

To make better plans Thomas had now spread all of the smaller maps out over the floor area so that they looked more like one large map with small stones holding down the corners of each one. Thomas had been at work for some time when he heard the sound of approaching footsteps; once again it was the faithful Fairley carrying a fresh mug of cafe and it was then that Thomas saw that the night had grown lighter and that dawn was upon him.

Thomas smiled at Fairley as the batman placed the cafe close to hand and then stood back and asked.

"Do you want something more to eat Sir?"

"No thank you Fairley, I still have plenty left to chew on until breakfast."

Fairley looked over at the table where a very clean plate sat; he smiled as the turned back to where Thomas was kneeling on the floor as he looked over the scattered maps.

"I don't think the plates can be eaten Sir; perhaps I can find a little more to tide you over until the fires are stoked."

"What? What do you mean Fairley, there's plenty left, I've hardly taken a bite so far."

Fairley lifted the empty plate from the table and tipped it on its side before saying.

"Then we must have a bad infestation of rats Sir."

"What?"

Thomas turned his head and looked up to see Fairley holding the empty plate; a look of surprise came over Thomas's face as he realised he had been eating as he worked and yet his stomach still seemed to need something more. Thomas shook his head at the smiling batman.

"Alright, no need to get smug; so I was a bit distracted; see what you can find and another cafe to boot."

"Yes Sir." The smiling Fairley said as he took the plate away as well as the other empty cafe mug while Thomas turned back to his spread maps.

Slowly a pattern was beginning to develop in Thomas's mind as he surveyed the maps on the floor; if only he had one large detailed map it would have made it easier. With a sudden realisation, Thomas came up with a new job for the hard working Major Smithson and his little group of mappers.

On looking over the existing maps and trying to make allowances for the gaps between them; Thomas worked out that if the French did have to retreat then they had very few options but it would all depend on how far the English could push them back to the French border.

Fairley was soon back with a replenished plate and a fresh cafe which he placed on the table just as Thomas stood up and absently reached for some meat and bread without really looking at what he was doing; Fairley deduced that it was what Thomas had been doing for most of the morning. Thomas looked at Fairley and then said.

"When the others have arisen would you please find the Colonels and Major's for me and ask them to come and see me as soon as they can."

"Yes Sir."

Fairley left the house and went in search of the Senior Officers; as he walked out into the rising light of a new day Fairley could hear the beginnings of the camp coming to life in readiness of a new day. Fairley soon found all of the Officers and passed on Thomas's request before turning towards the kitchens where he could hear the scullery's beginning to stoke the fires for another day of cooking to feed the masses of the small army.

At the sound of a knock on the door jam, Thomas looked up to see Carmelo and Estaban standing there watching him on his knees on the floor as he continued to pour over the small maps.

"Come in, I have a few things for you to think on and let me know what you think; are the others on their way?"

"Yes Patron, they should be here shortly." Carmelo replied.

Thomas stood up and glanced at the now empty plate and the two empty cafe mugs; he couldn't remember finishing either but turned back to his two closest friends. Before he could start, Thomas heard the rest of his Officers talking amongst themselves as they came towards the house. Thomas held up his hand to indicate to his friends that they would continue once the others had joined them.

With everyone clustered in the small front room of Thomas's house there was little space to move but each man found a place and waited for Thomas to begin.

"Sorry to call you all here before breakfast but I wanted to get things started early and I need some suggestions so I can finalise everything before we move the camp north. Major Smithson, once again I have to ask for your help and those of your mappers. Can you make a single map of the following areas and put in as much detail as you can fit on a large space."

Here Thomas showed Major Smithson the smaller maps he had selected as being of the most importance according to the information he had so far. Major Smithson took one glance at the number of smaller maps and gave a single nod that he could do as asked but told Thomas he would need a little time to make it work.

"How much time do you need Major?"

"If I need to go back and look over the areas once more then it could be about a month Sir."

"Then I will leave it all in your hands Major but I do need as much detail as you can get for us. Take whatever supplies you need for you and your men and get underway as soon as you can."

"Immediately Sir, we can leave within two hours."

"Thank you Major. Major Morgan?"

"Yes Sir?"

"How long to get all your guns to this point in the pass to Balbao with one Company of Infantry along as well?"

Major Morgan looked at the four maps that Thomas had spread on the table and followed Thomas's finger as he traced the route to the south western pass leading to Balbao. Major Morgan stood silently for a few minutes as he tried to work out the distances and the needs of his five Batteries and a Company of Infantry along with all the supplies they may need.

"At the worst Sir, I think about three weeks but if all goes well then we may make it in two."

"Good. Major Lorenco I want to put you in charge of the other Company of Infantry as well as your sharpshooters; I think it would be best if you made use of all our mules for supplies but that you remain as mobile as possible. Your place will be here to the west of Vittoria and covering the central pass; do you think you can be there also in three weeks if needs be?"

"Yes Sir."

"Good then once there I want you to have the men well spread out along the northern ridge so that you have an open field of fire down into the pass. Your job is not to directly attack any columns but to do what you all do best; harry them from maximum distance and keep your men safe from any retaliation. Again mobility is your safest ploy."

"Yes Sir."

"Major Jones I want you to make sure they all have everything they will need and once that is taken care of I want you to take over the defence of this camp until we return. Captain Maketja and the others will probably return after we have left, keep them here to assist you in the defence of the camp."

"Yes Sir."

"Carmelo I would like you to stay with me as we will be with Estaban and the three companies of Cavalry; while I have full confidence in the three Cavalry Officers I would like one of us in each Company to make sure we keep them mobile and they do not stop to make a full out fight with any French we may run into. If the English succeed in their push north then there are going to be a great number of French troops on the road and not all of them will retreat in haste once battle is joined."

Carmelo and Estaban just nodded that they understood and would do whatever Thomas asked of them.

"Right next thing is we have to make our first plans and once Mister Smithson has returned and finalises his map we will begin to make the last plan; for now I want you all to see to your men and make sure they have everything they may need. If this works out it could well be our last fight to get the French out of the country so I want everyone to check and double check that you have everything you will need to succeed and that the men under your command are as safe as we can make them."

Thomas looked at the many faces of all his closest friends; he had a feeling deep inside that this was the time that was going to influence their future and only a solid win over the French would secure that future.

Even after five years of war, Thomas was astounded by the amount of work that was going into the checking of the men's equipment. Major Jones seemed to be right in his element as he took stock of his many supplies and began to issue new items to all the men. Every musket and pistol was to have new flint whether they had been worn down or not; the barrels of their weapons were cleaned of any sign of rust and then coated in a very fine layer of refined whale oil for preservation.

Every knife and sword was taken out, oiled and then sharpened. Boots were inspected for over wear and replaced wherever possible or repaired with care. Saddlery and tack were also inspected and repaired or replaced and the men's large panniers to carry all they would need were checked for any damage. When the time came to move north there would be no wagon train; the army was going to move at speed and everything the men would need would be in their panniers or they would go without.

Major Morgan had every gun stripped to its smallest part, cleaned and inspected before re-assembling and testing. The gunners were put through their paces as they were brought up to as fine a set of gunners as had ever been seen on ship or shore. Lieutenant Wright had his men stripping the rocket ramps and inspecting every nut, bolt and sighting slide then oiling it all to keep off any chance of rust. His next effort was to reproduce what seemed like an endless number of rockets of which he had now become very proficient at making after receiving the plans from England for their production, via the ever helpful talents of Mister Percy.

Thomas had allocated ten of their mules for the conveyance of the extra rockets as Lieutenant Wright had proven their worth more than once since using them for the first time so long ago. It was at times like these; as they prepared for what may very well be their most defining battle so far that Thomas found himself with little to do but sign masses of paper that Major Jones put before him each day. It was an onerous task and one of the few Thomas did not look forward to.

As the day for their move north came closer; Major Jones began to issue the men with what they may need as far as extra powder and shot to make their familiar wax paper cartridges. Their food would be issued the night before they moved off and would be made up of smoked meat, cheese and rounds of thin bread, each man carrying enough for five days. They would be re-provisioned by making use of whatever was around them for which Thomas had given orders that each man was to carry two gold coins for any purchases of food from the local farmers as they needed.

It was mid April before Major Smithson re-appeared with his small band of map makers. They all looked as though once again they had gone without much sleep and were dressed in rough peasant garb to lessen the chances of discovery when so close to the French. Major Smithson's report and final details of the maps was concise and to the point as he revealed to Thomas what he had seen while he and his men filled in any blanks in his older maps.

From the Major's report it seemed the French were indeed preparing for the advance of Wellington as the passes were filled with supply trains and reinforcements which had made it just that much harder for the Major to do his job. It appeared the French were making good use of the main pass from Balbao east to Vittoria or further. There seemed to be hardly a pause in the long columns of men and supplies being transported east for the upcoming battle.

Seemingly without rest Major Smithson set his men to updating the maps and transferring them onto one very large piece of thick parchment that the Major had somehow pieced together from smaller pieces; it now covered more than a yard on each side and the Major and his tired men set to work to make a complete map of the area Thomas had wanted.

Knowing that the Viscount had plans to attack around mid May Thomas began to issue orders for the slowest column to begin its move north. It was to be the guns and Infantry to go first with the other Company of Infantry and the sharpshooters to follow two days later; Thomas and the Cavalry would follow on two days after that.

By the 4th of May Thomas had the large map before him, to his young eyes the map looked extraordinary with its fine detail with distances and ranges in small figures where needed as well as the height of the ridges and low mountains that could stand in their way. On the 5th of May Thomas gave the orders for the gunners and Infantry to move out once they had the location he wanted them to take a stand at.

Major Morgan carried a smaller version of the map he would need for the area he was to fight from as did Lorenco; Thomas carried the larger map rolled up in a thick leather pouch as he would need the full coverage of the Balbao pass and its environs so he could keep and overall view of the plan.

CHAPTER 20

Lieutenant Snot Morgan and Captain Maketja led the small force of ten men in their guide troop towards where they had been told they should meet up with the English General Sir Thomas Graham. Thomas's orders were still fresh in their minds as they held their horses to a ground swallowing trot; with luck they should either meet up with or sight the tracks made by the English force in the next one or two days.

Snot had been told that they should find the English at or around Villafranca where Maketja and his guides would then take over and lead the large column of men and guns over the mountains and well behind the front lines of the French further to their east and south. The tracks they would be following were mainly used only by smugglers and anyone not involved with that trade would never find them.

Each of the extra ten men had deep knowledge of some part of the tracks they were going to use and Maketja had told Snot that he would have to impress on the English General that his men would have to work hard on getting their many guns over the passes; there would be no space for wagons and any they had would have to be left behind and the supplies carried on the backs of the wagon mules or left on the wagons.

Ahead of them was a journey that could easily take two months and there was little doubt there would be losses amongst the English soldiers. The area they were going into was considered by many to be impassable although the smugglers had proved that theory wrong at every turn if one was adventurous and brave enough to be almost foolhardy.

Two days after leaving their camp at Braganza, Snot and Maketja came across the first signs of the English army; with more than 20,000 men in the column it was not difficult to find the first trace of them. The trail led towards the lower ridges of the Asturian and

Cantabrian Mountains and appeared to be very fresh; Maketja thought they should meet up with the column within an hour or two as they turned to follow the churned up ground.

The winter in these higher elevations still held a little sway and the deep marks of many wagons were easily seen in the torn ground; Snot wondered what the English were going to think when they were told to leave their wagons behind.

The rest of the English army which numbered around 57,000 were to be led across the wide plains of Castile by some of Wellington's Spanish guides and were to be used as a feint while Sir Thomas Graham's men were to be the main thrust on the French right flank. Wellington's road was a little easier as he wanted to be seen by the French while Sir Thomas Graham's corps stayed well out of sight and was given the most difficult of the land to cross.

Snot and Maketja came across the tail of the English army just as it was looking up at the mountains they would have to cross; the comments made by the rough English troops as the small column of youngsters rode by were incomprehensible to the Spanish boys but not so to the tender ears of Snot Morgan, although he kept his own mouth shut and refused to speak to the rougher soldiers of England; it was not his place to correct their ignorance.

"Well lookee ere lads, them foreigners is sending little boys to fight in this ere man's war." Opined one soldier as he saw the small group pass by; the reply he got from one of the older hands was not what he had been expecting.

"Shut it Grimes, thems is the men of the Rolica Drummer whats is a hero in this man's army so mind yer manners."

"What them little boys, come on Sergeant they should be at their mummy's titty not ridin around like real soldiers."

"I says shut it Grimes; next time it be extra duty ifin you got a mind to talk bad bouts one of our own. Ifin them boys is ere then there be a good reason; only time you see them is when trouble is about."

Snot could not hide the smile on his face as he rode away; it seemed his special General still had a few old hands around that had respect for what he had done nearly five years ago. The long column of men and wagons seemed to go on forever as the twelve riders moved forward. For Snot it seemed the column had to be at least two miles long. If this were so then they would never make it over the mountains in time; the column would have to be stripped down and pushed far harder if Wellington's orders were to be fulfilled.

As they rode past the long column, Snot saw many of the men struggling as they tried to carry their equipment and at the same time try to assist in pushing the over-laden wagons through some of the rougher ground where the mud had not entirely dried into dust.

As the small troop came up to the rear of the English Cavalry they garnered more strange looks as they passed by and rode towards the front of the column. It was only a short time later that Snot and Maketja saw the man they had been searching for. Sir

Thomas Graham was a portly man and showed the effects of his exulted position. He sat his large horse with the ease of a man used to being in the saddle for long periods.

Around the General were a large number of high ranking officers and all seemed to be not only in good spirits but totally unaware of the plight of some of their men behind them. Snot and Maketja soon caught up to the Officers ahead of them but before they could introduce themselves, Sir Thomas Graham turned his head to look them over with a very superior, if not disdainful look on his face; his words were curt and to the point.

"Who are you lads and what are you doing up here?"

"Sir, I am Lieutenant Morgan and this is Captain Maketja, we have been ordered by our General to escort you and your army over the mountains. I will be your interpreter as Captain Maketja and his men do not speak English."

The General lifted his hand to halt the column and slowly the long line of men and equipment came to a halt; most of the Infantry immediately found a place to sit and rest while others searched for their water bottles.

"And who would this General of yours be lad?"

"General Don Thomasino de Toro Sir; Commander of the 1r Regimiento Espanol Guerrillas. We are here at the request of Viscount Wellington; it is our orders to find a path through the mountains for you and your army Sir. Captain Maketja and his men were born in these mountains and know every path to take you through to the River Esla as the Viscount requires Sir."

"I see Lieutenant; well I hope your abilities are more pronounced than your years. You and your men may dine with the Junior Officers and other ranks; if there is nothing more then we can continue on our way; we still have another hour before we must make camp for the night."

"There is one thing more Sir."

"What is it now Lieutenant?" The General's tone of voice said far more to Snot than his words conveyed.

"Your column Sir, it is far too slow and cumbersome to make the River Esla in the time the Viscount requires; it is imperative that the column be lightened of un-necessary equipment and the wagons will have to be left behind."

"Are you insane Lieutenant; everything we need is in those wagons and the men will not be able to advance without their equipment. The whole idea is impossible; you will have to think of something else."

"Sir, if I may ask; what is the daily distance your column is making at this time?"

"Why do you ask Lieutenant?"

"Well Sir, if it is like other army columns then it is far too slow to get to the River Esla on time; the men will need to travel lighter and at a better speed, the wagons are far too slow for that and there is also the size of the paths we will be using. Captain Maketja has told me that none of the paths will be wide enough for wagons and they will not make the grades that we are going to climb, it will be very difficult just for your guns but no chance at all for fully laden wagons."

"Well then Lieutenant you and your lads will just have to find another way; you can't honestly expect Officers to travel in the field without their normal comforts and as far as leaving the wagons that is also impossible; most of our war needs are on those wagons. How will we get the powder and shot to where they need to be?"

"On horseback Sir; we will transfer as much of your war needs to the wagon mules; what we can't take we will have to be left behind. Now Sir I think the average distance for an army is between ten and twelve miles per day; for you to make the River in time we need to make at least thirty miles per day and that can only be done without the wagons."

"Preposterous Lieutenant, no man can make that distance on foot; especially over these mountains."

"No Sir it is not preposterous; the 1r Regimiento Espanol Guerrillas can cover as much as fifty miles per day when required and so can your men. Thirty miles should be easy for them to accomplish if they are prepared to put in the effort."

"Are you arguing with a Superior Officer Lieutenant; if so I will have you brought up on charges just as soon as it is convenient. Now then your idea cannot be done; it is impossibility and that's final."

"Very good Sir then I have no alternative but to return to my General and report your decision and that you have no further need of us; I'm sure the Viscount Wellington will fully understand when you do not make your appearance on the battle field, knowing how difficult these mountains are to cross."

"That is impertinent Lieutenant; you are about to cross a line that no Junior Officer should cross."

"Yes Sir, then if you have no further need of us we shall return to our own camp. Good bye Sir Thomas." Snot being as he was a Morgan could not resist a last jibe. "We do hope you won't miss the Viscounts battle it would be such a slur on your record. Toodaloo."

Snot turned his horse and began to ride away with the others following him as he changed to Spanish and began to tell them what the conversation had been all about. The small troop rode off back the way they had come; he had followed his orders and they had been refused by the most Senior Officer. As far as Snot was concerned his duty was done and it was time to go home and take up the fight with his friends.

The troop rode for another hour before Snot and Maketja heard a double whistle from the rear of the troop; without a pause, Maketja waved his arm to the left and right and the two ranks split and looked for cover on both sides of the valley they had been riding through. A double whistle was the signal that there may be danger approaching from their rear.

With all twelve riders now well hidden among the large rocks and scrub that covered the sides of the narrow valley; they took their muskets from their shoulders and got ready to fight if they needed to. In the quiet that now surrounded them Snot could now plainly hear the sounds of a fast galloping horse coming from behind them. The only other sound in the valley was the very distinctive sound of twenty four hammers being taken to full cock.

Captain Warren rode as fast as he could, the General's orders were not to be ignored even though Captain Warren had seen the look of dislike and even distaste on the Generals face as he issued his orders to the young Captain of Cavalry to find and return with the young foreign men.

Captain Warren was easily able to follow the hoof prints on the dusty road; he was hoping they were not also at the gallop as it would have made his orders so much harder to carry out. It was with a surprise that almost unseated him when he turned a bend in the valley and came face to face with the twelve men he had been in search of; the fact that he was looking down the double barrels of some strange muskets also gave him cause for concern.

Pulling hard on his reins to bring his horse to a halt before he ran into the young men that blocked his path; Captain Warren gulped as he looked down the mass of barrels and hoped the men behind them had a good steady hand as he reached down to calm his horse. Captain Warren decided he had better speak first before a severe accident happened and he was on the receiving end.

"Excuse me gentlemen, which one of you is Lieutenant Morgan?"

Snot kneed his horse a few steps closer to the Cavalryman and then said.

"That would be me and who are you?"

"Captain Warren of the 18th Hussars, Lieutenant. I wish to convey the Generals compliments and would you be so kind as to return and advise the General on how he may march to the River Esla."

Snot could not resist the temptation laid before him.

"And if I say no, what then Captain?"

"Uhm...well...ahh...I don't exactly know Lieutenant, the General did not tell me what to do if you refused; I ahh..."

The Captains voice trailed off into silence as Snot smugly enjoyed the moment. Before replying to the Captain, Snot turned to Maketja and the others and, speaking in Spanish told them.

"Seems old Rolly-Polly can't find his boot straps and wants us to go back and find them for him; what do you think Maketja?"

"Well it's why we're here; seems a shame to make him have to ask us for help and not give it to him, besides I want to watch those fine soldiers marching bravely over the mountains."

"Did I ever tell you that you have a very nasty streak in you Maketja?"

"Yes often but then we would not have so much fun would we Snot?"

"That's true, OK I'll tell this Captain we are coming back to save them but only so you can watch all those brave soldiers."

"Hrumph... like you really care what happens to them; you should have been born a Basque instead of an English, your mean steak is far wider than my own and you damn well know it."

"True but then you would be lonely and never have any fun if I stayed away."

"There is that, well you had better put this Captain's mind at rest so we can return to your Rolly-Polly and help find his boots."

Snot turned back to the Captain who had sat his horse in silence with a look of concern on his youngish face while the two strangers had discussed matters in a tongue he did not understand.

"Well Captain, if you would like to lead the way, Captain Maketja has decided to return and help the General only because he feels a sense of duty to our own General's orders."

"Thank you Lieutenant and please convey our thanks to the Captain. If you and your men would follow me Sir I will take you back; the General is waiting for your return."

Snot gave Maketja a small nod and the rest of their small troop un-cocked their muskets and slipped them back over their shoulders before once again taking up their normal two ranks and following along behind the two young Officers.

The ride back to Sir Thomas Graham's army was a little more sedate as they kept their pace to a steady trot; it was less than an hour before full dark when they came upon the large spread out camp. The smell of smoke from the cooking fires and the hubbub of voices gave them ample warning well before they actually rode into the camp.

Captain Warren led Snot and Maketja directly to the well appointed tents of the Senior Officers while the other ten troopers found a small place they could set up their own camp slightly away from the English troops. After the troopers had seen to their horses they set about getting a good fire going and preparing the evening meal, they would wait for their two young Officers to get back before eating.

Snot and Maketja were led by the Captain to the largest of the Senior Officers tents where a group of Officers were standing around talking. At the appearance of the two young foreign Officers, there was a sudden silence and the air about them seemed to suddenly take on a decidedly colder feel. Not all of the looks were friendly but Snot and Maketja appeared to just ignore them; as far as they were concerned, these Officers did not know them or what they were capable of. In the days to come those same Officers were to get an education that none of them were prepared for.

Captain Warren handed them over to the care of a Major who immediately escorted them inside the nearest tent and into the presence of the portly and well fed Sir Thomas Graham; the look on the Generals face was not one of joy or friendship but more one of resignation, he needed the experience of these two young Officers even though he did not like it.

Sir Thomas Graham tried as best he could to wipe away the frown on his face as the two Officers were shown into his presence; neither Snot nor Maketja had missed the look they got from the General but decided to ignore it for the moment, they had their own way of making sure they were not taken for fools but now was not the time.

"Well...hrumph...thank you for returning...uhm...gentlemen, let's call any past errors a mistake in translation and let bygones be bygones. Now then Lieutenant, you suggested a course of action that the Captain recommended and, after some consideration I have decided to listen to his reasons a little more closely. If you could enlarge on the Captains plans then I shall see what we can do. I do understand that it is imperative for us to make the River Esla in good time for us to succeed."

Snot took the opportunity to speak with Maketja as though he was asking him for advice; the language barrier now became their best advantage when dealing with the bellicose General.

As the plan to get the English army across the mountains had long been set, most of what Snot and Maketja talked about in Spanish had very little to do with what the General had asked of them, most of it was to do with what they would be eating for dinner or how comfortable they could get while on the move from this day on.

After a few minutes of chatter, Snot turned back to the General and made his false report while Maketja stood beside him with a look of something resembling devilish superiority. With Maketja it was hard to tell which; it was not missed that he seemed to be absently fingering the butt of his shouldered musket while watching the portly General like a hawk.

"Well Lieutenant, what does your Captain suggest for us to move onward?"

"As I mentioned before Sir, we will need to lighten your column or there is little hope of you meeting the Viscounts needs. Captain Maketja has seen that you have your wagons pulled by six mules; his suggestion is that you take four of the mules from each wagon and use them as pack animals; they are sure footed and can carry a good load if done properly. Whatever is left can be put in the wagons and perhaps returned to Portugal with the remaining two mules. Next are the guns, they will need to be stripped down and the eight horse teams used to carry them on their backs. Captain Maketja also suggests that your Cavalry horses be used to carry extra powder and shot as there will be little opportunity for the men to ride for most of the journey."

"I see, well if that is all then how do you propose we get all this done in good time Lieutenant?"

"The Captain suggests we take two or three days now to break down the supplies and ready the column for the mountains. Once everything is ready some of our men will lead the mules out first and also watch the way forward, the rest of the column should follow along no less than one hour afterwards. The column will need to be on their way at first light every day if they are to make the camp sites before dark. Captain Maketja has said there are large stopping areas throughout the mountains that his people make use of but they are about 30 miles apart and there are no places to stop along the way. The column will have to eat and drink on the move during the day if they want to camp in some comfort that evening."

"You seem to have high expectations of my men Lieutenant; I am not sure if they can make that distance in the time your Captain suggests; the men are not used to moving such distances and my Officers will need time to raise their tents each evening."

"If you will excuse me for a moment Sir I will have to ask the Captain about your concerns."

Snot barely waited for the General to nod before he turned to Maketja and spoke in Spanish.

"Well old Rolly-Polly thinks he's going to have tents for the Officers and the men are not able to make thirty miles a day; I think it's time he was told a few home truths about what they are going into."

"Yes I agree, let's try to frighten him a little and there is no way on this earth that they will have space for tents, perhaps one for Rolly-Polly as he will need a headquarters to work from. Can you explain to him that if they insist on taking tents for the Officers then they will have to leave either powder or food behind; they don't have enough mules or horses to carry everything they want."

"Yes I agree; I'll tell him and then see what he does after that but you can almost place a wager that he will want his Officers to have their comforts before he worries about the men and their needs."

"Then we will have to set the rules without his knowledge, he will not find out about it until we are thirty miles away from his supplies. Make Rolly-Polly the offer that we will use our own men to set up the loading of the mules and horses; it's probably not the sort of thing he is used to so we can get them loaded before he finds out about the lack of tents."

"Good idea, I'll make the offer and if he asks why I'll tell him it's because of the terrain ahead and that you and the others know what can be taken over the mountains and how it should be done."

"Sounds like a good idea."

Snot turned back to the impatient looking General and began to lay out the plan for the column on the pretext that it was all Maketja's suggestions.

"Sir, Captain Maketja has doubts about being able to take too much equipment over the mountains and so has suggested that you allow his men to advise on the loading of the mules and horses. He has suggested that we place two mules at your disposal for your personal tent and some of your chattels but the other Officers will have to do with only what they can carry on their own horses. All the guns will have to be dismantled and carried on the horses but we have some experience of how it can be done so will also help your gunners with that. Now Sir there is only the matter of time; the Captain has said we should set aside the next three days to ready the column for the trail ahead; the mules will go first and leave before first light with the men following once dawn breaks."

"This all seems a little unnecessary and cumbersome Lieutenant but if it is the only way we can make the River Esla on time then I will have to bow to your Captains knowledge and allow him to carry out his plans. We will camp here for the next three days as suggested but then we must away by the morning of the fourth day; I cannot allow my force to be seen by any French spies at this early stage."

"Thank you Sir, we can promise that the column will be well on its way four days from now. If I may Sir, could we have written orders to that effect, it may stop any mistakes in orders with the other Officers."

"Very well Lieutenant, I will have your orders written and delivered before nightfall, now then if that is all I am sure you and the Captain have plans to make and I have other business to attend to."

"Thank you Sir, the Captain will see to the needs of your force and make everything ready for your move into the mountains."

Snot and Maketja gave a rather lose salute and left with smiles on their faces; the Generals army was in for a surprise the next day as would be most of his Officers, the work of stripping down the mass of the army would start at sunrise the next morning.

Later that night the twelve guides got together and discussed what really needed to be done. The young teen that was familiar with this part of the country would take the lead on the first few days of their move; with him would be two others who would act as guards in the van at the head of the column. The mules were to be led out first as they would need the extra time to make the next camp site before the rest of the army.

For the next three days and after some confusion as to the rights of the young guides to give orders were finally settled, the camp then became a hive of activity as the soldiers began to strip down the supplies in the wagons and the forty guns were dismantled into their separate parts for transport on the backs of the horses. The Cavalry horses had been commandeered to carry extra food and powder much to the dismay and dislike of their riders but the Generals orders were direct and to the point. Snot and Maketja were looking forward to seeing the Cavalrymen trying to keep up while on foot and leading their mounts which were now to be used as pack horses.

It was still in the dark hours of the fourth morning when the camp was awoken to the sound of mules being shivyed into action as the first part of the column got underway. For those left behind it was the last chance to sleep in the confines of a dry tent, from this day on it would be sleeping under their heavy cloaks and on hard ground.

Dawn was just breaking when the sound of loud voices called for the troops to set out on what was to be one of the hardest marches any of them would ever make. At the head of the forming column were Snot and Maketja with Sir Thomas Graham and his

Senior Officers just behind. For the first hour little changed except for the ever increasing slope ahead.

For those who wanted to look up at the ridge they were to climb to get to the top of the range where they would follow the ridge line until they made the first camp site; it was almost with trepidation as they could just make out the toy sized figures of the mule line far above and working its way along what looked to be no more than a narrow goat track.

For those troops who had not believed they would not be stopping for lunch they were to find out that the strange young foreigners were indeed true to their word; even the Officers were given no rest as the youngsters cajoled and swore as they urged the men forward. By nightfall it was only the sight of distant small fires that told the foot sore and weary column that the camp site was within reach.

The climb to the top of the ridge had been not only tiring but also very dangerous once they were more than a hundred feet up. The track had narrowed until there was barely enough space for the horses let alone the men to walk in double file. That first day saw two men fall to their deaths as they grew tired and did not watch where they placed their weary feet.

It was more than an hour after dark before the tail end of the column finally made it into camp; those ahead of them were in little better state and their meal consisted mainly of hard tack biscuits soaked in hot water before they fell into a deep weary sleep. For those camped closer to the small band of guides that had made their camp off to one side of the main army there was an added torment. Somehow the small group had had time to get a good fire going and there was a distinct spicy smell in the night air as they cooked their dinner, it was not to be the only time the foreign guides ate better than the other troops.

Snot and Maketja had gone back and forth along the column sometimes on horseback and other times on foot as they pushed the men harder and harder to raise the pace. Both boys were even amused at the end of the day when they saw the tired face and slumped figure of Sir Thomas as he was helped from his horse by a Junior Officer; the two boys smiled at each other as they went off to find their friends at the small camp off to the side of the main army.

Two days later and sixty miles further along the mountain range and with the men now becoming used to the hard slog each day; there came one more test for the guides, one that was unforeseen and no one was ready for it. The Senior English Officers were taken entirely by surprise but not Snot and Maketja and it was the two boys that settled the affair in a quick and final way. It was reported afterwards that even Sir Thomas Graham could only say good things about the two young Officers.

CHAPTER 21

16th May 1813

Viscount Wellington's camp south of the River Douro.

Colonel Lewis approached the Viscount's tent with a rather jaunty step, the first report from Sir Thomas Graham's column had finally come in. It had been fully two months since they had last heard of the General and his 20,000 strong force. The dispatch rider had been a young Subaltern from the 18th Hussars and looked to have been through the mill if his condition was any indication.

The report was quite thick and held most of what had happened during the crossing of the mountains. As per usual Colonel Lewis had read it through quickly before making for the Viscount's tent where the most Senior Officer was known to be taking his bath after the long hot and dusty ride forward.

Colonel Lewis paused outside the tent and gave a small cough to let the Viscount know he was there; from inside came the gruff voice that Colonel Lewis knew so well.

"Well come in Colonel; no need to dally around out there just because I am at bath."

Colonel Lewis drew aside the flap of the tent and entered; the Viscount was recumbent in his tin bath and looked to be enjoying his moment of rest and silence, he looked up at Colonel Lewis and raised an eyebrow as though in askance.

"The first dispatch rider from Sir Thomas has just arrived with a report My Lord."

"Damn it, about time we heard something from them; well don't just stand there Colonel, tell me what it's all about. I presume you have already read it so tell me the general gist of it, I can read it in full later."

Colonel Lewis had indeed read through the ten page report even though it had been briefly and only the main points were taken note of.

"Well My Lord, it appears they had a little trouble at first and some of the men decided to mutiny because of the pace and lack of essentials which the guides had insisted upon. In all Sir Thomas's force have had losses of one gun, two Junior Officers and thirty seven lower ranks along with six horses. They had arrived down on the plains on the 12th and stopped to rest which is when Sir Thomas made out this report. Sir Thomas has now asked what you need of him."

"What of this mutiny Colonel, does he give details and how did he handle it at the time? I do hope that he hanged those concerned in front of the other troops. We can't have the ranks thinking we are going soft Colonel."

Colonel Lewis flipped a few pages until he found the one that detailed the event; with a quick glance through the page he found the most important parts and lifted his eyes to see the Viscount still happily recumbent in his bath. The viscount had rolled a small towel up and placed it behind his head as he lay back in the warm water; he now had his eyes closed as he concentrated on Colonel Lewis's details.

"From the report My Lord, he states that a Corporal had incited some of the men to mutiny because of the conditions of the march. It would appear the guides sent by General Marking to lead Sir Thomas through the mountains had set very strict limits on what the men could carry and the distance they needed to make each day. It would seem the Corporal took umbrage at being given orders by young foreign boys and he and five others decided to take action. From Sir Thomas's report the guides themselves took the needed action to quell the mutiny before Sir Thomas's own men could re-act. The head guide, one Captain Maketja took down the Corporal and one other with his pistol, which as you know My Lord, are double barrelled; and another young Lieutenant by the name of Morgan took down the other two. The fifth offender was killed by the said Captain with a knife stroke to the chest. Sir Thomas reports that the action lasted less than one minute and was over before any other action could be taken. It appears that there were no other incidents of mutiny during the remainder of the journey to the banks of the Esla. At this time My Lord, Sir Thomas awaits your orders to advance and in which direction it should be so."

"Damn those mutinous scum; well we can only be grateful for General Marking's men to have taken just care of the situation; personally I would have kept two of them alive so they could be hung in front of the army as a future warning to those low class scum. It is getting more and more difficult to keep order as this war goes on Colonel; I fear we shall see more of the same before Bonaparte is put in his place. Now then Colonel, I would like you to issue the order for Sir Thomas to advance his force along the west bank to the Ebro; there is now no need to keep his army out of sight, in fact it would be best if the French got a good look at him while I take my men through the centre and the Spanish and Portuguese advance on the left through from Valladolid and Tudela. If all goes well Colonel we should have the French nicely rounded up in a pocket, if the worst comes to the worst we can always push them back to Burgos and end them there."

"Yes My Lord I will see to it immediately. One more thing My Lord?"

"Yes, what is it Colonel?"

"What of General Marking's guides, shall I issue orders for them to return to his camp?"

"Oh yes, the guides; well Colonel they may still be of some use to Sir Thomas as he advances; make an order for them to place themselves under Sir Thomas's orders and they can advance with his troops, they may be of some use if the terrain becomes difficult. One thing is for sure, we know they can fight and are not scared of a little bloody work."

"Yes My Lord, I will send the order forthwith but I don't think General Marking will be happy about it My Lord."

"Then we won't tell him Colonel; besides it is only a couple of men and I'm sure he won't miss them. I will leave it all in your capable hands Colonel. Now if there is nothing else perhaps I can enjoy the rest of my bathing."

Colonel Lewis saluted and left the tent, if there was anything he knew about Thomas and his men, it was that they would no longer take orders from the English. If he received a report that the young guides had departed for their own camp it would not surprise him in the least but he still had his orders and duty to perform. He would of course couch the orders in such a way that they could be open to interpretation dependant on how one looked at and read them.

14th May 1813

Somewhere on the south bank of the River Ebro, thirty miles west of Miranda.

Thomas had called all of his forces to meet in one place for any final plans to be discussed, they were now camped on the southern bank near the head waters of the River Ebro and some thirty or thirty five miles west of the town they had once ravaged. All of Thomas's Senior Officers were present around the table that now had the full scale map that Major Smithson and his men had spent many hours in perfecting. From this day on his forces would be working almost independently of each other and it was imperative they all knew where each other would be.

Thomas had received a dispatch from Mister Percy and so he was now well aware that Viscount Wellington intended to move against the main French forces in the east; it was decided that Thomas and his men would try to make sure that in the event of a French retreat they would only have one way to go and would not be able to double back through the passes of Bilbao.

The discussions and planning had gone on for more than three hours before a final plan came about that seemed to fit all eventualities and still keep his men as safe as he could, that he felt there was going to be blood spilt there was little doubt but he wanted to make sure that very little of the blood would be from his own men.

The final plan looked good and, while it was not a full scale plan of attack it was certainly one that would give no lee way to any Frenchmen that tried to retreat through his lines. Across the River Ebro and three miles to the north lay the eastern pass that led directly through to Bilbao; it was here that Major Morgan was to dig in his guns along with the protection of the 1st Infantry Company.

In the valley west of where Vittoria was positioned at the far eastern end, Lorenco and his Sharpshooters along with the 2nd Infantry Company would secret themselves on both sides of the wide pass; from their hiding places they would snipe at any French retreating back towards Balbao or use the same tactics to disrupt any supply trains sent through from the north.

Until the time came for action, Thomas gave orders that everyone was to keep their heads down and not let the French know they were so close. The order to open fire on the French would be when they heard that Viscount Wellington had started his advance and not before. Thomas, Carmelo and Estaban would each take one Company of Cavalry to command, they would be the fast attack force when hostilities opened.

To get an overall view of the valley that lead through from Vittoria to Balbao, Thomas had one of the goat herders from this area show him any and all small goat tracks that entwined over the mountains before them; he planned to make use of them to reach the other side of the valley without being seen by any roving French patrols; he could then look down on the valley and see what lay ahead of them.

By the date of the 10th of May, all of Thomas's forces were well dug into their positions and awaiting the order to take advantage of the long lines of supply wagons and troops that were pouring into the region. It would be only days later when they got the orders they were waiting for.

 On the 25th of May it was the sudden increase of French troops and wagons in the passes that alerted Thomas that something was happening; not only were the troops looking as though there was something behind them to fear but there was an increase in wagons all of which seemed to be travelling, not towards the east but north back towards France.

While the columns were a little disorderly and there were troops among them, the vast majority appeared to be wagons but the feeling in the air was one of desperation and a need to escape whatever was behind them.

Thomas told Captain Diego whose Company he was with to send the message to those troops of Lorenco by the means of using a small mirror that they could now open fire on targets of opportunity. The signalling system had been suggested by Major Carterton and was an effective and silent means of communication amongst the different troops now that they were so well spread.

It was not long before Thomas and those with him began to hear the sound of musketry as Lorenco's men fired from ambush at the slower moving wagons and the few frightened guards accompanying them. The results were what Thomas hoped they would be which was to cause even more fear and uncertainty as French guards or wagon drivers were shot at from the men hiding up on the sides of the valley.

There were of course some of the more battle hardened French soldiers who tried as best they could to put up some resistance but it did not stop the sporadic sniping of the masses on the roadway of the valley.

For the next few weeks Thomas's men kept up their selective targeting which caused even more confusion and often the wagons or troops were stalled in the pass as the French soldiers attempted to force the sniping sharp shooters back into hiding so they could move their wagons forward. Over time it became a game of hide and seek as the French troops tried to force a way forward and the Sharpshooters tried to slow them down.

When night fell there was little relief as even in the dark of night those driving the wagons or those guarding them found that even their night fires did not stop raids being turned into stealthy attacks by black clad figures right inside the camps themselves which left small numbers of men dead in their sleep. On other occasions there were whole pickets taken out in the middle of the night without a sound being heard.

As the first weeks of June came there was a noticeable increase in cavalry patrols along the pass, these had to be handled with great care and it was now that Thomas, Carmelo and Estaban's men came into their own with fast riding attacks which culminated in a quick withdrawal as soon as the enemy Cavalry tried to intercept them. The hit and run tactics were the backbone of the Guerrillas and Thomas and his men had become so proficient that they never had to stand and fight to escape from the French Cavalry.

Fast riding attacks on the many wagons themselves were also used and these led to even more uncertainty as the mass of French tried to retreat to safety. While it would have been well within Thomas's troop's ability, the attacks were not carried out day after day but they would allow days between attacks so the French were never quite sure when or where the next one was to come from.

By the 20th of June Thomas and his hard fighting army knew something was seriously wrong with the French. The numbers of wagons retreating north towards Bilbao and the French border had increased markedly; there were also now large numbers of wounded trying to make it north although Thomas had noted that most of the wounds were older and all had been tended to by surgeons.

Thomas decided to send a small twenty man patrol to the east via the upper goat tracks along the ridge top towards Vittoria to see why there was such an increase in the wounded. Captain Diego was put in charge and also asked to speak with as many of the local Spanish as possible to find out what was going on further to the east.

Unknown to Thomas at that time, part of the answer was about to rumble its way into the pass in a form he least expected or could have presumed. On the 22nd of June the morning was filled with the loud echoes of shouting and fearful Frenchmen, the pass was almost clogged with wagons and the many troops appeared to only want to run from whatever was behind them.

The pass had suddenly become a scene of chaos and fear and the addition of hidden men sniping at them from above only increased the sense of desperation in those below the ridge where Thomas and his men sat watching. As yet he did not have the report from his Patrol and could only guess that something major must have happened to cause such all out panic in the French.

As Thomas watched he could make out what appeared to be horses once used for the guns that were now being ridden by men, their gun traces cut away to the bare minimum and all seemed to be making a headlong rush for the French border in the north. Next to appear was a larger force of well drilled Cavalry from the ranks of the Chasseurs, they were accompanying a large group of very Senior Officers and behind them was a very long line of heavily laden wagons; for Thomas and his remaining men of Diego's Company it was just too much temptation.

The Senior Officers appeared to be very frightened of something behind them and, at the first shots fired their way; the most senior of the Officers gave the order to gallop away with their escort and leave the wagons to their fate. The Chasseurs formed a solid wall around the now fast riding Officers but did not try to counter attack the oncoming force of musket wielding black clad troops.

It was to be some time before Thomas heard that he had been within musket shot of the onetime King of Spain known as Joseph Bonaparte, but the chance passed just as quickly as the escaping Officers could ride. With the pass temporarily empty of retreating troops and Officers, Thomas took the chance to procure a few extra supplies from the now stalled wagons.

The drivers had seen the Cavalry and Officers spur their horses forward to escape the sudden attack and had abandoned their wagons as well, they were now running as hard as they could for the end of the pass which was still a few miles away but the drivers must have thought that certain death was the only thing that awaited them if they stayed with their charges.

Thomas looked both forward and backwards and could not believe the sudden lack of retreating Frenchmen; it was as though his little world in the pass had suddenly become a place of peace except for the very long line of stalled wagons. As he sat and looked at all the vacated wagons, Thomas thought he could hear what sounded much like Cavalry some distance away but coming in their direction.

Not waiting to find out if they were friends or foe; Thomas gave the order to have some of his men take the first ten wagons and drive them towards the western end of the pass behind the retreating French and drive them to where Major Morgan had his guns holding the western pass; they would look over the wagons at a later date to see what they had garnered to assist their need for supplies.

Ten of the riders dismounted and immediately took a seat on the front ten wagons after tying their own horses to the rear wagon gate, within a minute the ten front wagons were moving towards where Major Morgan waited and Thomas waved his hand to send the rest of his now very small Company to cover around the next bend in the road as the approaching sound of fast moving Cavalry drew closer. He did not have the men to fight against a large force of angry French Cavalry until Captain Diego returned with his report from the east.

As Thomas rode around the bend he saw that there was help on the way in the form of both Estaban and Carmelo's Company's as they rode towards him from further west; Thomas had time to note that not all of them got away without a scratch as some of the oncoming riders were carrying wounds covered by hastily wrapped and sometimes bloody bandages.

With the added numbers, Thomas now had a chance against the Cavalry he had heard coming their way. With a sharp order he had the three Companies form up in ranks of four and extending across the road, if the oncoming Cavalry wanted to escape to the north then they now had a battle ahead of them. Thomas sent one rider forward so he could see around the bend in the road and then report back to Thomas as to the numbers they may be facing in the event of a fight.

Minutes later and the scout returned with some interesting news; the Cavalry were not French but English, Thomas called for his men to make ready to move back to the wagons to see what was happening.

Thomas with Carmelo and Estaban beside him; rode ahead of the three Companies as they made their way around the bend and towards the now halted Cavalry. Thomas made out the uniforms of the Cavalry ahead and saw they were English Hussars and at their head and sitting his saddle with ease sat a Captain watching his men dismounting to look over the stalled wagons.

As Thomas and his men appeared, one of the young Hussar Lieutenants noted them and informed his Captain. The Officer turned in his saddle and looked along the road to see the approaching riders. They were led by three young men in the van with the rest of the black clad riders stretched out in three ranks behind; the Captain had seen those uniforms before.

As many of the Hussars became aware of the new arrivals they looked to their Officers for orders and made ready to attack; for those Hussars already on the ground it was a mad scramble to remount and ready their weapons; being mainly pistols and sabres, not much weaponry against what they could see in the hands of the men riding towards them.

The Captain called his men to stand down as he was sure these newcomers were friends or at least friendly to England. Thomas led his men up to where the Senior Officer sat waiting for them. When Thomas and his three friends halted their horses facing the Captain he was about to speak when the Captain took the initiative; Thomas found the man's careful attempts to be understood rather amusing and so kept his own mouth shut as the Captain stumble with his words as he tried to make the foreigners understand him.

"Uhm...Guerrillas? Arh...Espana Guerrillas? Uhm...English...uhm...speaky?"

Thomas and his friends looked at each other as they tried valiantly to keep the laughter out of their voices and the smiles that wanted to force their way forward from their faces. It was a few more seconds before Thomas felt he should relent and let the Captain off the hook.

"Yes Captain, I speak English very well; that's if you can forgive my Limehouse accent. Who are you and what are you doing this far from the Viscounts forces?"

"I may ask the same question of you young man?"

Thomas heard a very soft cough at his side; turning he saw the faintest of smiles on Carmelo's lips and the hint of a wink. Thomas gave a small nod and let Carmelo take over, why should he be the only one to have fun.

"Captain I may be able to answer your question if you please?"

"And who are you?"

"I am Colonel Carmelo Grey, second in command of the 1r Regimiento Espana Guerrillas Captain so I am also your superior, now then who are you and what are your troops doing here?"

"Sir! Sorry Sir I had no idea, I am Captain Warren of the 18th Hussars, we were in pursuit of the remnants of Joseph Bonaparte's forces in the hope of making a capture.

My apologies Sir for my disrespect to your rank, I was unaware of the nature of your rank structure. May I presume that beside you is General Don Thomasino de Toro?"

Captain warren was looking not at Thomas but at Estaban when asking the question; it had already been ascertained that Thomas was a Londoner so he could not have been a Spanish General, besides he was far younger looking than the other Officer of the three before him.

While Estaban's understanding of English had improved over the last five years, it was still rudimentary at best but at times like these he did his best to continue with the game his friends were playing. Speaking in Spanish as was his wont, Estaban made a few suggestions as how they should proceed with this Officer. After a short exchange of ideas, Thomas and Carmelo agreed and Carmelo once again took over the conversation.

"Your assumption is quite correct Captain Warren; this is indeed General Thomasino de Toro." Carmelo made a wide ranging gesture with his hand which could have included both of the men sitting next to him without actually point to one in particular. He would like to know why your men are so far ahead of the English forces and what you are planning to do now."

"Well Colonel, as I just said we were chasing Joseph Bonaparte as the time of the French is now almost over. Viscount Wellington's forces have routed the French at Vittoria and they are now in full retreat back to France in total disorder. Now however with the finding of this baggage train that we think belonged to the ex-King my men and I will stay to watch over it until our forces arrive to take charge."

"And what gives you the right to oversee this baggage train Captain?"

"Sir with all due respect but this train is now under the command and power of the English forces; if what I suspect is in the contents of this train it will go towards some of the reparations for our efforts in the war. I am sure Viscount Wellington will agree with me Sir."

"Captain; do you honestly think this baggage train is that of Joseph; if it were so then the contents belong to the people of Spain and Portugal and not the English."

"That is not for me to say Sir; I am only saying that we will watch over the train until Viscount Wellington makes a decision on its eventual destination. It would be remiss of me as an English Officer to do otherwise."

At this point Thomas interrupted; he had heard all he wanted to from this Captain and deep inside he had a funny feeling that something was not quite right with the Captains words.

"Captain, I would ask why you deem it so important that you and your men should stand guard on this particular baggage train?"

Thomas was not impressed by the Captains demeanour as he straightened his back and looked down his somewhat long narrow nose at the younger man in black.

"Ahm...Colonel?"

"General."

"General!"

"Yes Captain, I am General de Toro, next to me is Colonel Estaban Colosio; I am also known by your Viscount Wellington as General Marking; you may want to enquire about that with him. Now then what gives you the right to stand guard on what I presume is Spanish property?"

"Well...uhm...Sir, my orders are to...erm...protect the Viscounts and England's interests. As an Officer of the 18th Hussars it is my duty to protect that which is at this time presumed to be booty illegally taken by the onetime King of Spain. I am sure you can see the right of this Sir and if you have any questions I am sure that Viscount Wellington will make time to discuss it further with you Sir."

Thomas still got the feeling that all was not right but he now had only one of two options to take from here on. Firstly he could insist that he and his men take control of the baggage train which could result in having to fight this Captains Hussars or he could step back and then make enquiries with the Viscount.

At first he was more inclined to use his superior and better armed force to send the Captain and his men packing but there was also the fact that the Captain might try to make it a fight and that could put Thomas and his men in the sights of the English army as rebels if his men fired on English troops. He was not happy about either way but for the moment he could really do little unless he wanted to start a new war with the English and he had no intention of putting his men into the English gun sights.

Thomas sat watching the Captain with narrowed eyes as he thought about the options, there was little doubt he would have to ride away and hope the Captain was a man of his word but deep inside the small nagging suspicion still held sway as he made his decision.

"Very well Captain, we will leave the train in your care but; I will be taking it up with the Viscount just as soon as I am able. The people of Spain and Portugal are trusting you with their goods, I hope we can rely on your honesty Captain; you and your men really do not want certain parties on the Peninsula to have to come looking for you if something is amiss."

"I can assure you Sir that you have the word of an English Officer that nothing untoward will happen until Viscount Wellington makes a decision on what is to happen with this baggage train."

"Very well then Captain, we will leave you to your duty; I would just ask you to heed my warning."

"Sir I am an English Officer, we do not give our word lightly."

Thomas looked the Captain in the eye for a few more seconds before changing to Spanish and giving the order for his men to pull back and make for the position now held by Major Morgan and his guns. Even as he led his men away from the sight of the massed wagons in the pass he still had reservations. English Officer or not, if the baggage wagons held the wealth of Spain then even the most devoted Officer may be tempted to purloin just a little for his own use.

A week later and Thomas's suspicions were proved to be correct but as he rode away from the stalled baggage train he had other things on his mind, the least of which was what he and his army were to do now that the French appeared to be in full flight back to France.

23rd June 1813

The township of Vittoria.

After the savage battle for Vittoria, the English had moved into the town and taken over the Municipal building for their headquarters. The Mayor's office was now used by Viscount Wellington and so soon after the battle this large space was a scene bordering on chaos as the hundreds of reports found their way to his overloaded desk.

Wellington looked as though he had not slept since the end of the battle two days ago; his jacket had been discarded and the normally neat cravat around his throat hung open, there was also a smudge of ink on one of the shirt cuffs.

Viscount Wellington looked up as he heard the familiar soft cough which usually announced Colonel Lewis's presence. Viscount Wellington looked at Colonel Lewis as he waited for the response of his Adjutant.

"Well come on Colonel, I'm well used to bad news after the last few days."

"Yes My lord. I have the final figures and a very disturbing report for you."

"Damn it Colonel, why is it always bad news before breakfast, one of these days you will have to find me something good so my digestion can improve. Very well Colonel, what is the butcher's bill, you may give me the other report afterwards; I can only take so much bad news in one day."

"Yes My Lord. Well My Lord, while we did completely rout the French forces the numbers would not make you think so. The French have 5,200 dead or wounded and we have captured another 3,000, unfortunately My Lord our numbers are not much better. We have also lost about 5,000 dead and wounded but we did capture all one hundred and fifty one guns the French had held so they now have few or no guns to oppose us in the future."

"Well the capture of the guns is one point in our favour, can you explain why our numbers of dead and wounded are almost identical, I sent the 18th Regiment of Hussars to the left flank for the sole purpose of attacking their flank; their numbers should have been far greater."

"Well My Lord, the next report does concern the 18th Regiment of Hussars and may go a long way to explaining why the French managed to not only escape but also have time to form their present resistance on the Zadorra and are stopping us from breaking through to Salinas."

"Well get on with it Colonel, you've managed to ruin my breakfast, you may as well destroy my lunch as well."

"Well My Lord, the report I have states that the 18th Hussars were advancing as ordered but, before they came into contact with the enemy to close the pass to Salinas, they came across the baggage train of what we now know was that of Joseph Bonaparte. The baggage train had been abandoned due to the intervention of General de Toro and his troops earlier and the guards and drivers had fled to avoid capture or death. With the baggage train undefended the 18th decided to take it and in the process ignored your orders to close the pass and take the French in the rear. The report states that the troopers of the 18th were then seen to be selling off the valuables and goods of the baggage train to other troops at the end of the main battle. I fear My Lord that we may have a very serious situation on our hands."

Colonel Lewis could only watch as Viscount Wellington straightened up from the desk, his normally hard eyes now turned steely as he reached up to remove his cravat and throw it with great contempt onto the desk.

The Viscount's face went as rigid as stone as he looked down his prominent nose; Colonel Lewis could almost see the Viscount begin to shake with rage at the conclusion of the report; his next words boded ill for someone and Colonel Lewis could only stand and wait in silence as the atmosphere grew to one almost resembling and explosion of gun powder.

"By God they will pay a heavy price for their ignorance. What do we have here Colonel? Is this man's army filled with nothing but low life scum? I gave orders to take and hold the pass and those low life scum stop to pillage and have probably caused the deaths of brave men by their actions. Will you please go and call Colonel McPherson of the Scottish Regiment and ask him to present himself to me immediately. Next I want you to send an order for the army to assemble outside of town on the plain to the south for a full parade on the morrow at 10 of the clock. When you have done that I want a special order sent to the 18th Regiment of Hussars that they are to parade the full Regiment at that time. Do we have the name of the Officer in charge of the Baggage train raid?"

"Yes My Lord, he was one Captain Warren; he has served for five years with the Hussars and this is the first time we have had note of him."

"Then Colonel you will make damn sure he is present with those scum he calls Hussars."

"Yes My Lord."

Colonel Lewis turned and left the office to the sounds of a very irate Viscount; his words of anger could still be heard as Colonel Lewis walked away to carry out what was to become a very distasteful duty.

Colonel Lewis took a little time to find Colonel McPherson but once told of the Viscount's request he immediately left while Colonel Lewis set about getting out the orders for the morrows parade.

Colonel McPherson was a large man and well known for his hard stance on any who crossed his path with bad intentions; as he entered the office of the Viscount he could feel the coldness in the air. Coming to attention and saluting his Commanding Officer, he then waited for the Viscount to speak.

"Colonel I have a very distasteful duty for you and the men of the Scottish Regiment to perform on the morrow."

"Aye My Lord and what would that be?"

"I have just been informed that certain members of the 18th Hussars took it into their own hands to make a raid on a Baggage train when they had been ordered to take and hold the pass to Salinas, not only that but they then proceeded to make profit from the baggage after good men had died due to their blatant disregard of my orders. On the morrow I would ask you to assemble your Regiment on the periphery of the parade ground to act as guards; they are to have fixed bayonets and charged muskets. Next I want you to find a number of carpenters; they are to erect five gibbets and five ring posts at the centre of the parade ground. Once this has been accomplished I would ask for your most experienced Sergeant Majors ready to carry out punishment. Is there anything else you may need Colonel?"

"No My Lord, your orders are clear and will be carried out as ordered."

"Thank you Colonel, you are dismissed and may God watch over us for what is to come."

"Aye My Lord."

Colonel McPherson left to carry out his orders, that there was trouble afoot there was little doubt but he was sure his men of the Scottish Regiment could well handle anything that may arise.

The next morning dawned clear and already hot, the large area set aside for the parade was already being set up with the five posts and five gibbets. By 10 of the clock the full army that was present in Vittoria had assembled along both sides and at the eastern end sat all of the Senior Officers with Viscount Wellington astride his horse at the centre; Colonel Lewis and Colonel McPherson sat their horses on each side of the Viscount.

At the western end of the long parade ground were the Cavalry with their mounts. The Scottish Regiment were lined along both sides with fixed bayonets and facing out towards the mass of troops, their polished bayonets shining in the bright sunlight like a forrest of steel thorns. Viscount Wellington turned to his left where Colonel McPherson sat waiting for his orders.

"Colonel McPherson will you call for your Regimental Sergeant Major to present himself before us."

"My Lord."

The Colonel urged his horse forward a few steps before calling out the order.

"THE REGIMENTAL SERGEANT MAJOR WILL ADVANCE FOR ORDERS."

The power of the Colonel's voice was startling in the rigid silence of the parade ground. Within moments a very tall Sergeant Major in full kilt and red jacket with his black bearskin Busby flowing as he moved, broke away from those guarding the sides of the parade ground and marched purposefully towards where the Officers sat waiting. When the Sergeant Major arrived before the Officers he came to a smart halt and performed a perfect salute before waiting for orders.

Viscount Wellington used his hard edged voice to give his orders to the Sergeant Major; he was easily heard by all those nearby.

"Regimental Sergeant Major, you will give orders for the 18th Hussars to advance to the centre and dismount."

The Sergeant Major gave another perfect salute, turned about and, in a voice that could have awakened the dead called out the order.

"THE 18TH REGIMENT OF HUSSARS WILL ADVANCE TO THE CENTRE AND DISMOUNT."

From the western end of the parade ground came the sound of massed Cavalry moving forward at the walk, when they were level at the centre of the parade ground they halted and then dismounted and stepped to the heads of their horses to hold the reins close to the horses head as they all stood at attention. No one at this stage really knew what was to come but it had to be something serious for such a parade to be called at such short notice.

The Sergeant Major turned back to the Officers once he had seen that the 18th Hussars were in position and stood as stiff as a board while he waited for his next instructions.

The Viscount looked at the ranks of Hussars before turning his flint edged eyes back to the Sergeant Major but his voice rose so that he could be heard even in the furtherest part of the huge parade.

"SERGEANT MAJOR, YOU WILL SELECT A PLATOON OF YOUR SCOTT'S AND ADVANCE TO THE LINES OF THE 18TH HUSSARS, ONCE THERE YOU WILL SELECT ONE CORPORAL AND FOUR LOWER RANKS FROM EACH COMPANY AND ESCORT THEM BEFORE US."

The Sergeant Major once again saluted and turned to carry out his orders. Once the Sergeant Major had selected his men from those standing guard he marched them in perfect formation to the ranks of the 18th Hussars. Within minutes his platoon of very large Scottish Infantry guards had the twenty five men inside their cordon and began to march them smartly back to stand before Viscount Wellington and the assembled Officers.

Viscount Wellington then raised his voice so he could be heard clearly.

"CAPTAIN WARREN WILL PRESENT HIMSELF BEFORE THE ASSEMBLED OFFICERS."

There was a sudden movement at the front of the 18th Hussars and then Captain Warren handed the reins of his horse to a nearby Subltern before marching down the parade ground and coming to a halt before the Officers where he stood at attention. Colonel Lewis could see the look on the face of the hapless Captain as it began to dawn on him why the parade had been called in such a manner. Viscount Wellington continued but in a more subdued voice.

"Colonel Lewis you will read the charges and penalties."

"My Lord."

Colonel Lewis hated this part of his duties but for such an occasion this time it was needed to restore some sort of order back into the army.

"This parade has been assembled to witness punishment to the members of the Regiment of the 18th Hussars for dereliction of duty, failing to carry out a lawful order and the crime of looting. As the whole Regiment cannot be punished in a fitting manner, those assembled before us will be held as an example to the rest of the Regiment. The penalties are as follows. The five Corporals will be hanged by the neck until dead. The twenty lower ranks will each receive twenty strokes on the bare back. Captain Warren will be stripped of all ranks and privileges and discharged with severe prejudice and dishonour. Sentences to be carried out immediately."

There was an immediate rumble of discontent as the ranks of soldiers around the parade ground heard what was to happen; it became immediately silent when the loud clear sound of muskets being cocked by the throng of ever vigilant Scottish guards lowered the barrels to be aimed at the front ranks before them. Viscount Wellington sat his horse stoically as he gave the final order to Colonel Lewis.

"Colonel Lewis I would ask you to strip all ranks and insignia from Captain Warren, on completion he may reclaim his horse and walk from this parade ground once all punishment is complete; he will not ride his horse. Captain Warren, you will surrender your sabre into the hands of Colonel Lewis and stand by to witness punishment of the men you led so disgracefully. Colonel Lewis, carry out your orders."

Colonel Lewis dismounted and then stood directly in front of Captain Warren; he could see in the man's eyes a certain amount of anger but, deeper in those eyes was the unmistakeable look of guilt; it was this that Colonel Lewis used to make the final steps in the destruction of an Officers reputation and career.

Colonel Lewis reached out his left hand and took the sabre and scabbard; with his right hand he took a firm hold on the gold braid epaulettes and; with a solid wrench tore them free of the Captains jacket. Colonel Lewis's next action was to also tear away the campaign and service ribbons on the man's chest.

Dropping the items on the ground at the Captain's feet, Colonel Lewis then took out the pistol from his sash and cocked it before standing at the Captains side; it was very obvious what the pistol was to be used for should Captain Warren decided to not watch what was about to happen next to some of the men his actions had betrayed.

Viscount Wellington's voice was next heard as he addressed all those present.

"Regimental Sergeant Major you will take the five Corporals to the gibbet, there you will hang them one at a time so the army can see what happens to looters and those who disobey my orders. Once complete you will assign five of the Sergeants of the Scottish Regiment to administer twenty lashes to the others; the surgeon is not to interfere until all punishment has been carried out."

The Regimental Sergeant Major snapped a fine salute and then turned back to his duty. In one hour all punishment had been completed and the twenty men with backs that looked more like raw beef than human flesh lay on the bare ground as the surgeon and his aides went to work on them. As the parade ground quickly began to clear of the assembled army only the Officers stayed until the last act which was to silently watch as the one time Captain Warren led his horse from the parade while on foot; it was the final act of shame for the ex-Captain.

CHAPTER 22

With the taking of the ten wagons Thomas decided it was time to return to Braganza to consolidate his forces and see where they were to go next. That the end of the war was near was easy to see now that Wellington had forced his army almost to the edge of the French border. There would still be hard fighting ahead but Thomas was not sure he wanted to once again move his whole camp to the north; he did not have any ambitions to invade France.

In the first week of July Thomas led his men into the camp at Braganza; it had been improved somewhat by the efforts of those left behind and was now once again a reasonably comfortable camp. The first few days back were almost like torture for Thomas as Major Jones laid pile after pile of reports and messages before him to read or sign.

By the third day Thomas had had enough paper work and wanted some fresh air and something else to clear his mind. Thomas called the army together and asked for a volunteer troop of twenty men to go north and send back reports on what they saw as the allied armies moved into France; as far as Thomas was concerned his promise to rid Portugal and Spain of the French had been fulfilled and there was now little need for him to chase after the retreating army.

With the hastily held meeting at an end it then came time to open the ten wagons and investigate their contents, they had been held under guard since their arrival at the Braganza camp. Once again it was Major Jones who took over as the many items were removed from the wagons and laid out on large canvas tarpaulins that had been placed on the ground to protect the contents.

It was only after a few pieces had been taken out that everyone knew what they had stumbled upon; it was a vast treasure trove as well as very high quality furniture and the paraphernalia of the rich. There was so much wealth in the ten wagons that most of the army could only stand back and look in total dismay, there was hardly a soul who had ever seen such wealth and now it was all in their hands.

The contents of the ten wagons made Thomas wonder just how much was in the wagons they had left in the hands of the Hussar Captain and if any of it ever reached the Viscount. With the huge pile of goods and wealth now piled in a great mass on the ground, Thomas called for ideas; there was a gleam in many eyes and Thomas knew that some of it would have to go to his men, it was only fair after they had sweated blood and tears to win it back from the French usurper.

There were those among the army that were good Papists, their request was that the items of a religious nature be returned to the church as was proper for any religious icons; the rest, they said should be distributed amongst them all equally; as most saw it, it was only fair they should be paid a little extra for their many troubles over the last five years.

It was Pablo that volunteered to take a troop of twenty men north to watch what was going on; he would send back dispatch riders at intervals with reports for Thomas so he could keep track of the final stages of the war with France. Pablo knew that he and his men would be looked after with a fair share when the time came to break up the ten wagons of loot.

It took Major Jones the rest of the day to note everything from the wagons before it was all replaced and once again put under guard until he had it evenly divided, there were only three crates of religious items and he wasted little time noting them and then having it all packed way and put aside to be given back to a church at a later date.

Thomas was now left with what to do with his little army now that most of the fighting was at an end. Fully one third of his army was made up of men and boys that no longer had homes or families or had been living precariously on the streets of Portugal and Spain so had little to look forward to once the war was over; these were the ones that most concerned Thomas.

On the Tuesday of the second week of July, Thomas was alerted to a dispatch rider coming from the south; one glance at the riders uniform told him the man was from the Prince, he wondered what it could be as he thought the Prince had gone north with the Viscount and so it was strange to see the rider coming from the south.

The message was clear and simple; the Prince had made his headquarters at Benavente and wanted Thomas to meet him there to discuss what was to be done now that the French were routed and in full retreat. Thomas had two days to make the trip which was easy as he was sure he could make the distance in one day from where they were now camped.

The next morning Thomas found he had Carmelo and Estaban sitting their horses outside his door and waiting for him; it was evident that his two oldest friends in Spain were going with him. Even though there was little chance of trouble Thomas noted that he still had a twenty man escort mounted and waiting behind his two friends. With a resigned sigh, Thomas mounted his waiting horse and led the small group from the camp; Lorenco had volunteered to remain and watch over the camp until their return.

Thomas and his friends were approaching Benavente by late afternoon; they had not tried to push the horses too hard and so all arrived reasonably fresh. It took only a few words to find out where the Prince was staying and they were soon dismounting outside the low walls of the villa he was using, the guards took note of the black uniforms and immediately came to attention and saluted while one of their number opened the double gates into the villa.

It did not really surprise Thomas to see the young Prince lounging happily in a cane chair with a glass topped table by his side on which were a number of bottles and plates of food. Once gain the Prince was partly dressed and seemed to be enjoying the late afternoon breeze as his guests arrived and joined him in the shade of the veranda. Without rising from his chair, Prince Pimentel casually waved his hand at the other empty chairs before saying.

"Welcome Don Thomasino, I had a feeling you would be here today and I'm very glad to see you have Don Carmelo and Don Estaban with you; it will make this so much easier. Come sit and relax, dinner will not be for some time yet so there is some wine or brandy and a few small snacks to fill an empty belly until dinner."

Thomas and the other two took a cane backed chair and relaxed after opening their jackets and loosening their cravats and top shirt buttons; some of the Princes hostlers arrived to take their horses while a guard from the gate led the mounted guards to a place they could also relax and wait for their Officers to finish their business.

"Your Highness I was not expecting to see you so far back from the front lines so your request to see me was a little unexpected."

"Thank you Don Thomasino but I have many duties to perform and not all of them are to do with the war at the front. I have asked you here because there have been some rather interesting, and dare I say it, disturbing things happening that I need you to be aware of; not only for your own sake and safety but also that of your followers."

"I see Your Highness, and what are these concerns, if I may be so bold as to ask?"

"Ask you may my dear friend. As you know the war for Spain is nearly over; already Marshals Joseph and Jourdan have been replaced with Marshal Soult by Napoleon and from what I understand he has been given orders to halt Wellingtons advance into France. With Soult's tactical ability he may just succeed but I personally doubt it, however it raises a thorny question. If Soult does not succeed then the King will return sooner rather than later; if this is true then we may well have a problem on our hands if my informants are correct."

"What would the problem be and how can I and my men help you Your Highness?"

"Ah, this time Don Thomasino it is I that must help you, there is little you can do this time; any attempt to involve yourself in the affairs of Spain will probably bring down the wrath of the King. There are already plans afoot by the Royalists to demand certain harsh conditions on you and your men and; unfortunately there is a faction within the Cortes that also have their own plans to limit your movements. What I am about to propose does not make me happy in the least but my first concern is for your safety and that of your men that have for five years fought so valiantly for Spain's cause. It would pain me greatly to see you and your reputation destroyed by greedy and self serving politicians and Royalist sycophants."

"This does not sound good Your Highness, while I can fight my own battles I do not want to see the men that have trusted me to watch over them for five years be discarded for some political gain or forgotten by the very people they fought and died for."

"That is the reason I have asked you to join me here rather than in some place where there are far too many ears. Let me explain what I think is about to happen. Most of this is based on my own spies within the Royalist camp and the Cortes so I am fairly certain it will be close to the truth of the matter. There is little doubt the King will return early next year; of this fact you can be certain. When he does he plans to ask for Viscount Wellington to be given a Dukedom in recognition of his valiant efforts to save Spain from the French. I have little doubt he will receive it. Next the king will have to recognise the efforts of those Spanish forces that helped Wellington to attain his victory; this also will be expected by the people and the Generals."

The Prince paused for a few seconds before he continued; it was obvious to all that what he had to say did not sit well with him.

"Now this is where you and your men come in. There are those in the Cortes that have an unhealthy fear of your reputation within the military and so they are making plans to recognise the efforts of you and your men in public but, behind the scenes there are plans to have your force disbanded and spread throughout the country in the hope you can never reform your force to threaten their plans in the future. Now then, unfortunately the Royalists are also afraid of you and your reputation. The King knows of your popularity with the masses; this is something he cannot allow or bare, he would feel that it undermines the power of the throne even though I personally know better but, in this case I have little say in the matter. Do you see where this is all going Don Thomasino?"

"Yes I think so Your Highness, half of them are scared we will attack them and the other half are sure we will so they both want us well out of the way."

"Yes that's very close to the mark and very astute of you to recognise the fact; however I think I have come up with a way to circumvent some of their plans but it will take a lot of thought and many considerations on your part and the part of your men. Do you wish to hear what I have thought of Don Thomasino?"

"Of course Your Highness, if it is to keep my men safe then I will listen to any reasonable plan."

"I thought you might. You know Don Thomasino, my own father would have liked you; he would have said you and I think and act in the same way. If you were not English we may have been born brothers; anyhow I digress. When the treasure wagons were pillaged by the English, the King was most upset; you may not be aware but the King, even though he is still being held in the chateau in France can still get reports both in and out from his Royalist friends in Spain. When he heard of the pillaging of the wagon train he decided that there must be a price to be paid for its loss and the loss of the treasure it contained; to this end he has decided you and your men shall pay the price one way or another. Now I have it on very good authority that you are going to return the items of religious significance back to the church; for this I can only commend you highly, however the rest of your ten wagons could be another matter and so; to this end I have spread the rumour that they were the only ones the French managed to escape with."

"Your Highness, how could you know of this?" Thomas sat back and thought for a few seconds while watching the Princes features; it then suddenly struck him when he saw the faint smile on the Princes lips. "You have a spy in my camp Your Highness?"

"Yes Don Thomasino, don't worry he is very faithful to both you and I, as time passed it was more and more difficult to get him on side or to report the goings on in your camp but, Don Thomasino, it was not that I did not trust you; I placed him there so that I would know if or when you need help. Besides, even a Prince must have his little games. Now then back to our problem. When the King returns and the war is over there will be great festivities in Madrid; Wellington will receive his Dukedom, the men of the forces will have their big parades and the people will cheer the return of the King and his loyal subjects.

However, and this is where the first part of their plan involves you and your men. You will be asked to attend the celebrations but only you will be allowed to march with the Officers and men of Spain; all your other troops will not be allowed to be seen by the people. The King will also not allow you to have your drummers with you as it might incite the people to your side and he fears that more than anything else. You see Don Thomasino, your reputation at this time even exceeds his own and the King is not the sort of man that could stand that to happen. Your Spanish troops will be placed at the rear of the parade, you will not be allowed to carry or show your battle colours and they must all march unarmed. The members of the Cortes that are against you are also part of the group that want you to be as small as possible in the peoples mind."

Thomas sat stony faced as he listened to the Prince detail what the elite of Spain had planned for him; while he was not concerned for himself he thought the proposed actions as a direct insult to his men and to those who had lost their lives fighting for those same people. Thomas gave a small nod that he understood what the Prince was saying and for him o continue.

"As you can gather Don Thomasino, I will not have anything to do with this; I have made it clear to those involved that I will not be available for the parade in Madrid and that is final regardless of the King's request to the contrary. Now here I can only assume but I think I am fairly close. The King is furious about losing the wealth of Spain to the English soldiers but there is little he can do directly, especially as the Viscount has taken the appropriate action on those who were involved. However the King still wants his own revenge and so he has decided on the one threat left and that is you and your men. The plans I have heard are thus. At the end of the parade and after everyone is over the excitement, The King will declare all your lands, titles and estates to be annulled and they will all be taken by the crown or given to friends of the King; you will then be declared an outlaw and given one week to leave Spain or be arrested, this also goes for Don Carmelo as he has an English father. The Englishmen that are in your army will be rounded up and placed on ships to be transported back to England, hopefully in disgrace. The King and the Cortes hope to destroy your fine reputation amongst the people so the King can then sleep better and safer in his bed at night. Your Portuguese troops will be asked respectfully to leave Spain for their own homeland. Now Don Estaban will be held up as the great saviour of Spain in your place, his lands will be increased and a new title will be offered to him. The King and the Cortes does not want any non Spaniard taking the glory of Napoleons defeat here so they want to sacrifice you for their cause."

Prince Pimentel watched the look on Thomas's face as he passed on his information; it almost brought a tear to his eyes as he watched some of the fire being wrung out of the young man he personally thought of as a dear friend, not only to himself but to Spain. It was painful to watch but the Prince had a plan and he felt he had better get on with it before his friend lost all hope.

For Thomas it was like being shot in the gut, after five years of fighting and watching those who trusted him fall to the muskets of the French he was now being told he was going to be treated like a common criminal. The feeling in his stomach began to sink into a dark abyss; had it all been for nothing? Prince Pimentel began to speak again in an attempt to bring back the fire in his friend's belly.

"However Don Thomasino, there are those who have been fortunate enough to see the writing on the wall and can do something about it. Colonel Cruickshank along with some other friends as well as myself have found a way to keep your reputation intact. Do you wish to hear what we have come up with?"

Thomas could only nod his head in agreement while his mind was trying to work out the meaning of the shocking information he had just been told.

"Over the last month we have all been working on this problem. There is little doubt in our minds that you rightly deserve and should continue to have all your titles and ranks and to this end there is one way for you to keep them and for your men to hold what they also have. We have estimated that the war will be over some time during or shortly after the end of March. There is little doubt the French will be able to hold out after that. Now then, if you and your men were to voluntarily disband before that time you could under Spanish law be able to hold onto your titles and ranks and there is little even the King can do about it."

The Prince got a look on his face that told Thomas a plan had already been put into effect.

"Next the problem of your estate and land. If you were to sell it off to either your men of others before the end of the war then it could not be given into the hands of those in the Cortes or the friends of the King as long as those who bought it were Spanish by birth. Of course if they were to buy your land and Hacienda and then had to purchase such things as wines and ports from a certain company in Oporto, they would have to send monies to pay for it all and; who can say how much that would cost them. Now the next thing we have observed is that there are ten French ships being held in the port at Malaga. The crews had to surrender under the guns of the English Navy but the English had little time or use for them at that time. Because of the speed of the English advance, the ships were put into the hands of Spain to be disposed of and any monies collected were promised to the English Navy; less a small fee for the work. I believe they are looking for someone to buy them; perhaps you know of someone that could use ten good ships in their company? I believe one Prince Pimentel is the person you have to negotiate the price with and that he was asking for one thousand ducats a ship; perhaps you may like to discuss it with him when next you meet. Now lastly, I believe Don Estaban has his lands that border on your own, he may like to purchase some of the lower flat lands to add to his own, I'm sure he could come up with a little gold to purchase it on a long term lease, say perhaps ten years at a time with the option to renew?"

Thomas could now see what had been going on behind the scenes to make sure his welfare and that of his men were taken care of before the politicians and sycophants of the King could cause too much trouble. For the first time in the last half hour Thomas showed a small smile on his face as he watched the twinkle in the Princes eye grow to a sparkle.

"Now Don Thomasino there is only the matter of Don Carmelo. As I have stated with his father being English even though his mother was Spanish, the King and his...err...advisors still want to leave him with nothing, to this end I have decided to enlarge my own holdings and am looking to lease some fine land in Castile where I can run my bulls and horses on more open ground. Of course it would probably cost me as much as a thousand ducats a year to lease this land if I can find it but at least one day the owner may come back and can then fully claim it back for his family. What do you think Don Carmelo, do you wish to lease your land before the King and the Cortes can claim it for their own?"

"Well Your Highness I was planning to accompany my friend on his future journeys but I was going to put it off as the land held me here but, as you say you may be able to take it off my hands for a time and it would relieve me of the responsibility until I have finished my travels with my friend."

"Good then that is settled, now then Don Thomasino, what are your views on our future plans?"

"Well Your Highness if all you say is to come to pass then I can only agree with you and your friends to follow the plan you have devised. I will have my Adjutant send a letter to my agent in Oporto and have ten thousand ducats sent to you via Malaga for the ten ships, you may then like to get them underway for Oporto where we can have them undergo a refit for our needs."

"Ah that's good to hear, I thought you may think that way as the ships left Malaga four days ago and are underway towards Oporto as we speak; there crews are a little mixed and you may want to find your own when they arrive at Oporto, most of them will want to return to their families once the ships are delivered. Now then it only remains for you to see to your army. I will have all the necessary papers drawn up for the transfer of lands for both you and Don Carmelo. Any alterations needed for any of your men that may want to take up some of the land for their own use can be made out by your own Adjutant if they so desire. Now then Don Thomasino, enough of all this intrigue and planning, it's time for a good hearty dinner and a lot of wine. Tonight my friends we will drink until the sun rises and then use the next two days to suffer for it; what say you?"

The next day, sometime after midday Prince Pimentel's words turned out to be prophetic. All three of his guests rose with their mouths dryer than ever before and their eyes could not stand too much light; their heads pounded and food was the last thing they wanted to think of. It took all three nearly a half hour to dress and finally make their way outside and into the glare of the bright sunlight; each was shading his eyes with one hand as they almost stumbled to the table where the Prince sat; he was not in much better condition by the way he was slumped in the chair.

It was only minutes before one of the Princes servants arrived with a large silver jug and four glasses. Thomas was almost praying that whatever was in the jug did not contain any alcohol; it was the last thing he wanted at this time. Thomas and the others watched as the servant poured a thick red looking mixture into each glass and then stood back to wait while the Prince took up a fresh egg from the plate on the table and cracked it into his glass; he then pushed the plate over to Thomas and indicated he do the same.

Thomas looked at the raw egg floating in the red mass and felt his stomach try to rebel at the thought but then pushed himself to do as the Prince had done; he was quickly followed by Estaban and Carmelo. It took a big effort for Thomas to swallow the concoction straight down in one huge gulp as the Prince had done; it was only after swallowing as fast as he could that he felt the raw heat of the chilli that had been added to what he then knew was finely squashed tomatoes.

After a long and very loud burp Thomas settled back into his wicker chair while still shading his eyes from the afternoon sun, the others were in much the same state. It was not long before each of them began to feel a little better but food was still very low on their list until the servant reappeared with a wood platter which had only bread, cheese and olives on it.

"There we are Don Thomasino." Prince Pimentel said with a thin smile on his face. "Just the thing for young men who over indulge the night before, please help yourselves, you will find that it is needed before dinner."

The Prince reached for a knife and cut off a slice of cheese before breaking the round loaf of bread and taking a few green olives, the others followed his example as the hot chilli was still making their throats constrict as the heat almost seemed to increase with every breath they took.

"So Don Thomasino have you had any thoughts about what we discussed yesterday?"

"Yes Your Highness. I plan to take all my men back to Oporto where they will all be paid off what is owed. I know there are a number that have lost everything or had nothing to start with have had offers from the people of Vimeiro, I plan to see that they make their way to the town without delay. I have a number of English sailors and gunners that I feel sure will want to take a place on the new ships and those who want to return to England will be given free passage on one of my ships. With the papers for the land in Spain signed I think I would like to take passage on a ship and see a little of the world but first I will look for a little land in Portugal and ask Senor Forsca if he can teach me about trading. I would like to think that you and Estaban would keep me posted so I may one day return to Spain."

"Of course we will keep in contact, there is much going to happen over the next few years and; if the King has his way, a lot of it will not be pleasant for some. Have you given thought to your land and the Hacienda?"

"Yes, your suggestions for Don Estaban to take some are sound so I will allocate most of the low land to him and his cousins, perhaps they can take three thousand acres and the rest divided up between the men who have spent their lives working it, I will have to send messages to them and find out. The Hacienda I want to leave to my two servants, they are Spanish born and deserve to have it, they will also watch over it with great care."

"Who are they Don Thomasino so that I can get their names registered and the Hacienda signed over to them?"

"Their names are Carlito and Sergio, for now they have taken my surname but I am sure it will be safer if they have another until this is all settled."

"Think nothing of it Don Thomasino; I will make arrangements so they can hold your Hacienda for you."

"Thank you Your Highness, it will be one small thing off my mind, the two boys have been with me from the start and I don't want them to have to return to their old life if I can help them."

"Fear not Don Thomasino, I will make sure they are well settled and cannot be touched by others. Now is there anything else I can do for you?"

"Not at this stage Your Highness but if I may call on you if needed at a later date I would be forever grateful."

"Of course you may Don Thomasino and think nothing of it, Spain owes you far more than it can ever repay. Many may forget but those of us who really know what you did never will. Now then, let's spend the rest of the day relaxing, I am sure you will want to return to your men and tell them what their future may hold."

"Yes thank you Your Highness, we could all do with a quiet night before leaving for Braganza early on the morrow."

The rest of the day and early into the night was spent relaxing and trying to rid their systems of the heavy drinking of the night before. When the sun rose early the next morning the Prince was waiting for them over breakfast. As soon as all had eaten their fill the horses were brought around and his guards arrived to escort them all back to their camp; with such an early start they hoped to arrive back at Braganza well before dusk.

The small force left Benavente at a fast walk. There was no need to hurry as they had a full day to make their camp and apart from the news they now carried, there was little need for speed. They had made it about half way to Braganza when the lead guard in the van raised his hand to halt the column; with the column halted the guard turned back to his Officers and waved them forward as he slipped his musket off his shoulder and held it ready in his hands.

The three friends rode up and sat beside the lead guard; as they looked forward they all saw a sight that almost brought a smile to their lips. Riding ahead of them was a small group of others, they were all dressed in rough peasant clothes and some wore old bloody bandages; the two riders at the head of the small group looked to be tired and were almost slumped in their saddles.

Estaban turned to Thomas and Carmelo with a wide smile as he pointed something out to his friends; on the backs of every one of the riders were the familiar double barrelled muskets and while the men and their clothes looked more like rags than anything his men would wear, Thomas could only nod as a glint came into his eye. With a quick whisper to Estaban and Carmelo, Thomas took his own musket from his shoulder; checked his two friends had done the same and charged at full gallop towards the tired men in front of them.

It was difficult for Thomas and the others to keep the laughter out of their voices as they yelled and called loudly at the startled men ahead of them; perhapss if the men had been more rested they would not have been caught out so easily but the temptation for a bit of fun could not be denied as the men ahead tried to turn and at the same time reach for their own muskets as the black clothed ranks charged at them over the open ground.

When Thomas and the others had grown close enough for Maketja and Snot to work out who they were, the three friends at the front were almost laughing loudly as they drew close enough for the others to make out who they were. It took a little time for Snot to stop cursing in English while Maketja was doing much the same thing but in French or possibly Basque as Thomas and the others slowed so they could stop beside the returnees; the course language only made the three friends laugh even louder.

Once Thomas had caught his breath and stopped laughing, he turned to Maketja and asked.

"Well Captain, where have you all been, we expected you back almost a month ago?"

"Patron, should you do this again and we may never come back, my heart is now ten years older."

"So where have you been?"

"The English General Rolly Polly wanted to keep us to fight for him but we decided we did not like his orders so we saw them to the Elba and then left in the night. Unfortunately the French were like fleas on a dog when we tried to make our way back so we had many small fights and other times we had to hide away for days while they fought their battles. The English gave them a very bloody nose and once they ran for Vittoria we were able to start back again. As we moved back we had to change our clothes so we were not so noticeable by the French whores but still we had small fights to get through. Now Patron we are nearly home and our own friends come charging at us like wild animals; it does not make for a happy homecoming Patron."

The three friends were still trying to stop their laughter as they watched Maketja frown at them before he too smiled and lifted a finger which only had one meaning in any language. When everyone was calmer Thomas told Maketja and his men to join them for the ride back to their camp in Braganza; it was good to have the company with the men they had lost track of for so long; Thomas was sure there would be a great fiesta for the returnees.

It did not take long for the two groups to combine into one force and lift their horses to a faster trot; Thomas knew that now his long lost patrol had returned there would be even more for him to do to get his little army ready for what lay ahead. It was time to think of something else but war, hardship and loss.

CHAPTER 23

With the two groups joined up, the ride for their camp at Braganza became more lively. Although Thomas had taken notice of how tired and worn the newcomers looked he tried his best to maintain a light hearted atmosphere as he was very glad to finally have them all on the way home again with no losses.

Dusk was approaching just as the group arrived at the camp; immediately Thomas called for the cauldrons to be filled and placed on the fires for Maketja and his men to bathe; it had been a long time for them since the last good bath and he wanted them to have a little light pleasure before the rigors of reporting their travels took place.

While Maketja led his small troop of guides to find a place to unwind while they waited for the water to heat; Carmelo took over and went to the kitchen to find some extra food for them.

The rest of the evening was spent resting while Thomas put on his thinking cap and began to work on the problem of what to do next. During dinner that evening Thomas asked for Major Jones to join him in his tent where he had new orders for him to carry out. Next Thomas told all the men present that there would be a full meeting of everyone the next day after lunch where he had a number of important decisions for them to think over and some final decisions to be made for their future.

After dinner Thomas returned to his tent and began to work on a long list of things he would now have to take care of; he was soon joined not only by Major Jones but also his three closest friends and Senior Officers. Thomas began to throw out some ideas of what he wanted to do and asked for any suggestions the others may have.

It was far later than he thought it would be when the meeting finally broke up for the night; the plans and decisions had now all been made and it was time to put things into practice just as soon as the sun rose the next morning. Major Jones had been given the responsibility to organise things in Oporto and would take Sergio and Carlito with him to help as well as two of the mules laden with some of the treasure from the ten wagons.

Carmelo and Estaban would see to organising the movement of the camp from their present position to one they would have selected by Major Jones in or just outside Oporto. The two old friends were also charged with making sure everything was ready for the move by the 10th of September when it was hoped Pablo would finally be back from his escapades further north.

Now that the final decision had been made that the small army had no further need to prepare for a fight, Thomas allowed the men to begin to look forward to a different life after the war. Most of the mornings were spent by the men in relaxing or inspecting their equipment, the first three hours of the afternoons were spent with the many preparations that would be needed once they began the return to the west and the final stop in Oporto.

Thomas had received two reports from Pablo in the north, the first was just after Viscount Wellington had been pushed back by Marshal Soult at Maya, and the second was about how the Viscount had then turned the tables on the erstwhile Marshal Soult at Sorauren on the 28th of July and was once again on the advance towards France.

Thomas sent a message back with the rider for Pablo to have his scouts back before he moved the army out to Oporto during the month of September; all was now ready for their last long push back to safety at Oporto and the final assembly of his loyal troops; he hoped the plans he had made would be appreciated and remembered by those who had for so long fought beside him.

When the time finally arrived for them to leave their camp north west of Braganza and Pablo had returned with his force of twenty, Thomas set the pace much slower than they normally would have moved; he was happy for the column to make a mere twenty miles a day and, even with the increased number of wagons they now had, the column moved in a good and orderly fashion; even the two Companies of Infantry did not mind the slower pace.

As the outskirts of Oporto came into view on the 8th of October, Thomas saw the three black clad figures waiting for him on the side of the road. Major Jones and the two boys had been keeping watch every day for the last week as they waited for their friends to arrive; everything that had been asked of Major Jones was now put in place and ready for the big day that Thomas had planned.

The three waiting men sat straighter in their saddles as Thomas and the others drew up beside them; Thomas was the first to speak as was only proper.

"Major, Lieutenants, has everything been arranged?"

"Yes Sir." Replied Major Jones before he continued. "I have managed to procure the lease on some land just a little further along this road; it is about two miles from the outskirts of Oporto so we should not be disturbed during the parade or while we are in camp."

"Good, well done Major; and is the owner happy with the arrangements?"

"Yes Sir although he would only accept half the payment offered, he said his duty to the Patron would not allow him to take more. He has vacated his house for you to use during your stay and there are barns the men can use and plenty of open fields for the animals. At the front of the main house there is an area large enough for you to hold the last parade without congestion."

"Thank you again Major, and is everything else arranged as we wanted?"

"Yes Sir, Senor Forsca and his sons have been most helpful; he was able to find a good foundry for our use and the owners put their entire workforce at our disposal. Senor

Forsca's sons also helped to make up the wages for the men and have double checked to make sure none are short changed according to my records."

"Good Major and what of the ships? Did they arrive on time and what has Senor Forsca arranged for them?"

"Yes Sir, the ships are at anchor except for one of them which is undergoing work in the dock but Senor Forsca would like you to call on him for further information on that matter Sir."

"Very good Major, well let's get the men to their new home so they can settle in. Lead the way Major."

Major Jones turned his horse and began to lead the way to their new home; it was only about three miles away and it was not long before the long column of men and wagons were beginning to find places on the open farmland to settle for their stay. While the Officers of each corps found a place for their men, Major Jones led Thomas, Carmelo, Estaban and Lorenco up to the house where the rooms had been readied for their use over the next few weeks by Sergio and Carlito.

The large front room had been set aside to use as the main office where it was far easier to greet anyone looking for Thomas or the others. Within minutes, the ever hovering Fairley had selected the best room for Thomas and was already seeing to his many bags and cases while Thomas looked for somewhere to sit while he waited for the other three to find their own room before going out to inspect the rest of the men.

By mid afternoon the kitchen in the house was filled with the rattle of pots and pans and the general noise of boys working on the evening meal for the Officers. Out by the two barns the scullery boys had set up the large mess marquee with the help of a number of the Infantrymen and were now working hard over the freshly dug fire pits with a number of sheep now cooking on them.

By early evening and only about a half hour before meal time, the camp had quietened down and the men were sitting around in their groups as they talked about the end of their war and what they would now do when the time came to leave all of the last five years behind. Many had already decided that their friendships within the small guerrilla army had to be maintained at all costs; they were all brothers of spilt blood and all had lost good friends to the French.

The next morning Thomas called for Major Jones once again; there were still a few minor details he wanted to check over before he left the new camp to visit Senor Forsca. When Major Jones had arrived, Thomas and the others were seated in the early morning sun and enjoying their cafe; Thomas indicated for Major Jones to take a spare chair and join them.

When Major Jones was comfortably seated and was given a fresh hot cafe by Fairley, Thomas began.

"So Major how are things going?"

"Everything is on time Sir; there are only a few minor details I have to finish with concerning the parade."

"And what would they be Major?"

"Nothing of real importance Sir; I have had a few requests by others to be allowed to be present for the parade and was working on something or somewhere for them to stand and view the proceedings."

"Do you wish to enlarge on that statement Major?"

"Not at this time Sir, there are still arrangements to be made."

"I had not allowed for guests Major, this was to be a small and final parade before we disband."

"And so it will be Sir, these are just small and minor points I wished to take care of before that time comes."

"Very well Major, but I do hope there will be no disruptions to our plans."

"I will see to it Sir, now is there anything else that has you concerned Sir?"

"I just wish to check that all is going well. Are the foundries on time?"

"Yes Sir, I have it on good authority they are well within the time span."

"What of the carpenters and seamstresses? Are they also on time?"

"Yes Sir, in fact the seamstresses are almost finished with all their goods and the carpenters will be finished well ahead of time. The only ones having to take a little extra time are the engravers but they have extra personnel working day and night to finish everything we ordered."

"Good and what about printers? Were you able to find one that could do the work we needed?"

"Yes Sir, Senor Forsca had knowledge of a good print shop and they are attending to everything needed; with luck they should also be done by the end of this week. If you wished for my opinion Sir, I would suggest the parade be held in about a week; say about the 15th of October?"

"Yes that sounds good Major; you can inform everyone who needs to know that we will be on parade on that date. Now would you also inform the men of the date and that in the mean time I would like at least two hours a day set aside for practice, the rest of the day they may use to rest or look to their equipment; anything that needs replacing I will leave in your hands Major."

"Very good Sir, I will see to it."

"Thank you Major, now all I have to do is go and visit with Senor Forsca. Colonels Colosio and Grey will remain here if anything is needed while Major Lorenco accompanies me to Oporto town."

Carmelo was the first to speak up as the Major disappeared to carry out his projects.

"Patron, we have been talking and all three of us think you should plan to spend three or four days with Senor Forsca; you need a break away from us and a place to just sit back and rest. There is little more to do here that we cannot take care of and all of the planning for the parade is now done. Besides, perhaps you can leave Sergeant Fairley here to watch over us so he too can have a small break from your continued desire to keep moving and planning. I swear Patron the poor Sergeant must be nearly on his last legs the way he watches over you day and night."

Thomas looked at Carmelo as his friend tried so hard to look innocent while Estaban took great care to look up and watch the cloudless sky while pretending to whistle silently as he twiddled his thumbs in his lap.

"What the bloody hell are you two up to? And don't go telling me it's nothing; you both look about as innocent as a five year old with a stolen plum in his hand."

"Ah Patron, you wound me deeply; would I, your brother, truly lead you astray."

"Yes Carmelo you bloody well would if you thought you could get away with it."

"Oh Patron now I am wounded deeply, we only want for you to get away and rest without worrying about the small day to day things of the Regimiento; everyone must have a break from the daily grind of leadership; even the great El Toro."

"Bull dust Carmelo, you and the others are up to something but I suppose you will never tell so I will just get out of your hair for a few days and enjoy the company of a man who will not tell me tall tales."

"That is good Patron; do not fear, all will be ready for the parade when you return."

"It's not the parade I'm worried about Carmelo, but I will do as you advise and take a few days in Oporto; perhaps I will stay in a tavern instead of riding back here each day."

"A very good idea Patron; we, your brothers will take good care of your army while you relax in the town."

"Alright Carmelo, I get the hint you don't want me around for some reason but; I warn you I will find out what you are all up too sooner than later."

"Of course you will Patron that is if we are actually doing anything."

"Oh you are doing something, of that there is little doubt; I just don't know what yet."

"Have no fear Patron, we will take care of everything for you. Go now and enjoy your holiday from the rigors of command; your brothers have full control."

"That's what I'm bloody afraid of. Very good Carmelo you can call for Fairley to bring my horse and that of Lorenco, we will get out of your hair immediately and leave the rest to your machinations."

It did not surprise Thomas in the least to see Fairley walking around the side of the villa leading Thomas's horse while another of the younger Cavalrymen was leading Lorenco's; the fact that Thomas's panniers were also tied to his saddle told Thomas this had been well planned in advance; all it did was raise his suspicions that his friends were up to something.

While the trip to the main dock in Oporto did not take all that long and Thomas knew he could return to the camp within an hour; it also gave him a sense of freedom from the rigors of command, just as Carmelo had said. On arrival at the dock, it did not take long to find Senor Forsca and his sons working hard in the main warehouse office; what did surprise Thomas was the sight of three large ships of war anchored in the stream not far away from the dock itself.

Thomas gazed open mouthed at the three large and heavily armed ships as he tried to think of a reason they would be there, the war had moved far to the north and for Thomas there was no earthly reason for ships of war to be there. Thomas dismounted at the large doors along with Lorenco; he did not miss the new painted sign over the door.

It was painted in large letters on a pale blue background, the design looked very familiar and almost brought a smile to Thomas's lips; at the centre in black was the stylised bulls head and between the two horns were the letters, M.S.C. When the two friends walked inside the warehouse they were quick to spy Senor Forsca with a ledger in his hands as he counted baled goods on the floor.

Senor Forsca looked up as he heard the two pairs of boots walking over the wooden floor of the warehouse towards him. Senor Forsca stopped his work and, with a wide smile greeted his visitors.

"Patron, it is so good to see you once again after so long; what is it I can do for you?"

"Senor Forsca, it is also good to see you again, how goes the warehouse and the ships?"

"Excellent Patron, with the war moving north there has been a great increase in trade for us but, alas for others it is not so good; the fact you have your own ships has been a real boon for us."

"How so Senor Forsca?"

"Well Patron, the other dock owners are struggling now that the war effort has moved to Spanish ports; it has left them with very little business. I was fortunate to be able to make an offer on three other docks so now your company has the full length of these docks for our use."

"Do we really need so many; after all we only have a small fleet; how can we keep the supplies coming in to warrant buying the other docks?"

"A small fleet Patron? With the arrival of the extra ten ships you now have a sea going fleet of fifteen ships but it is not only those we cater for. There are now other companies that make use of our docks and labour, of course they have to pay a small fee for that use but they must also take anchor if one of our ships needs the dock. There are also the dock workers; they all work for us under a contract so the foreign ships must also pay for their work. The end result Patron is that you are now very wealthy and I have had to have constructed a second currency house at my home; soon I will have to find some trustworthy men to keep guard as my sons are becoming more and more involved with the running of the four docks."

"I think you will have no problems in that direction Senor Forsca, I am sure I have some men who would like nothing better than an honest day's work with the company. Now I must ask you of those war ships; for the life of me I can see no reason for them to be anchored so far from any battle lines or naval action with the French?"

"Ah yes Patron, the three forty gun Frigates; well Patron it is up to you as to what happens to them."

"Me?"

"Yes Patron, you. The ten ships you bought from the Prince Pimentel included those three Frigates. They are fine French ships; one is less than two years old and would make a fine company flag ship with a little refit."

"Flag ship? I have no intentions of becoming an Admiral and certainly not going looking for a war with them."

"I did not think you would Patron but the ship would make a fine flag ship for you to go wherever you desired. I have spoken to some of the shipwrights and they say they can do the work in less than two months to make it liveable for the owners use. I thought the other two could be used as escorts for some of your new fleet when they go far afield in search of cargo."

"That sounds like a good idea, where were you thinking they should go?"

"There are many places Patron. The Dutch are opening many places in the Mir Pacifica and are carrying spices and other valuable cargo to the continent at great cost, perhaps you could have some of your ships journey in that direction. There is also the huge trade now coming from the new world and the demand for tobacco and cotton is very much in demand; another smaller fleet could be sent there."

"Thank you Senor Forsca, it is something for me to think on. What of the other ships sent by Prince Pimentel?"

"They also need a little work to turn them into good cargo vessels but it can all be done in good time. You have three good and solid Sloops and four Brigantines that will convert nicely. I did think that perhaps the three Sloops could be used in the Mediterranean; there are many countries that abound it and we could make fine use of their trade. The Brigantines and one of the Frigates could be well used in the Mir Pacifica, I am told there are many pirates that operate in those wild seas but one of your Frigates should soon put them to flight; forty guns is a very good persuader Patron."

"Yes Senor Forsca, a very good deterrent as you say, now then I must go and find a tavern for us to stay, I have been told by my Officers not to return for a few days and can take my ease away from the army. There are one or two things I would like to discuss further with you but I would like to find accommodations first."

"There is a very good tavern not far from the end of the docks Patron and I would also like to extend an invitation to once again dine with my family later tonight if you are not otherwise employed."

"Thank you Senor Forsca, I would look forward to the pleasure and to once again meeting your generous wife. Shall we say seven of the clock, I hope by then to be settled at the tavern and could really do with a good homely meal after my boy's cooking for so long."

"Seven of the clock would be fine Patron, I will tell my wife of the arrangement and look forward to seeing you both then."

"Thank you again Senor Forsca; seven of the clock it shall be, I bid you a good day for now and will look forward to the dinner with great anticipation."

The two friends shook hands and Thomas led Lorenco outside to reclaim their horses and go in search of the tavern recommended to them. As they turned to walk their horses along the busy docks, Thomas noted that the next three warehouses all carried the newly painted sign which he had not taken notice of when first arriving. Along the dock were five ships being either loaded or unloaded. Thomas noted that there was a mixture of ships and their flags denoted their country of origin; the first two were Dutch, the next was Spanish and the last two flew flags that Thomas did not recognise but assumed they were not of any country he was aware of.

As he looked out into the main stream of the docks to where his newly purchased ships lay at anchor; Thomas saw movement on the deck of the newest looking Frigate. With some concern Thomas turned his horse back to the warehouse where Senor Forsca was at work. He had to tell the man that their ships were being raided; what affected Thomas the most was that the thieves were doing it in broad daylight and seemingly without fear of any retribution.

Thomas was soon back at the doors of the warehouse and caught sight of Senor Forsca who was once again busy with his ledger and also looked to be instructing one of his sons at the same time. Thomas jumped from his horse and raced to Senor Forsca's side, he then quickly reported what he had just seen on his new ships. Much to Thomas's surprise, Senor Forsca turned around smiling and completely unfazed by Thomas's report.

"Ah yes Patron, the men on your ships; forgive me I should have told you sooner but I thought this evening at dinner would be in time; I had no idea you would notice them right now."

"But who are they Senor Forsca? From the dock they looked to be armed and were not in the least afraid of being seen."

"They are some men I hired to protect your ships while they are at anchor. I was very fortunate that a cousin of my wife's sister's husband had a friend who said he could find enough men to guard your ships. I have found out since that he was once a navy man but was wounded so grievous that he now has to stay ashore but he does know how to control the ruffians he has watching over your ships, I have to give him that much."

"Where does he come from?"

"A small village just across the northern border with France; he is not a Frenchman but the man who recommended him has traded with my family for three generations and I trust his word. So far the man has proved to be more than adequate to the task, he has shot one man for trying to steal and another he hung from the main brace so every man in the harbour could see him; his charge was for attempting to murder a fellow guard over a dispute. I shall organise a meeting with him if you wish, I am sure he will fit your needs for a good guard on the ships while they await refitting."

"Thank you Senor Forsca, once more you have gone far above my expectations; I look forward to meeting the man, perhaps he may even take a permanent place once the ships are ready for sea."

"Of that I do not know Patron but he does carry some grave wounds, perhaps he may not want to take ship again."

"Well I can only ask him I suppose, any man who can bring order with a bunch of ruffians deserves to be asked if nothing else."

"I agree Patron; I shall set up a meeting on the morrow with the man so you may ask him for yourself."

"Thank you Senor Forsca, perhaps we can be taken out to the ship so I can see what condition they are in at the same time. What is the man's name Senor Forsca?"

"He calls himself Pierre, Patron."

"Just Pierre? Nothing else, no other surname?"

"No Patron, he only answers to Pierre although his accent is a little strange but that could be because of his injuries, they are quite bad."

"Well Thank you again Senor Forsca, tomorrow will tell us all we need to know about him and then I can get on with my relaxing just as my Officers want me to do."

"I am sure they have only your best interests at heart Patron, now if there is nothing else where I can be of assistance I will set about arranging the meeting with your guards."

"Thank you again Senor Forsca, I will leave you to your business and find that tavern you recommended. I shall see you again for your kind invitation to dinner."

Thomas turned back to where Lorenco sat his horse and was holding the reins of Thomas's. Within a few seconds the two old friends were riding slowly towards the tavern where they planned to stay while in Oporto. After finding a pair of good clean rooms for themselves and a good stable for their horses, Thomas and Lorenco set about sorting their clothes and organising for a good hot bath before having to go to Senor Forsca's house for dinner.

Thomas and Lorenco decided to walk to Senor Forsca's house as it was not that far away. As they strolled through the darkening streets, the two friends could smell the salty air and hear the sounds of the night-watch as they kept watch on the docks so that no thieves could take advantage of the vacant warehouses.

It was only minutes before seven of the clock when Thomas and Lorenco arrived at the gate to Senor Forsca's house; his youngest son was waiting for them as they arrived.

"Good evening Patron, my father waits for you in the front room."

"Thank you, would you please lead the way, as you can see we decided to walk so there are no horses to attend to."

The youngest son bowed and led them through the gate and back into the house where Senor Forsca and his family were waiting for them. It did not take long for everyone to get comfortable and the rest of the evening was one of laughter and relaxation as the two visitors were regaled with small stories by the men of the house. It had been silently agreed that no business would be discussed until after dinner and when the small group of business friends could relax with a fine Oporto wine.

With dinner done and the lady of the house seeing to the clean up; Senor Forsca took his guests into the front room where his sons joined him for an hour or two of business talk. By the end of the evening Thomas had been brought up to date with everything that had been going on since his last visit so long ago.

The business of war had been a real boon for the new company and Senor Forsca had been more than wise with his dealings and decisions; he had even had to build a second vault for their combined wealth. At this stage Thomas had not mentioned to Senor Forsca the fortunate capture of the ten wagons and what it could mean for their ever burgeoning finances.

At the end of the evening Senor Forsca told Thomas that he had arranged a dory to take the two men out to the anchored Frigate where they could meet the man in charge of the guards; it was decided to catch the morning tide at 10 of the clock which would give Thomas and Lorenco time to sleep a little later than usual. After their good nights the two friends slowly made their way back to the tavern where they soon took to their beds for what they thought of as a good night's sleep.

The next morning was slightly overcast and reminded Thomas that the full force of winter was not far away. There was a distinct damp chill in the air but as yet the raging winds and heavy rain had not made their usual appearance much to Thomas's delight.

By ten of the clock, Thomas and Lorenco were standing on the dock with senor Forsca as they watched a small six man dory tie up to the landing below them. The two men at the oars looked to be old sea hands in the way they manoeuvred the dory and placed it at the dock side with the ease and familiarity of those born to the sea.

The three men stepped down into the dory without a word being spoken and the two oarsmen released the dory and turned for the closest Frigate; it was to be a trip of ten minutes before they came under the high side of the Frigate's gunnels. Above them Thomas could see that the two decks of guns had been run out and it was obvious the

Frigate had been built not too long ago as the woodwork looked to be undamaged in any way and the furled sails looked to still be white and clean.

A rope ladder had been hung from the side and far above them Thomas could see the heads of some men standing in line waiting for their guests to arrive. It was now plainly obvious the men were used to the traditions of the navy in the way they had assembled and were standing steady. Once Thomas had clambered up the rope ladder he could see that at the end of the line of men stood the one in charge. Thomas could immediately see that the man had been well and truly in the wars at some stage. The man stood erect but with difficulty as it was obvious he had once been badly wounded in his left leg by the way he stood with a little more weight on his right leg.

The man was dressed in a mish-mash of clothing which was nothing really unusual for this country. He wore what appeared to be a very old and faded blue jacket which may or may not have had brass buttons at some time in the past. His shirt was the typical red striped shirt of sailors worldwide and his white canvas trousers he wore right down to his black shoes although from what Thomas could make out, the man may have been wearing boots of some description.

Around the man's waist was a wide black leather belt which carried a brace of pistols with both their butts facing to the right for ease of use by the man's single useable arm; on his head was a worn felt hat with a wide floppy brim in the style of the northern peasants of Spain; only the lower part of the man's face could be seen and Thomas could just make out some bad scarring around the man's lips. The left sleeve of his worn and faded jacket was folded back at the elbow where his forearm had once been.

In the man's right hand he held a wide mouthed blunderbuss that had been shortened for the man to be able to carry in his single hand; Thomas had little doubt the man could make good use of the evil looking musket. Thomas turned his back and looked over the side of the ship to watch both Lorenco and Senor Forsca climb the ladder to the deck. As he watched he heard the sound of footsteps behind him and turned around.

Limping towards him was the disabled man and as he came closer the man halted, brought himself to a form of attention and then after resting the strange musket under his left armpit; removed his floppy brimmed hat with his right hand. As the man swept the hat off his head to reveal his face, Thomas suddenly felt queasiness in his stomach as his legs threatened to give way on him just as the man spoke.

"Hello Mister Marking, I was wondering when we would meet again; I hope you will forgive my appearance but I had a little bother with a French Man-O-War."

"SCULLY! What...how...Oh my God we thought you were dead, even the navy told us so."

"Yes it was a bit of a bother and I'm sorry if I was the cause of any distress to you but I have not been myself for more than a few years and by then things had changed a lot."

"Bother be damned, what happened? All we got was a report from the navy that you had died and gone down with your ship."

"Well rather than stand out here, let me take you down to the Captain's cabin where I can assure you there is some very fine French brandy; after all this was a French ship.

Alfredo, the men can stand down and return to their duties, I will be in the Captain's cabin if I'm needed."

One of the young men standing in line stepped forward and touched his forelock before replying in Spanish.

"Yes Sir, is there anything you will need Sir?"

"No thank you Alfredo not for now, I will let you know what the plans are after I have spoken with Mister Marking."

The young man turned and gave the order for the others to dismiss and see to their duties as Mister Scully led Thomas and the other two through to where the Captain's cabin was situated. The three old friends along with Senor Forsca were soon seated in the large cabin set aside for the Captain of the ship and Mister Scully was in the process of pouring a good measure of brandy into four glasses.

After the four had taken a hefty gulp of the French brandy, Thomas looked at Scully and said.

"Alright Mister Scully, what the hell happened and why didn't you try to make contact with us; there was not a dry eye in the camp when we heard of your demise. I still have your possessions and have valued them because of whom they belonged to. I can only say I will be well pleased to return them all to you at the earliest opportunity if you are willing."

"Are you saying I have a position with your company then?"

"A position with my company? Are you mad Mister Scully, you will damn well take command of this ship as its Captain and will be the Commander of the Companies fleet or by all that's holy I will have you strung up higher than any mast in this harbour before the sun is set, and I brook no arguments about it Mister Scully."

"The rope will probably break Mister Marking; if the French could not finish me then there is little hope of anyone else getting me to the pearly gates before I'm ready; now then let's get down to tin tacks. What do you want to know?"

"Every bloody thing, after the tears I lost over you I want every detail of how you managed to walk away from certain death."

"It's a long story Mister Marking so we had better top up our glasses before I get started or we will all have parched throats."

Scully passed the bottle around the table once more and waited until everyone had a full glass before starting his story.

"Well on the day the Man-O-War came after the convoy I decided to try to slow it so the others could escape; I thought we had done enough damage to it to make the ship turn back to port but unfortunately it seemed to have other ideas and I promise Thomas, I had no idea what or why I did what I did but it seemed the right thing to do at the time. When I got the few men off the ship that I could spare and the two men on the forward guns refused to leave the ship, all I could do was set course to ram the Man-O-War and hope for the best. When we got to within distance I raised your battle flag and tied off the wheel; it was then that they fired their first broadside. The guns killed the two men on the forward guns and I felt myself hit with something and thrown high into the air, the next thing I knew I was in the water with bits and pieces of the ship falling around me. I suppose it was the shock but at that time I did not know I was injured until I tried to grasp onto a broken spar that landed in the water just yards from me. When the pain finally caught up I had managed to somehow tie myself to the spar with my one good hand. The last thing I remember seeing was the Man-O-War turning for the French coast, it was then I knew we had been successful in saving the convoy but don't really remember much after that until I felt someone pulling me from the water."

Scully paused to take a large gulp of brandy before continuing, the others stayed silent as they waited for him to drink and then get his thoughts straight so he could continue with his story.

"The men that saved me were fishermen; they had seen the battle and were trying to stay well out of the way until after the Man-O-War left, they then came forward to find any salvage and instead found me. The flash had damaged my face and a large splinter had gone through my leg and something large had torn my arm to shreds. The fishermen did what they could to stop the bleeding and turned their boat to shore. When we arrived at the small town of St Jean De Luz which was their home, they found someone with medical knowledge and set about repairing what they could. The Medicante had to take my lower arm off but managed to save my leg; he said it was the salt water that saved my face from further damage from the burns but it left me with no memories for a long time. The villagers although living in France did in fact have close ties with families over the border in Spain. We did hear about the war and how the English were making great advances so the villagers kept me well hidden from anyone who may give me up to the French authorities. For some time I worked as a fisherman mending nets with the men that had saved me and it was not until a request from Portugal came asking for help with guarding some captured ships that I decided to return to Portugal; not in the hope of once again joining you as I did not know the Company belonged to you but as a means to earning enough coin to return to England one day."

"Well you will return to England one day but it will be as Captain of this ship and no other way."

"My, my Thomas, you have become bossy since I last saw you; did you make Major or are you still a lowly Captain?"

"Neither, for the next few weeks I am a General and don't you bloody forget it Captain Scully or I will have every man of the Regiment down here rattling their drums when you are trying to sleep."

Scully laughed as he lifted his glass to take another sip while he watched the smile broaden on Thomas's face; the old comradery was settling in once again as the two friends began to relax into a long lost familiarity. Thomas could only think of all those who had been lost over the last five plus years and now, here was one that had returned from the dead, it gave him hope that all the fighting would perhaps have some happy moments after all.

After a short pause for everyone to let the harrowing tale of Mister Scully's return sink in, Senor Forsca raised the question of renaming and crewing all the new ships; it was suddenly time to get down to the practicalities of a shipping company. Thomas was the first to speak and was to set the tone of the meeting.

"Well firstly I think as to renaming the ships; I have given a lot of thought to this just as soon as I found out the Frigates were part of my purchase, however, with the sudden appearance of Mister Scully in the flesh I may be the cause of a little embarrassment to him but I am going to proceed as I originally thought. The two older Frigates are to be named after my two adopted sons so they will be the M.S.C. Sergio and the M.S.C. Carlito. Now this ship being as it will be the flag ship of our fleet and the newest of them all shall now be known as the M.S.C. Scully; and Captain Scully there will be no arguments; it is the name I had settled on before your revelation. Anyone with other thoughts?"

"Yes but I'm sure you won't listen to me about it all." Scully replied with a smile.

"Probably not Captain, this is one discussion where you don't get to choose. Now then I have something else for you to do to get your mind off the naming of the ship. With ten new and unmanned ships we will need full crews and I have no idea how or where to find them. The English navy has taken most of the men from shore so we may be hard pressed to get the men we want. Captain! Do you have any suggestions?"

"Yes General." The using of Thomas's rank was said with a wide smile which Thomas could only put down to his own insistence in using Scully's new rank and was his way of getting a little revenge. "You have a lot of contacts both here and in England, or have you forgotten the cane you carry? There is also the fact that the war is winding down and very soon there will be more sailors ashore than asea, we can wait and take our pick. With the winter coming and work still needed on the new ships there is time yet before we will need them."

"A good idea Mister Scully, let's work on that and I will get a message off to Captain Morgan about looking for good honest Captains for the other ships and perhaps putting the word out that there will be crews needed for the ships here. Now then Senor Forsca, I plan to find some land to build a home here in Portugal; is there some way it can be done?"

"It would depend on what you were looking for Patron and where you wished to have the land."

"I was hoping we could find somewhere close to our old bay near Vimeiro, the one the boys called Toro Bay; we already have a good dock built there and the bay could easily take the Frigate and perhaps one or two other smaller ships. What do you think Senor Forsca? Is there any chance we can purchase some land for a small house there; perhaps overlooking the bay or at least close by."

"Leave it all in my hands Patron, if it can be found then I will see it is done; I should have an answer for you within a week if I move quickly now."

"Well gentlemen I think there is only one thing left to do. Major Lorenco, I would ask you to accompany Captain Scully to the nearest tailor and have him completely fitted out with all the necessary clothing and uniforms that would now be fitting for his new position as Commander of the Company Fleet. I will get with Senor Forsca and see what victualling needs we will have to purchase for the new ships once they are refitted to our standards and purposes. Mister Scully is there anything you will need for this ship?"

"Yes General, most everything was stripped from the ship that would have been used on a daily basis, they left most of the shot but we have no powder and the food stocks are nonexistent as is most of the plate wear and cooking utensils and bedding; practically everything that could be carried off has been done so; it's going to cost a pretty penny to refit it completely."

"Don't worry Mister Scully, that's my problem not yours and I can assure you it is little of a problem as you will one day find out. Now then the last thing I have to mention is that we are having a small parade to disband the Guerrillas; it's the only way we can give the men a little hope of a future without being hunted down once the Spanish King has returned. Mister Scully I would appreciate it if you would also appear for the parade, it is after all your one time home and the men would be overjoyed to see you alive and kicking. Senor Forsca perhaps you may wish to also join us for the day; your invaluable help throughout our campaign should be recognised; perhaps your sons would like to join you also?"

"Thank you Patron, you do us a great honour to include my humble family; I shall see that my sons are present for the honour."

"Good, thank you Senor Forsca. Mister Scully, your Answer?"

"I suppose I had better turn up or you will hound me to the grave although I must admit there are a couple I would like to see again so when and where?"

"Our camp is about two miles to the east of town, you can't miss it; we plan to hold the parade on the 15th of October and would like to see you at about nine of the clock."

"Thank you Thomas, for everything; I'll not let you down and I will also be there to watch the men parade out on the 15th. Now then let's get off this ship and do some long needed shopping Major Lorenco or this may turn into a morbid recounting of past mistakes."

The four friends rose and left the cabin; once on deck Scully called for the oarsmen to ready the dory to take the small group back to land, there was a lot to do and it was better to get an early start. Thomas sat facing the scarred face of Scully with a wide and very contented smile as the two men worked hard on the oars as they rowed against the tide to make the steps of the dock; once the four men were ashore the dory would make the return journey back to the ship while the four friends went about their day.

CHAPTER 24

Once the two oarsmen landed the four others on the dock they turned back towards the ship leaving Thomas and the others to continue with their day. Thomas asked senor Forsca if he had knowledge of a good tailor so that Scully could have his uniforms made at speed. With a recommendation from Senor Forsca, Lorenco took Scully off towards the centre of Oporto in search of the tailor.

Thomas and Senor Forsca turned back towards the warehouse and on arrival saw a small black clad figure waiting for them. Lieutenant Morgan snapped to attention as he saw Thomas walking towards him; his smile told Thomas that the young Officer had something important to tell him or at least something that Thomas hoped was good news at the very least.

"Lieutenant, what are you doing here?"

"I have a message from Colonel Grey Sir, and then he has ordered me to wait for some new arrivals and escort them back to the camp on their arrival."

"Well what is it and what have those two been up to?"

"Sir Colonel's Grey and Colosio have asked for your presence on the morrow for a final planning session for the parade. They have asked for permission for me to stay here until the persons arrive on the Avante in the morning and then escort the passengers to the camp for the parade in two days Sir."

"Passengers? Visitors? What the hell have they been up to Lieutenant?"

"I'm sorry Sir I'm not at liberty to say at this time under direct orders from Colonel Grey."

"You do know I am not only your superior Officer but also theirs so it may be wise to tell me what's going on."

"Yes Sir, but they are far more scary when they want their own way Sir and I don't really mind being a Private again if I have to too keep their secret; even though I owe you everything and find it very difficult to keep their plans from you Sir."

"You really are not going to tell me what's going on, are you Lieutenant?"

"No Sir, they want it all to be a surprise for you."

"I could order you to tell me Lieutenant."

"Yes Sir you could, but then I would have to take my chances and return to the kitchens as a Private."

"Well it looks like threats won't work on you; how about bribery? Will that work?"

"Sorry but no Sir, the thought of the Colonel's revenge would even wipe away any thoughts of bribery."

"Damn it all, just what are they up to? Well Lieutenant I suppose I will just have to go and see for myself, you have permission to take a room at the tavern around the corner and join us for dinner later; I expect you to pay for the wine tonight; if I can't get you to spill the beans then you are going to have to stay on my good side until I leave on the morrow."

"Yes Sir, thank you Sir, I will see you at table tonight Sir."

As Snot Morgan walked away towards where the tavern was situated, Thomas spoke in a voice loud enough for the disappearing young Lieutenant to hear.

"Senor Forsca, where can I find the most expensive wine in this town; if young Morgan is not going to tell me anything then I'm going to make damn sure he pays a heavy price for keeping secrets."

Senor Forsca could only chuckle as he led Thomas back into the warehouse where the two spent the next hour going over Thomas's requirements for a small piece of land in the area of the bay north of Vimeiro. Much to Thomas's satisfaction, the land he liked had not been claimed and was said to be open land, he asked Senor Forsca to proceed with trying to purchase some for his small villa overlooking the bay.

It was later in the afternoon when Thomas returned to the tavern, there was no sign of Lieutenant Morgan but Lorenco and Scully were sitting at a table at the rear of the main barroom and talking quietly as they waited for the sun to go down on another day. It was not long before the other two were told about Thomas's meeting with Lieutenant Morgan and what had transpired. Both Lorenco and Scully then gave their report about the uniforms; a dress uniform would be ready the next day and the other three working Captains uniforms would take a little longer but they had been assured that the uniforms would be ready by week's end.

The three friends had been reliving old times when they were finally joined by the young Lieutenant Morgan. At first Snot took very little notice of the extra person sitting with his Officers, it was not uncommon to see injured men in this day and age; the five years of war on the Peninsula had taken a toll on just about every family in the country. Snot did not know he was in for a surprise as he sat where Thomas indicated at the end of the table.

"Lieutenant Morgan, I would like to introduce you to an old and dear friend and now Captain of the Marking Shipping Company fleet; Captain Roger Scully, you may have heard some of us discussing him at times."

Snot looked at the injured man and tried to think back to when he had first heard the name Scully. After a short time his eyes opened wide and his jaw dropped as he put two and two together. Was this man really the one all the others had said died at the hands of a seventy two gun French Man-O-War. The three friends watched the dawning comprehension on the young Lieutenant's face. It took a few more seconds before Snot could get his voice to work.

"He...he's a dead man come to life?"

"Yes Lieutenant, the most solid ghost you will ever see, say welcome to Captain Scully before you go to purchase more drinks for us; I do hope you brought a good heavy purse with you this evening."

"Ahm...yes Sir...but Sir...uhm...how...ahm...I mean what?"

"All I can say Lieutenant is that sometimes good things happen and this is one of them, now off you go and get our tankards filled."

"Yes Sir."

For the rest of the evening there was a sense of renewed comradery although poor young Snot Morgan could only sit with the others in awe at the resurrection of Mister Scully with his mouth agape; that a dead man could return, albeit badly wounded and scarred, was to Snot a miracle of the times. The small group retired early in the evening so they could rise early and make their preparations for returning to the campsite.

The next morning, with everything being made ready for their departure; Thomas, Lorenco and Scully were sitting outside the tavern with a last cafe when they were approached by a middle aged and very well dressed man. Accompanying the man was one a little young and he held what could only be the dress uniform for Roger Scully. Both men looked as though they had slept little and Thomas would not have been surprised to learn they had been up all night working on the uniform so it was ready by the time required.

Lorenco addressed the man as Scully stood to take receipt of the offered uniform from the hands of the younger man. The older man stood with wide eyes as he looked at Thomas while Lorenco passed on who he was. The man stepped forward and bowed to Thomas then once erect again he took out what appeared to be the bill for the uniform and tore it into small pieces before dropping it on the ground where the gentle breeze scattered it far and wide as the man spoke to Thomas for the first time.

"Forgive me Patron De Toro, I had no idea the uniforms were for you. There is no charge for them as they have already been paid for in full with the blood of your men when they defended us from the French invaders. Please accept them as a small part of the payment due to you and your men for our freedom."

"Senor, I thank you for your offer but it has always been our way to make payment on anything we purchase from the people. I must insist that you give me a full accounting of the costs so I can make recompense in full."

"Patron I must again apologise but I cannot accept any payment for such a small effort; as a man of honour it would grate upon my conscience to do so. I must beg you to accept this small offering on behalf of all free Portuguese."

"Senor?"

"Lacante, Eduardo Lacante Patron."

"Thank you Senor Lacante. We are honoured by your gesture Senor Lacante but I find it difficult to accept such generosity when others must put food on their tables from the sweat of their brows when I can pay for anything we need."

"As I said Patron, you and your men have already paid in blood, there is no need for any other payment as far as I am concerned. It is little enough after what you have done for us and I would implore you to accept it as a gift from those who owe you so much."

Thomas looked at the honesty on the man's face and could only resign himself to having to accept so as not to seem ungrateful for the tailor's efforts.

"In that case Senor Lacante I accept on behalf of my men and I am sure that Captain Scully will wear your uniform with pride."

"Then I am truly honoured Patron. The rest of the Uniforms will be ready in two days if they can be collected then at your convenience or as soon as the Captain has need of them."

"Thank you again Senor Lacante, your generosity will not be forgotten."

Senor Lacante bowed with a wide smile showing on his face, he then turned to his young assistant and led the way back towards his shop where there was work to do. Thomas watched the receding back of the two men before turning to Roger Scully.

"So Roger, now you have your uniform and it looks as though you have more braid than is allowed, I swear you will stand out even more than I will, which is a good thing as far as I am concerned. Now then we have a road to take; the parade will not wait for us. Where is that damned Snot got to?"

From behind Thomas came the nervous voice of Snot Morgan as he stepped out of the tavern.

"I'm here Sir."

"Good, when does the ship arrive at the dock so you can get yourself back to camp on time?"

"I was told it should be at the dock within the hour Sir so I must be away to meet it, I still have a lot to do according to Colonel Grey's orders Sir."

"You're still not going to tell me what you are up to are you Snot?"

"Sorry Sir but I am under strict orders not to reveal anything on pain of Colonel Colosio's boot Sir."

"Well I suppose under such a threat there is little I can do to change your mind; just make sure you are on duty for the parade on the morrow and don't be late Lieutenant."

"No Sir, I shall be there as ordered."

Thomas just smiled at the young Lieutenant before turning back to his friends.

"It's time to get back and find out just what those two have been up to. We will see you on the morrow Lieutenant, don't forget, be on time or the Colonel's threat will seem very minor if you are late."

"Yes Sir." A blushing Snot replied as he watched the three walk away to where their horses were being held. Snot turned towards the docks, he had other important business to attend to and had little time to waste if he wanted to be on the dock when the Avante arrived with its very special cargo.

The ride back to the campsite was taken at a gentle pace as it was a trip of only two miles and they would be there well before the midday meal was served in the general mess. On their arrival back at the camp, Thomas noticed the looks on the faces of some of the men as they watched the trio ride into the camp. Many of the men had not been around when Roger Scully was a part of the army and so he was being viewed as a stranger, especially with the way he was still dressed in his rough sailors garb; his new uniform was carefully wrapped and placed inside Thomas's pannier.

It was not until they were closer to where the Officers were housed in the small villa that the looks changed from inquisitive to ones of utter disbelief as those who knew Scully began to recognise the battered features of the third rider. The whispers started out with a sense of awe as they watched the three horses pull to a halt close by the villa and the three men stepped down to look around.

It was almost as though a gate had been opened as all those who knew Scully suddenly began to shout with joy and disbelief at his return to their midst. The sudden rush of bodies took Scully completely by surprise as old friends quickly surrounded him and began to slap him on the back with looks of awe on their welcoming faces. Thomas and Lorenco stood back and let Scully have his moment in the sun as they were quickly joined by Carmelo and Estaban; both of which looked as dumb struck as the others with the sudden rebirth of an old friend and ally.

It was fully a half hour before things began to settle down to a sense of normalcy and Scully was able to break away from the masses after Thomas told them all he would make sure that Scully would be allowed to relate his miraculous escape during the evening meal but for now he needed to have Scully go inside with him so they could make the plans for the parade on the morrow.

Once they were all back inside the small villa, Thomas watched what he thought was a most touching scene as Fairley appeared from nowhere and stopped to stare at Scully; as the tears ran from the young Sergeant's eyes he could not help himself and ran into Scully's chest to hug him so tight he may well have broken a rib or two. Roger Scully could only look at his onetime cabin boy and hold him close before saying.

"Well Fairly you've grown a bit since I last saw you." Thomas and those with him could only watch the young Sergeant Batman nod his head in tearful silence as he kept a tight hold on his long lost and supposedly dead friend.

With old friendships renewed, Thomas asked about the preparations for the next day's parade; he was assured by both Carmelo and Estaban that everything had been taken care of and Thomas could rest easy. That statement alone raised a few questions in Thomas's mind of what the two may have been up to but he was kept in the dark and given only innocent looks every time he brought up the subject during the evening meal.

Once dinner was finished the mess remained seated to the last man as Thomas asked Roger Scully to once again repeat his own story of escape; it was late in the night before he finished his story and then answered the torrent of questions that were asked. There were many tears shed by those who listened to the miraculous tale of escape and for those who knew Roger on a more personal level shed even more. It was a tired group that finally made it back to the villa for the rest of the night, the morrow would bring a long day and no doubt tears as the final parade of the 1r Regimiento Espana Guerrillas was held.

As was normal for the army, the men rose early to carry out any last minute cleaning of their uniforms and equipment; Thomas was kept inside the villa with many small jobs for the final part of the parade while outside he was sure he could hear the sound of wagons moving along the road that led past the villa to the west. In the dimming light of the last sunset, Thomas had looked over the ground that had been prepared for the parade.

The grasses had been cut with scythe and sickle and there was now a very large area of reasonably level ground to be used for the men to assemble. At one end of the large field the stone wall had even been broken down to enlarge the area needed for the full Regiment to parade. About half way down the huge area the men had set up one of the large marquee that was normally the mess; this was to be used by the Officers and any dignitaries that may be present.

The road ran to the west of the cleared ground and to the east was more open ground which made up smaller fields for the Hacienda on which Thomas and his men were camped. Although Thomas knew something was going on with his long time friends, he never had a real chance to find out what it was. Even at these last hours before the parade he seemed to always be diverted at the last minute.

The parade was called for eleven of the clock but Thomas was kept busy with one small task after the other until it was nearing ten of the clock, nothing really unusual as there were so many last minute things to be seen to for such a great occasion and he did not want his loyal men to not be recognised in a proper fashion for their last parade. Thomas was kept so busy he did not realise his friends were keeping him well out of the way of anything going on outside.

Although Thomas did hear the sounds of wagons moving along the roadway, he never thought too much about it as it was obviously a market day and many of the farmers would be heading into Oporto for the event.

At ten of the clock, Thomas felt he had finally done all that could be done and was ready to move to the marquee which was now a temporary pavilion with the front and both sides left open for a better view of the parade; Thomas could not really understand why it was needed but kept his peace as the other Officers seemed to be well aware of everything that was needed.

As the time for the Officers to move to the temporary pavilion arrived, they all took one last check of their formal dress uniforms. It was quite a show with all the plumes, medallions and ribbons on display; what most of them thought of Thomas's fancy plumed Bicorn and mass of decorations was kept to themselves as his looks of discomfort at such garish displays went against the grain even though the newly attired Roger Scully had to now wear a very fancy Captain's uniform with long white trousers of good cloth. Around Scully's waist was a sash of light blue with a black outer trim. Scully's jacket was also a pale blue with the cuffs festooned in gold braid and on his head was a plain black Bicorn hat with a rosette of pale blue with the black edging.

Thomas could not resist his next actions; returning to his bedroom, he returned quickly with the fine Toledo sword he had been given by General Martino. Thomas still wore Scully's sword and had done so since receiving it all those years ago; it was the one thing he never left behind when on the move.

Thomas approached Roger Scully and held out the fine Toledo steel sword.

"I want you to have this, a Captain should have his own sword and I feel I cannot return your own as it means a lot to me but this one is as fine as I have and I want you to have it."

Scully looked at the fine sword and a tear slipped from his eye as he reached for it; he was well aware how Thomas had gotten hold of the sword and what it must have meant to him; that Thomas wanted to keep Scully's plain looking Junior Officers sword was beyond him but he was not about to look a gift horse in the mouth and especially not from a friend like Thomas.

Scully rested the slightly worn sash over his shoulder and checked that the scabbard was properly seated at his hip before reaching out to give Thomas a light and friendly one armed hug. The two broke apart before it was too noticeable just how much Scully had been missed over the years.

With everything now ready it was time to walk out to the pavilion and start the parade. Thomas was closely followed by all his Senior Officers as they walked down the field to the pavilion. They had not made it half way before Thomas stopped and stared at what was before him; it was just now that the hum and buzz of conversations were noticed.

Thomas looked to the field behind and to the sides of the pavilion and could not believe his eyes as he looked over the huge mass of people gathered there. Some were sitting around in small circles apparently in a picnic mood while others were forming small crowds along the edge of the double sized fields where the parade would take place. Out on the road Thomas could still see many other wagons, carts and even small carriages still coming towards the fields, amongst them some very fine looking carriages that could only belong to some very wealthy people.

Thomas was taken totally by surprise by all the activity, none of this was in his original plan and he could not work out how so many had found out about the last parade of the Espana Guerrillas. Had he taken time he may have noticed some very sly looks between his long time friends as they took note of his surprise at the mass of people forming all around the parade ground.

By half Ten of the clock there was a solid mass of spectators all around the parade ground; in the distance where the barns that the men had used for their accommodations, there was a very large spread of fabric that hid the area around the barns, Thomas could just make out the shadows of men moving behind the screen; another addition he had little knowledge of.

Thomas was led to the pavilion where he noted that most of the chairs from the villa had been set out with his own large carved chair at the centre; at the back of the pavilion were a pair of trestle tables with food and drink displayed for those who would like to partake during the parade. It was now plainly obvious what his friends had been up to while he was out of the way but he could still not understand why or how they had managed to gather such a huge crowd to observe the last parade.

Thomas was escorted to his large chair but before he could sit he was directed to the front of the open pavilion and surrounded by his Senior Officers. Just as Thomas was about to ask what was happening, a black coach turned into the gate on the far side of the parade ground and turned towards the pavilion. Thomas took a moment to stare at the passengers and could not believe his eyes when he recognised the small plump figure sitting in the back of the carriage.

Thomas watched as Mister Percy's carriage approached, it was not the sight of Mister Percy sitting in the back but the fact he had what appeared to be two passengers with him. The extra passengers sat with their backs to the driver and so where not recognised by Thomas but, the fact that one of them was a women and the other was in a red English uniform on which Thomas could just make out the Sergeants stripes on the sleeve of the right arm. All this did raise some wonder in Thomas's as he had not given orders for any English troops to be present at the parade, his mind also took notice that Mister Percy was talking to someone at his side but Thomas could not see who it was as the person was hidden by the high sides of the carriage.

Mister Percy was in full dress uniform which was also an unusual event for Thomas to see and he waited while the carriage came to a halt in front of the pavilion; suddenly Thomas's breath caught in his throat as he began to recognise the two passengers.

Thomas felt as though his boots had been nailed to the ground as he stood transfixed by the sight in front of him. The familiar face of Mister Percy's driver had jumped from the driver's seat and was opening the small door of the carriage as Thomas's father stood up and made is slightly ungainly way with his wooden peg leg making it a little difficult. Once on the ground beside the carriage, Cromwell Marking turned back to help his wife Matty from the carriage before turning back to face Thomas.

Cromwell's uniform was that of the 33rd Yorkshire Regiment and Thomas was taken completely by surprise as Cromwell came to attention as best he could on his single leg and saluted Thomas.

"Sir, Sergeant Cromwell Marking reporting for parade duty Sir."

Thomas forgot all of the niceties of protocol and somehow overcame his sudden paralysis and did what no General should ever do, although for Thomas it would not have made any difference at that moment. Thomas left the pavilion at speed and flew into the arms of his father as everyone looked on with tears and smiles, that Thomas was a General seemed to be ignored as a great roar of encouragement went up around the large parade ground by the entire large crowd watching the event unfold.

Thomas could only hold on tight as his sobs and tears fell onto the bright new uniform of his Father; that hundreds of strangers were watching the event did not even penetrate Thomas's awareness; his Father was the only centre point in his present world.

Although it was only a few moments, for Thomas it seemed a life time as he held his Father tightly; eventually it was the calm voice of Cromwell that brought a sense of decorum back to the meeting.

"Come now lad, you is an Officer and have duties to perform; brace up and show us what it is you been up to. There be plenty of time for family after you have done your duty."

Thomas sniffed as he stepped back and looked to where his Mother was now standing with her hand resting on Mister Percy's arm and her left hand holding the hand of a young boy of about five years old who appeared to be trying to work out what all the fuss was about; after all he had been on a big ship all the way across the ocean and now he was watching an older boy make a big fuss of his Da in a strange place where everyone talked funny.

It took a few seconds for Thomas to realise the little boy was his brother and he wasted little time in giving his Mother a hug before looking down at the Brother he had only seen as a young baby; it suddenly made him realise how much time had passed since he had been around his family and all the things he may have missed over the last five years.

For Thomas there was very little time to take it all in as Mister Percy escorted Matty Marking to the central chair under the shade of the marquee and placed her in Thomas's large chair; for Thomas's brother there was so much to look at and he could be seen trying to pull away to go and investigate other things; it was the ever present Fairley that took over and removed the little boy somewhere outside the pavilion; unknown to those in the pavilion it would be some time before they saw the small boy again and, when they did it created quite a stir among those watching.

With everyone moving inside the pavilion where they could relax and make ready for what Thomas thought was to be the beginning of the parade; they were suddenly interrupted by the arrival of another carriage; this time Thomas could not believe his eyes as two familiar figures emerged from the carriage and made their way towards where he stood; the smile on Mister Percy's face told Thomas how this had eventuated.

The smile on Thomas's face only increased as he watched Peter Morgan and his aging father step from the coach, both were resplendent in smartly cut suits which were becoming the fashion of the day and it was only their rolling gait that told those in the know that they were both old sea hands; in their right hand was the very familiar silver topped black cane. Subconsciously Thomas's hand tightened on his own black baton as he watched the two older men approach where he stood waiting.

"Well Captain Toro, we see you made it all in one piece." The elder of the two said as he walked with amazing agility towards Thomas; any sign of his age was put aside now that he was dressed so well and his appearance of an old man huddled in a dark tavern was no longer apparent. Thomas had not missed the large driver of their carriage either; it was the formidable shape of George; he was to return and join them once the carriage had been driven away and parked out of sight.

The next carriage carried the family of Senor Forsca; the pavilion was filling quickly as the special guests continued to arrive. Matty Marking could only sit and watch in awe as the arrival of more of her little boy Thomas's friends increased with every carriage that arrived; she could not quite understand how her little Thomas could possible know all these varied people.

The next carriage's arrival only went to confuse Matty even more. The carriage was very fancy and was accompanied by a full troop of mounted Cavalry in foreign uniforms and all carried long lances. In the carriage were three very important looking men also in full dress uniforms, the long plumes on their Bicorn hats waved in the breeze as the carriage pulled to a halt in front of the pavilion; there was a sudden hushed awe from the hundreds of spectators at the arrival of the large black carriage with the coat of arms on the side.

The Cavalry troop had lined up behind the halted carriage and, as Prince Pimentel stepped from the carriage to be followed quickly by General Livorno and General Martino; the Cavalry troop lowered their lances in salute, not to the three men but to Thomas. With the salute done the troops immediately began to move off behind the empty coach as it made its way from the parade ground.

Prince Pimentel led his two friends up to where Thomas was standing with his mouth agape, these three men were the last ones Thomas would have expected; Thomas did not see his Mother lean forward to hear a little better as the Prince stopped in front of Thomas.

"Don Thomasino I thank you for your kind invitation to join you in your final parade; had not your fine Officers notified me some time ago I would have missed it and it would have been one of my great regrets. I have prevailed upon General Livorno and General Martino to accompany me which they did only too willingly."

"Your Highness, thank you for coming but I must admit I had little knowledge of it and therefore must apologise for my tardiness."

"There is nothing to apologise for Don Thomasino; your fine Officers have it all in hand; after all, is that not what Officers are for? Now then whom do we have here?"

The Prince had turned towards the others waiting under the marquee as Thomas tried to hide his blush. Thomas led the Prince further into the tent and stopped in front of his Father who was standing beside his seated Mother.

"Your Highness may I present my Father retired Sergeant Cromwell Marking and my Mother."

The Prince looked at Cromwell with a discerning eye and made note of the way the Sergeant was standing which indicated he had a serious injury.

"Sergeant Marking it is indeed a great pleasure to make your acquaintance; it is an honour to meet the man that could raise one such as our dear Don Thomasino; it is easy to see where he got his bravery and strength from. You must be very proud of him and his many endeavours."

"That I am Your Highness. May I ask Sir why you would call him by such a title, it is not one I am familiar with or was aware he held?"

A large smile spread across the Prince's face as he turned to look at Thomas.

"Don Thomasino shame on you; are you to tell me you have not revealed your true self to your own father? Never mind I will do it for you and then we can watch the parade in complete familiarity. Sergeant Marking your fine son is the holder of several titles and achievements that many lesser men would be proud to boast of. That he did not even pass them all on to you; his Father is quite the wonder. Let me explain this young man to you as it would seem he would prefer to keep his true nature to himself. Your Son, Sergeant Marking holds the title of a Cavalier De Espana as well as the title of a Hero of Spain; they are much like the English title of a knight and so we refer to him as Don as the English refer to their knights as Sir. He has land holdings in Spain of five thousand acres but unfortunately they are being brought under threat by the political situation which is developing at the moment but, I can assure you Sergeant Marking, there are plans afoot to make sure his holdings are held in trust for when he can return to his rightful place in our country. Senora Marking I must also congratulate you on your steadfastness in our favourite General's rearing. We say in our family that a man is given courage by his Father but his strength comes from his Mother, for this we must all thank you. Your son was truly one of our most valued saviours in our fight against the French invaders and there is little we will ever be able to do to repay his valour."

Thomas could only stand to the side as the prince revealed many things he would rather have kept to himself; he also noticed that his Mother was both nervous and proud at the same time as she tried to thank the important man standing before her with a friendly smile.

With Thomas being revealed before everyone and trying to hide his blushing face; he turned and directed the Prince to the other guests standing with their mouths agape at the revelations. Thomas tried to push aside his embarrassment as he took the Prince among the visitors and introduced them before he turned back to the open and still empty field which waited for the parade to begin.

Thomas looked around at his gathered Officers and was about to ask for the parade to begin when Carmelo stepped forward with a smile to indicate he would start the proceedings. Thomas just nodded and took a half step back as Carmelo straightened himself up and looked out onto the empty field before yelling out in his loudest voice which almost echoed over the empty space. The hundreds of spectators immediately drew quiet as they heard the loud order echo around the field.

"Captain Perrin will present himself before the Officers for orders."

From somewhere behind the pavilion Tommy Perrin marched out to the front of the marquee; he was dressed in his best formal uniform and much to Thomas's surprise was carrying Thomas's drum on his hip. Tommy Perrin came to a smart halt at attention and saluted the Officers and guests before Carmelo continued.

"Captain Perrin, as the original drummer and one who has stood by our General's side since the start of hostilities we would ask that you beat the cadence for the colours to be paraded."

"Sir."

Tommy Perrin about turned and stood erect as he moved Thomas's original drum to the front and prepared his sticks for the Cadence. Tommy Perrin began with the long drum roll and then swiftly went into the call for the colours. As Tommy beat the cadence Thomas watched the far end of the field as the screen in front of the barn was drawn aside and the colour guard appeared with all the flags flying high and Major Carterton at their head.

Directly behind Major Carterton marched both the flags of Portugal and Spain side by side, just behind came the battle flag of El Toro's forces and behind that came the English flag, it was not lost on those watching that the English flag had been positioned in the place of a secondary banner. Thomas was surprised that there were two more banners but both were still under their covers and had not been revealed.

The colour guard marched the long distance in perfect step until they were standing before the marquee and came to attention; all four flags were then lowered as a salute before being raised again and Major Carterton held his salute as he reported to Carmelo.

"Sir, the colours of The Regimiento De Toro are all present and correct and await your orders."

Thomas did not miss the change in the Regimental name but kept his silence to see where it was all going as Carmelo gave his next order.

"Major Carterton, the colour guard will move to the right and take stand."

"Sir. The colour guard will move to the right! March."

The colour guard smartly left turned and marched the few steps to the end of the pavilion where they came to a smart halt and stood at attention with the colours softly waving in the gentle breeze that had sprung up. Carmelo continued with his orders; Thomas was now finding out he had little knowledge of what his Officers had set in motion.

"Captain Perrin, you will beat cadence for the Originals to assemble on parade."

"Sir."

Thomas stood and watched as Tommy Perrin began to beat a cadence he had not heard before but almost seemed to be part of a number of other cadences worked together to make a very distinctive beat. From behind the screen Thomas watched all of the original surviving members of the Drum Corps appear in ranks of four, at their head was Sergio who was carrying a large staff while directly behind him was one of the drummers who was playing the marching beat on his single drum; the rest of the Corps held their drums on their hip as they marched in rank towards where the Officers waited.

Tommy Perrin had stopped playing as soon as the single drummer had started and he stood at attention as the ranks came forward until they were all at attention before the pavilion. Tommy Perrin stepped forward until he was standing next to Sergio where he then turned and faced Carmelo.

"Sir, the drums of the Regimiento De Toro are all present and correct and awaiting your orders."

"Captain Perrin, the drums of the Regimiento De Toro will call the army to parade."

Tommy Perrin turned about and gave the order.

"The drums of the Regimiento De Toro will beat the army to Parade."

It did not take Thomas much thought to recognise the start of the De La Guerra and, as the drum roll at the beginning of the tune rang out, Thomas heard what could only be the sound of massed horses and wheels as the guns rode from behind the screen with Major Craven Morgan at their head. The twenty guns and the smaller Rocket Battery bringing up the rear rode in perfect formation as they came forward.

The guns moved at a well paced trot as they made their way along the western side of the parade ground and; as they drew level with the pavilion and all its important Officers and guests, the gunners turned their heads to the right and threw up a one handed salute before turning back to the front as they moved past.

With the drums still playing Major Morgan lifted his arm high and swung it in a circular motion, the guns behind him immediately turned inward and came to a halt with the guns facing outward to the west. The gunners jumped from their seats and saddles all except a single rider at the head of the six horses who would take them away once the guns had been unhitched.

As the guns were set in place the next to appear were the two large companies of Infantry lead by Major Oliver Perrin at the head of the 1st Company and Major Trent at the head of the 2nd Company. The men were in three ranks and marched in perfect time to the resounding call of the De La Guerra as they came down the centre of the parade ground.

Once again the men all turned their heads to the right as the Officers saluted those standing in review in the pavilion as they marched past until they were all turned to the right and halted along the eastern side of the parade ground where they formed two long and tight formations and leaving the centre empty for the next force to appear.

As the drums continued the next to appear from behind the screen was the young upright figure of Lieutenant Morgan and Major Jervis while behind them marched Sergeant Fairley as they led the three perfect ranks of all the boys that were now known as "The Auxiliaries" as there was not a man in the army that felt calling the youngest of their men 'scullery lads' and even worse was in the best interest of some of the hardest working and devoted troops they had and there were many among them that had also fought alongside the rest when a fight came their way.

The youngest were all dressed in their full uniforms and carried their arms with pride as they marched past the pavilion and gave the salute by turning their heads towards the

Senior Officers; only the young Officers at the front raised their hands to salute. Behind the main force of Auxiliaries came a wagon that had been altered so that there were a number of boards laid across to form seats on which sat those who could no longer march because of amputations and severe injuries. Sitting on the seat alongside the driver was the very erect and proud figure of Lieutenant Flores De Silva. Once past the small force of the Auxiliaries formed up just to the right of the pavilion and only ten paces away from the end of the 2nd Company of Infantry.

Something had been niggling at Thomas mind ever since the Artillery had appeared but he could not quite put his finger on what it was; it was the appearance of the 1st Company of Cavalry that it finally came to him; that and a rather strange sight as the Company rode at a slow trot out onto the parade ground, there was no sign of the other two Company's.

The Cavalry troop rode four abreast with Pablo riding alone at about halfway down the column on the right hand side. The troopers had their muskets over their backs and were carrying their sabres in their right hand with the blade resting on the right shoulder. While the column of smartly turned out riders received the same loud cheers from the hundreds of spectators that surrounded the parade ground, it was the sight that everyone saw as Pablo rode erect on his horse.

Sitting on the saddle in front of Pablo with obvious joy spread over his small face was Thomas's little brother. Pablo had his left hand holding the little boy around the middle as the boy held the reins of the horse as though directing it; he was obviously not aware that Pablo controlled the beast with his heels and toes but the little boy's smile said it all; as far as he was concerned he was the leader of the troop of Cavalry and no one was going to tell him different.

At the sight of the little boy riding on the large horse with Pablo, Thomas heard a gasp from behind as his mother now saw what had happened to her other little boy. Cromwell Marking had a smile on his face as he told his wife to stop worrying and hush herself so they could all enjoy the moment. Thomas could not stop the smile on his own face as he saw his little brother seemingly having the time of his life; the men had even found a small French style white Kepi with a blue and black band for him to wear.

As the 1st Company drew level with the pavilion, Pablo lifted his sabre high and brought the blade down in a slashing movement before raising it out to the side, the rest of the Company came to an immediate halt and Pablo then called the order.

"The 1st Company of Cavalry of the Regimiento De Toro will turn to the right."

The crowd of spectators and everyone else had grown quiet as the troop turned to the right and faced the pavilion. It was as though every man in the Company had been tied with a string as they raised their sabres so the haft was level with their lips and the bright shining blade was sparkling in the midday sunlight. Again with a slashing movement the blades came down and Pablo called the next order.

"The 1st Company will turn to the left and advance at the walk. March."

Thomas did not miss his little brother lift his hand in his own salute; as though to make sure he had done it right, the little boy looked over his shoulder at Pablo to get conformation; the returning smile was all the boy needed before taking hold of the reins once again; it was such a tender and touching moment that the spectators gave a mighty cheer that made one or two of the horses give a little jump of surprise before settling back into the walk pace as they rode further down the field.

The 2nd and 3rd Company's followed in the same order with each stopping to give the salute just as Pablo and his men had done. It was as Thomas watched the 3rd Company move off that the little niggle finally got answered. It was the sash the men were wearing and it took Thomas completely by surprise when he realised that every man had changed from the well known and well worn red and gold sash to one of pale blue in the centre with a wide band of black on the top and bottom.

A little further along the parade ground, Pablo and his Company had taken a place at the centre of the parade ground and the 2nd and 3rd Company's formed up behind him. Silence had descended over the parade ground as the last rider took his place at the back of the Cavalry lines as Pablo's voice echoed out over the hushed scene.

"The Company's will prepare to dismount."

There was the sudden sound of steel blades being returned to their scabbards in readiness for the next order.

"Company's Dismount."

The three hundred or more riders moved as one single entity as they dismounted and then stepped to the head of their horses to hold the reins close under the horses head; for Pablo there was one extra duty to perform as he turned back and reached up for the smiling little boy to jump into his waiting arms which he then placed the smiling bundle at his side where the little boy reached up and took hold of Pablo's hand; it was a touching scene and the spectators let everyone know they had seen it.

With the army now all in their places, Carmelo waited for the last few notes of the De La Guerra to finish. The sudden silence seemed to draw out for a long time although it was only about ten seconds before Carmelo called out.

"The Regimiento De Toro will salute the colours. Salute."

There was the sudden sound of over seven hundred booted feet coming together as everyone stood at attention and saluted the flags standing beside the pavilion. After a few seconds Carmelo gave the next order.

"The Regimiento De Toro will stand at ease."

Again the sounds of boots moving filled the open space before Carmelo turned towards where Thomas stood to give his report.

"Don Thomasino De Toro, the Regimiento De Toro is present and correct and awaits your orders."

This was the part that Thomas had not been looking forward to; it was time for him to take control and set the orders for the dissolution of his brave and dedicated force, the very men and boys who had followed him through such torrid times. Thomas suddenly found his throat constricting and the feeling of tears trying to force their way through his eyes as he looked out onto the expectant faces of men he considered more friends than troops. Thomas straightened his shoulders and forced himself to carry out his duties for the day.

In a voice that was almost ready to betray his feelings, Thomas began his speech to the men. Without thought he spoke in Spanish as had all the others when giving orders; he had forgotten that his parents and the Morgans did not know what he was saying but a saviour had come to his rescue. While Mister Percy translated for the Morgans, Prince Pimentel took the place of translator for Thomas's parents.

"I know that today is, for all of us a sad day in that this is the last parade of our special army. All of you came together to fight a common enemy when there was little left for you or your country and today will see the end of our era. On the morrow there will be a special parade for all of you to receive your dues that have been faithfully kept by Major Jones until the day you had a need and that day has arrived. On the morrow you will also be asked to sign your papers of discharge which have been dated until the 2nd of January 1814, until this date you will remain on full pay but noted as being on formal leave. I have hope that this will give all of you time to find a new place but I must first tell you that I will be in need of a large number of men with your abilities for the shipping company, especially the men who are gunners. I know that many of you younger ones have been offered homes and families with our second families in Vimeiro; I hope you will take up those offers. Major Jones has informed me that our home valley at Vimeiro is open to those who wish to make a new life there and the mayor of Vimeiro has said they will welcome any who want to make use of it to create a home."

Thomas paused his speech to let his words sink in and for some of the men to think about what they wanted to do in the future before he continued.

"There is little else for me to say except to thank you all for your bravery and dedication to our cause and that not a single one of us must forget those who gave the final sacrifice so that we could all be here today. There remains only for me to ask two of our special guests if they will accompany me in presenting you all with a rightly deserved campaign ribbon and medallion of commemoration for the years of your service and duty. Colonel Cruickshank; Your highness; would you do us the honour of presenting my men with their honours?"

Prince Pimentel replied for both of them.

"The honour Don Thomasino De Toro will be entirely ours and we will do it willingly."

Before more could be said or done, Estaban came close to Thomas and held out a new sash of pale blue and black trim.

"Patron you will now need this; it is the new colours of the Regimiento De Toro. If you will allow me we all wish that your Madre has the old one as a token of our esteem and so that she will always know that you have friends no matter where you go."

Thomas suddenly found his throat constrict at Estaban's words but, with slow and deliberate movements he untied his old blood stained, worn and frayed red and gold sash and handed it to Estaban before slowly replacing it with the new blue and black. Once complete and Estaban had had time to speak with Matty Marking in his slightly broken English and give her the old sash for her to keep, Estaban returned to stand in front of Thomas and await the next orders.

"Colonel Colosio you will call the men to attention if you please."

"Yes Don General."

Estaban turned about and then took the five steps to be outside the pavilion and raised his voice so that he could be heard the length and breadth of the parade ground.

"THE REGIMIENTO DE TORO WILL COME TO ATTENTION...Ateeeen-shun."

There was a ripple of sound as booted feet came together in unison amid the softer jingle of iron wear on the horses as they shook their heads or swished their tails. With all the men now standing at attention, Estaban called out the next order.

"Captain Thomas Perrin will present himself before the Officers and the colours."

Tommy Perrin about turned smartly from where he had been facing the other drummers, took two steps forward until he was almost face to face with Estaban and then brought his hand up in a perfect salute. Tommy Perrin was to be the first of a long line of presentations but, as he was the only other soldier that had been in the war from the very first battle to the last fight at Thomas's side, all had agreed he should be the first one recognised. It was going to be a long and in some cases, tearful day.

CHAPTER 25

A hush came over the large crowd that was watching as Thomas, Mister Percy and the Prince stepped from the pavilion and towards where Tommy Perrin stood waiting. Just behind the three senior Officers came Major Jones and in his hands he carried what looked to be a small wooden tray with some small items on it.

When they were standing in front of the waiting Tommy Perrin; Thomas spoke in a softer voice but was still heard by those close by.

"Captain Perrin, you have stood by my side since the first shot was fired in this war and for that I thank you. Many times you were my rock and even though it was never said, I am sure I could not have faced all that we have without your support. I truly wish that there was more I could do for you and your dedication to our cause and find that the small presentation I have is quite inadequate for the honour and effort you put into your duty to the colours. Captain Perrin I will ask Prince Pedro Pimentel to present you with the campaign ribbon which you truly deserve and hope that it will always remind you of not only your honourable stand but also our long friendship. At the top of the ribbon is a gold six pointed star; it is to remind others that you were the first Original and have stood at my side through thick and thin. All of the major battles we fought together are marked with the gold bar; those of a lesser nature are presented by a silver bar. Colonel Percy Cruickshank will present to you a medallion in gold which will carry all of your details including your length of service to the people of Spain and Portugal. Captain Perrin, I feel this is less than you deserve but at this stage it is all I can offer as a means of informing you of the value that we all hold you in. Your Highness?"

Prince Pedro Pimentel stepped forward and took the long blue and black edged ribbon from the small tray. After taking the short step in front of Tommy Perrin he smiled as he pinned the long ribbon onto Tommy's chest before saying.

"Captain, if there was one person that was responsible for the safety of our most valued General De Toro then it is yourself. I am sure that without your dedication to duty we may well have lost the General many times over. I am honoured that I was asked to make this presentation and will remember your name for a long time in the future. The people of Spain and Portugal sincerely thank you for your service and duty."

Thomas almost smiled as he saw the red blush tinge the cheeks of what many would consider to be a hard bitten fighting man as Perrin heard the Princes words; if he thought he was going to get off so easy he was mistaken as Colonel Percy stepped up to replace the Prince. In his hand he held a small wooden box with a glass top which he had taken from the tray held by Major Jones.

Inside the box it was lined with black velvet and, sitting in the centre was a large gold medallion which was about 4" in diameter and must have been at least a quarter inch thick. On the face of the medallion was engraved a drum with two sticks crossed above it and on the obverse was Perrin's name, rank and length of service which was written as 1808-1814.

Colonel Percy smiled at the blushing Perrin and then said.

"Captain Perrin, as you may know I have been in the service of the King for a good many years and in all that time I do not think I have seen more valour or dedication to duty than I have seen from you. It is a great honour to present this medallion to you and thank you for your service and dedication to duty."

Colonel Percy Cruickshank gave the boxed medallion to Tommy Perrin and then stepped back and raised his hand smartly in salute before turning back to stand just behind Thomas. For those close enough it was not difficult to see the appearance of small tears in the eyes of the young Officer; after all he had just turned nineteen years of age and his emotions were beginning to show through his slightly scarred and tough demeanour; it was the first sight of the boy that had been hidden for so long and took some of those who knew him best by surprise.

Tommy Perrin could only gulp as he waited for Colonel Colosio to call out his next orders and, although this had all been practiced while Thomas was out of the way, it still caused him to show his softer side; he did not have to wait long before he heard Colonel Colosio call out.

"Captain Perrin you will call the drums of the Regimiento De Toro to order for the presentation of campaign ribbons and medallions of remembrance."

Tommy Perrin did a smart about turn and faced the ranks of the originals.

"Originals...atten...shun. The Originals will form ranks of three...march."

Everyone including Thomas was surprised at the smartness of the formation and how precise and quickly the phalanx of drummers formed the three ranks and then stood at attention awaiting further orders from Captain Perrin.

"The Originals will open order...march."

The front rank took three smart steps forward while the rear rank took three steps back; there was now a wider gap between ranks which would make it far easier for the Officers to move through as they presented the ribbons and medallions to each drummer. While the ranks were being formed two of the boys from the Auxiliary's marched forward with a large wooden tray laden with the small wooden boxes with the medallions while another appeared with a tray full of ribbons. Major Jones now had one of his large ledgers in his hand and open at the first page.

It was no wonder to Thomas that Major Jones would be so well organised but he did wonder how the men had found the time to plan everything in such detail and then find the time to practice it all. It was to be one of those little secrets that his friends had kept from him and continued to do so even though he asked them after the parade for details. As usual for his friends they just smiled and shrugged their shoulders as though they had no idea what Thomas was talking about.

Once the three senior men were standing in front of the first rank, Major Jones looked at his ledger and read out the first name and first the Prince and then Colonel Percy stepped forward and presented the ribbon and medallion. Thomas stepped up and shook hands with the drummer and said a few words before moving along the line to the next man.

It was not a surprise for Thomas that the men were all lined up according to the list of names in the Major's ledger; in fact he would have been surprised if they had not with the way the parade had been organised so far. When the last of the seventy six remaining drummers had been presented with their ribbons and medallions the small group of Officers marched to the front of the force and all saluted the men before turning back to stand just outside the pavilion.

Major Jones had closed his ledger but only stepped to the side while the three boys' of the Axillaries disappeared presumably to refill their trays for the next part of the presentations. Estaban called out the next order for everyone to hear.

"Captain Perrin, the Drums of the Regimiento De Toro will retire to the left flank and take stand for the duration of the ceremony."

Tommy Perrin once again turned about and called out the order for the drummers.

"The Originals will close order and retire to the left flank...March."

Tommy Perrin took up his place at the centre mark of the quickly reformed ranks and marched with them to the left of the pavilion where they all came to a halt and then performed a right turn and faced out into the centre of the parade ground. Once the manoeuvre had been completed they all stood at the ease position while Colonel Colosio called the next order.

"Captain Perrin, the drums will strike the cadence for the Auxiliaries and Infantry to advance and present themselves before the Colours."

Tommy Perrin saluted and then turned about and gave the order to his drummers. The beat of the Infantry advance soon filled the air as the two company's of Infantry and the smaller force of Auxiliaries came to attention, turned left and then marched forward until they were lined in ranks before the pavilion.

When the troops stopped and stood at attention in front of the pavilion they had the Auxiliaries at the front and then the 1st Company behind them and the 2nd Company at the rear. Major Jervis had been given the privilege of being the Senior Officer in charge to give the orders.

Thomas also noticed the men had given the place of pride at the front of the formation to the young Auxiliaries. Major Jervis stepped to the front, saluted the Officers in the pavilion and then about turned and gave his orders.

"The 1st and 2nd Company and Auxiliaries of the Regimiento De Toro; will open order...March."

Once again the presentation was orderly but this time it took a while longer as there were so many more to receive their ribbons and medallions. Thomas was determined to personally thank each and every man that stood before him which only added a little more time to the event but in his own mind he couldn't have cared less for such minor details as the right time or keeping to a schedule. His many friends amongst the men were far more important to him than what others may think or plan.

The Infantry and Auxiliaries medallion was similar to those given to Captain Perrin and his men except they had a pair of crossed muskets engraved on the face side. Once all had been presented the Infantrymen were dismissed and returned to their place to the right of the pavilion while Estaban called out the next orders to Captain Perrin.

"Captain Perrin, the drums will beat the cadence for the Artillery to advance and present themselves before the Colours."

"Sir."

Tommy Perrin raised his drum sticks up to his top lip as the signal for the rest of the drummers to prepare to play a cadence and then called the order to the originals.

"The drums will beat for the Artillery to advance and present themselves before the Colours."

Captain Perrin dropped his sticks to the drum top and began the double time beat for the Artillery to advance. At the far end of the field Major Craven Morgan called for the gunners to assemble in front of their guns then take their muskets from their backs and carry them at the trail as they marched towards the pavilion in double time and then came to attention in perfect order before the waiting Officers.

For this presentation, Thomas had asked Colonel Cruickshank to do the honours as Major Jones followed along behind to call the name of each artilleryman until; almost a full half hour later, the last man was awarded his ribbon and medallion and the small group of Officers returned to the front to give a final salute to their gunners. The medallion for the gunners was the crossed barrels of a pair of guns as it should have been for such a force. Major Morgan called his men to attention and returned as they had come to the faster beat of the double march to where their guns waited.

With the Artillerymen returned to their place on the western side of the parade ground, Estaban called the last order for Captain Perrin.

"Captain Perrin, the drums will beat the cadence for the Cavalry to advance and present themselves before the Colours."

Tommy Perrin once again took up his drum sticks and began the beat for the Cavalry Advance with the rest of the Originals soon joining in and the double beat echoed out over the countryside.

Pablo called for his men to remount and at the same time gave a small tug on the reins of his own horse. As everyone watched, Pablo's horse knelt down which allowed the smaller figure of Thomas's little brother to scramble a little ungainly up into the saddle and take hold of the reins. Once he was seated Pablo drew his sabre and stepped easily into his saddle and took hold of the smaller boy around the chest as he toed the order for his horse to regain its feet.

Pablo lifted his sabre above his head and then swung it in a circle before once again resting the tip on his shoulder while the three Troops reorganised themselves until they were now spread across the parade ground from one side to the other and in three ranks with each Troop about five yards apart. As the drums beat out in the early afternoon sunlight, Pablo raised his sabre and swept it forward as he toed his horse to advance at a slow trot with the other two Troops moving in unison. The manoeuvre was carried out with precision and the ranks of Cavalry now looked almost threatening as they advanced towards the pavilion before Pablo swung his sabre once again as his Troop came level with the waiting Officers.

With the sabre raised above his head Pablo then swung to the left and back to the front. Pablo's Troop began to swing around from the left end of the line until they were all now facing the pavilion and then slowed the pace to a walk until close to the pavilion where Pablo gave the signal for them to halt. The other two Troops followed suit and were soon lined up behind Pablo's Troop and still with about five yards between them all.

Pablo gave his horse the order to once again kneel and then; after he stepped to the ground he called out while helping the young boy to also dismount.

"The Cavalry of the Regimiento De Toro will prepare to dismount and take station in ranks." There was heard a tinkle of metal and a few snorts from the horses as their riders rose in their saddles in preparation for dismounting.

"Dismount."

The sound of boots hitting the ground and then all stepping almost in a single movement to the heads of their horses could be heard by even those who were on the far side of the parade ground and then there was silence as the watching crowds waited for the Officers under the pavilion to come forward for what they thought was the final presentation.

Thomas turned to the Prince and asked.

"Your Highness, would you do the honour of presenting the awards to the Cavalry? Many if not most are from both Spain and Portugal and have been without a doubt our most effective force. I am sure that they would appreciate the presentation being done by a fellow Cavalryman."

"I would certainly like that honour Don Thomasino and I thank you for the generous offer and will think fondly of it for many years to come."

Prince Pedro Pimentel stepped forward from under the pavilion and marched forward until he was standing before Pablo who had his hand on the shoulder of the young boy. Major Jones was close to hand as were a number of the younger Auxiliaries with the awards trays. Prince Pimentel began by speaking to Pablo after Major Jones had introduced them from his ledger.

"Captain Cavalino, I must offer the thanks of the people of both Spain and Portugal for the dedication and heroism of your troopers. Don Thomasino De Toro has told me nothing but great things about you and your men and I can only agree with his assessment. It is with a sense of gratitude that I present you and your men with these ribbons and medallions so that others will never forget your valour."

The Prince took the long blue and black edged ribbon from Major Jones and pinned it on Pablo's jacket; after presenting Pablo with the medallion in its small wooden case, the Prince looked down at the young boy standing perfectly still under Pablo's hand but with a look of awe on his young face as he looked up at the very fancy uniform that the Prince and the others with him were wearing. That the boy had not understood all the foreign words being spoken had also given him a bemused look.

The small boy suddenly got a surprise as the foreign looking man knelt down on the ground on one knee and asked him in perfect English.

"And who are you, young man?"

The young boy blushed and then straightened up a little more as he spoke in his best and most polite manner as he had been taught by his Da.

"I am Thomas Cromwell Marking, Your Honour and I'm going to be a famous Cavalry man just like Uncle Pablo."

"Are you indeed? Well Thomas Cromwell Marking, you carry very famous names, where did you get them?"

Little Thomas smiled and blushed at the same time as he lent forward a little as though he was going to tell a big secret like all small boys are won't to do.

"I got a big brother who went to fight in the war, Mummy says he is very brave but I don't member him cause he went away when I was real little."

"Is that a fact, and you never met him again?"

"Oh yes Your Honour, Mummy says that's him there with the funny clothes on." Little Thomas was pointing to Thomas where he stood just behind the kneeling Prince.

"My, my Master Thomas Cromwell Marking, this famous young man is your big brother? Well I never, and to think I never knew that; so you are the brother of the Famous Don Thomasino De Toro? Well Master Thomas Cromwell Marking, you should have something to remember your brother by. Let me ask the good Major here what we have for you. Major Jones! Is there any chance you have something put aside for this young Cavalryman?"

"Yes Your Highness, as it happens we had prepared for such an event."

Major Jones reached over to the nearest tray and took up a small silver medallion that had been attached to a pale blue and black ribbon. Thomas was now getting the idea that this had all been arranged well in advance and, yet again he had been kept in the dark by his friends and Officers. Major Jones gave the small medallion and ribbon to Prince Pimentel who immediately looked it over before reaching out and pinning it on the young boy's lapel.

On the front of the small silver medallion were the crossed lances of the Cavalry and on the obverse was engraved the small boy's full name with the dates of 1813-1814. Little Thomas tried as best he could to look down at his own personal medallion and ribbon as the Prince stood back up and then stepped back and gave little Thomas a smart salute. Little Thomas tried his best to emulate the salute but the wide smile on his face took some of the solemnity away from it and there was a soft chuckle that went around the grounds at the unforgettable sight before them.

The Prince smiled as he stepped past the small two man tableau and began the long task of presenting every trooper with his ribbon and medallion. With Thomas also taking the time to thank every individual trooper as they went it was nearly an hour before the last one was done and they were able to return to the front where Thomas could see his little brother had been sent back to stand beside his mother. It was obvious that Pablo had thought the small boy should not have to stand out in the hot sun for over an hour and had sent him into the shade of the pavilion. Little Thomas was still trying to look at his special medallion and ribbon while at the same time also trying to show his Mummy and Da.

The voice of Estaban broke the family scene being played out before Thomas.

"Captain Perrin, the drums will beat the cadence for the Cavalry to retire."

The drums were soon beating out the withdrawal for the Cavalry and, when they were all back in their places at the far end of the field and the drums drew silent; Carmelo stepped forward and faced Estaban at the front of the pavilion.

"Colonel Colosio, the men of the Regimiento De Toro request permission to call the roll of the fallen.'

"Permission is granted Colonel Grey; please convey the order to Major Jones."

As the two had been talking, some of the boys from the Auxiliaries had carried one of the long trestle tables out in front of the pavilion where they set it up and then disappeared over to their Company while others appeared with more trays on which were what appeared to be a large stack of wooden picture frames which were all lying down and stacked one on top of the other.

Once again it seemed that Major Jones in his own orderly way had prepared everything as he stepped forward with another of his ledgers on which was fixed a black band of cloth diagonally across the front cover. Major Jones opened the ledger as silence descended over the whole parade ground and every soldier as well as every civilian that was wearing some form of hat removed them and bowed their heads as the first name was read out aloud for all to hear.

"Drum Sergeant Peter Clement of the Original's, fallen at Talavera."

As Major Jones finished speaking, one of the boys close to the trays took up a picture frame and stood it on the table at the very front; it was held erect with a small fold out arm at the back of the frame. As the frame was placed on the table; from further down the parade ground came the loud stentorian voice of Major Craven Morgan.

"Number one gun of the first battery...Fire."

The boom of the single gun surprised most that were there and as the echo rolled out into the countryside there was faintly heard the first of what was soon to be many sniffles as memories of the fallen began to return to old friends at the sound of each and every cannon shot. In the picture frame sat the ribbon and medallion which was fixed in place on a background of black velvet and around the wooden frame was a thin black line; there was little doubt what the frames were representing. Major Jones called the next name.

"Drummer David Smith, fallen at Vimeiro."

As the frame was stood on the table the next gun boomed out over the silent parade ground as they waited for the next name on what was a long list of fallen; many of whom no one knew about except the men of the regiment and the friends they had made during their duty to the colours. There was one name that struck a particular cord for Thomas; even more so than all those he had watched being lost to the cause they had all signed up for. The name caught him in the throat once again and he was not ashamed of the tears that spilled from his eyes.

"Private Marcelo Marking, fallen at Albuera."

Thomas did not see the startled look on his mother and father's faces nor did he see the hand of his mother fly up to her mouth to stifle a cry as she heard the name of someone she had never heard of but was using their own family name; it was something she would definitely have to get her Thomas to tell her about.

When the final name was read it had been counted that the list of the fallen had covered one hundred and sixty eight names; far more than any except those in the Regiment had known about. As the last gun salute echoed out over the countryside there came a soft shuffling of feet as some tried to get a closer look at the trestle table now filled with small wooden frames all standing up so they could be seen.

The glint of silver and gold medallions along with the sun reflecting off the glass fronts only went to prove that the onetime small guerrilla force had had more than its share of losses and the friends that had stood by their side had little intention of ever forgetting any of them.

Estaban about turned and faced Thomas where he stood back under the pavilion between the Prince and Mister Percy.

"Sir, The men of the Regimiento De Toro ask for permission to retire the colours."

Thomas straightened up and replied to the request.

"The Regimiento De Toro has permission to retire the colours Colonel Colosio."

"Sir."

Estaban turned back to face out towards the parade ground once again.

"Major Carterton, the Colour Guard will furl the colours and pass in review. The battle flag of the Regiment will be given into the hands of General Don Thomasino De Toro for safe keeping while the others will be held in safety at Vimeiro."

Thomas watched as the men of the colour guard began to furl the colours; once done the three flags of the nations were marched away to the end of the company of Auxiliaries where they stopped and waited. The furled battle flag was brought forward and the guard stood at attention to the left of Thomas. Without further ado, Estaban then turned back to the last two men who were standing at attention with the two new flags furled and covered; this was a part that Thomas knew nothing about.

"The guard will clear the colours and parade in review."

Thomas watched as the two colour guards removed the thin cotton covers from the two flags and then unfurled then. Once the two flags were revealed the two guards placed the butts in the small bucket around their waist and lowered the flags as a salute before turning about and marching with the flags flying high for all to see as they progressed down the centre of the parade ground.

Thomas could not work out how his friends had kept the secret of the new flags from him; not even Fairley had given any hint that they were being made but, if he thought that was all they had devised as a surprise for him, he was greatly mistaken. The first flag was the Portuguese flag but the second was a new flag for his company and the reference to his being the Patron El Toro was not missed.

The new company flag had a panel of red on the left and a panel of pale blue on the right; at the centre was the ever present black bulls head but this time the horns were more curved and the three letters of M.S.C. Company were set between them. On the return of the two flag bearers they took up a stand to the left of the pavilion where they held the flags high for all to see.

It was Carmelo's turn to take over and he stepped to the front of the pavilion where he turned to face Thomas but kept his voice loud enough for all to hear.

"Sir, there is one award not yet given and the Officers and Men of the Regimiento De Toro ask permission for it to be presented?"

"Permission granted Colonel."

"Thank you Sir. Lieutenant's Marking will present themselves before the officers."

Thomas did not see the strange look his two parents sent his way at the sound of his name being used for what was obviously someone else; it was something he would have to explain to them at a later time.

Thomas watched as Sergio and Diego appeared carrying a large object covered in a black cloth. It was evident by the slight strain on their young faces that the piece was heavy but, as soon as they were standing at attention before the grouped Officers two of the younger Auxiliaries appeared with a low bench from the mess and placed it on the ground in front of the two Lieutenants.

Thomas watched the two as they set one end of the item on the bench and then, once they stood erect they carefully took away the black cloth to reveal a very large wooden carved frame. It was about three feet high and covered in finely carved scroll work which had been done by a master carver. The frame was also about three feet wide and at its centre were two plaques of what appeared to be gold.

The two plaques were laid out like a double page in an open book and the engraving was also done by a goldsmith with exceptional ability; Thomas could only stare in disbelief at what his friends had been able to do without him finding out about it all. Carmelo continued as he watched the stunned look on Thomas's face.

"Sir, the Officers and Men of the Regimiento De Toro wish to present you with a record of your service to the countries of Portugal and Spain and hope that it will hang in the entrance to your new villa or wherever you decide to call your home as a reminder to all who see it that it was your valour that held us all together and enabled us all to defeat our common enemy."

Thomas did not feel the sudden silent tears falling as he looked over the large frame. As he had noted at the first sight, the frame was surrounded by finely scrolled woodwork and the two joined plaques at the centre must have taken more gold than he thought as they were both about a foot wide and a foot long. The engraving was finely done and detailed everything Thomas had done from almost the first day he had stepped foot on Portuguese soil until the last attack at the pass of Balbao.

At the top of the first plaque was the outline of a drum and crossed sticks and below was the first entry.

'Drummer Thomas Marking 1808 Victory at Rolica'

The next entry also told its own story as many knew but this plaque was for posterity and the friends had even thought of that for him.

'Drum Corporal Thomas Marking 'The Patron' 1808 Victory at Vimeiro'

And so it went in the long list of his accomplishments which took both plaques by the time every fight he had been involved in both major and minor. Thomas did not know whether to be happy or embarrassed by the attention but the thought that his friends had gone to all this trouble just for him was hard to realise. For Thomas there was to be one more surprise which again was totally unexpected.

With the small ceremony over it was the Prince that stepped forward next and smiled at Thomas before speaking again in a voice so all could hear.

"Don Thomasino, we have been friends for a long time and I have watched your rise with great interest. The dedication you have shown not only to the defeat of our common enemy but to the safety of your men has left me in no doubt that you richly deserved the honour of your title. To this end I have taken it into my own hands to make sure that your final presentation should be one of honour and one that all people will recognise for the value you are held in by those who know fully what you have been able to accomplish."

The Prince raised his hand and from behind the pavilion came a bright new carriage with two matched pairs of horses. On the side of the carriage doors was a crest and coat of arms painted in gold, black and red with some added blue. At the centre was a small outline of a shield of which one half was gold on which had a small bundle of red arrows held together with a black band. On the other half which was red was the signet of crossed muskets in black. Around the shield were scrolls of gold and the whole was surrounded by what appeared to be gold laurels.

The crest at the top was once again the symbol of the black bulls head with a small gold coronet above the horns.

"Don Thomasino, this is the true coat of arms for your title of Cavalier de Espana and we hope you will display it in its rightful place in your home wherever that may be. Please accept this as a very small token of what is truly owed to you for your unflinching service to both our countries."

Thomas could only stand and stare at the beautiful black coach with its bright shiny coat of arms displayed on both sides; for the first time in what seemed forever he found himself speechless and could only stand and let the small trail of tears fall down his cheeks unhindered. It was finally the loud voice of Carmelo that brought Thomas back to the here and now.

"The Officers and Men of the Regimiento De Toro will pass in review and retire to barracks. Captain Perrin, the drums will sound the cadence of the Regimiento De Toro."

Immediately the drums began the familiar beat of the De La Guerra as the army formed up on the parade ground for the last time. The order for withdrawal had been planned by Carmelo and Estaban and the first to leave the parade ground were the heavy guns; they were soon followed by the three troops of Cavalry with the Infantry and Auxiliary Companies bringing up the rear as they marched from the field for the last time to the sound of their marching tune; the De La Guerra.

As the small army moved towards the far end where the barn was still covered from those on the parade ground; they were led by the three troops of Cavalry with the Artillery following and the Infantry and Auxiliaries bringing up the rear. The mighty roar of approval from the hundreds of spectators filled the air as the troops marched past the pavilion giving a salute as they did so. Thomas turned to everyone else that was standing in the pavilion once the troops had passed.

"Your Highness, Generals and Colonel Cruickshank; I would like to invite you and everyone else back to the villa for refreshments and where we can relax and let the men enjoy the fiesta that is arranged for them in peace and without any Officer's watching over them."

Thomas then indicated the arriving carriages and took great delight in handing his Mother into the new carriage. Cromwell had the look of a very proud father as he lifted little Thomas Cromwell into the carriage beside his Mother and then stepped in as the rest of the people began to enter their own coaches. It was only a short drive to the villa and, once there everyone began to ease tight clothes and find a good place in the shade from the mid afternoon heat.

Once again Fairley seemingly appeared from nowhere and began to set out food and drinks for those who wanted them; Thomas could see that his Mother had many questions for him but most he did not want to answer and so tried to lead the conversation away from his past endeavours. Prince Pimentel seemed to gather what Thomas was trying to do and gave his own help to keep any awkward questions from arising.

"So tell us Don Thomasino, what are your plans now for the future; I am sure that with a shipping company to run there will be many chances for you to see more of the world."

"Yes Your Highness, I have one of the ships being fitted out for just that event. Many of the men from England have wished to return home to see families but also have said they would like to take a place with the company if there was one after they have seen friends and family. I believe that the Captains Morgan's sons also wish to join the ship as well. Don Carmelo will be with me or take charge of the estate at Toro Bay once the villa has been built. Senor Forsca, how have the negotiations gone for the land there?"

"Don Thomasino, they have been very successful and the price for the land around the bay is very reasonable and I have ventured your money towards that. Your Major Carterton has already begun to draw up plans for the villa and the Portuguese Government have made a suggestion that you look at acquiring the land on the other side of the road. There is five hundred acres available if you choose to take it. Personally Don Thomasino I think it would be a good venture, there is good soil for the cultivation of olive trees and further up the ridge there is some good land for a vineyard."

"Can we afford to make the purchase senor Forsca?"

"Without a doubt Don Thomasino; perhaps you are not aware of the value of the coin you now have. The war was a great benefit for your coffers and the Shipping Company has been an outright success. There is one small thing that I need to tell you though. Don Thomasino I have now reached an age where it is time to take my wife back to our homeland and retire; to this end I have left my eldest in charge of your Company business where he will work even harder than I to make sure of its success and my other sons have all wished to stay behind and help in any way they can. I hope this does not cause any inconvenience for you but at my age I feel the need to stand back and let the younger ones make their own way in the world."

"Thank you Senor Forsca, I can only add that without your honest support I would never have been able to accomplish a half of what you have done for me and my men. I hope that you will find comfort in your retirement and look forward to dealing with your sons in the future and I can only add my thanks to you for your honesty in all our dealings."

"You are most welcome Don Thomasino; should you ever need my assistance then I hope you will not hesitate to call upon me."

Old Henry Morgan then spoke up from where he was seated on a chair with none other than little Thomas Cromwell sitting on his knee with what appeared to be a large smudge of food colouring around his lips and a twinkle in his young eyes of pure pleasure.

"So lad you want to go venturing across the seas; and where might you be wishing to go?"

"I had not thought too much about it at this stage Captain Morgan but the idea of seeing new lands has caught my attention but where that is just yet I am not sure."

"Perhaps I can make a suggestion and even offer a small tip or two."

"I would be delighted to hear anything at all Captain Morgan."

"Well lad, I was thinking about my young grandsons and their need for adventure. Now I know you have given them more than enough for most men over the last few years but I have one man that seems to think you should have an adventure like none other; that is if you feel adventurous enough to take it on?"

"And what did you have in mind Captain Morgan?"

"It would seem lad, that our savage George has a desire to return to his homeland; now if you were to give him passage on your ship I am sure he would see his way to find new adventures for you; especially in those far off seas of the Mir Pacifica. There are new lands far away on the other side of the world and a young man with adventure in his blood could well make something extra of himself if he were to be that way inclined."

"It's indeed a good idea and I will give it all my considerations but first I have to spend time with my family and there is the refitting of the ship that needs to take place before I can make a final decision, but it does raise my interest."

"Well lad you know where to find me when you make a decision. Oh, and while I think of it, there is something else I need to discuss with you but it can be done at a later date if it's all the same to you."

Thomas did not miss the slight raising of the black cane in Henry's hand which told him it was Brotherhood business but instead said.

"Thank you Captain Morgan, I will indeed let you know just as soon as I have had time to rest and have time with friends and family."

The discussions now turned to other things as everyone relaxed; Thomas was impressed that the Prince spent so much time with his Mother and Father and by the look on his Mother's face there were things said he would much have preferred she knew nothing about. Thomas's little brother seemed to be happy to sit on the old man's knee as Henry told him stories about pirates and great sea battles he had seen; his little brother was lapping up the attention as well as rather large quantities of food that seemingly never failed to appear on the table or carried in on trays by the young cooks.

Thomas looked around the room and even with the great number of people present he still managed to find a quiet corner to contemplate the day and what the retirement of his army would mean for so many. He was well aware that his men had been taken care of, many of whom wanted to continue with him in the shipping company or as farmers or guards at the new villa once it had been built. Many of the younger ones had homes to go to at Vimeiro or would take over the home valley and make their own home there.

Estaban would take many of the Cavalry troops back to Spain where he was still welcome and a number of the English troops would also return to their homes but with the proviso that they could return to Thomas's side should they ever wish to.

Thomas was starting to feel as though a part of his life was ending now that the army was in theory no more; there was only the pay parade on the next morning and his many friends and protectors would be signed out of the force for what he thought of as the last time. Thomas was almost taken by surprise at the sudden feeling of sadness that crept up on him as he stood and watched all those around him chatting as though they were all old friends and not having just met, most for the first time.

Dusk brought a new feeling to the room as young men appeared to light the many candles while outside the old large table had been set up by the ever vigilant Fairley for all of Thomas's guests to sit for dinner. Thomas did not miss the fact that all of the best dishes, silverware and cutlery had been laid out on the table; it seemed that Fairley was going to make this last formal meal of the Regimiento De Toro one that would be remembered by all those present.

Three days later Thomas found himself once again on the docks at Oporto along with his family, the Avante stood at the dockside and waited for him to board along with all those returning to England; it was going to be as fast a trip as the Captain could make it and even the weather gods would not delay him.

The Avante caught the tide in the late afternoon; Thomas stood with the Captain on the quarterdeck and watched Portugal recede into the lowering light of dusk, it was at times like these that Thomas often wondered what the future would bring for him but for now his concern was only for returning to his family's home and spending time with the brother he had had so little time with.

Thomas turned to the west and looked at the sun as it lowered into the calm sea, the ship was directed west by north and should be once again in England within five days; it was time for Thomas to sit back and try as best he could to forget the horrors of the war now that for him it was over. Thomas was yet to know that those same horrors could rear their ugly head at the worst of time for many years yet to come.

The End.

Made in the USA
Middletown, DE
14 August 2018